DEMANDED SUBMISSION

PIPER STONE

Published by Stormy Night Publications and Design, LLC.
www.StormyNightPublications.com

Stone, Piper
Demanded Submission

Cover Design by Korey Mae Johnson

CHAPTER 1

 lexandra

"I hate Miami!"

With my head sticking out the window of my car, screaming at the top of my lungs, even in traffic people probably thought I was nuts. What I'd learned from being in the overcrowded, oversexed, and over-opinionated city was that everyone was a little crazy. They had to be to put up with the nasty, horrible people who lived here.

Huffing, I thumped back in my seat, honking on my horn like at least ten other drivers were doing. Although we weren't going anywhere quickly. Even the timing of the traffic lights made life miserable. Okay, I'd had the worst week of my life, so I was obviously jaded, but after the last job interview, I was fed up with assholes who thought they were all that and a bag of chips.

1

I'd been forced to parade around in front of four men in the required cocktail uniform, pretending to serve them drinks. The entire time they'd studied my ass, not my ability as a cocktail waitress. No. They'd ogled my ass with their tongues hanging out. And who the hell forced their waitresses to wear five-inch heels? Hissing, as the traffic started moving again, I had an instinct to slam my foot on the accelerator, stopping myself at the last second.

Adding a wreck to the toxic mixture of events certainly wouldn't put me in a better mood. At this point, only a bottle of red wine and a pint of chocolate ice cream would. Pint? Try a gallon. When the traffic came to another screeching halt four car lengths from where I'd been, steam was rolling from my ears. At least I was first in line at the obligatory traffic light. I could zoom out with glee, maybe making it through the next light before it turned red.

I tapped my index finger on the steering wheel, remembering the last nasty barb I'd heard after finishing my walk of shame.

"Honey, you have the coordination of a moose. Maybe you should consider another profession."

At least the backhanded comment wasn't as embarrassing as my ass being compared to two gigantic pumpkins stuck together. I should sue the bastards for sexual harassment. Yeah, that would work. With the three hundred and forty-two dollars I had in my dwindling bank account, I could only imagine the attorney I'd manage to hire.

So I wasn't a skinny-minny like more than half the women in the city. So what? I had healthy curves, a place for a man to grab onto while he fucked my brains out. How would I know? I couldn't remember the first, only, and last time I'd had sex. I shuddered even thinking about the fumbling turkey I'd allowed to take my virginity.

Nine interviews and not one bite. At this rate, I'd be forced to go home to Montana with my tail between my legs and I refused to do that. Thank God, I was living with my cousin for the foreseeable future. I wouldn't get very far living on the streets.

Huffing, when the light turned green, I became a driver in the Indy 500, peeling out with just enough oomph my tires squealed. I'd never had one of those life-altering moments when time barely crawled, allowing you to see danger heading your way. I did at that moment, glancing quickly to the right before some asshole plowed through the intersection.

My entire world jerked to a halt, the sound of shattering glass all I heard. As my car was spun three hundred and sixty degrees, my mind spiraled to the silliness of why I was laughing. When the hunk of metal came to a solid jerking halt, I gasped for air, amazed my poor ole clunker of a car had survived the impact. The slow motion continued as I looked toward the other vehicle involved. All I could see was a stunning red sports car shimmering in the late afternoon sun, the guy sitting behind the wheel dressed like a movie star.

Or a gangster. It was tough to tell the difference in the city.

"Great. I bet he has fantastic insurance." After taking a deep breath and checking myself, I realized I couldn't go off on the asshole like I wanted to. Oh, hell, yes, I would. He caused the accident. An adrenaline rush jetted into my veins, anger placing a close second. I opened the door, determined to give him a piece of my mind. When my car suddenly jerked, I threw my head over my shoulder.

Hold. The. Fuck. On.

The asshole had backed up. Now he was turning his wheel. Wait a minute. Was the ass-wipe really going to flee the scene? Oh, no, he was not. Without thinking clearly, I barged into the intersection, positioned with my legs spread wide open and my arm thrown out, palm up. The bastard was going nowhere.

Yet he kept driving.

He was coming closer.

Traffic wasn't moving to allow him to get through.

There was only one way to go.

Directly through me.

Fuck that. I refused to play games, glaring at his cracked windshield.

The second I smiled in my bitchy little way, I knew I'd made a mistake. The dude behind the wheel had no intentions of stopping. And I was suddenly frozen on the spot.

Whoosh!

I expected pain tearing through me like a blasting furnace as my mangled body was slammed onto the pavement.

Instead, I felt the warmth of a hard body pressed against mine, my feet lifted off the ground until it almost seemed as if I was flying. If this was what heaven felt like, I was all in.

All I could hear at first was the rapid thudding of my heart. Was this the angel sent to guide me through heaven? Then I could swear people were clapping. What? Maybe I wasn't in heaven after all.

That's when I realized two important things. One, I wasn't dead. And two, I'd been whisked off my feet by what could only be described as a mountain man on steroids. When I was gently placed on the ground, the carved god stared into my eyes, and I thought for certain I'd melt into a huge puddle right there. Even the embarrassment would be worth being caught by him again.

Lord have mercy. The three words were the only thing that crossed my mind. My hormones were going wild. Now all sound stopped except the rapid beating of my heart colliding with my exploding core.

With a chiseled face and steel-gray eyes rimmed with flecks of amethyst, I could swear I was peering into the man's soul. This had to be a delicious dream. For a few spectacular seconds, my mind rushed to dark and filthy things. His hands all over my naked body. His tongue tasting every inch of skin. His cock spreading my pussy wide open.

Dear lord, the savior's cock was rock hard.

Exhaling, I swallowed the lump in my throat and blinked to try to focus. Then the beautiful haze that had surrounded me faded, faces popping from everywhere.

5

My savior eased me back by a few inches, forced to lower his head to keep looking in my eyes. He was gigantic, a solid foot taller than me, built like a Greek god. Unfortunately, the stern expression on his face dragged me all the way back to reality.

"Are you alright?" the stranger asked, his tone so husky goosebumps popped across every inch of naked skin, the sound gravelly and dominating.

"Uh-huh." Really? I was in the hands of a god and all I could say was uh-huh?

"You're not hurt? Not even a scratch?" he pressed.

"Nuh-uh."

"Can you stand on your own?"

I licked my lips, trying to form a decent coherent sentence. "Sure." Oh, my God. I'd never acted this way around any man, but with his thick hair I longed to run my fingers through, muscles that his jacket couldn't hide, and luscious lips meant for kissing for hours on end, I was a goner.

My breath hitched. Electricity soared through me like rocket fuel, igniting every single one of my senses. Wow. That was the only word to adequately describe the moment that seemed locked in time, spiraling to a dark and deliciously dangerous place. I allowed my gaze to roll over the man, his massive shoulders and long legs creating a wave of desire. The entire universe stopped at that moment, my mind caught in a capsule of lust and need that was so overwhelming I was lost. His heated gaze was forceful, his eyes stripping me bare.

"Did you hear me?" The question oozed from his lips, forcing me to acknowledge him with something other than carnal desires.

"Yes."

"Show me."

The stranger forced me to demonstrate I was able to stay upright. Then he exhaled, the sound exaggerated.

"I'm glad you seem to be okay. Now, what the fuck were you doing standing in the middle of a busy intersection? Did you know you could have gotten yourself killed? Did you have any inkling that driver had no intention of stopping?"

Nothing ever flabbergasted me.

Except for this man.

He stood with his arms crossed over his barrel-sized chest, antagonizing me. Chastising me like I was a bad little girl who'd misbehaved.

"I… No. I mean maybe. I didn't think." I gave myself another mental high five for sounding like an idiot.

"That's what I thought. You. Didn't. Think. I should turn you over my knee right here, right now and give you a spanking you won't forget."

And just like that, the fantasy was tossed out the window.

CHAPTER 2

 ameson

"Excuse me?" The girl with a death wish threw me a nasty look, the glimmer of sun unable to hide her fury.

Her two words were laced with venom. She had no idea how close she'd come to being run over by the asshole determined to drive away from the scene of an accident he caused, and she was glaring at me with her hands on her hips.

"You heard what I said. You need a hard spanking," I retorted, uncertain where my snappy reply had come from. The fact I'd jumped from my car, which was four lengths behind hers, sprinting so I could grab her before she became pavement art hadn't fazed her in the least. "I think I'm going to make certain that happens."

"Like hell you will."

"I won't mind adding washing your mouth out with soap if necessary. You need to understand that risky behavior has direct and often brutal circumstances." While her hateful glare remained, I sensed she knew I was right, her mouth twisting as she tried to figure out how to counter my proclamation. There was no suitable reply. "Good. We'll take care of that when we sort through this mess." I still couldn't believe she'd risked her life doing something so stupid.

"Well, aren't you an asshole, just like everyone else in this wretched town. I'll have you know I was doing just fine taking care of myself until the big he-man jumped in my way." She was exasperated, ready to throw a tantrum.

"To save your life in case you've forgotten." Holding her close had been like grasping a stick of dynamite in my hand. The instant attraction was unusual if not disturbing. I'd caught a whiff of strawberry I'd thought was the scent of her shampoo, but I'd realized the fragrance was from whatever she'd used on her lips. Which were naturally rosy. I'd fought the urge to crush my mouth over hers to find out if the taste was just as tantalizing.

"Bullshit," she huffed, raking her fingers through her long blonde hair. Suddenly, my mind went to several filthy places, which was totally inappropriate.

They all involved shackling her to my bed. I squinted from the sun, trying to pull my mind out of the gutter.

"Way to go," a bystander said from behind me.

"You're a regular hero," some lady chirped, although her tone was as caustic as the girl standing in front of me.

"Give the guy a medal." The third comment brought a smirk to the mysterious girl's face.

Grimacing, I glanced toward her wrecked vehicle. The heap of junk had definitely seen better days, but the accident had likely totaled it. When I pulled out my phone, she wrapped her hand around my wrist and a bolt of electricity slammed into my system.

"Who are you calling?" Her eyes opened wide in acknowledgement of the current tearing through both of us. When she jerked her hand away, fisting her fingers, it was all I could do not to smile.

"The police, to report the accident."

"There's no time. I need to go after the scumbag." She pulled away, trying to shove her way around me. I stopped her cold, grabbing her wrist as she'd done with mine.

"You're not going anywhere."

"You can't tell me what to do."

As I took a step closer, she sucked in her breath. "Maybe that's what you need in your life, someone to control you." When she opened her mouth to issue what I knew would be a nasty retort, I pointed to her car. "It's not drivable. Two tires are blown, the axle and the frame likely bent."

She slowly turned her head with a ragged moan. "Oh, shit. I need my car. God, this week sucks donkey turds."

At least the girl still had a sense of humor. "After we deal with the police, I'll give you a ride to your home. I know a body shop. My buddy will have your vehicle towed there."

"First of all," she snapped, jerking her arm away. "I don't know you. You could be a serial killer or rapist in cahoots with the crazy driver. Second, I don't need anyone's help. And third…"

"Yes?" I crowded her space, ignoring the honks that blasted all around us. "You were saying?"

Her face flushed and she looked down, but not before I noticed her bottom lip was quivering. With her breathing still ragged, I was drawn to her taut nipples poking through the thin tee shirt she was wearing. I wanted to wrap my lips around one, pulling the tender flesh between my teeth. Jesus Christ. She was half my age. What was I doing thinking about sex at a time like this?

"Like I said. You could be a monster for all I know."

"While the jury is still out on whether or not I'm a monster, if I'd wanted you hurt, why bother saving your life?"

She chewed on her inner cheek, debating my answer. "What do I do about the dude who hit my car?"

I continued the call. "Don't worry, princess. I managed to get his license plate number. I also happen to know the chief of police." I turned away from her, dialing the number, Manuel Gonzalez answering on the first ring.

"Hey, buddy," he answered. "How've you been?"

"No too bad, my man. I haven't seen you at the club lately."

11

"Work. I'm chained to my desk. An upturn in cartel shipments. It's keeping me busy, but I'll make a point to drop by. I need some TLC bad. What can I do for you?"

"I have a situation with an accident I witnessed, the son of a bitch driver taking off."

Manuel laughed. We went back to the first days after I'd opened the club. He wasn't chief of police then, just an officer told to keep an eye on the kinky club. Somehow, we'd become friends after a half dozen arguments. "Let me guess. Mr. Eagle Eyes got his license plate?"

"I did." As I relayed the number, I watched her pacing near her car. Then I noticed the Montana plates. She was a long way from home. My body remained tense, a heavy dose of adrenaline still trickling through my veins but only partially from my impulsive reactions. Shit. The girl was stunning, her cornflower blue eyes and blonde hair accentuated by a voluptuous body. It was the kind a man could sink his teeth into.

Or his cock.

There I went again, my mind dragging me off in unwanted places. There was too much on my agenda to be fantasizing about some wayward girl with a bad attitude.

"You there, buddy?" Manuel huffed, yanking me away from the delicious image.

"Yeah, I'm here."

"The plate came back immediately."

"Let me guess. Stolen."

"Not stolen," he answered. "Owned by Diego Santiago."

"The fucking cartel leader?"

"The very one. This accident will be testy to handle. Even if we do a report, it's doubtful I can do anything about it. I'll get shut down by the bastard's attorney in less than thirty minutes. Whoever this victim is, I'm not sure you want to put him or her through a nightmare. I won't tell you what happened to the last guy who challenged Santiago."

"Girl," I said absently. "And she's from Montana." If I had to guess, I'd say new to the city. I hated the fucking cartels ravaging the city, acting as if they owned every square inch of Miami. It wasn't like the old days where the bad guys were tracked down and sent to prison. Santiago had a team of lawyers, the man never serving a day behind bars or even connected to a traffic offense. He was virtually untouchable.

"Ah... Well, then."

Exhaling, I ran my hand through my hair. "You do your job and I'll figure out what to do with her. Have an officer take a report."

"Will do."

I ended the call, immediately contacting my buddy at the garage. At least he would prove more helpful than law enforcement. "Hey, Jake. I need a favor."

* * *

Alexandra Kingston sat with her arms folded, staring out the passenger window of my car, a scowl on her face. She

13

was shoved so far against the door that if it wasn't locked, I'd be fearful she'd fall out. I'd only learned her name from overhearing her telling the police officer. She'd said almost nothing to me except grumbling one more time she could take care of herself.

"Where are we going?" I asked.

"The Perigon."

I almost laughed. The Perigon was one of the most expensive, luxurious residences in the city. I quickly glanced at her torn jeans and tennis shoes, the scuffed purse she was clutching against her chest. While looks could be deceiving, in a town where opulence and pretense meant everything, she was either hiding her true identity or she'd found herself embroiled in a love affair with a wealthy sugar daddy.

When I didn't say anything, she turned her head in my direction. "What?"

"Nothing."

"You'd had plenty to say up until now. Are you making fun of me?"

Her haughty attitude continued, the thick suit of armor she wore becoming impenetrable. "Expensive location."

"So what? Are you saying I can't afford it?"

"Can you?"

"Well, no, but that's all I've seen since arriving in this lousy town. Skyscrapers for the rich and famous. I'm neither. Satisfied?"

"Why is it so lousy?" The girl had a boulder on her shoulder, not a chip.

She shrugged. "The people are holier than thou. They act like I'm some hick who couldn't possibly offer them anything worthwhile. Bastards."

Every word that slipped past her luscious lips was laced with acid. Her behavior was reckless. The unruly girl definitely needed control in her life, rules that she would be required to follow. The dom in me hungered to wrap her in chains to keep her from hurting herself. "What happened?"

"Why do you care?"

"Maybe because you're sitting in my car."

Her laugh was bitter, yet the lilting sound tightened my balls. "Well, since you asked oh-so nicely, I've had several interviews this week and every time I was treated like shit."

"You went to an interview dressed like that?"

"Oh, please." She acted offended then pressed her hand against her leg, but the way she was tapping her foot on the floorboard meant she was nervous. I couldn't blame her. "Every interview required me to put on a costume, parading myself like some whore. I'm not a whore. I just... I just need a job. No one will give me a chance."

Sighing, I tried to think of something to say that wouldn't cause her to lash out as she'd done before. "What kind of job?"

"Cocktail waitress. A lousy fucking cocktail waitress job and I've been told I'm fat and ugly."

"Whoa. Hold on. Some asshole said that to you?"

"Not in so many words, but several pompous men implied it. They sat in their expensive suits and their TAG Heuer watches, their manicured nails screaming they'd never done a hard day's labor in their precious lives, watching me walk in front of them like a trained seal."

As I headed onto the freeway, I shook my head, anger furrowing inside. Miami was a tough town, especially for a young girl as beautiful as she was. Granted, there were thousands of gorgeous women, but so many were created by wealthy surgeons. This girl was the real deal, innocent and vulnerable. Shit. I had to get my mind out of the gutter. I was furious she'd been treated with such disrespect, but I knew far too many men exactly as she described. Hell, the majority of members of my exclusive club could be shoved into the same category.

"Why move to Miami if you hate it so much?"

Snorting, she immediately pressed her hand against her lips, unable to keep from laughing. "I'm sorry. I make noises when I'm nervous."

"You have nothing to be sorry about, except your ridiculous behavior," I told her, the twitch in my cock because of her anxiousness.

"Funny. You're a real comedian." She shook her head several times. "My parents are going through a nasty divorce. I couldn't take their constant bickering. Plus, they kicked me out of the house. My cousin offered me a chance to get away even for a few months. I thought a change of scenery would do me some good. I'm staying with her until I get settled, although at this rate, I might be forced to return home. I don't like failure. But that's what I feel like. One big, fat failure. At least I regrouped and told the last group of pigs off. I stood right in front of them and told them exactly what I thought about them and their interview."

Whew. This girl had balls, her chutzpa not only keeping me intrigued but aroused as well. "What exactly did you tell them?"

"That the reason they were acting like dicks was to compensate for their itsy-bitsy cocks and that they could shove their interview up their tight butts."

Jesus. Christ. The girl's mouth was going to get her into a hell of a lot of trouble. By the flicker in her eyes, I could tell how much their comments had hurt and embarrassed her. Men were pigs. What the girl needed other than discipline was someone who could help her see how special she was.

"Alexandra. I realize you don't know me and have every right to be afraid of sitting next to a stranger in a city that hasn't welcomed you like they should with open arms, but you need to listen to me. You are not a failure. You're also not fat and ugly. In fact, you're probably the most beautiful woman I've ever met. You can do anything you want with your life. Never allow anyone to take that away from you, especially pompous men who treat women like possessions. Do you understand?"

The silence prickled my senses. I casually glanced over my shoulder. Seeing a shimmer of tears in her eyes pulled at the protector inside of me. She wasn't used to praise, only condemnation. Suddenly, I wanted nothing more than to be the controlling, nurturing factor in her life, a man who could guide the budding flower into its moment of brilliance.

I wanted to be the man who provided her with compliments when applicable, discipline when necessary, and the man she'd eventually call Master.

CHAPTER 3

 *lexandra*

Tears.

I had freaking tears in my eyes. I never cried. Not for anything or anyone. Well, maybe once or twice from sad movies, but certainly not from some hulking mass of gorgeousness praising me when he didn't even know me.

But after all the words that had hurt me so deeply, to hear a stranger complimenting me with feeling behind his statement, I was in a mild state of shock. A lump had formed in my throat, butterflies in my stomach, but worse than that was the wetness between my legs. As crazy as it was, I wanted to please him, as if that was the only thing in my life that mattered.

My throat was so dry I had difficulty breathing. Even as I tried to look away, I couldn't. My head and body were frozen on the spot as his kind words reverberated throughout my system.

Along with explosive heat.

The chemistry I felt with the stranger was bizarre, initially uncomfortable, but at this moment it felt right. "Thank you." I wasn't entirely certain he heard me, the hoarse whimper I issued unrecognizable to myself. The wretched long days had put me on edge, memories of the real reason I'd run far away from home lingering in the back of my mind like a tight vise that would one day strangle me. I was overwrought, the emotional rollercoaster I'd been through the last few weeks taking an ugly toll.

I'd thought moving away from the harsh realities would not only do my aching heart some good, but would be easy as well. I'd been wrong, so very wrong.

As I dragged my tongue across my lips, I allowed another salacious study of his muscular physique. The stubble attached to his chiseled chin was groomed, adding to his utter dominance. While others might think the man imposing, there was a distinct light in his eyes, a hint of amusement that suggested a complex layering of control and playfulness.

No man was supposed to be so good looking, every muscle carved from the finest stone, and hands that could crush someone easily. He had to be at least six foot five, dwarfing me easily. I'd felt protected, cared for even while the police officer had taken my statement. Wow. What was I thinking?

"I meant it."

We remained silent as he headed toward the beach, although I had about a million questions I wanted to ask him. He was obviously rich, given the Porsche he was driving. Did every wealthy man have a flaming red vehicle in Miami? Maybe he was a drug dealer.

Good going, Alex. You know how to find the best people.

That wasn't fair. I didn't even know his name. "Who are you?" My confrontational tone had returned.

He chuckled, the deep baritone fluttering all the way to my damp pussy. "Jameson Stark."

"What do you do, Jameson, besides playing Superman in your off time?"

"I own a club."

"A club. Like a dance club?"

"Something like that."

I bet he catered to the rich and famous. "I'm oh-so sorry to inconvenience you."

His gaze was a combination of admonishment and disbelief. Maybe I was acting a little over the top. I blamed exhaustion. He'd likely blame my upbringing.

"It's not a problem," he said more quietly than I'd anticipated, which made me feel even guiltier for my behavior.

Whew. I couldn't stop trembling from the sound of his voice. I stole another glance and sighed. He was much older, the hint of gray hair at his temples adding to his aristocratic look, but there was a roughness about him that attracted me more than anything. He was a man who took control.

Why did that make my heart flutter?

As the minutes passed, I grew more uncomfortable being around him. His presence was powerful and even without uttering a word, his aura ticked off every box in my fantasy about the perfect man.

If there was such a thing.

As my cousin's building came into view, I stiffened. I had no method of transportation, no job, and a bleak outlook on life. Even my little voice was laughing at me, the taunts fueling the encroaching despair.

Failure. Failure. Failure.

I reminded myself of what Jameson had just told me and my insides fluttered all over again. How could a stranger's praise mean so much?

"You can let me off here," I told him as he pulled into the parking lot leading to the garage.

"That's not going to happen." His tone was brusque, obviously not used to anyone trying to tell him what to do.

"You've taken too much time already."

"Nonsense. I need to make certain you're alright."

It seemed my refusal to allow medical attention continued to bother him. I was shaken, no doubt about it, but my knocking knees and hammering heart had more to do with being in his presence.

"Really, it's not necessary. I'm a big girl."

"Obviously, it's necessary, Alexandra. You are in clear need of direction in your life. And you will obey me."

Obey. The single word brought another flutter in my heart, the draw to him so intense I realized I was holding my breath.

He made the statement as if he'd known me for longer than sixty minutes and I found myself unable to respond, nodding instead. As if the man knew what I needed in my life better than I could discover for myself. Why did the words 'yes, sir' play clearly in my muddled mind?

Was it because he was older that I wasn't issuing my usual retort? I wasn't certain but as he drove into the garage, lowering the window as the uniformed guard behind the small structure leaned in, I shuddered all the way to my core. As he arranged for his car to be placed in a protected space, I couldn't help but notice he'd tipped the young man a hundred-dollar bill. Whether or not he was trying to impress me lingered in the back of my mind.

After pulling the impressive vehicle to the side, I watched as he climbed out, his intensity and control absolutely clear in his choice of vehicle and the way he moved. Every simple action he took elicited a powerful surge of lust that felt uncontrollable. I'd never been so flustered around any man, especially those around my age.

He took his time walking around the front of his Porsche, opening the door and extending his hand as if we were attending a fabulous soiree. When he pulled me to my feet, I'd never felt so small and invisible in my life. Yet the way he pressed his palm against the small of my back as he directed us toward the elevator set off another series of thunderous fireworks.

"What floor?" he asked, and I had to think about the question.

"Um, the top. I think. Yes, the top floor."

He chuckled but said nothing, his refusal to say anything adding to the nervousness electrifying my system as much as his touch.

Once inside, he refused to move his palm, especially when another resident raced into the confining space, angrily slapping his hand on one of the buttons. The pressure of Jameson's fingers became more possessive, moving his body slightly in front of mine. As I looked up at his face, the way his jaw was clenched defined his features. His expression was also one of warning, ruthless especially after the other man dared make direct eye contact with me.

Suddenly, the testosterone in the elevator was overwhelming. Jameson remained tense even after the unwanted visitor exited.

I had no idea what to say to him, but his utter possessiveness kept me tingling all over. As I fumbled to find my keys in my purse, I prayed Charlotte hadn't left work early. I had no idea how to explain his presence or the fact I'd wrecked my car. My cousin had been so accommodating, telling me at least a half dozen times not to worry about paying rent for a couple of months, but I wasn't the kind of girl to accept handouts. I hadn't been brought up that way.

When I tried unsuccessfully to slide the key into the lock, I realized tears were fogging my vision. Crying twice in one day was unheard of, but I was ready to break down into heaving sobs. I was broke and didn't even have reliable transportation to get back home. Home. My parents were selling the house I'd grown up in, both moving to other cities. I felt like I didn't have a home any longer.

Jameson said nothing as he wrapped his massive hand around my shaking one, pulling the keys into his fingers. A single tear slipped past my lashes, the lowered angle of my head allowing the salty bead to drop to the floor. I was stronger than this. Maybe if I hadn't lost my temper with the group of men who'd insulted me then I might have a job.

Oh, who was I kidding? It had been obvious from the second I'd walked into the room they had no intentions of hiring me. Yet I'd been made to go through the process, the skimpy outfit barely hiding anything. The entire last few days had been humiliating.

When Jameson opened the door, ushering me inside instead of the other way around, I'd never felt so helpless in my life.

Another tremble rolled through me as I scanned the condo for any sign of Charlotte, breathing a sigh of relief realizing she was still at work. Then I heard the jingle of keys as he placed them on the entrance foyer table, his thudding boots on the marble floor jarring.

"Nice location."

I shrugged and tossed my purse onto the couch, gazing out the wall of windows at the rolling ocean waves. "It's okay."

"At somewhere in the neighborhood of ten million dollars per unit, it's more than just okay."

I spun around, gawking at him. "Ten million dollars?"

"Easily. Maybe more. I'm curious what your cousin does for a living."

"Um… Well, she goes to an office every day. I think." I was stymied by the price tag, my mind suddenly blank. Charlotte had told me what she did, or had she? We'd been close once, a long time ago when she'd lived only five miles away from my parents' ranch. What did I really know about her any longer other than she had a wardrobe to die for and worked odd hours?

"Interesting." While he wasn't exactly criticizing me for my lack of knowledge, he was just as amused as when I'd berated him about saving my sorry ass.

"She's a free spirit. Men flock to her like flies to honey." His expression of amusement remained, and another giant wave of heat crested across my jaw. The man made me as nervous as a kitty cat. I was rarely tongue-tied but around him, I couldn't seem to think clearly. I'd been so angry before that I hadn't paid attention to the way he was dressed.

Instead of the slicked-back appearance I'd seen all week, with suits that cost more than a year's salary and not a single hair out of place, he had a slightly rough around the edges look about him: tousled hair, an open shirt, and a casual suit jacket with no tie topped off with snakeskin cowboy boots. I almost felt a little taste of home standing in the middle of a condominium that seemed cold and uninviting.

"I see."

"Um. Thank you again for bringing me home. As you can tell, I'm perfectly safe. You can go about your merry business."

Instead of responding, he removed his jacket, placing it over the back of the couch. Then he returned his attention toward me as he unbuttoned one sleeve of his shirt. I found myself in awe of what he was doing, my mouth going completely dry as he rolled the material over his elbow, exposing colorful ink on his forearm.

"Would you like something to drink or eat? I think I can make you a peanut butter and jelly sandwich." What the hell was wrong with me? A peanut butter and jelly sandwich. I'd completely lost what was left of my mind. Thankfully, he didn't burst into laughter, humiliating me even more than I was already feeling.

The larger-than-life hunk of the year kept his eyes piercing mine, so silent that I could hear my heart thumping. He repeated the action with his other sleeve, every movement deliberate. When he walked closer, I almost backed away, his presence overwhelming. But it was easy to sense he wasn't going to hurt me.

"You're overwhelmed by the move. Correct?" he asked.

I thought the question was strange at first, but the softness of his voice and the way he continued to look into my eyes made it easy to answer. "Very much so. Up until coming here, the furthest I'd been away from Montana was to my brother's wedding in Denver."

27

He nodded as if he completely understood, taking another step in my direction. "You've been acting out more than usual, allowing your anger to speak for you?"

The way my lower lip quivered was annoying even more so than the fact he was right. "Yes, sir." Sir. I'd never called my father sir. Why him?

He shook his head, a complete look of understanding crossing his face. "Your behavior indicates you're crying out for someone to take the burden off your shoulders if only for a little while, guiding you so you can breathe more easily. Isn't that correct?"

Jameson had no idea how right he was. "Yes. Yes, sir." I lowered my head, cognizant that he'd closed the distance. When he lifted my chin with a single finger, I clenched my fists by my sides.

"You crave a firm hand providing discipline when needed to help keep you on track."

His last words weren't a question but a statement, yet I found myself answering, drawn into the moment. "Yes." As soon as I admitted what I was feeling at that moment, relief flooded my mind. I'd never felt so free, as if a burden had been ripped from my shoulders. The thought was shocking since I'd never wanted anything like this before.

I wanted to look away, but he pinched my chin between his fingers, the act more intimate than if we were kissing, which I couldn't seem to stop thinking about.

He nodded, the smile crossing his face and the intense shimmer in his eyes as if my admittance had pleased him.

"Good girl. I'll take care of that for you."

Good girl. Why did his words cause such a powerful physical response? My legs were shaking, my heart racing and I even sensed my panties were damp.

Suddenly I allowed him to lead me toward one of two luxurious leather chairs, watching as he eased down onto the edge of the seat. I was in a daze of some sort as he began to unfasten my jeans, taking his time. The fog was thick enough I wasn't stopping him. I had rules I followed, yet I had or was about to break just about every one of them.

Rule number one: Never get into a car with a stranger. Check.

Rule number two: Never encourage a bad guy by talking to him. Double check.

Rule number three: Never allow a dark, wildly attractive bad guy into my house. Triple check with bells on.

Number four: Never become insanely hungry for a delicious hunk of a man who I wasn't sure I cared was a super bad dude. That one I was still adding checks to plus gold stars.

Now I was adding rule number five. Never allow a dark, dominating hunk of a god to expose my bare bottom for a hard spanking.

As he yanked my jeans and panties over my hips, pulling me over his lap, I realized I should give myself a failing grade.

 lexandra

I'd never had a single spanking in my entire life. That wasn't how my parents handled discipline. They weren't what my father called 'those' kind of people. The word had been specifically chosen, used for every person or situation he found unsavory. He'd preferred more civilized punishments including taking away one of several electronic devices for seventy-two hours.

Since my brother had almost landed himself in prison, it would seem the discipline provided hadn't been strong enough. Now, as I pressed my hands against the expensive Nourison Twilight area rug Charlotte couldn't stop raving about, I was strangely calm about the moment.

Jameson was as well, taking a deep breath as he pressed his hand against the small of my back just like he had when guiding me through the parking garage. The gesture was comforting even though my stomach remained in knots.

"Hopefully, this will be an excellent reminder that life is precious and that you deserve happiness. However, reckless behavior won't help you achieve your goals."

He didn't warn me before bringing his palm down twice, the cracking sound of skin against skin forcing a yelp from my throat. I struggled to suck in enough air to continue breathing, shocked by the swiftness of his actions instead of reacting or feeling any pain.

"Good girl. Stay in position."

Good. There was that word again, one of acknowledgement for my obedient deed as well as praise for keeping my shit together. When he brought his hand down four more times in rapid succession, a series of stinging sensations quickly moved into unadulterated pain exploding down the back of my legs.

"Fuck!" I couldn't stop the word fast enough, gasping as I wiggled on his lap.

"Watch that mouth, young lady. That's why you didn't get the job you applied for, not for any other reason."

I wanted to disagree, but he might be right. Okay, so he was undoubtedly correct in his assumption. Still, yelling at the wealthy dudes had made me feel a lot better.

"Calm down or I'll start over."

Calm down? Shit. Heat was building across my bottom. I wasn't entirely certain how I was supposed to pretend everything was just dandy. He continued the spanking and I wasn't aware that I'd tried to crawl off his lap until he jerked me back with force. What I did realize was that he was hard, his cock throbbing against my stomach.

The little flutter of butterflies in my system turned to a swarm. I was actually giddy that I'd made him aroused all over again. Now he had his arm firmly planted around my hips to hold me in place. His cracks against my bottom became more brutal, his hand coming down rapidly.

Within seconds, I was panting, writhing in his hold as pain turned into anguish. Shock tore through me from the powerful surge of electricity, the combination disturbing. That's the moment I realized in addition to the utter discomfort crawling down every inch of my legs, I was completely aroused. Enough so my pussy clenched and released twice. I was mortified at my body's reaction, needing desperately to get out of the situation before he realized my condition.

Shit. Shit.

Every brutal smack of his hand only added to the heightened level of excitement sweeping through my system. I was on fire, especially my aching buttocks, finding the level of desire I was reaching unfathomable.

"Stop. Stop!" I threw my arm back to cover my aching bottom and within two seconds he snatched it away, his fingers digging into my wrist as he pinned it against the middle of my back.

"Breathe, Alexandra. You're taking your spanking well."

The way he said my name was intoxicating, every muscle tingling. The deep, rich tone was sensual while being utterly commanding. I immediately took a deep breath, holding it as he continued the round of discipline. It was difficult to keep from squirming, the enjoyment of feeling his engorged cock pressed against me irresistible.

Crazy thoughts of whether my juice was staining his expensive trousers entered my mind, a nervous laugh popping past my lips. And dear God, the scent of my desire wafting in front of my face was so strong I cringed. It was a flashing neon invitation to explore carnal sin.

When he stopped, I thought the round of embarrassment was over, that I could finally hide my face for days. Oh, I was so wrong. He was merely caressing my skin, allowing me to catch my breath as he prepared for round two.

"Just remember that every misdeed has its own set of consequences, some more harmful than others."

His statement pushed me into a lull, but I was listening intently. Maybe I was seeking some crazy method of finding salvation or at least answers.

"We're almost finished." He hitched me up further on his lap before starting again.

Maybe I was immune to the anguish or resigned to accepting my fate, but I dropped my head, allowing him to finish unhindered.

And the entire time impure thoughts rolled through my mind, desire refusing to be driven aside. He continued the round of punishment, the tingling sensations increasing. I was breathless, trying to ignore how wet I'd become yet it was impossible.

When he was finished, he took a deep breath, patting my aching, heated bottom.

"I'm very proud of you."

"Thank you." Thank you? I was thanking him for treating me like a child? Oh, I'd dropped to a new level.

As he turned me over, cradling me against him, the entire situation seemed normal, as if I was meant to be in his arms, protected and cared for.

Until it wasn't.

Another dose of reality slammed into my mind like an icepick being driven into my brain. I was sitting half naked on the lap of a man I barely knew and I'd thanked him for the spanking. This was about the craziest thing I'd done in my entire life.

A tremendous amount of fear and uncertainty shattered the comfort I'd just felt and I jumped off his lap, almost falling onto my face given my jeans were being used as shackles. Fortunately, I managed to catch myself before dropping straight into hell from another round of embarrassment.

My face was on fire, my mind a fuzzy blur of madness as I stumbled forward, trying to jerk the tough material over my hips. I couldn't look at him, couldn't stand the thought of seeing my reflection in the mirror. What he must think of me. An errant girl who needed daily punishment for being so childish. How could I be so stupid to try to stop the driver? Even worse, how had I managed to lose a good portion of my mind by allowing this... this... atrocity to happen?

Oh, he was extremely good at being a conman alright. If I had to guess, I'd say he'd done this before, the hero stint just his method of operation to get a girl... okay, so most men didn't offer up spankings like candy, but in a city like Miami, I'd already learned anything was possible.

My fingers refused to work, so stiff I couldn't zip my jeans, let alone button them. To hell with it. I spun around, taking long strides in his direction. "How dare you."

The hunk rose to his full height and I swallowed hard.

"How dare I what, Alexandra?"

Damn his sultry voice too.

"How dare you..." *Think, stupid girl. Speak.* Ugh. I hated the little nagging voice more today than probably any other day in my life. Forced to tilt my head at an awkward angle given his height, I took a deep breath, narrowing my eyes. "How dare you act as if you know what I need in my life."

He cocked his sexy head, the same look of amusement that I'd found charming before now irritating as hell. "The truth is, Alexandra, I think I do."

I was so shocked by his commanding statement that I was even more rattled, trying to come up with a crafty rebuttal but my mind was one blank canvas. That prompted me to do something that I knew with certainly I'd regret but I had no self-control with it came to my anger.

35

The hard crack of my hand across his face was as unexpected for me as it obviously was for him. "Oh. My. God." I heard my whisper but no longer recognized the tone. This was bad. This was really bad.

When Jameson closed his eyes, his nostrils flaring, I backed away, covering my mouth with both hands. I'd never done anything quite so impetuous in my life.

When he finally opened his eyes, there was fire in them unlike anything I'd ever seen. He took one step in my direction, and I took one step back. Then he took another, and I countered with two. The expression on his face changed, the look in his eyes dark and temptingly dangerous. I'd never been as attracted to anyone as I was at that moment.

It was as if I'd drawn a line in the sand and I'd dared him to cross it.

With a single long stride out of the blue, he had both his massive hands wrapped around my wrists, yanking them free of my face. When he pulled me onto my tiptoes, dragging me closer, all I could think about was how it would feel to kiss his lips. I licked mine and he exhaled, his heated breath blasting across my face.

"You shouldn't have done that, Alexandra." If his voice got any deeper, he'd suck me straight into a vacuum lined with velvet.

"Why is that?"

"Because those who do pay for their sins." He brought me even closer, his chest heaving.

"So, I'm a sinner?" I whispered.

"The worst kind."

"So what punishment do I deserve?" I arched my back, barely able to keep my eyes off his full lips.

"One befitting the crime." He lowered his head until our lips were just a tiny inch apart. The man smelled of citrus and sandalwood, spices and a hint of the ocean, the combination creating a firestorm of need deep within.

Somewhere in the back of my mind I knew this wasn't a good idea. It was obvious so did he, but God help me, I'd never wanted another man as much as I wanted him. He made me feel more alive than I had in my entire adult life.

"Then I'll accept your punishment."

"Good. Girl." As he crushed his mouth over mine, an immediate explosion of sensations rocketed through me. My mind soared into the stratosphere as he tempted my lips, his hold strong and dominating. When he slipped his tongue past my lips, I heard a rumble, a growl coming from deep inside his chest.

He released one wrist, allowing me to press my fingers against his chest. I'd wanted to slide my fingers under his shirt since the moment I'd been able to focus. I tangled my fingers in his few chest hairs, tingling all over. In turn, he wrapped his hand around the back of my neck, grinding his hips back and forth.

Holy cow, he was huge. My mouth watered at the thought of wrapping my lips around his cockhead while a portion of my brain tried to figure out if he'd fit in my tight pussy. His hold was even more possessive, his fingertips digging into my skin. I managed to unfasten another button, dragging my fingernail down from the base of his neck.

The kiss was exquisite, the taste incredible, the hint of peppermint refreshing. He swept his tongue through my mouth, taking his time to explore. But seconds later, I sensed his need increasing, the electricity surging between us.

I was breathless, my pussy aching as much as my heated bottom. I wanted this man. I needed to feel his cock buried deep inside.

Seconds later he broke the kiss, immediately ripping the tee shirt over my head. Then the two of us were in frenzy to remove our clothing. When he was finished, he stalked toward me, cupping and squeezing my breasts.

The look in his eyes was indescribable, as if the man was preparing to partake in a feast of all his favorite foods. I allowed my gaze to fall down the length of him, moaning as I gorged visually in the sight of his cock. It was a thing of beauty, the tip purple, the thick veins on the sides throbbing much like the cords in his muscular neck. When I wrapped my hand around it, my fingers barely came together because of the thickness. I was enthralled, stroking all the way to the base.

He issued a throaty growl and I purred in return, my mind blown by the fact we were doing this. Crazy. I was a crazy girl, but nothing would stop me from enjoying time with the gorgeous man.

When he dropped his head, pulling me onto my toes once again, I threw my head back, laughing nervously. As he pulled my nipple into his mouth, I closed my eyes, still swooning from being in his hold. How could anything feel better than this?

He took his time sucking then swirling his tongue around my hardened bud. Every sound he made kept the butterflies swarming, so animalistic that I knew the man planned on devouring me. He rolled his lips to my other breast, dragging his tongue underneath before outlining my nipple with the tip before engulfing it completely. This time, he bit down, the flash of pain oh-so delicious.

Moans slipped past my lips as lights flashed in my field of vision. I was floating on a cloud, no longer recognizing myself, so uninhibited I was worried I'd do a freefall.

Jameson's actions became rougher, squeezing my breasts until vibrations jetted down to my toes. When he finally lifted his head, his eyes appeared dilated from extreme lust. I was taken aback at how wolfish they seemed, the dimming sunlight refracting off the now darkened color.

He lifted me into his arms, cradling my bottom. I entwined my feet, tangling my fingers in his hair as he took several steps. I was shocked when he tumbled us over the back of the couch, laughing as he managed to roll me over so he was on top. I couldn't help but be thankful the posh leather was oversized, or the larger-than-life man wouldn't fit.

His grin was dark, almost demonic, and as he rose onto his elbows, peering down at me, I was struck by how close I felt to him. That wasn't really possible and this certainly wasn't about anything but the simplicity of what we were doing, the joy of sharing passion, but that was fine by me.

"You are so beautiful, Alexandra. Don't ever allow anyone to make you feel otherwise. Do you hear me?"

"I do. You make me feel beautiful."

He captured my mouth as he'd done before, using his knees to push aside my legs, pressing his shaft against my aching pussy.

I was so wet, my nipples already tender and swollen. As I raked my fingers over his shoulder, another tickling series of sensations rolled through me. When I eased my other hand between us, he lifted his body, allowing me to slide the tip against my swollen pussy lips.

After breaking the kiss, he chuckled. The sound was darker than before, a promise of things to come. He pressed his forehead against mine briefly, catching his breath and allowing me to do the same, but we were too crazed for each other to wait for long.

Seconds later, he yanked first one hand over my head then the other, easily wrapping his fingers around both wrists. The passion exploded between us and as he drove the tip of his cock inside, I arched my back, wrapping both legs around his hips. Several scattered whimpers left my mouth as my muscles struggled to expand wide enough to accommodate him.

Gasping, I closed my eyes, my core aching as he nearly split me in two. When he was fully seated inside, he nipped my lower lip then pulled almost all the way out, driving into me with such ferocity the couch moved. Or maybe the entire earth moved. I wasn't certain but I knew if anyone could do it, he could.

There was such darkness in his eyes where there'd been light before, as if his needs had driven him to another level of desire. He never blinked as he fucked me, thrusting harder and with every stroke of his fabulous cock, I spiraled closer to something I'd never experienced in my life.

A mind-blowing orgasm.

His actions were primal, so much so I struggled to breathe, my natural tendencies shining through as I tried to free my arms. There was no way. His hold was too strong. I bucked against him, but he shook his head, another subtle but effective reminder that he was very much in charge.

As he swiveled his hips, grinding into me, the switch in the angle forced a series of strangled gasps. "Oh, my. Yes. You are..." Laughing, I was thrown into a shimmer of electric jolts that had my mind incapable of processing what was happening. "Oh, no, you're going to make me..." Why was my face beet red? I knew it was. Was I actually embarrassed that I was ready to explode into a powerful orgasm?

"Not yet. Not until I say you're allowed."

"Oh, you wouldn't dare."

"Yes," he whispered hoarsely as he slowed his grinding actions, "I would."

"No. No!" I tossed my head back and forth, the ripple effect of trying to keep from experiencing what I'd looked forward to for years insane. Yet that small part of me still wanted to obey him. Why? Why?

Every time I blinked, stealing a glance at his eyes, I could tell he was grinning, waiting for me to disobey him.

"Please, let me come. I'll be a very good girl."

"I don't know," he muttered.

I struggled with his hold to the point I managed to drag one arm away, pushing hard against his chest. With another move I didn't see coming, he flipped us over onto the floor. This time the force he used shoved the glass coffee table across the artistic rug I'd heard so much about I'd rolled my eyes by the end. I wonder what Charlotte would say when she knew two people had fornicated on it.

"Such a little tease," he muttered before pulling his cock all the way out.

"No!" I reached for him, horrified that he'd leave me like this.

"Don't worry, little country girl. I'm not done with you yet." Without any exertion, he tossed me onto all fours, smacking his hand across my bruised and aching backside. Before I had a chance to react or tumble forward, he fisted my hair, tangling his fingers in my long curls.

Then without any hesitation, he drove his cock deep inside, filling me once again.

Holy smokes, I couldn't breathe. He'd filled me so completely I'd lost all the air in my lungs. This wasn't about anything romance but brutal, animalistic fucking. Lights swirled in front of my eyes, and I clawed the short nap of the carpet, the sounds erupting from me ones I'd never heard before.

He remained on his knees, rocking me as he plunged into me, using my hair as a leash. This was dirty and delicious, the most sinful thing I'd done. Within seconds, he drove me straight back to the moment where all rationality was lost, sinful pleasure crowding its space. I couldn't stop trembling, ready to beg him to allow me to come.

So I did.

"Please. Let me come."

"Mmm…" He pumped several more times then gripped my hip with one hand. "Come for me. Come on my thick cock."

The man didn't need to tell me twice. A giant wave crashed over me, drowning me in sin and shame and I loved every second of feeling so out of control.

Unrecognizable sounds erupted from somewhere inside, my mind spinning as the pleasure intensified. As my pussy clamped down on his cock, I sensed him tensing. One moment of rapture led to another and I lost control of myself completely, clawing the rug, my movements jerking us both forward.

"Oh. Oh. Oh!" While I doubted anyone could hear my screams, I did my best to bite down on my lower lip. It wasn't working. The moment of pure ecstasy was more powerful than I'd been led to believe. I would do anything to feel like this again. Anything.

He stiffened, his growls becoming something even more guttural. Then I knew the second he was prepared to erupt deep inside. When he jerked me up from the floor, wrapping his arm around my waist, grinding into me, I melted against the man from the explosive heat.

As he filled me with his seed, another crazy thought pushed through my mind. Maybe I didn't hate Miami so much after all.

CHAPTER 5

 *ameson*

Fuck me. What had I done?

I'd lost control. There was no other way to describe the idiocy of my actions. I never lost control. I was the man my best friends called the most demanding and unforgiving of all of us. The three amigos. The three musketeers. Three crazy guys who'd had a desire to develop and build an exclusive BDSM club that would rival every other successful kink club in the country. Soon, we'd be expanding overseas. The franchise in France was already underway and the one in Milan was taking shape.

The creation might have been thought up by three college kids getting ready to graduate, but the design was all my baby. Hell, I'd been the one to think of the name. Carnal

Sins. It had a nice ring to it if I said so myself. After college I'd dug in deep with my dad's commercial construction firm, never realizing how valuable the work would be when finalizing the architectural designs for the first club. It had literally taken an act of Congress to make the purchase, tearing down an old factory. The legal aspects had been one nightmare after another, but we'd persevered.

I'd never forget the day we broke ground. We'd felt like kings of the world. Smirking, I headed toward the photograph of the three of us at the illustrious groundbreaking ceremony. It had just been the three of us and a dude we barely knew taking pictures. For that, we'd had to buy him dinner. We'd had big plans and even bigger dreams. Most had come true.

Lachlan McKenzie ran the club in DC, Grant Wilde the one in LA. And I held down the fort in Miami. With the franchise opportunities, Carnal Sins Inc. would soon be considered a multibillion-dollar company.

The club catered to the wealthiest and most powerful men and some women. The promised anonymity and exclusivity including a private entrance with a gated garage where license plates were blacked out kept all three clubs with an extensive waiting list. With a hundred-thousand-dollar application fee and yearly dues of five hundred thousand to one million depending on the level of membership, only the most influential power mongers were listed on the rosters. Our security system was top notch, our computers networked together.

Members were allowed to visit any of the clubs in the corporation, which had proven to be popular.

We kept a pro dom and pro domme on staff, other masters of various kinks, bouncers and spotters trained to ensure that every fantasy was fulfilled, no matter how dark the kink. Impact play, Shibari, wax play, cupping, needle play, praise play, and bondage were some of the more popular kinks we catered to.

There were strict rules, guests allowed but only with a background check. In addition, every club had a separate party zone where anyone off the street could gain entrance. The Blackout Club had proven to be well worth cost of the addition on all three clubs, lines of people waiting for hours to get in almost every night.

Blacklights and a neon lit dance floor were only part of the festive decor. Every bartender and member of the waitstaff had special uniforms that glowed in the dark. Even special software had been developed for use with 3D-style glasses. When a guest arrived, they were required to fill out a short but very useful form highlighting likes and dislikes in various areas of their life, which would help when searching for a compatible partner. Once a guest was within two feet of someone else, they could read details about the other person near the frame of the lenses.

It had proven to be another hit. We'd also added merchandise available for purchase and the proceeds were unimaginable. We were freaking rolling in dough.

The fact was the three of us were filthy rich and considered some of the most powerful men in our respective cities. It didn't hurt that our members walked various upper echelon floors of the world. Politicians, corporate moguls, judges, artists, actors. All walks of life were represented, but the owners of Carnal Sins held their privacy and proclivities in the palms of our hands.

All of it was exciting and good news, our profits for the year soaring, yet I was an unhappy man and had been for some time. I faked it well, schmoozing with guests as necessary, but when I went home at night, I took off the invisible mask of pretense and bullshit.

I was a country boy at heart, preferring my Harley and cowboy boots to tuxedos and fancy parties. I'd long since lost my Southern accent and almost never revisited the days of being a star football player. They were long gone. Just like the fresh-faced kid lucky enough to get a full ride to the University of PA. If I hadn't, I'd likely still be lugging at my father's construction firm.

I thought about my father for a few seconds and sighed. He'd hoped I'd be married giving him grandkids before he'd died. I'd been the playboy for the first few years, falling victim to believing my own hype. Then I'd fallen hard for one girl. That hadn't worked out, and I'd failed him once again. Going down memory lane wasn't in my best interest.

That's why what had just occurred with Alexandra was so completely out of character for me. I moved through the club toward my office, ignoring basically everyone who acknowledged my presence.

I was in a grumpy mood and there was no reason for it. When I passed by one of my bouncers, a man I considered a friend, I sensed he was following me. He always knew when something was wrong.

After throwing open my office door and storming inside, I headed straight for the bar, yanking a glass off the shelf. I heard the door close behind me with a soft click. There was no sense in turning around. He wasn't going to be here very long. I'd see to that.

"You want to tell me about it?" Jagger asked. Jagger Sanchez had been many things over the years. Star linebacker in high school and college, a formidable and decorated Marine. Now he served as head of my security team, muscle when necessary.

"Nope."

"Why?"

"Because it's not worth talking about."

"Uh-huh," he chastised. "That's why you're hiding behind closed doors prepared to drink yourself to sleep."

I finished filling the glass with scotch before turning around, glaring at him. "First, I'm not hiding. This is my office in my club that I own. Second, I never drink myself to sleep." Hissing, I took a massive gulp, polishing off almost half.

He lifted a single eyebrow as he folded his arms, his look of amusement pissing me off.

"What?" I barked.

"That's what I'm waiting to hear. I'm not leaving until you spill it."

"Get out."

"No."

"I'm your boss."

"So the fuck what?"

"You're fired."

"You make me laugh."

I shook my head, finally able to grin. He had a way of carving through the bullshit with both my garbage and with every person who walked through our hallowed doors. That's why he was so good at what he did, his observation skills keen. His glare remained and I knew how the man operated. He wouldn't leave until I tossed something juicy in his direction.

"Fine. I did something terrible."

"Like soon to be in prison terrible or I should lock down the club in case the cartel shows up terrible?"

"Well, pretty bad." I laughed at his suggestion. There could be a little bit of both.

"What did you do?"

"I saved a girl's life." The admittance brought an exaggerated breath from deep inside my chest.

He narrowed his eyes, his brow furrowing. "Call me crazy but the last time I checked, saving someone's life was a good thing, possibly heroic. I'm not sure where this could end up being something terrible."

"Yeah, well, you don't know the rest." I gulped more, hoping the burn of the liquor would help but it was too smooth.

"That's what you're going to confess. Just think of me as your priest."

"Funny. So damn funny." Sighing, I couldn't seem to get Alexandria's face out of my mind. She was beautiful, far too much so and in my mind forbidden. I knew there were relationships with huge age gaps, but I wasn't that kind of guy. Wait. Relationship? Oh, hell, no. I had no intentions of ever getting involved with anyone again under any circumstances. It wasn't just about Alexandra's age or her obvious vulnerability.

I simply had no further desire for commitment.

"What else?" he prodded.

After easing into my office chair, I sat back, staring up at the ceiling. "She was involved in a car accident. She almost got herself killed by jumping in front of the driver as he sped away from the scene."

"O-kay."

"I jumped in and pushed her aside."

"Like I said before, I don't see the issue."

"For one thing," I said as I thought about the condo her cousin supposedly owned, "the car was registered to Diego Santiago."

"Oh, shit. That's interesting."

"And she wants to press charges."

"Don't blame her; however, doesn't she know who Diego is?"

"She's from Montana. Just moved here."

"Hmmm..." He scratched the scruff on his jaw. "I assume you explained it to her."

"It didn't come up."

"You obviously think there's an issue."

"Well, she's living with some girl at the Perigon. The penthouse."

"Fuck me. Doesn't Santiago have a stake in that building?"

"You got it."

"You think she's a main squeeze for Santiago. Don't you?"

I'd thought about that several times since leaving the condo. "If she's not, her roommate who happens to be her cousin is, which still isn't the best of circumstances. She'll be recruited the moment Santiago gets a look at her. Given the girl is hurting for money, my guess is she'll think it's a sweet deal being a mule."

Diego Santiago was a brutal son of a bitch, the kind of man who believed he owned the world. His empire stretched from Florida through parts of the south, his products coming from South America as well as portions of Europe. He owned a portion of the local law enforcement, who looked the other way when sudden, savage murders occurred that could be directly linked to his organization. Several of the men he held in his pocket were members of the club. What I'd learned early on was that by allowing them to enter the club, I could keep better tabs on what was occurring throughout the city and beyond.

After all, information was power.

He laughed, shaking his head. "Yeah, that is a mess. I assume you walked away and told her to have a nice day."

"Not exactly."

"Is this where the part about you did something bad comes in?"

"Partially. I had to take her home since her car might be totaled."

"Let me guess. You called your buddy Jake to handle the situation."

"Yep. That's not all." Jagger had seen me at my worst, carting me home after a drunken night out on the town. Admitting the carnal event was somehow worse. "I might have enjoyed spending time with her." I lowered my head, lifting a single eyebrow.

Jagger's entire face was suddenly made of stone. "You fucked her."

"And I spanked her for being reckless."

"Jesus motherfucking Christ. What the hell is wrong with you?"

"That's what I'm saying. And she's barely out of school."

When his mouth dropped open, he cursed in Spanish under his breath then headed for the bar. "You're shitting me."

I laughed to myself as he tossed bourbon into a glass of his own. "I wish I were."

"How young?"

"Young."

"Please tell me she's at least over eighteen?"

"I think she is."

"You think." He stormed closer to the desk, his grip on the glass as firm as mine had been.

"I'm pretty certain."

"You're right. This is bad."

Another vision of her sexy body floated into my mind. Her scent still covered my skin, the taste of her managing to linger in my mouth. "I told you."

"Please tell me that's it."

"Not exactly."

"Do I need to be sitting down?"

"Maybe." I took the last swig of my drink, thinking about the Carnal Sins business card I'd left with her including my personal cellphone number. "I offered her a job."

CHAPTER 6

 lexandra

"Hello, sunshine!"

Charlotte blew into the condo as she always did, dramatic and on fire. One day, I hoped to have the same confidence she did.

I glanced over my shoulder as I grabbed the carton of ice cream, surprised to see her home so early. She wasn't dressed in her usual fancy attire, dresses I would kill to wear let alone own. While she'd told me I could borrow anything in her closet more than once, there was no reason to wear something so exquisite. I had no boyfriend, no parties to attend.

Now I didn't have a car.

"You're home early," I muttered as I grabbed a bowl from the cabinet, still sulking.

"Not much going on tonight. I figured we could order in pizza and have a girls' night in." She moved into the kitchen, immediately grabbing a bottle of wine from the counter, peering over my shoulder as I scooped out three spoonfuls of the gooey delight. "I hope that's in celebration of getting the job."

"Hell, no. The fuckers were assholes. I told them so too. Then they had security escort me out of the building."

"Ouch. Are you kidding?"

"Nope. I lost it bigtime."

She laughed, the sound something I'd remembered from before. The gesture was one of the few aspects about her that remained the same. Everything else about her had changed. Her hair color. Her attire. Her attitude. Even the way she carried herself was laced with a hint of arrogance. The gorgeous condominium she'd invited me to stay in wasn't a true reflection of her. It was too... perfect. However, I couldn't look a gift horse in the mouth. I was lucky I wasn't on the street.

"I'll give you points for flair," she said.

I was content with feeling sorry for myself, swiping my finger through the frigid deliciousness. The moment I brought it to my mouth, I thought of the insanely gorgeous man who'd... I would never be able to get over the embarrassment of being spanked. Ever. "It was almost worth it seeing the shocked looks on their faces. I thought the

56

toupee was going to drop off one of the guy's heads. Granted, I'd thought about yanking it off and feeding it to the other Garanimals in the room."

"Whoa. I don't think I've ever seen you this... *spicy*," she purred as she swiveled her hips. "Are you sure something else didn't happen?"

Nothing much other than Thor saved my life then tossed me over his shoulder for good measure, spanking and fucking me like a wild animal. Yeah, that would go over well.

"Isn't that enough for one day?"

She gave me a fake frown, batting her long eyelashes. "I'm sorry, cuz. You'll find a job."

"I know. It's just so depressing. Moving here was a bad idea."

"Don't say that," Charlotte encouraged. "You needed to get away."

She knew enough of the reason I'd agreed to her offer to live with her within seconds of me getting her on the phone. "Yeah, I know." I hated that I was so transparent, a trait I'd done everything to bury.

"Well, I might be able to help," Charlotte said almost in passing as if it was a trivial idea.

"Meaning what?"

There was a hint of resignation on her face. "Meaning I know some people who would give you a job."

"As a waitress? A teacher?"

Everything about her laugh was entirely different. "Oh, God, no. Do you think I'm living here in this fabulous condo based on the income from being a waitress? And why are you so intent on becoming a teacher?"

"Maybe because that's what I studied in college."

She wrinkled her nose. "Bo-ring. You deserve an exciting life, girl, especially after everything you've been through."

"Then what are you suggesting?"

I hated when she shrugged, as if she was blowing off my obvious concern. "Running errands for some powerful people."

"What kind of errands?"

"The kind you don't talk about."

All the times I'd pressed her about what she did for a living. Now she was scaring me.

"Don't look at me that way. It's a great opportunity," she insisted.

I thought about the business card Jameson had given me before he'd left. *Carnal Sins.* The black card had little else, but the name of the club in the center, his on the bottom, both embossed in gold. Then he'd penciled in the phone number of the person I was supposed to call on the back while insisting I provide mine. Which he'd programmed into his phone. When I'd hesitated before giving it to him, he'd reminded me he would need to call me about my poor little car.

"I don't know," I said, thinking about Jameson again.

"You'll make a lot of money." Her singsong voice continued to trouble me.

She'd alluded to being able to get me a job before and I'd declined because of my pride. Given the way Jameson had reacted to the condo, I was nervous for her, curious what she was really doing and who she was working for.

"Thanks, but there's a chance I might have a job." Jameson's job offer came at the tail end of our time together, almost as an afterthought. I hadn't told him how desperate I was, with barely enough money to grab a few groceries, but somehow, he'd known.

"Okay. Tell me more. Every little detail. I knew something else happened. My instinct is never wrong." She poured two glasses of wine then took the spoon from my hand, digging into the ice cream. The way she moaned while taking the bite reminded of the few porn movies I'd seen over the years.

"I had a wreck coming home. Not my fault. Some fucking rich asshole T-boned me. This guy saved me from certain death. He even brought me home. Then he offered me a job. That's pretty much it. I told you nothing else much happened today."

The spoon was in midair as she turned her head toward me, her jaw dropping. "Excuse me?"

Laughing, I grabbed the glass of wine, leaving the ice cream for now and heading into the living room. The lights of Miami were beautiful at night, neon colors of cobalt blue, intense tangerine, and fuchsia creating a sinful backdrop for a city that partied until the wee hours of the morning. "It was a little crazy but all true."

"Who is this guy?" She trailed behind me, moving to the couch and flopping down.

"He owns some club and he thought I might be a good fit."

"What kind of club?" Her words were more biting than playful.

"I don't know. He didn't tell me anything about it."

Snorting, she moved onto the edge of the seat. "There are several clubs in town you don't want to have anything to do with, cuz. I'm serious. Bad people own them. They handle illegal activities behind closed doors. I think you know what I mean."

She was only two years older but acted as if I was naïve as hell. I might be from Montana, but I read the news. I watched television. I knew Miami was considered an illegal drug hub and there were cartels in place to handle the billions of dollars in business. "I think he's legit. Besides, he saved my life."

"You don't know anyone in this town. Men are slick fucks who believe women are tools and nothing more. Do you know his name?"

"Of course I do. I'm not stupid enough to consider going to work for a man without finding out who he is." I'd planned on searching the internet, but on top of everything else crappy that had happened earlier, I'd forgotten my laptop charger was in the last bag I'd yet to bring into the building.

I'd tried to get into her computer, but it was locked down tight.

"Then what do you know?"

I opened my mouth then frowned. "Okay, so I haven't checked yet." I yanked the card from my pocket, rubbing my finger across the lettering before handing it to her.

Charlotte scowled as she snapped it from my fingers. As soon as she glanced at the front, she whistled. "Holy fucking good fortune."

"What? Do you know it?"

"You said this guy who saved you was the owner?"

"That's what he told me. Jameson Stark."

I thought for certain the poor girl was going to hyperventilate. She placed her wine on the table, jerked up and raced toward the bedrooms. What the hell was she doing? When she returned a couple of minutes later, she had her iPad in her hand, her finger bouncing across the screen furiously.

Then she handed it to me. "Is this the guy you met?"

I glanced at his picture first and my stomach started to do flips. Jameson was at some event, dozens of people in the background, champagne flowing. Dressed in a tuxedo, he was surrounded by women, the same glittering smile I'd seen more than once on his face. He was even more stunning than he'd been, his eyes holding the kind of fire that had attracted me to him in the first place.

"This is him? Answer me."

"Stop being so forceful."

"Come on," she snipped. "If it is, then you are one lucky woman."

"Fine. That's the dude who acted as if I was some nutcase for trying to keep the driver responsible for the wreck from speeding off." Now I was flustered, heat building behind my ears, my pussy aching from being stretched and taken roughly. Oh, God. What was wrong with me?

"Whew," she moaned, fanning her face. "You know how to pick them."

"I didn't exactly pick him. Fate did." Fate. I'd never believed in the concept, especially not after everything that had happened. I scrolled down, skimming the article.

Miami's Hottest Bachelor Donates One Million Dollars to the Children's Hospital

The tagline was just the beginning, the article highlighting him as man of the year. "Who is this guy really and what is Carnal Sins?"

"The man is exactly what that article states. He's rich, famous up and down the East Coast, powerful and sought after by every woman who still has a pulse in the city. Carnal Sins is *the* hottest club in town, although you and I will never get an invite." She huffed, returning to the couch and grabbing her wine. "Was there a maintenance worker in the condo today?"

I noticed she was staring at the floor covering and winced. While the units in the building were all owned by someone, there was a special maintenance team supposedly providing everything from replacing lightbulbs to fixing plumbing leaks. I'd never asked her who owned this unit. I had a feeling the subject was off limits. At least it was a plausible excuse to probably ruining her precious rug.

"No, why?"

"There are scratch marks in the rug. Damn it. Anyway," she murmured and heat shifted across my jaw for a second time as I remembered our act of filthy sin from earlier. "Carnal Sins is a members-only kink club."

My pussy still ached from his wide girth. Just thinking about the way he'd fucked me made me tingle all over. What she'd just said suddenly registered. "Kink club? As in BDSM?"

"You got it. I've heard anything goes there for a price. I think it's like a million dollars a year or something like that."

My skin suddenly crawled. "I'm not into kink."

"Yeah, I know. Did he say what he'd hire you for?"

"Not exactly, but he knew I'd applied as a cocktail waitress all around town with no success."

"Then maybe he wants you to work at Blackout, the sister business. It's a dance club accessible to the likes of you and me. Pretty hot too. I've been there a couple times."

"Oh, yeah? With who?"

She laughed, the sound throaty yet practiced. "I have a few men who treat me like a lady."

The implication was that she wasn't always treated that way. A cold chill drifted down my spine. I thought about what Jameson had said when he'd handed me the card, which wasn't much. *"I might be able to get you on board at my club. We'll talk."* That had been it.

"So, how close did you get to your *savior?*" she cooed.

"Oh, I don't know. He brought me home." Why was it that everything that popped from her mouth sounded dirty? *Because you initiated a sinful, filthy act. I most certainly did not. It was all his fault.* Now I was having a conversation with my inner voice. Maybe I had to consider I was cuckoo.

"Yeah?" Charlotte lifted her eyebrow.

"We talked. That's it." My throat started to tighten.

"O-kay. Come on, girlie. I can tell there's more. What was he like? Did the photographs lie?"

Sighing, I revived the screen on the iPad and shook my head, doing my best to keep from drooling. "No. He's perfect."

I couldn't stop the heat from continuing to rise, suddenly embarrassed.

"Oh, my God. Did you fuck him?"

"No! Of course not." *Liar, liar, pants on fire.*

"Holy shit. You did. Don't you lie to your cousin. Tell me everything. That man is the hottest hunk of meat to set foot in this town. I heard he's rich, like filthy rich. He's graced all the hottest magazines. I also heard he's the ultimate in dangerous, dressed in Armani suits."

I laughed at her exuberance. "He didn't seem like the Armani type."

"You're not skirting around telling me every juicy detail."

"Nothing happened. He was just very protective."

"Hmmm…"

"I'm serious."

"That definitely means you fucked him." The expression on her face was devious.

"Charlotte!"

"What?" she huffed, giving me a pouty face. "I'm just looking out for your best interests."

"Sure you are." I rolled my eyes, suddenly needing more than just a glass of wine.

My cousin took a sip of her drink, her face furrowed to the point I was concerned she was having an attack of some kind. "I'll get it out of you one day. I say take the job. What do you have to lose?"

She was right, but that didn't mean I wasn't nervous about doing so. Every good event in my life had been followed by black clouds.

"Unless you'd prefer working with me." The change in her tone was odd, as if she was trying to warn me to stay away from whatever she'd fallen into.

"No. As long as I'm not involved in the kinky side of their club, I'm okay with working for him."

She nodded, glancing toward the window a few seconds later. "Let me know if by any chance there's another job in the fancy joint for me."

I moved toward the couch, sitting down. Only then did I realize she had a bruise on her cheek that she'd done a very good job covering up with makeup. When I reached out, she pulled away, laughing.

"What happened?" I asked, curling my fingers and pressing my hand into my lap.

The sudden shimmer in her eyes yanked at my insides. "I was a bad girl." While she continued to laugh, keeping her face turned away from me, my gut told me she'd found herself in a very difficult position.

"Talk to me."

"Nope," she said, her expression brightening. "This is a celebration. You're going to knock them dead, kink or no kink. But I'd consider allowing him to tie you to a cross, flogging your ass."

"Charlotte! I'm not that kind of girl." Even as I made the statement, a little tremor of excitement coursed through me.

She lifted her glass and for the first time since I'd arrived in Miami, I noticed how much pain she was in, her eyes haunted.

Charlotte noticed I was staring at her and jerked to her feet, holding her arm as she walked toward the window. The sudden tension between us was unusual. We used to tell each other everything, our conversations on the phone and sometimes in person going late into the night. We'd shared our passion for boys, thoughts on our futures, and so many hopes and dreams that we'd almost built a fantasy world around us. She was so different it scared me.

"Charlotte. Tell me what's going on. You can't possibly afford this place on your own."

"It's Char. Remember? Charlotte apparently isn't sexy enough."

Exhaling, I headed toward the window, keeping enough space she wouldn't walk away. "You're too sexy for your skin."

She flitted a look in my direction, her laughter more like I remembered. When she wiped tears from her eyes, I wanted to wrap my arms around her, but she wouldn't let me get but so close. She'd shove me away, telling me for the fifteenth time how fabulous her life was. I knew better but not knowing what she was going through left me in a difficult position.

"I think Jameson is a good guy from everything I've heard. Don't allow this opportunity to pass, cuz." Her statement was said in a kind of reverence that unnerved me even more.

"I'm going to find out if they need another waitress."

"Ha. You'd do that for me?"

"We're family. Right?"

She pulled me into her arms and the way she was shaking nearly destroyed me. "Make the call to Mr. Stark. You'll be safe working there."

Safe. I shuddered from the way she muttered the word.

What had my cousin gotten herself in the middle of?

 ameson

"Ginger," I said as I headed to the bar where she stood.

"Hiya, boss man."

I glanced down at her outfit and grinned. "So that's another version of the festive wear you mentioned?" Ginger Coleman, my director of recreation was perhaps the most creative employee I'd hired to date. She had a flair for costumes, providing dozens of suggestions for updated versions of the black-on-black attire the employees had worn since inception in the Blackout Club. Even though we'd settled on a flashy costume including built-in LED lights, she'd constantly tinkered with improvements.

"What do you think?" she asked, twirling in a full circle.

"I think you're brilliant at what you do and I'm not certain what I would do without you."

"Uh-huh," she purred. "You're buttering me up for something. I can tell."

"When have I ever done that?"

"When you asked me to host an event for Slade, the pompous rock star. Remember?"

Wincing, I couldn't help but laugh. It had been her first week on the job and I'd tossed her into a den full of lions. The aging rocker had met his match with her, ending his night screaming at me that she was a bitch. "Oh, that."

"You owe me."

I held up my hand. "I promise you this one will be much less of an issue to deal with."

"You do know that man almost became a soprano that night. Right?"

"Is that why he hasn't returned since the event?"

She fanned her face and winked. "What do you need?"

"How are we on waitresses?"

"As in do we have plenty of employees?"

I nodded.

"For the most part, although if business keeps up this way, I'll need a couple more. Who do you want me to hire, your niece?" Ginger asked.

"Ouch and no."

"Just teasing."

"There's a sweet girl down on her luck and I thought she might make a good fit." The funny thing was that as I scanned the crowded bar, I could see Alexandra giving the dudes who got handsy hell.

"Sweet girl, huh? What's her name?"

"Alexandra Kingston and I might have already offered her a job." I stood back, giving her my usual commanding look that she typically ignored.

"Should I ask any questions?"

"Don't you dare."

"Okay. You're the boss man. Have her contact me directly. What if she doesn't work out?"

"Then let me know and I already gave her your number," I told her. When she gave me a mischievous twitch of her nose, I waved her off, laughing at her bravado. At least she kept me on my toes.

"Of course you did."

I strode through the club, doing my single nightly check. Then I headed back to my office to sulk.

Before venturing out to talk with Ginger, I'd sequestered myself behind my office doors for two hours, still trying to process why I'd slipped off the edge of a cliff. For most men, indulging in a beautiful and very young blonde for intense passion would be considered a reason for celebration. So why was I sulking behind closed doors? I drummed my fingers on the wooden surface of my desk as I scrolled through my phone numbers until I found Alexandra's. I continued to have a sense that she was in danger, although I had no firm reason why the nagging thought remained.

As expected, her car had been totaled, the fifteen-year-old vehicle soon to be put out of its misery. I'd taken the liberty of checking out what I could find on her background, confirming that until recently, she'd been living in Billings, Montana. She had no arrest record, not even a single parking ticket. Thank God, I'd also been able to confirm her age. A ripe old twenty-three. Shit. It still felt like I'd robbed the cradle.

Well, since our encounter was a one time and done, I wouldn't need to worry about how bad my decision-making processes had been. That didn't change the fact I'd offered her a job. So far, she'd yet to make contact. I wasn't certain if I was pleased or offended. What I hadn't managed to find was anything worthwhile regarding who owned the condominium. It was listed in a company name. I didn't need to search to know it was a bogus entity, nothing more than a shell to make everything seem on the up and up.

I didn't think I'd get long odds if I bet Santiago's accounting minions had paid for the unit as well as several others throughout the city.

Groaning, I closed my eyes and tossed my phone onto the desk.

The knock on the door drew my attention away, and I almost bristled from being interrupted. "Yes?"

Jagger had a sheepish grin on his face as he walked in. "That replacement senator has requested your presence."

Replacement senator. I almost laughed. Since Marshall Winston had been found guilty of several insidious crimes, his attempt at hamstringing my life and the club had shifted into blissful peace. While I knew little about the man who'd taken his place after a special election other than he'd been a member of the club for several years, with a name like Wallace Collins, I'd labeled him in my mind as a staunch conservative. Since his election, he hadn't returned to the club. I was curious as to why now he'd decided to approach me and what he had to say.

"Where is he?"

"With his buddies in the Red Room. They waited outside for an hour for it to become available."

"Christ."

"That's what I said. Maybe Miami is getting ready to burn down."

His summation was believable.

His grin forced me to laugh. The suite of conference rooms all had specific names. The Gold Room. The Silver Room. The Red Room. The monikers had been selected after a night of drinking with my two partners. They were listed the same for all three clubs, now made a requirement in the contracts for all franchises. It was funny how the Red Room was selected most often by the members. For some, it meant the warm blush on the bottom of their submissive after receiving a harsh round of discipline.

For others it was a clear warning to whoever was on the receiving end of the required discussion.

Then for others, it meant a dangerous statement that blood could be shed depending on the outcome of the meeting.

I'd learned that the hard way, the single incident outside the club creating a buzz with the police, leading to Senator Winston's attempts at destroying the club's reputation. The room was where the most pampered, pompous assholes were catered to until I decided as to whether they'd remain a member. When someone was insistent on the room in particular, I knew trouble could be brewing.

"His buddies," I repeated as I stood, buttoning my jacket. "I'll be curious as to who they are." I'd spent an hour in my private gym in my attempt to work off the continuous flow of testosterone, which hadn't worked. Even the hot shower where I'd fisted my cock to the point of leaving it raw hadn't pulled my mind away from my intense desires.

"I figured the senator was just another one of the lifeless few."

Jagger had a saying for the various levels of members, his creative use of the English dictionary amusing. His reference denoted someone who'd become a member for the sole reason of confessing their illustrious membership, which added credence to their level of wealth and influence. "An excellent judge of character."

"That's why you hired me."

He flexed his muscles on purpose as I walked by, his sense of humor ever present. "Any idea who he brought with him?"

"A bodyguard, the CEO of Welsh Pharmaceuticals, and from what I can tell some piss-ant attorney."

The combination was interesting and since I was a betting man, I'd say the senator was fishing about the same man who continued to haunt my mind over the last few hours. Diego Santiago. I'd heard through numerous channels that Santiago was attempting to strong arm several smaller pharmaceutical companies, his desire to get into the pain management business widely known. I remained surprised the DEA had yet to get involved, although I wondered if Santiago's reach was more encompassing than anyone originally thought.

If my assumptions were correct, I wasn't certain why I'd been called into a meeting. Santiago had been refused membership twice, his reaction certainly not endearing the man in my mind.

I'd been threatened numerous times in my life, including from women who believed I was the sole reason their husband preferred spending time with a submissive. Diego's threat had been personal, so much so I'd taken it to heart, installing another layer of security around my home.

I also had an arsenal locked away behind closed doors with enough ammunition to start a war. My fellow college buddies would laugh their asses off if they knew the formal football star had taken up target shooting as a hobby.

"Any word from the girl?" he asked almost sheepishly.

After throwing him a look, I grinned. "No, but you don't need to worry about the police knocking on our door."

His gesture of rolling the edge of his hand across his forehead was exaggerated. "Whew."

I gave him my middle finger, shaking my head as he laughed before heading down the stairs, not bothering to knock on the door before entering. Three of the four men remained standing; only Senator Collins was seated, drilling his fingers on the conference table.

"It took you long enough," he said, his caustic words amusing me.

"I didn't realize I was working on your schedule," I answered. No one came into my club and acted as if their shit didn't stink. I couldn't care less about how much money they spent or their connections in the world. Neither meant anything to me.

The obvious bodyguard snorted as if he was a bull in heat. He was a tank in stature, the same size as Jagger but his bulk was comprised by eating one too many cannolis.

"What is it that I can do for you gentlemen?" I asked, not intending on indulging them with but so much of my time.

The entire group except for the bodyguard appeared uncomfortable. When I counted ten seconds of silence, I turned toward the door.

"Wait a minute, Stark."

The attorney's voice was gruff and I was already in a piss-poor mood. "That's Mr. Stark to those I don't consider a friend." I shifted toward the man in question, driving my hands into my trouser pockets. I stood several inches taller, a solid fifty-pounds-plus additional muscle.

"Forgive my colleagues for their rudeness, Mr. Stark. I don't believe we've met. I'm Donald Welsh, CEO of Welsh Pharmaceuticals."

I turned to my head toward the man speaking, my photographic memory providing the last article in *Forbes* magazine, the article championing his successes.

"I know who you are, Mr. Welsh. The question is why you requested this meeting. If it's about aspects of the club, that's something my assistant handles."

"It's not about your damn club, Stark," Collins huffed.

Donald exhaled, slowly looking at the man. "As you probably know, Diego Santiago is making a pitch to get into the pharmaceutical business."

I chuckled. "In a manner of speaking. What does that have to do with me?"

"It's come to our attention that Mr. Santiago has requested membership in your club."

"And you are?" I asked the other stiff shirt in the room.

"Parker Redman. Attorney for Mr. Welsh."

"Mmm..." I said as I rubbed my jaw. I had no doubt where they were going with this. "Let me guess. You want me to allow his membership so you can have an up close and personal opportunity to set him straight about his intentions in complete privacy. Am I correct?"

"That is the general idea, yes," Redman answered, although far too smugly for my liking.

"While I understand your concerns, gentlemen, I'm not in the habit of playing politics or having the cartel dancing within my club. I prefer to keep my members safe."

"You have dozens of criminals as members, Mr. Stark. I wonder how your more affluent clientele would take if they knew you allowed mafia kingpins into your hallowed halls." The smirk on the senator's face was enough to almost have me revoke his membership. Men like him believed the limited power they'd gained in office precluded them from engaging in the golden rule. That's why my partners and I had developed what others would affectionately call a little black book of members' sins.

No one was off the hook unless they were squeaky clean. Admittedly, neither Lachlan nor Grant had been required to use their scathing information but on rare occasions, given the caustic atmosphere Miami had been shoved into over the last few years, I'd found the detailed dossiers quite useful.

I slowly placed my hands on the table, leaning over as I planted a smile on my face. "My guess is about the same as they'd feel about learning their newly elected state senator had a penchant for young men. I am curious. Does Elsie know about your overzealous proclivities?" I was almost never required to go any further than shoving the possible leak of information in their faces. I also never made a claim I couldn't back up.

"How dare you!" The senator jerked to his feet with enough force it knocked the chair over.

I stood to my full height, smoothing my hands down on my jacket. "I don't dare, Senator Collins. I deliver. I think this concludes our meeting. Don't you?"

Mr. Welsh seemed more piqued than before, the lump in his throat growing larger. My guess was the man had a personal reason in wanting Santiago out of the game of legal drugs. However, it wasn't my cause to undertake.

"Have a pleasant evening." I walked out, immediately heading for the main entrance of Blackout where Jagger was stationed for the evening.

"That was fast," he said as he stepped away from the door.

"You know how I feel about pompous assholes, my friend."

"Are they in one piece?"

"For now. Watch them. If they cause any trouble, throw them out."

"Will do, boss." He grinned. "You going to see the new snack?"

"Rude, Mr. Sanchez. Very rude. I'm headed out for the evening."

"Wow. The chick really wiped you out." He threw up his hands in surrender. The only other men who got away with taunting me were Grant and Lachlan. And that was only because they'd known me as the runt of the football team so many years ago that I didn't want to remember.

It only reminded me I was getting old.

Laughing, I returned to my office to grab my keys. It was time to go home.

To an empty house and a hell of a lot of bad memories.

The slight chime on my watch forced me to glance at the time. I hadn't realized I'd been sitting in the same place in the den for over an hour. The almost full drink was still in my hand, which wasn't like me. I wasn't the kind of man to succumb to depression, but the last few years had worn heavily on my mind.

Lachlan had said it was because I needed to get laid more often.

Grant had said something about taking more vacations. But the club was my life. In the beginning, the long, arduous hours had excited me. Seeing my artistic creation come to life had kept me on cloud nine for years.

I moved from the chair, heading to my office. The one rule I'd made for myself after the first club in DC had opened was that I'd never bring work home. I'd followed the rules with only a few exceptions. That didn't mean I hadn't handled business, but it had been on other projects.

I couldn't remember the last time I'd been inside the room. Between adding the Blackout Club in Miami as well as dealing with Philip Dumas, the Frenchman who'd recently come into the Carnal Sins family in Paris, I'd had very little time to myself. Now, with construction of the first franchise well under way, my visits to Paris had been reduced to once a month for only a couple of days at a time.

Blackout was running smoothly. Hiring Ginger had turned out to be a godsend, her efficiency off the charts. In other words, I had all the free time in the world if that's what I wanted. Jesus. Was I suddenly throwing a pity party for myself?

I flicked on the light, leaning against the doorjamb. The reason I'd never brought any club work home was that I'd continued designing buildings for the first few years after the DC club opened. The location had always been Lachlan's baby. I'd lived in various small apartments, not setting down roots due to my traveling schedule.

The flexibility had allowed me to design several award-winning buildings, dotting the skies of Los Angeles, Seattle, and Baltimore. Then I'd stopped designing altogether. I'd told myself that I'd been too busy with the club, which had been true in the beginning, but with the employment of competent people, the lie hadn't been as easy to swallow.

I walked inside, glancing at the framed designs. I'd been so proud of them, longing to share them with my Pops. He'd died before I had an opportunity to show him that I wasn't just creating what he'd called a 'goddamned sex club for freaks.' As I ran my finger across one of my favorite pieces, I took a deep breath. I no longer had the drive to continue creating.

Even the laptop that remained in the center of the desk needed software updates. I'd all but shut down another side of my lucrative business. Half laughing, a bitter taste left in my mouth, I headed toward the door.

Going down memory lane certainly wasn't going to change my foul mood.

And it certainly wasn't going to make me forget the past.

CHAPTER 8

 *lexandra*

"You're okay with this?" Charlotte asked as she pulled her car in front of the club.

"The job? Absolutely."

"No, me leaving you here. How are you going to get home?"

"I'll catch an Uber if I need to," I told her.

"That's crazy."

I gave her a look as I opened the door. "I'm a big girl. I can take care of myself. Besides, hopefully Jameson will have some information about my car."

"Maybe he can take you home. Ooh-la-la. After a little kinky time."

"Stop," I admonished, although the thought had crossed my mind. Not about the kink but the ride.

"Did you call the body shop?"

"I did," I lied. He'd taken care of everything, and I couldn't even remember the name of the tow company who'd arrived. I knew it was stupid putting all my faith into him, but I'd been a little bit out of my mind by that point, maybe even in shock. "I think Jameson had it brought here."

"Girl, there's no way the damage could have been fixed that quickly. Call me and I'll come get you. Okay? That is if that hunk doesn't grab you first." She was in an unusually good mood, far too giddy for someone who'd been labeled a 'bad girl.'

"What about your work?"

She shrugged yet was unable to hide the shadow that crossed her face from the overhead light. "I can get off for a few minutes. They owe me a favor or two. Don't worry about it."

There were so many things I wanted to say to her, begging her to find another job, but now wasn't the time.

A few minutes. The drive here had taken almost thirty. I had to fend on my own. Besides, I had the distinct feeling that pulling her away from her important duties would be frowned on. She looked as if she was headed to a glamorous party, her sequined dress sparkling in the neon exterior lights of the club. "Let me see what happens. Okay? I'll be fine."

"I worry about you. That's all."

I climbed out, thinking about something I'd wanted to ask her once again. When I stuck my head back in, I almost didn't do it, but something prompted me otherwise. "You're not doing anything illegal, are you? With your job, I mean."

While she laughed, I sensed she was prepared to give me the answer I needed to hear. "Now, you need to stop worrying. I'll tell you more about what I do later. Okay?"

In my mind she was running drugs for the cartel.

Somehow, I doubted she'd come clean with me no matter how many times I asked. "Okay. Be safe. I'll ask about the job."

"Thank you. Now, go have some raunchy fun."

I backed away, waiting until she was out of sight before taking a deep breath. The truth was I was anything but okay. While I was flustered and worried I couldn't handle the job I'd been offered, I also had reservations about seeing Jameson again. His domineering actions had remained with me long after he'd gone. It wasn't just about the round of discipline, but also because I'd enjoyed pleasing him, being praised. It made no real sense. I'd never been that kind of girl in my life.

My daddy used to call me a tomboy, more likely to pick a fight with a boy than play with dolls. He was right. I'd never been comfortable around girls, especially my age. Maybe that's why I'd liked spending time with Charlotte. She took no shit from anyone.

At least I could pretend to be something I wasn't tonight. Confident. I threw my head back and headed for the door, noticing a line had already formed outside the building. I'd talked with Ginger for a little while over the phone. She seemed very nice, albeit I could tell a little baffled about why Jameson had offered me a job. I certainly wasn't going to tell her he probably felt sorry for me.

Or that we'd... fucked.

Ugh. I had to stop thinking about it. When I opened the door, a huge man advanced like a predator, stopping in front of me. The look on his face was menacing. And holy cow, he was huge.

I was forced to lift my entire head to be able to try to look him in the eyes.

"You'll need to get in line with everyone else," he told me in a brusque tone, folding his arms over his massive chest.

"I... work here. I mean this is my first night. I mean I'm supposed to see Ginger?"

He narrowed his eyes, scrutinizing my jeans and sneakers. "What's your name?"

I tried to swallow the huge lump in my throat, anxiety tearing through me. "Alexandra Kingston." The man acted like I wasn't going to be given entrance. Then he grabbed an iPad, running his fingers across the screen. When a huge grin popped across his face, I shrank back.

"So *you're* Alexandra."

Uh-oh.

"I'm her. Who are you?"

"Direct. That's good. I'm Jagger. I'm one of the men who will protect you. You'll hear this in your introduction, but no one touches the merchandise. If anyone bothers you, all you need to do is let me, Stone over there, or Colt know, and we'll take care of the situation."

"Jagger. Stone. Colt. You guys should be depicted in romance novels."

His laugh was hearty. I had a feeling I'd like this guy. "I'll take that as a compliment. I heard you had a little attitude on you. That will prove to be helpful."

"Hmmm... I'm not sure I like that."

His grin was knowing. "I'll take you to Ginger."

Why did I have the distinct feeling he knew exactly who I was and why I was here? I almost backed out then chastised myself. I'd been a damn good waitress while attending college. Granted, it had been at a honkytonk bar, not a club for the wealthy, but I could do anything if I put my mind to it.

He led me inside past another huge dude and once I walked down a long corridor, the room I entered reminded me of being in Disneyland. There were neon lights everyone, strings of them floating down from the ceiling, walls covered with various sharks and flamingos. Even the bar was backlit with them.

Employees were wearing costumes, every one of them lit. Some were even flashing. There were dozens of standing tables, all made of acrylic tops allowing another warm glow of sparkling lights. Even the drinks had a neon straw nestled inside. There were also blacklights everywhere, creating gothic shadows and the dance floor was one of the largest I'd ever seen. I noticed a DJ in a booth far above the crowd, the snazzy dressed buff man dancing to the powerful thumping music.

I hadn't realized I'd made gasped loud enough to be heard over the almost tribal music until he laughed.

"You haven't been in the club before, have you?"

"No. This is amazing."

"You haven't seen anything yet. Come on. Ginger will give you a tour."

My hands were like ice as he led me toward a hallway to a set of locked doors. Using a keycode, he gained access. The quiet as soon as the door closed behind us was unnerving. The area must be soundproofed. I couldn't imagine the amount of money spent on building the club itself.

He tapped on a partially closed door before pushing it open.

The girl on the other side wasn't what I'd expected, although at this point, I was certain I'd be wrong about everything.

"Your new employee," Jagger said with amusement still in his tone. Did everybody know I'd slept with the boss? That wouldn't bode well for being the new girl or with being accepted.

"Thanks, Jag. I'll take it from here."

"Remember what I said," he told me before walking out.

Ginger moved closer. "Stunning."

"I'm sorry?"

"I was told you were stunning and Jameson is right. You'll be an instant hit with the customers."

"I, um… I hope I'm getting this job because I'm qualified. I don't want any handouts. As a matter of fact, maybe there's been some kind of mistake. I'm not that kind of girl. I don't do kink. I wouldn't even know what a St. Christopher's cross looks like let alone want to be strapped to it. I'm not into pain, although I've heard with pain comes pleasure, but I don't know if I believe that so… So, I'll just shut up now." I rambled when I was nervous and I'd crossed over into being terrified.

She chuckled. "First of all, you're working the Blackout Club side of Carnal Sins, not the kinky side. Second, while physical beauty is a positive trait that helps our girls and guys make higher tips, I don't hire on looks alone. Third, and hopefully Jagger told you this already. I don't allow any of my people to be touched inappropriately. I also don't allow dating amongst the ranks. This is a fun club with an amazing reputation and I won't allow that to be tarnished."

Uh-oh. I'd already broken at least one rule, although I'd hardly call Jameson amongst the ranks. "Yes, ma'am."

"Please. I don't call my mother ma'am. I'm Ginger. And lastly although just as important," she said as she walked closer. "But so you know, it's called a St. Andrew's cross."

She grinned mischievously and I knew instantly I was going to like her.

"Oops."

"It's alright. I'm sure Jameson will provide you with a tour of the other side of my world. It's good to know what we offer but you will never be forced to submit. Okay? I wanted to make certain you understand that."

I shuddered when she used the word. That's what I'd already done, submitted to Jameson. "Okay. Thank you."

"Relax. We do try and have fun here. Let's get the nasty paperwork squared away. Then I'll give you a uniform and take you on a tour. Tonight you'll be shadowing both one of our bartenders and one of the servers. If you're comfortable, you can take a table or two. Then I'll get you on the schedule."

I felt relieved more than anything.

But I was also excited. The only trouble was my intense enthusiasm was based on my hope of seeing Jameson again.

Somewhere in the back of my mind I knew it wasn't the best thing all the way around, but a girl wants what she wants.

God help me, I was doomed.

* * *

Heaven's mercy, he was watching me.

The chiseled god himself.

I'd never felt so nervous in my life. My hands were shaking and that was nothing in comparison to the clunkiness I felt in my legs. I wasn't used to being on heels for one thing, but the moment I'd realized Mr. Stark himself was watching from the shadows, I turned into mush. I'd suffered through drunk cowboys and oil riggers, their hands-on approach as much of an irritant as their lewd slurs.

I'd been confronted with a crazed asshole determined to steal my purse. The stupid jerk had been completely shocked that instead of cowering like a girl, I'd thrown two hard punches in a row, knocking him to the pavement, taunting him to see if he wanted more.

And for kicks and giggles, I'd fought off a big, burly guy determined to roughhouse my best girlfriend.

But this... this was as if I was walking a tightrope over quicksand. Even from thirty feet away, I'd felt Jameson's eyes capturing my every move. My instinct told me he wasn't merely assessing his latest hire. He was contemplating what he wanted to do with the girl he'd fucked. Shit. Shit. Shit.

Ginger had allowed me to work a couple of tables, keeping an eye on me for the first few minutes. Then she'd disappeared, which had given me confidence. Now, as I made my way to a table of five rowdy guys, I couldn't seem to keep my arm or the tray holding beers and shots from shaking.

"Here comes the babe," one of the dudes said. I didn't need to hear the slurping sound he made as he dragged his tongue around his lips to know it was disgusting.

"I think she needs to be our party favor tonight," another jerk commented then barked like a dog.

With the boss watching, I couldn't provide the answer I usually did, even if it was apparent the jerk could use a swift kick in the balls.

"Hey, babe. I think you're coming with us. Maybe you can handle all five of us."

"I might consider it if even one of you had a decent size dick." I knew the comeback was childish at best, but I wasn't in any mood to deal with bullshit since my life was currently still hovering just over the toilet.

"What did you say?" one of them growled, jerking to his feet.

"You heard me, or are you lacking in other areas as well?" I gave him a snarky look and was certain even in the sparkling lights that his face was turning bright red.

"You want to see, sweetheart? I'll be happy to show you."

"Right here?" I challenged. I'd heard this kind of trash talk back in high school.

"I think she needs to be taught a lesson."

I was about to hand out the first drinks when bottom feeder number four decided to grab a handful of my ass. The moment of sickening slow motion wrapped around my ugly little world, and the tray of drinks went flying toward the jerk and his buddies.

"You little fucking bitch!" the ass grabber snorted, jerking up from the table with enough force he knocked his chair over. He didn't hesitate to grab my arm, yanking me against him.

"I suggest you get your hand off me now or I won't hesitate to ensure you won't be allowed to make a return visit," I snarled.

"You obviously don't know who we are."

Laughing on purpose, I shifted my gaze around the table. "No, I got it. Little boys with little dicks."

When the bastard lifted his arm as if to hit me, I was shocked enough I didn't respond right away.

I didn't need to.

The son of a bitch was grabbed around the back of his neck, lifted into the air then slammed on the floor as if he weighed nothing. Then my hero dropped to the floor, pressing his forearm against the jerk's neck.

I had to blink twice to realize the man who'd come to my rescue wasn't one of the bouncers but Jameson Stark instead.

"You don't treat women that way," Jameson roared. He used the full weight of his body in pinning the guy to the floor, so much so I heard the kid gagging as he flailed his arms.

"Hey, man. You're killing him," a buddy shouted.

"We were just fooling around."

The look Jameson gave the guy who'd just made the mistake of speaking was pure evil.

Suddenly, Jagger was there as well as the other bouncer.

"We got it from here, boss," Jagger said, sneering at the entire table.

Only Jameson didn't seem very interested in letting the now choking man go. In fact, he leaned over, his voice low enough I couldn't hear what was being said, but I did notice the look of terror on the guy's face. Then my boss rose to his feet, raking both hands through his hair. Everything about the incident seemed surreal, including the fact no one in close proximity seemed bothered by any of it.

The dude scrambled to his feet, huffing and puffing as if he was going to attempt to take Jameson on in a fight. I wasn't a betting girl, but I'd be happy to slide a C note on this one given the kid was at least six inches shorter and a solid eighty pounds lighter.

"Now, apologize to the young lady," Jameson hissed, snapping his head in the dude's direction. At least the kid had the good sense to back off.

The arrogance of the four remaining guys remained strong, one of them folding his arms and laughing.

"Not gonna happen, bud."

I was certain that Jameson was going to fly across the table at the guy for his haughty attitude alone, but instead he took a deep breath then planted his hands on the table, leaning over. "The five of you are banned from my club, gentlemen. Now, you will apologize, or I'll personally have you tossed out of here instead of any of you being able to walk out on your own. It's your choice."

"My father will hear about this." The statement was made by the one who'd grabbed my ass.

Jagger seemed surprised at first then grinned, mimicking the jerk's movements by crossing his arms over his massive chest.

Jameson took a deep breath, moving closer once again. "Do that. It changes nothing. Apologize or you're going to get hurt."

The five looked back and forth at each other. Finally, the one who'd been completely silent throughout the entire floor show cleared his throat.

"We're sorry. That was rude of us."

One by one the others gave their sorry excuses for an apology, the ass grabber coming in an oh-so shocking last. When they grabbed their things, acting as if they were going to leave without paying, Jagger smashed his fist on the table.

"Money, boys. And make certain you tip our server generously for the bullshit you just put her through." Jagger's voice boomed over the music.

Ass grabber cursed under his breath, yanking out his wallet and tossing several bills onto the table. When he walked past, he brushed against me with enough momentum I had to take a step back.

"Out. Now!" Jagger winked at me before leading all five away from the table. I took a deep breath, about ready to provide thanks to my boss when I realized he'd walked away, disappearing into the crowd.

I started to shake all over again. Within seconds, another employee was there to clean up the mess. I grabbed the money and tray then backed away, taking several shaky breaths before sliding behind the bar. As I shook off the glass, returning the tray to the holder, the bartender eased behind me.

"Delicious excitement on your first night," Troy said, the bartender grinning as he made some frothy beverage.

"Ugh. I shouldn't have insulted them, but they plucked my last nerve." I held out the wad of cash, noticing ass grabber had stopped long enough to take another spiteful look in my direction.

He took the cash from my hand, immediately cashing out their check. When he handed me a crisp hundred-dollar bill, I almost kissed him. "Your tip. At least they were generous."

"Only because they were made to do so. Jerks."

"You got that right. I'm glad someone had the balls to say something to them. Spoiled little rich brats with trust funds. They've been troublemakers since the day they were born. I oughta know. I had to go to high school with all five of them."

"Ouch!" I shoved the money in my pocket, grateful to have some additional cash.

"You can say that again. I'm curious. What did you say to them to get them all hot and bothered?"

"Oh, something about their tiny dicks."

He burst into laughter. "I knew I was going to like you from the second you walked around my bar. At least the owner doesn't allow that kind of shit to happen."

"I'm curious. Does he do that often?"

"Mr. Stark? He usually doesn't need to go that far. Folks know his reputation and try not to piss him off."

"His reputation?"

"That he's a take no shit kind of man. He's some big ex-football star nicknamed the Cruncher for his ability to break bones." His grin had me more than curious. "I will admit he was more possessive than I've seen him. That means he likes you." His grin made me blush.

Possessive. I wasn't certain I liked the word any longer. I'd seen his look of fury, the kind of anger than made a man do very bad things.

"Great. Not the best first night."

He laughed. "Stop worrying. You did what you had to do. Now, back to work."

I took a deep breath, unable to pull my mind off the way Jameson reacted or how sexy he was. No one had ever come to my defense the way he'd just done. I searched the crowd for him once again, shaking my head. I had to get over my crush. When I noticed Ginger coming around the corner, I cringed.

"So, what do you think so far?" she asked as she approached the bar where I was standing and watching the bartender tripping out over the glorious drinks he was making. The man was an artist, flipping glasses and high-flying bottles of liquor all in time to the music.

The gorgeous and very buff blond was a hit with the ladies and he knew it. Every delivery was personal, including licking his lips in appreciation of the beautiful woman who'd ordered the cocktail. But he'd already let me in on a little secret.

Troy was gay.

He was also intoxicating, his tips reflecting his skill and prowess. If I could be half as good as the man one day, I'd make a fortune.

"She's doing fabulously, darling Ginger," Troy said in passing, giving me a wink.

"You're a flirt," she answered, lifting her eyebrows.

"Other than the jerks who grabbed my butt, I love it."

Ginger laughed. "That's why we pay our bouncers very well. I assume they took care of the wayward customers?"

"No, Mr. Stark did."

She seemed taken aback. "Wow. That's very rare, as in it never happens. You're high on his radar."

I wasn't entirely certain that was a good place for me to be.

"Everything about Blackout is incredible. There's so much energy and the crowd loves everything, including the cages hanging from the ceiling." I glanced up at the performers, young men and women gyrating in similar costumes to the beat of the music, tossing out candy to passing customers. The entire scene was like a free-for-all party.

"A recent addition," she noted. "My creation. Jameson thought I was nuts."

"They don't strip, do they?"

"Oh, heavens, no. They don't need to. They're providing an illusion of upcoming sin, a fantasy that allows our customers to believe in anything they desire."

"Maybe I could perform one night. I can dance." My exuberance continued to amuse her.

"We'll see. Let's make certain you master the art of serving our often raunchy customers first. Troy. Will you make Mr. Stark his favorite drink?"

"Why, of course, darling. Is he going to indulge our latest victim in a traditional walk of shame through Carnal Sins?"

His laugh was infectious. I already knew he and I were going to be best buddies.

"Ignore him."

"Jameson asked to see me?" Uh-oh. I had the distinct feeling I was in trouble for what happened.

Ginger smiled in a slightly provocative way. "He did, but I doubt it has anything to do with what happened. Don't be nervous. He invites every new employee into his lair to give his final approval and he does enjoy providing a tour of the club he designed."

"Wow. He's talented."

"He has two partners, friends since college. The three clubs are their babies. One is in DC and another in LA. There's a lot of money to be made in sin." Ginger kept a smile on her face.

"What's Jameson, I mean Mr. Stark's drink of choice?"

"A very special and ancient bottle of Macallan scotch. A nod of approval by the way," Troy said in passing as he slid the drink in my direction. "That's when you know you've already received an A grade from someone inside the club. That someone would be *moi*." He pressed his hand against his chest, his dramatic flair cracking me up.

"Troy!" a chorus of girls yelled from the end of the bar.

"I'm wanted and it's so exhausting. You'll have to excuse me." He floated off, returning his masculine mask.

"I adore him already."

Ginger burst into laughter. "I think the feeling is mutual. I'll take you to the private entrance for the corporate offices. Your hand scan should work now."

"I feel so official." I grabbed the drink then glanced at the neon straws. The playful side of me couldn't resist, placing two of them in the glass.

She snorted and walked toward the end of the bar.

Why not bring an entirely different kind of sunshine into his life. Right? What could it hurt?

Ginger moved through the crowd to a darkened space, pointing toward the door. "Remember that no one who isn't employed here or specifically asked by one of the executives is allowed behind that door. No one. No exceptions. Our exclusive members have access from a different location in the building."

"Yes, ma'am. I mean Ginger. I won't forget."

"Knock him dead. If everything works out, you'll be on the schedule for tomorrow. Don't worry. I'll take it easy on your first night."

"One question. Are there any other openings?"

"Anything is possible at this point. Why?"

"I just might have a friend interested."

Ginger nodded. "You can tell her to give me a call."

"Thank you!"

Now if only I could convince Charlotte into switching jobs.

For some reason, I was even more nervous. I bit my lower lip then pressed my fingertips against the keypad. Within seconds, a light turned green. They took security very seriously around here.

As I walked in, I felt almost instantly disoriented. Unlike the other corridor, this one was brightly lit, the deep burgundy walls screaming of power. I could only imagine what Jameson's office looked like. I headed up the stairs, my heart going pitter patter the entire time. I found his office easily, although I slid against the wall for a few seconds to catch my breath.

My nerves were in high gear, my pulse so high I was light-headed. This was crazy. It wasn't like I didn't know him... carnally.

Oh, God. If anyone found out, I would die.

I knocked on the door, still breathless. Then I heard his deep voice and another flutter of butterflies and some other creature turned my stomach into a rumbling mess.

As I opened the door, I held my breath. At first, I didn't see him. I closed the door behind me and bit my lip to keep from gasping. His office was magnificent, the rich, bold colors exuding the kind of power that I knew he held.

The furniture was leather, and there was a gorgeous rug that I could imagine rolling around on it.

Or fucking...

No. No. I had to shove the lurid thoughts aside. I was now his employee and nothing else.

His desk screamed executive, the wooden legs and all glass top adding an artistic expression. There was a bar at one end, a credenza on another, and a massive computer system with four monitors to the side. He could run a country from here.

When I finally noticed him standing, staring out the window at the Miami skyline, my heart skipped several beats. He was a dreamboat in all black and for a few seconds, I couldn't breathe. Then he turned around and I had the same reaction as when he'd saved my life.

I swooned, my mouth suddenly dry, my mind unable to process a single coherent thought. Everything around me seemed to shrink, making me feel small and inconspicuous.

The shadowed light accentuated the dark stubble on his chiseled jaw, his eyes penetrating mine with a level of heat that singed every nerve ending. With the obsidian shirt and dark trousers, his presence was the epitome of raw and very brutal power. Only with him, it was no illusion. He was a dominating master.

And for a few seconds, I felt like his prey, his possessive nature penetrating the room as he allowed his heated gaze to fall slowly to my shoes then back to my eyes.

As he walked forward, I remained frozen, uncertain I was still holding the drink in my hand.

"Alexandra," he said, his voice booming in the room.

"Yes, sir." I'd suddenly lost control of everything. My mind. My resolve. Somewhere in the back of my frazzled brain, my inner voice was shouting that around him I had no control over my body, but I wasn't listening. "I'm sorry about the incident in the bar. You didn't need to come to my defense. I could have handled the creeps."

There was surprise in his eyes from my statement, but he said nothing. However, his presence made me nervous. I suddenly felt like I'd been a very bad girl.

He walked closer and my entire body tensed, my pussy throbbing as my desire increased. His intoxicating scent was all I could concentrate on, fixating on the exotic scents that I could swear I was able to pick out one at a time.

Cinnamon. Cardamom. Juniper berries. Chile. Smoked paprika. When he was only a few feet away, I sensed my body was swaying. No man had ever had this kind of effect on me. When he spoke, I wasn't expecting his demand, nor was I anticipating my longing to please him.

"When you come to my office, Alexandra, you should immediately drop to your knees."

CHAPTER 9

 *ameson*

Alexandra's eyes opened wide, the dazzling blue color shimmering in my office lighting. She was also searching whether I was being serious or not. I wasn't entirely certain of the answer.

As she slowly dropped to her knees, lowering her head without being directed to do so, the sadist dom in me roared to the surface. Every filthy vision I'd had before doubled, my desire to thrust my cock deep inside insatiable. I wanted her shackled to my bed, writhing in my hold as I fucked her several times.

I wanted her between my legs, sucking my cock as I tangled my fingers in her long blonde strands.

Jesus. The effect she had on me was incomprehensible.

The sight of the beautiful woman fighting off assholes had had an unexpected result. I'd immediately turned into a caveman, going into attack mode. I'd reacted without thinking, wanting nothing more than to pummel the guy's face without hesitation. Not only was I no longer prone to enraged acts of jealousy, I also usually allowed Jagger and his more than capable team of bouncers to handle situations of that nature.

The option hadn't even been on the table, my possessive side taking over.

She'd become mine to protect.

Period.

Granted, I'd wanted a reason to toss the judge's arrogant son and his buddies out the door more than once. I couldn't care less if they ran home and told their daddies. The fact Judge Garber was still considered best friends with the former senator who'd made my life a living hell hadn't mattered. I almost laughed at the thought of how many times I'd been threatened over the years. The judge had made certain to track me down at a party and tell me that he had it out for me.

My answer?

I'd told him to get in line.

Exhaling, I studied the lovely woman in front of me as I thought about what to do with her. She'd held her own with the young men at the table, but it worried me. Her habit of confronting anyone who irritated her could get her hurt or worse.

Alexandra remained where she was, holding out the drink as if serving me this way was a requirement of the job.

I'd issued the command before I'd realized what I'd done. What I also hadn't anticipated was for her to comply with minimal hesitation. I had seen her look of confusion, which drifted almost immediately into questioning whether or not she could or should comply. Then it was as if a mask had been lifted, revealing a portion of the girl underneath.

I'd witnessed that in all of ten seconds.

She held out the glass in her hand, her chest rising and falling as I finished my approach. I was playing a dangerous game with her, but I couldn't ignore my hunger. I'd also seen the look in her eyes, a building need that would only continue. Our connection was unusual, so much so I'd already contemplated training her as my pet. The fact she'd obeyed my command without pushback or hesitation meant I'd been right about her longing to submit to someone who could take care of her, nurture her needs.

A part of me felt atrocious while the other was completely aroused, determined to follow this through.

"You don't need to be sorry for protecting yourself, Alexandra."

"They insulted me." She snapped her head up, looking for some hint of salvation for her act. "But I can tell I did the wrong thing."

"I employ people to handle unruly customers."

"Then why did you do it?"

"Because I won't allow anyone to treat you that way."

Her smile was brief, her eyes imploring. Goddamn it, I wanted this woman.

"Alexandra," I stated firmly, expanding on the moment by lifting her chin with a single finger. Her eyes shimmered, searching for acknowledgment. I nodded, offering her a smile. "You are a very good girl." The hard pull to the girl was strong enough I found myself lost in the moment. The entire situation was ridiculous. She was now my employee, something I couldn't forget. I'd been the one to insist that no fraternization rules applied across the board. I stroked her jaw, her breathless response exactly what I was looking for.

The few words of praise brought light to her entire face, a smile to her lips. It was amazing what a single compliment could do. My balls tightened from the thought.

"Thank you, sir." Her voice was subdued, which was another surprise. I expected her fury, not her compliance. Even if what I'd commanded hadn't been planned.

"Get to your feet," I told her, taking the drink from her hand, guiding her to a standing position. The touch was as electric as before, perhaps more so.

She chewed on her bottom lip as she obeyed, still eyeing me carefully. She was a nervous wreck, which I couldn't blame her for. In any other business, my direction would be considered sexual harassment. In this environment, allowances were made, even expected depending on the position within the company. Several submissive women and men were employed for members without guests.

However, I wasn't that kind of man, not during business hours.

"I'm sorry, sir. I didn't know. No, that's a lie. Jagger told me he'd take care of rude guests, but the jerk caught me off guard." She seemed slightly confused by her words, uncertain what she was saying was respective of her needs. The sudden look of denial regarding her wants was almost immediate.

"He won't be allowed to bother you any longer. We'll talk about club rules later. Come. Sit down with me." If anyone else in the club had witnessed my initial interaction with her, they'd think I'd lost my mind. I never mixed business with pleasure. Every employee knew me to be tough but fair, unyielding on the rules.

Christ. Here I was thinking about not only breaking them but smashing them to oblivion.

She was stiff but obeyed my order, moving to one of the couches, sitting on the edge, her discomfort evident. That's when I noticed the colorful straws added to my drink. I had no doubt she'd added them at the last minute. She was playful and had a flair for the dramatic. I already adored her kick-ass nature, yet it was her vulnerable side that called to me.

I eased down on the chair, studying her intently. "What do you think about my club, other than being accosted on your first day?"

Almost immediately her demeanor changed, her face lighting up as if I'd just opened Pandora's Box. In a way, I had, allowing her to be herself likely for the first time in her life.

"It's incredible. The lights. The energy. The power exchange. The music. Everything is spectacular. I heard this is your design?"

She leaned forward, more excited than I'd seen anyone when venturing into the club for the first time. "It is. A long time ago a couple buddies and I thought it would be a good idea. We never imagined the success or good fortune."

I took a sip of my drink as she scanned my office, taking note of every piece of art, the various pictures on my walls.

"Is that the three of you?"

There was no need to glance over my shoulder. "Yes, when we were much younger."

"You're all very handsome." She chuckled slightly. "Of course, you most of all."

She had a way about her that made me laugh. "Of course." When her face flushed, my cock twitched all over again.

"Mr. Stark. I would like to see Carnal Sins. Please. I need to learn every aspect about your world. I want to experience everything. I know that sounds crazy but I'm so curious. Granted, I've never done anything like being caged or beaten but there's a first time for everything." She seemed reticent in her words, a stark difference from less than thirty minutes before. It would seem I made her nervous.

"Only certain members enjoy the art of caging their partner, usually in the privacy of their home and no one is beaten inside my club. That's not allowed."

"Oh. I... I know I sound naïve, but I don't think we had a kink club in Billings. And I doubt a single cowboy, including my worthless ex-boyfriend would be caught dead in one."

Her innocent answer made me smile. "My guess is that there are several of them in every state. Often their locations are by word of mouth or private websites. And you'd be surprised how many cowboys have memberships."

"See. I don't know shit." She laughed at herself, pressing her hand across her mouth. "Maybe I can try something. Maybe something simple. Oh, God. What am I saying?"

She reminded me of myself when I'd finished the first design, so eager to show off the intricate details to my buddies. Her freshness was a welcome change. "I'll gladly show you the private side of the club. However, you're not ready to experience anything just yet."

"Why not? I'm a big girl. I can handle pain."

The girl had a lot to learn.

And I was the man who wanted to teach her.

"I'm a good judge of character, Alexandra, and you're not ready."

"Why not?" She wasn't exactly defiant, more curious than anything.

I was surprised that not only had I never been asked that before, but I wasn't entirely certain of the answer. As I contemplated what to say, she never blinked.

"Because what you've obviously read about the lifestyle is only partially the truth. Because it's not something to be taken or entered into lightly. I won't forbid you in the future, just not now."

"The lifestyle is about giving up control, right?"

"For one party in the relationship, yes. Sometimes our couples switch."

She narrowed her eyes. "One becomes the top when she was the bottom?"

"Yes. It can also apply to a man as well. Many powerful men who reign over multimillion-dollar companies during the day prefer to surrender to their mistress at night." The innocence of her questions was far too enticing.

"Do you... I mean are you..."

Laughing, I shook my head. "I've never been interested in being a bottom. I'm far too controlling."

"Oh. I can see that. I may not know you very well, but I can tell you're a powerful man." Her face blossomed into another lovely shade of pink. "So am I allowed to see the club?"

"Absolutely." I took a sip of my drink, then placed it on the table before rising to my feet. A part of me was excited that she'd made the request. While I'd once considered the costumes Ginger had selected overkill, seeing the festive attire on Alexandra gave it new appeal.

"By the way, I like Ginger," she said absently as I led her from my office, determining which rooms I wanted her to see. The last thing I wanted to happen was to scare her off. Even though I'd been advised in several languages against sharing even a single experience with her, I had the distinct feeling I would eventually ignore my own good advice.

"She's been an excellent find."

"She's sharp and very organized. How many members do you have?"

"Close to two thousand, although only a few hundred are active at any given time."

"Wow. So many men into kink."

Chuckling, I decided the tamer the better tonight, leading her down two flights of stairs. "We have dozens of female members, Alexandra. At least half have never participated in any activities behind these walls." I noticed every time I used her full name, she shuddered visibly.

"Then why pay an ungodly sum of money? A million dollars a year?"

She'd been doing her homework. "Prestige."

"Plus, I bet it's a good place to do business as well as to show off. Do you have a special keycard or emblem the members can use to brag?"

I pulled out my wallet, tugging on my personal membership card. When I handed it to her, I gauged her reaction, the way the corners of her mouth upturned as she rolled the tip of her index finger across the C and S in the center.

"A black card with gold initials. No phone number. No member number. Impressive."

I opened the door to the floor, guiding her in before answering. "The chip imbedded in the card provides all the information needed. That eliminates imposters."

"Do you have many of those?"

"You'd be surprised how many times someone has attempted to infiltrate the organization."

"Why?" She glanced up at me.

I stopped outside a door and leaned in. As soon as I did, the electricity shooting coursing through my veins threatened to become toxic. Even after a couple of hours on Blackout's floor, her soft floral fragrance tickled my senses. "Because there are many who think what occurs behind closed doors is either based on criminal activity or on my hunger to gain more power."

"So I was right. You are powerful."

"Yes."

"Does that make you a bad guy?" Her tone was teasing but I sensed she wasn't certain.

"There are many people who would tell you that I'm dangerous. It remains to be seen if you agree." I opened the door, ushering her in. The room was occupied by a handful of members and their guests, most casually enjoying their drinks while watching a lovely, blindfolded brunette being punished.

I wasn't certain what kind of reaction I anticipated but to see the way her eyes glistened as she studied the couple was fascinating. It was also easy to sense she had a dozen or more questions. When the dom in the scene brought down his belt across the sub's naked ass, the cracking sound brought purrs from several of the female guests.

As Alexandra turned her head toward the audience, I followed her gaze. She seemed fixated on the two submissives who were on the floor next to the male members. Both were collared, leashes attached. One of the women had her head on her master's knee, peering up at him as he stroked her head lovingly. The other had likely been banished from viewing the round of discipline for some infraction. Her forehead was resting on the floor, her arms shackled behind her.

Both were naked.

When the member stroking his pet's head noticed the attention, he gave Alexandra a nod and she shrank back against me.

The crackle of fire was intense, my cock shoving painfully against my trousers. I allowed her to watch for another few minutes before taking her to another room, merely opening the door this time. I'd interrupted a meeting, which surprised me since it had originally been booked for a Shibari demonstration. There were four men inside, all with submissives of their own. One was between a member's legs, deep throating him as they conducted business, her wrists shackled with thick leather straps. This wasn't what I'd anticipating walking into.

It would seem my mind had clearly been on anything else but business.

Her slight gasp was lost in their conversation, but only seconds later, one of the members noticed our visit and rose to his feet. His smile was genuine, one of the few members whose tastes bordered on tame in comparison.

"Mr. Stark. I was hoping I'd run into you tonight." As he walked toward me, the submissive crawled behind him on her hands and knees.

I felt a change in Alexandra, a tenseness that hadn't been there before. I'd been correct in only providing her limited access. Her unblinking eyes drifted from the girl sucking cock to the one purring by the movie mogul inches away.

"Mr. Longmire. It's good to see you. It's been a few months." I gritted my teeth seeing one of the people he was actively engaged in conversation with. Grigori Aleksei was Pakhan of a dangerous mafia organization, rival to the Santiago Cartel. He was reported responsible for dozens of brutal murders throughout the city. That didn't concern me nearly as much as the fact he was well known for recruiting young women against their will, training then selling them in the open market.

His methods of training were heinous by any standards. He'd been refused membership twice, which made his appearance as a guest disturbing. I made a note to speak to Jagger later. There was no sense in making a scene at this point.

"Unfortunately, yes, but I do enjoy visiting the club in LA. Grant is a fascinating young man." To someone of his age, I was considered a young boy. Even at almost eighty, Austin Longmire remained a powerhouse in the movie industry, often using Miami in his various films.

"He's a character. What brings you to Miami?" I returned my gaze to Grigori, who was paying far too much attention to Alexandra's presence.

Austin laughed, suddenly noticing Alexandra as well. "Why, making a movie, of course. This time on a dangerous crime syndicate controlling the beautiful city of Miami. To that end, I was wondering if you would consider allowing me to use the club for a couple background shots. I assure you my production team won't interfere with either club." He absently stroked his pet's head as she rubbed her face against his leg. Then he noticed my angry gaze toward the Russian.

"Mr. Aleksei was good enough to offer some background information while I was here," Longmire said in passing.

I thought about his request, noticing his acknowledgement of Alexandra was turned enough into a leer that a hint of jealousy almost spiraled out of control. That hadn't occurred in years. "I don't see an issue with that. Why don't you make arrangements with Anastasia Wilde in our DC office? She coordinates media events for us."

"Excellent. We'll start filming in about a month." He reached out to shake my hand.

I accepted the gesture while sensing Alexandra was becoming more uncomfortable. "I look forward to seeing your return."

"It's always a pleasure. By the way, young lady," he said as he pulled a business card from his suit jacket. "You have a certain look about you that is very appealing. Take my card. If you'd like to be tested for a small part on my upcoming film, call my secretary and she'll make certain you get on the list."

She hesitated before taking the card, refusing to do so until I'd nodded in approval.

"Thank you," she said, although her hint of defiance was noticeable.

He gave her another look of admiration before smiling. "I'm glad to see you're finally enjoying the perks of your own club for a change. She's spectacular."

"Oh, I'm not with him. I mean I am, but only because I work here. Nothing more." Her quick response and insistence were amusing. "I don't think I could handle anything so sick." Her last words were hissed.

Her insolence was immediately noticed by all four guests, their looks of admonishment adding to her bristled tension.

"She needs to be punished for her insolence," Grigori snapped, the other unknown men immediately uncomfortable. "She has no respect. If you'd like, I will be happy to teach her a lesson." The fucker was goading my anger, every muscle in my body tensing.

She leaned against me, but it was easy to tell her hackles were raised, ready to issue a tart retort. I pressed my hand against the small of her back, glaring at the pompous Russian.

"You are a guest here, Mr. Aleksei and as such, you are not allowed to touch another inside this club. Is that understood?"

He fisted his hand and Austin gave him a hard look. "Forgive my friend. He often doesn't know how to represent himself in any other manner but what he was forced into."

Austin's terse words were followed by Grigori baring his teeth.

"Come, Alexandra. Let's leave these gentlemen to their business." After narrowing my eyes and staring at Grigori for another few seconds, I pulled her out and by the time I closed the door behind our exit, she'd headed down the hall, her arms clasped against her chest.

I waited for a few seconds before going after her. She shot her head in my direction as I approached, uncertain of my reaction while knowing she'd crossed an invisible line. I couldn't be angry with her given the circumstances. She had no understanding of certain protocol. And in truth, I loathed some of the holier than thou attitudes exhibited by far too many of our wealthy clients.

Grigori had crossed a line himself and at some point I'd be forced to deal with his arrogance.

The fact they believed they got a pass for everything they did within the club had become more than just an irritant.

I'd tossed out several members for mistreatment of their submissives. I'd also cast out a half dozen others for berating employees.

"I think our tour is over for this evening." I guided her to the elevator, wanting to get her away from the floor quickly.

Once inside, she turned toward me, fire in her eyes. "Are you going to punish me? Maybe use your belt this time?"

I'd expected her outburst. I crowded her space, taking my time to answer. "Is that what you want?"

"Want? Are you crazy? I mean…" Sighing, she looked away.

I gripped her chin, pulling it back to me. "As I said before, there are rules, but in this case, the man making the demand had no right. Only I'm allowed to punish you, and it would never be because you were pulled into a room you shouldn't be in."

"Why? Because I'm just the hired help?"

The elevator doors opened and I shifted my grip to her elbow. While she didn't fight me, I could tell she was conflicted as to what she'd seen, more so than what Grigori had said. As soon as I walked her into my office, she pulled away, another flash of uncertainty crossing her face.

I thrust my hands into my pockets, keeping just enough distance not to drive her away. "No, Alexandra. Because I never want to make you feel uncomfortable either in your job or around me. There are some men who enjoy acts that you would consider twisted. However, that isn't why people engage in acts of BDSM."

"Then why? Is this all about pain?"

"For some, it's a moment of being able to lose themselves if only for a night. Often, there is no escape from the day-to-day drudgery of the hamster wheel they're on. Whether they top or bottom, they're free from their inhibitions, finding pleasure through taking or shedding control. While pain is a part of the lifestyle, for a club of this nature, that's not the driving force. Nor will I allow it to become one."

She eyed me warily, nodding once. "I can handle it."

"That's not what I want from you or for you, Alexandra. You wanted a tour, but I should have known you weren't ready. That's part of my job not only as owner of the club but also as a master dom."

"So that was... normal in there?" She had more confidence in her words, dozens of questions in her eyes.

"The word normal is relative and different to everyone. What Carnal Sins offers is a facility for our members and their guests to feel unencumbered and be satisfied by other methods than vanilla sex."

"You mean bondage and flogging."

"Yes, but there's much more to it."

"Were those submissives being abused?"

"That's not allowed. Entering into the lifestyle was their choice."

"So those women wanted to be on their knees, treated like some furry pet?"

I dared walk closer. "No, Alexandra. Those women longed to feel pampered and loved. Even when they're being punished, they will tell you that they felt more adored than ever."

"That's crazy."

When I brushed my knuckles across her jaw, she visibly shuddered. "Is it really?" I purposely lowered my voice.

Alexandra nodded. "I guess you're right. I still don't understand but I want to learn more."

Her tenacity was beguiling. "Then I suggest we enjoy a late dinner together and you can ask all the questions you'd like. Is that suitable?"

"Only if I can get a ride home?"

"Deal."

CHAPTER 10

 lexandra

Stunned.

The word was the only one I could think of as Jameson followed the host to our table. He'd kept his massive hand against my back from the moment he'd parked his Porsche. Before I moved to Miami, I would have shied away from men who were insistent on opening doors and guiding me like I was a waif who needed help. I'd been the girl most likely to end up alone since I didn't like men doing anything for me.

Not changing a tire.

Not repairing a broken pipe.

And certainly not ordering for me.

Since the minute I'd met him, it was as if I'd lost a part of myself, comfortable when he took control. I was dumbfounded by the realization, angry with myself for feeling that way, but Jameson had such confidence that I couldn't resist allowing him to be the dominating force.

When he walked into a room people noticed, men and women alike. It wasn't only because of his gargantuan stature but the way he carried himself.

What I'd seen had been unnerving, more so than I cared to admit at least to him. The closest I'd ever gotten to anything remotely like what I witnessed was by watching a movie. I'd thought about what Jameson had said in his office. While I hadn't wanted to believe he was right about the women enjoying being treated like a puppy dog, I'd seen it in their eyes, joyous from feeling loved and protected. However, I still couldn't grapple with why I hadn't been able to take my eyes off them.

And for a few seconds, I'd wanted to be them, but only with Jameson.

I took a deep breath, my stomach rumbling. I hadn't been able to eat all day, too nervous about the job and seeing him again. Now the wafting scents of charred meat and spices made my mouth water almost as much as being on the arm of such a gorgeous man.

He hadn't asked me where I'd like to go and I hadn't asked. Now, as he eased me into a chair on the open deck of a garishly lit six-story building, the table located next to an ornate railing overlooking South Beach, the ocean only yards away, I was reminded of just how rich he was. He fit in with the crowd in his luxurious attire while I remained in my jeans, tee shirt, and sneakers.

The breeze was light, music coming from all directions, flickering candles on every table. I shouldn't feel as comfortable as I was, but he was as charming as he was dominating, the draw to him undeniable.

"What would you like to drink?" he asked as the waiter immediately approached the table.

"Red wine is fine."

Without hesitation, he ordered a bottle I'd never heard of, conversing in Spanish. I turned my attention to people watching, enjoying the scent of the ocean as well. Then I sensed he was studying me as he'd done so many times before.

"What?" I finally asked.

"I'm waiting for your barrage of questions."

"Truthfully, I don't know what to ask that won't sound ridiculous."

He lifted his eyebrows. "No question is ridiculous. Why don't we start with easy ones."

"Who are you?"

"What do you want to know?"

I shrugged. "Why do others think you're dangerous?"

"In a town like Miami, people feed off information to use against others. Given what I do for a living, I'm privileged to learn secrets and admissions that certain members would prefer to stay locked away."

My smile was instantaneous. The man was becoming more intriguing by the minute. "Oh, my God. You blackmail people."

"No, I offer advice should it prove to be a prudent aspect of my life."

"How very astute of you. Do you still break bones?"

"What?" He shook his head, feigning fury but I could tell by the glint in his eyes he was enjoying our conversation. "I can see that you've been chatting with Troy. Let's discuss my pedigree before we go any further. Yes, I used to play football in college, lucky enough to get a scholarship. Three times in my career I made a tackle that cause a few broken bones and the name has stuck with me twenty years later. I'm a scotch drinker, own a Harley and a Dodge Ram. I live on the water, although not in one of those fancy houses you've seen up and down South Beach. I don't have any pets or kids, but who know, maybe one day I will. I don't appreciate or tolerate pompous assholes, as evidenced by the jerks who accosted you. Oh, and my mother used to call me the apple of her eye. That about sums it up. It's your turn."

Talking about myself was more difficult than I could express. "I bet your mother is a hoot. Let's see. My life is not nearly as glamorous as yours. I was raised on a huge ranch in Billings. My parents were ultra conservative, which meant my brother and I were rarely allowed out of the house, a different kind of leash. I love animals and kids too. I have a degree in elementary education that I'm not certain what I want to do with yet. Hmmm…" I cocked my head, using my resume to bring up the car. "And I used to have a little Corolla that got me from Montana to Florida with no problems, but some asshole decided to tear her apart. That's about the only interesting thing about me."

"I think everything about you is interesting, Alexandra."

Goosebumps popped along my skin. "Why do you use my name? I mean not a lot of people do. They usually say chick or dude after they get to know someone."

"Alexandra is a beautiful name that fits a lovely woman, and I will never call you a chick."

I could feel his heated breath all the way across the table, the dark husk of his voice creating little waves of desire rushing through my core. "Speaking of my car."

"We'll take care of that in the morning."

"What does that mean?"

"That means you'll find out."

The way he made the statement was a dismissal of the conversation. "That's no fair, but I appreciate you taking me home." We sat quietly for a few seconds, but he never blinked.

"What did you think about what you witnessed earlier in Carnal Sins?"

"Truthfully? I don't know what to think other than I realize the life I've lived up until now has been very sheltered. It just seemed… wrong. That might be based on my father's often irrational influence. He hated everything."

"Because you don't understand something doesn't make it wrong. As I told you before, your job doesn't entail having anything to do with Carnal Sins. I'm not a monster forcing my employees or women in general into anything they don't want to do. Besides, I don't think you have any understanding of what goes on inside a club like mine."

"You're right about that. I shouldn't place judgment on something I have no clue about. But you'll tell me the truth about all the kinky little acts?"

His laugh sent shivers down my spine. "I have no reason to lie to you about any aspect of the club, Alexandra. I'm not embarrassed in the least about the proclivities people enjoy. Ask away."

Why was it that every time he said my name my stomach fluttered? "You said there was more to BDSM than cages and whips."

"Absolutely. The lifestyle is about a power exchange. Usually, one partner is the top or the dom, the other considered the bottom or the submissive. It's all completely consensual. There is nothing forced allowed."

"But that happens?"

Even in the dim lighting, I could tell he was troubled by my question. "Unfortunately, yes. That's one reason there are so many misunderstandings about BDSM."

I allowed my thoughts to drift to Charlotte. "Then help me to understand the basics. What kind of acts do people enjoy?"

"Bondage is very popular. You also witnessed impact play with aspects of humiliation. There's pet play, cupping, breath play, anal play, medical play, figging, knife play, praise play, needle play, Shibari or rope bondage, age play, suspension. And many others."

I had no idea what to say. "Knife play?" I had a feeling my skin had paled.

"Rarely done in truth. We have a structured system in place, so no one attempts certain acts without supervision." He was studying my reaction, no doubt certain I'd freak out. "Few people are into that anyway. It's considered very advanced."

"Wait a minute. There are people who are considered experts in playing with knives?" I felt myself paling, glad the waiter had already returned as he was opening the wine.

"Absolutely. I hire the best in the business. We also offer classes in certain kinks as well."

A disturbed look must have crossed my face by the way he laughed.

"I assure you that there are strict rules that apply to everyone regardless of who they are or their level of experience. Every room no matter if it's private is monitored. The lifestyle isn't about injuring anyone. Is there pain involved? Yes, and some people are considered sadists while others are masochists and thrive on the higher level of pain. However, there is a certain level I won't allow. The liability alone would kick my ass and shut me down if anything should happen."

"Has it?" Pain. I thought about the spanking from before and tingled all the way to my toes. I'd enjoyed it. Wow. That was completely insane.

"We've had some incidents," he said, waiting as the waiter poured a taste. Jameson didn't bother swirling the liquid before gulping the small amount, nodding his approval.

"What is praise play?" I whispered, fearful the young man handling our table would overhear our conversation.

Jameson leaned forward. "It's being made to feel appreciated by subtle actions or behavior."

"That's why you called me a good girl." My words sounded accusatory.

"Yes. That's what you need in your life, a craving you've yet to have fulfilled."

"You think you know so much about me. You don't."

"We all have secrets as well as armor we tidily hide behind so as to not allow ourselves to get hurt. Isn't that the truth?"

There was no reason for me to be annoyed at his words because they were the truth. Maybe I was just so terrified of opening myself up again that I needed to lash out at someone. I'd been hurt enough that I wasn't certain why I'd agreed to dinner. "I'm an open book. I have nothing to hide." It was another lie. I had so many plates of armor surrounding me I no longer recognized myself.

"Then why is your lower lip trembling?"

I felt my muscles tightening. I'd felt amazing after he'd complimented me, something I rarely had before in my life.

"My father would say praise is for the weak. Up until now, I believed him. Straight A's. I held down two jobs in high school while taking courses at the community college as well. I helped on the ranch, often getting only a few hours of sleep. All without getting a pat on the back or a thank you."

"Interesting," Jameson countered. "I'm sorry to disagree with your father, but everyone needs to hear they've done a good job in their lives. Including you."

"I assume you're right, but not about me. I was raised to be a strong woman. My father was a tough man, ex-military. He believed in hard work and discipline, but his methods of showing approval consisted of not yelling at his children for something they'd been unable to accomplish. My brother hated it. I learned that it made me tougher."

"Is that what you want to be? A tough girl, the one I saw almost get herself killed? The five guys you told off have the wealth and standing to get away with waiting for you after work and having their way with you."

There was admonishment in his tone and I hated it.

"What I don't want is for anyone to think they need to take care of me. I'm a big girl and I can handle anything life throws my way. Maybe that's something you should keep in mind." Where was this coming from? Because he was being so generous, taking me out to dinner? Because he'd offered me a job when no one else in the entire city would?

He remained quiet and I tried to laugh it off, immediately reaching for my wine. I hadn't realized I'd remained nervous until I almost knocked the glass over, drops spilling on the table. "I'm sorry!"

When he placed his hand on mine, his grip firm, I was almost instantly calm.

"There is nothing to be sorry about and I'm not your father."

"And I'm not looking for a surrogate." As soon as the words left my mouth, I was horrified. "I…"

"Shush, Alexandra. What you and I shared together had nothing to do with age play. I'm not looking for a little girl."

"Little girl?"

"Another form of kink."

"Oh, as if you'd become my daddy." My retort was clipped, but the light flutter in my heart had yet to cease. He had that kind of effect on me, and it scared me to death. I'd allowed him to see and experience the most vulnerable side of me and when I did something so stupid, I either turned into a bitch or crawled into my shell.

"Yes. That's not my thing." I could tell he was irritated that I was crossing him, acting like an impetuous child.

"What is your thing?" I was afraid to ask.

He sat back in his seat, but his hand never left mine, his thumb brushing aimlessly across my knuckles. "Someone I can enjoy life with, a woman to make feel special. However, I'm a dominant, so that means I will be always in control within the relationship."

Was he testing whether or that was something I was interested in? I couldn't tell.

"So you require a woman to remain at your feet? Would that woman eat out of a dog bowl too?" *What are you doing?*

My little voice pinged me hard. Challenging my boss when he was being so open was a very bad idea.

"Wow. If the woman I adored and trusted wanted to share her meals with me on the floor at certain times, I'd encourage it, but that is a choice between couples." He narrowed his eyes, the slight shake of his head a reminder of how dominating he truly was. "But yes, I do prefer a woman to submit to my needs."

"What exactly does that entail?" Great. Now I was grilling him. I leaned over the table, running the tip of my finger around the wineglass. He shifted his gaze toward the sensual action, his chest heaving.

"What are you asking?"

"If for some crazy reason we were together, what would you expect of me? That I'd drop to my knees when you came home? That I'd remain shackled to the bed waiting your return so you could have your way with me?" I was arousing myself with the ridiculous questions, uncertain if he'd answer me or not.

As he'd done so many times before, he took full control over the situation, acting as relaxed as ever, enjoying a sip of wine before carefully placing his glass on the table. When he leaned over, his lips were only a few inches from mine. I gathered a scent of his aftershave and every nerve ending was sizzled, desire roaring through me, my nipples swelling.

"I'll be happy to tell you, sweet Alexandra. If you and I were together, you would be required to be completely naked when I arrived home no matter the time of day. You'd be on your knees, your arms behind your back. Your head would be down, your eyes to the floor. You wouldn't speak until spoken to. Then I'd inspect what belonged to me, the woman I possessed. After that, I'd enjoy the feel of having her wet mouth wrapped around my cock."

When he paused, I could swear I'd leaned further forward, my mouth suddenly dry, my heart thudding against my chest. Was he being serious? I dragged my tongue across my lips and was certain he was going to kiss me.

He lifted his hand, bending a single finger then rolling it back and forth from one side of my jaw to the other as he continued taunting me with the darkness.

"I'd enjoy every moment of face fucking you, driving the tip of my cock against the back of your throat with such ferocity you gagged. When I climaxed, I'd fill your mouth with my cum, requiring you to lick my shaft clean."

"Oh." The single word came out as a moan, visions of the act he'd just described creating the kind of desire that was blinding.

"Does that sound like something you'd enjoy, Alexandra?" The rumble of his voice set my entire body on fire.

I found myself answering him before I could stop it. "Yes."

"That's yes, Master."

The half laugh escaping my throat was jittery, almost embarrassing, but he was also as aroused as I was.

"Say it for me," he commanded.

There was suddenly no breeze, no sound other than his words filtering into my ears. "Yes, Master."

"Good girl."

As he continued brushing his fingertips across my jaw, I realized I was holding my breath, quivering from pleasing him.

"Then that's what we're going to do. After that, I'll tie you to my bed and share with you the magic of pleasure and pain that you've been seeking your entire life."

Pain and pleasure. I was strangely attracted to the thought of what he would do. Could I handle being shackled, my wrists and legs bound so I couldn't move? The butterflies in my stomach said yes while a part of my mind continued to tell me I was out of my mind for even thinking about it.

"First, we're going to enjoy a lovely dinner. Just the two of us."

"Yes, *Master.*" My words were barely audible, said with continued uncertainty.

He made the connection, our lips lightly touching. I arched my back, hungering for more but he was in full control, tasting me then pulling away. I was mesmerized by his eyes, terrified yet scintillated.

I sucked on my bottom lip, the nerves getting the better of me. After taking a shallow breath, I glanced toward the ocean, attempting to think of something brilliant to ask, but I was so out of my depth it was ridiculous. "So, you're not in a relationship?" The elephant in the room. I doubted he was the relationship kind of guy, but I had to ask.

He chuckled darkly as if my question was one he'd antici-pated. "Not for a very long time. I'm far too busy with work, including being the general contractor for the new club being built in Paris, to consider anything permanent."

I nodded, the same small part of me that had appreciated his compliments wishing this could be more. "That's exciting. Paris I mean. I'd love to see it one day." I looked away, fearful of him seeing disappointment in my eyes.

"Then perhaps I'll take you one day. For now, we'll enjoy some dinner."

"And afterward?"

His answer was matter of fact, as if he was ordering food, not taking full control.

"Then we're going to my home. Make no mistake, Alexan-dra. As of now, I *am* your master."

 *ameson*

Rational thoughts had been tossed out the window.

First, I'd claimed possession of her. Then I'd become determined to allow her to enter into my world.

In bringing Alexandra to my house, I was subjecting myself to possible angst or difficulties in business later on. I was a private man, usually preferring to spend my nights alone. Sadly, the last few weeks had me questioning my reasons why I hadn't been able to move on after the hearing about Pamela's death. We'd broken up long before, but news of her passing had hit me hard, a reminder that I wasn't getting any younger.

As with saving Alexandra's life before, the decision to open a portion of my privacy wasn't something I'd planned or thought through. But with her questions, her curiosity, my cock had spoken for me.

She'd remained flirtatious through dinner, although our conversation had turned to intellectual discussions regarding typical topics for two people getting to know each other. While she was timid with regard to the club and what she'd called 'creepy proclivities,' that's where her reticent side remained. In everything else, she was a woman on the edge. Her opinions were based in knowledge, not on what she'd learned on social media.

I found our banter and her exuberance refreshing as well as surprising. What she refused to talk about was almost everything about her past other than her love of horses, dogs, and just about every other animal on the planet. Her insistence that her past would remain there told me in no uncertain terms she'd run from something traumatic. Maybe her parents' divorce was the reason but a slight nagging in the back of my mind told me otherwise.

Maybe she was ready to sow her wild oats finally after living such a conservative life. Who was I to judge or condemn her for wanting to start a new life entirely on her own?

I'd left her alone on the deck while I'd made us a drink, hoping to calm her nerves. My house wasn't grandiose in Miami's terms, an older house in a quaint neighborhood that had long ago been considered for the wealthy and powerful. It suited my needs, which were simple. Plus, I'd spent time and money on making repairs and renovations, although I had a ways to go before I'd consider the project finished.

When I walked to the open set of sliding doors, I took a few seconds to watch as she enjoyed the ocean view front, stars providing a slightly blueish glow across the ocean water. She sensed my presence, tipping her head to the side. I could smell her fear, which had a distinct scent, but she was also excited, her eagerness to learn keeping the sadist in me close to the surface. However, she wasn't like submissives employed in my club. With her lack of experience, whatever I considered would need to be done carefully.

The term 'playing with fire' was never far from my mind. She was my employee after all. Eventually, someone would talk or notice a distinct behavioral difference. While being the owner should mean I couldn't care less, I honored the rules not only by requiring them but by living them.

"You didn't lie to me. You don't live in a mansion," she said absently as I flanked her side. "This is far better."

I handed her the cognac, her request another slight surprise, taking a quick glance at the quiet beach. "I'm glad you approve. Besides, I'm not in the habit of lying and glamour and opulence doesn't suit my style."

"But you have all the money in the world. What do you do with it?" She took the glass from my hand, our fingers touching. The crackle of electricity was the same as before, intense enough she murmured something under her breath. "Is that too personal?"

Snickering, I resisted fingering the strand of hair that continuously whipped across her face. "No, that's not too personal. My bankers are happy. I invest and reinvest."

"How intelligent of you, but that's no way to live. You only live once, you know."

"It's what I know and how I grew up. My parents didn't have a lot of money, so we learned the value of everything we owned." I hadn't told anyone about how I'd been brought up, including Pamela. Mostly because it had never come up. This girl was terrified to let her guard down.

"No wonder you're so grounded. Very admirable."

I leaned over the railing, contemplating whether or not her assumption was correct. "I learned a long time ago that money isn't about happiness or the future. Yes, it provides security, but it can also be damning."

"Everyone wants a piece of you."

"Exactly."

"I wouldn't mind experiencing living a lavish lifestyle for a little while, but in the end, I love the mountains and where I grew up. Miami is beautiful but could never be my home."

"Never say never."

"Too cliché, Mr. Stark."

"But something to remember, Ms. Kingston. I'm curious about your cousin. What's her name?"

"Charlotte, although she goes by Char now. Evidently Charlotte is too passé for her job."

"Her last name?" Red flags continued to rise.

She eyed me curiously. "You want to check her out. Don't you?"

Shrugging, I wasn't going to lie to her. "I'm concerned about you living in that building. Only the rich can afford the kind of condominium where she lives."

"Don't be concerned about Charlotte. She wouldn't hurt me." When she looked away briefly, I sensed her trepidation as well.

"It's not about whether your cousin would hurt you but the friends she's keeping possibly could."

"She's a tough girl as well."

"In this town, no one is tough enough to fight off the cartel."

Her deep and ragged breath was an indication she'd already thought about that as well. "Her last name is Darlington. She is different than I remember but she's not a stupid woman."

"Stupid doesn't usually come into play with the people I'm worried she might have gotten involved with. They are cunning, tossing out lures that most people find difficult to resist. Once hooked, the requirements can be lethal. Just be careful. There are some very bad people in this city."

"So you've told me."

There was such emotion in her words and the way she kept her gaze pinned on the ocean waters fueled anger more than desire. One of the first things I'd do in the morning was to find out everything I could about her cousin. While I knew better than anyone that any arm of a tight family could present problems through the years, I had the distinct feeling Charlotte was in deep with Santiago's cartel.

If that was the case, Alexandra couldn't continue living at the condo. I'd find her a more suitable location even if I had to pay for it.

There I went again, playing her hero, which I had no business doing. She slipped her fingers through her hair, her nervous glances in my direction continuing.

"What are we doing here?" she asked.

"I think you know the answer."

She studied me for a few seconds, taking another sip of her drink. "I don't want to get hurt."

"And I don't intend on hurting you, at least emotionally. Will there be pain involved? Yes. But I know that's what you want and what you need."

She couldn't deny what I was telling her.

"Come here, Alexandra."

"Why?"

"Because I commanded you to do so."

She studied her glass for a full ten seconds before obeying, lifting her head as she approached. "Yes, Mr. Stark?"

I took her glass from her hand, placing both drinks on the outside table. Then I cupped her face, rubbing her jaw as I'd done before. Within seconds, tension eased, the bright moon adding a shimmering reflection to her eyes. She was without a doubt the most beautiful woman I'd ever met. "I need to see all of you. Every inch."

"You have."

"Not enough." I lowered my head, kissing the top of her forehead. "Undress."

She shuddered at my touch, her answer breathless. "Here?"

"Right here."

I sensed she wanted to glance at the beach, worried someone might see us. "Obey me, Alexandra. When I give you a command, you will comply immediately. Understood?"

"Yes, sir. I mean Master."

I kept my grip for a few additional seconds before lifting her chin higher. "Have confidence in yourself. You are exquisite."

Another look of relief crossed her face. No one had ever taken the time to provide encouragement or adoration. That brought out the angry beast in me. She was a precious jewel, a creature to be treasured. I let her go, leaning against the railing as she backed away, still nervous but excitement lingering, the crackle of electric current running strong.

As she pulled her shirt from her jeans, I took a deep breath. Our passion from before had been explosive, so much so that I hadn't taken the time needed to indulge in her magnificence. Tonight I planned on changing that. She would learn that I could be trusted, which would allow her to trust in herself.

Something she sorely needed.

Very carefully she folded and placed the shirt on a chair, crouching down to untie her tennis shoes. Part of me felt like a bad man, but we both needed this, not only a release but closeness that was rare. When she returned to a standing position, her eyes roamed my chest, dropping lower. Then she dragged her tongue across her lips. My balls immediatcly tightened, the thought of collaring her in the forefront of my mind.

She would look even lovelier with her nipples pierced, a delicate chain connecting them. I scrubbed my jaw with my palm as she unfastened and unzipped her jeans, peeling the dense material away. Then she took a deep breath before slowly lowering them past her voluptuous hips. She had the perfect hourglass figure, rounded curves meant for a man to grab onto.

My cock was uncomfortable, throbbing like a son of a bitch against my zipper. While I wanted this to last, I'd need relief soon.

When they were lowered to the floor, she kicked out of them, almost tripping. Her embarrassed laughter floated toward the sky, the nervous skitter adding fuel to my raging hunger. Now she stood in a bra and matching panties. If the light reflected them accurately, the color was a soft pink, a reminder of the baby doll she was.

I wanted to think she'd chosen them with me in mind. She slid her hand in front of her mound, looking away briefly. The intimacy from before was nothing in comparison to being commanded to undress in front of a basic stranger. She raked her other hand through her hair, more nervous than before. Yet the scent of her desire was strong, filtering into my nostrils.

My mouth watered from the thought of feasting on her pretty pink pussy once again.

Alexandra turned around. Then the second I cleared my throat, she froze.

"You will never turn away from me unless you are told to do so. Understood?"

"Yes, sir." Her movements more awkward, she slowly turned to face me, reaching around her back to unfasten her bra. Then she eased one strap over her shoulder then the other, her eyes never leaving mine.

I nodded in appreciation, hopefully giving her more confidence. She responded with a smile, removing and tossing the bra toward the chair. Now she stood in a thong only and I was ready to rip it off with my teeth.

"Touch yourself for me," I told her, keeping my tone low and intense.

She stiffened initially, taking several shallow breaths. Then she rolled the tips of her fingers down the side of her neck, stiff and uncertain. I said nothing as she trailed them between her breasts, hesitating before rolling a single finger around her already taut nipple. My pulse was rising, my needs increasing.

"Like this?"

"Just like that."

As if encouraged, she moved her other hand under her breast, squeezing before toying with her hardened bud.

"Pinch it between your fingers," I directed, enthused when she did so immediately. Seconds later, she added her other hand, now kneading both breasts as she toyed with her nipples. I could watch her for hours, appreciating a spectacular show, but my hunger was too greedy.

When she rolled the flat of her hand down her stomach, my breath hitched. I was curious how far she'd go. A nervous laugh pushed past her lips as she gyrated her hips to the music coming from inside the house. Her stiffness eased within seconds, allowing her to enjoy the sinful moment.

The second she pressed her fingers against her lace-covered pussy, my heartrate sped up even more. As she rubbed herself, filthy images floated into my mind. I also wanted her clit pierced, a tattoo placed in an intimate location indicating she belonged to me. Then my mind drifted to purchasing a cage, the idea creating far too many salacious thoughts.

When she crawled her fingers under the thin elastic of her thong, I held my breath, eager to see how far she'd go. She never blinked as she teased her clit, rubbing gently at first then rougher as pleasure rolled through her. I watched her facial expressions, the shivers coursing through her body until I knew it was enough. I would satisfy her rapture.

"Enough, baby girl."

A playful look of disappointment crossed her face but she immediately removed her hand.

"Lick your fingers clean for me."

Now her eyes opened wide but she lifted her arm, staring at her glistening fingers for a few seconds before complying. When she drove them into her mouth, the suckling sound she made excited the hell out me. I hadn't enjoyed anyone this much in so long, I'd forgotten how much I relished asserting control over someone, both body and soul.

And there was no doubt that she belonged to me.

"Take them off," I told her, my cock aching to the point of pain.

She smiled and I could sense another round of embarrassment, but she didn't glance toward the beach worrying about someone seeing her. She lifted her head in defiance as she slipped her fingers under the thin lace, pulling them over her hips then shimmying them to the floor. As soon as she kicked out of them, I sensed a coat of armor falling, revealing her increasing desire. I could also tell she was eagerly awaiting my next command.

"Crawl to me."

Unlike in my office, she dropped to the deck slowly, her lips pursed and her eyes never leaving mine. As she began to follow my order, I took several breaths. The anticipation of having her in my arms had never been so intense, the dom inside of me still planning on how far I wanted to go with her.

She controlled her actions, still skittish yet able to enjoy the moment, tossing her hair back and forth in another attempt to tease me. It was working, too much so. I could lose myself with her, which was something neither one of us needed. When she was only a few inches away, she stopped, waiting once again for me to tell her what to do.

"Come here."

The second she crawled between my legs, I closed my eyes, pressing my hand against her head and guiding her face to my thigh. Few would understand how close I felt to her or how calming it was to have utter control of someone in this way. There were no words needed, no actions required, just an understanding passing between us. A moment of power exchange and trust.

And it was very powerful, more so than any other act.

She relaxed even more, her breathing even. When I finally lifted her head, I could swear there were tears in her eyes.

"Suck me." The deepness of my voice was surprising, not the need. I wanted her wet mouth wrapped around my shaft, deep throating her till my cum coated her throat.

Alexandra shifted, running her fingers along the insides of my legs. I kept a single finger under her chin, forcing her to keep her large eyes locked on mine. As she rolled her hands across my cock, a deep growl erupted from deep in my chest. If I wasn't careful, I'd lose all control with her, fucking her like some crazed animal.

She slowly crawled her fingers to my belt, taking her time to unbuckle it. She was doing so on purpose, her way of attempting to maintain some control of her own. When she finally tugged the thick leather free, a part of me knew I'd use it on her, marking her bottom. It wouldn't be entirely about punishment for mouthing off to customers, but also to mark her as mine. The thought was exhilarating.

As she slowly unzipped my trousers, she licked her lips in such a provocative way I was certain she'd been planning this. When she finally freed my cock, the air sending tickling sensations all the way to my balls, I fisted her hair at the scalp. She tugged the material past my hips, freeing my balls. She blew across my cockhead, the seductive action forcing another husky growl.

I could almost read her mind, the vixen inside of her coming into her own. I couldn't take my eyes off the beauty, sucking in my breath as she darted the tip of her tongue across my sensitive slit. She slipped her hand under my balls, rolling them between her fingers as she wrapped the fingers of her other hand around the base of my cock. She was determined to continue teasing me, sliding just the tip of her tongue around my cockhead as she squeezed my testicles.

The combination of her heated breath and the hint of pressure on my balls forced me to jut my hips forward. Where the few submissives I'd enjoyed spending time with had performed the act as required, she was enjoying the moment, her wet tongue creating electric sensations.

My muscles were surprisingly tense, so much so my body was shaking. I allowed her to continue tormenting me, dragging her tongue down the underside of my cock several times. When she pulled the tip into her mouth, I threw my head back, gasping for air. Fuck. The woman's mouth was so freaking hot my blood was on fire.

As she took another inch inside, I lowered my head. "Do you like having my cock in your mouth, baby girl? Do you like knowing that someone could be watching us?"

She murmured her reply, reveling over swirling her tongue back and forth across my shaft. This was something else I could do for hours, or at least I tried to convince myself even though I knew I was lying. She was far too tempting. The way her tongue caressed the ridge was far too enticing. When she started to pick up in speed, I pulled her head away.

"Slow down, baby girl. Take your time." Christ, my heart was beating so rapidly I was out of breath.

Her eyelashes fluttered across her cheeks, and she opened her mouth wider, waiting as I pushed my shaft back inside. She shifted on her knees, using a combination of her tongue and jaw muscles, sucking with just the right amount of pressure. I was so into the moment that I was forced to grip the railing with one hand to keep my body from rocking.

She kept one hand wrapped around the base, pulling her head back until the tip popped from her mouth. There was a more devilish look in her eyes as she licked down the underside, taking a testicle into her mouth. The woman's mouth was hot, the wetness and sounds as she sucked keeping me on edge. Even my legs were shaking.

"Jesus."

The feel of her wet tongue stroking my aching cock was incredible, my thirst for her increasing. I had a feeling she sensed my increasing need, opening her mouth even wider.

"That's it. Take all of me." My eyesight had already become hazy, but as her head bobbed up and down, I concentrated on what she was doing. However, I wasn't a patient man by any stretch of the word. After a few seconds, I took full control, thrusting the remaining few inches deep inside. When the tip hit the back of her throat, she gagged enough I backed off, but that wouldn't last for long.

Moans slipped past her lips, the moon in a perfect position to allow me to see the glimmer of need in her eyes as well.

"Hands behind your back," I instructed as I gripped her head with my other hand. Then I rolled onto the balls of my feet, pulling almost all the way out then driving into her again. Savage thoughts remained in the forefront of my mind as I fucked her pretty little mouth, images so brutal they surprised me. I developed a rhythm, sliding in and out, savoring every moment.

Every sound she made continued to fuel the fire, my cock swelling even more. I thrust with enough force her body rocked, my balls swelling to the point I could easily erupt deep inside.

Her entire face glowed in the moonlight, my animalistic actions unable to stop the excitement in her eyes. I pulled away, taking several deep breaths as I stroked her face, hungering to taste her swollen lips. After yanking my trousers into position, I bent over, sliding my arms under hers to pull her into a standing position.

"What now?" she asked, her voice breathless.

"Now, my beautiful submissive, we begin your training."

CHAPTER 12

 *lexandra*

Training.

The word had so many connotations to it that my mind was a flurry of thoughts.

My heart was also drumming an unknown beat but certainly faster than the music on his stereo. It had been so easy to submit to him that I remained in awe of his prowess and control. I'd felt so ridiculous before asking questions that a woman of my age should already know. In my defense, I'd never considered going to a kink club. Not once.

Sure, I'd seen a few kinky things in movies, including *Fifty Shades*, so I wasn't a prude by any means, but dropping to my knees without hesitation in order to please him? That

152

girl wasn't me. She was some go-getter chick determined to shift completely out of her comfort zone.

No, it was an attempt to pretend my past didn't exist. Maybe I was fooling myself but for the first time in as long as I could remember, I felt wanted. Jameson had been nurturing with his answers, allowing me to feel comfortable in asking another. And another.

He hadn't laughed or shoved them aside, providing detailed answers.

He was so experienced and powerful that a part of me remained in awe, but that wasn't what he wanted. He wasn't attempting to belittle me or treat me as if I was a nothing but a fling he would toss away. Although I refused to be a fool. This also wasn't forever, merely a pleasant blip in time. He needed someone to work out the 'kinks' in his heavy and tense schedule and I needed...

Someone to continue nurturing me. Admitting that was surprisingly easier than I'd believed it would be.

I'd loved the taste of his cock, the pre-cum lingering in my mouth. He had a musky scent that was uniquely him, more intoxicating tonight than I'd noticed before. I'd gathered a sense that he could have required me to continue the intense stimulation for some time, which I wouldn't have minded. As with every other experience I'd had with him before, I longed to please him.

His entire demeanor was different, now so dominating that I didn't recognize his voice. As he spun me around, cupping my breasts as he held my back against his chest, I could feel his rapidly beating heart. There was something deliciously filthy about the fact he was completely dressed while I was devoid of any piece of clothing.

The light, warm breeze tickled my skin, creating dancing sensations yet he'd already awakened every one of my senses. I was on a cloud of bliss, desire blooming more every passing second.

He caressed my skin, his massive hands forming a cradle under the heaviness of my breasts. When he kissed the top of my head, I eased my hands against his legs, arching my back.

"You will do everything I command you to do."

"Yes, sir," I answered, still unsure about whether I was required to call him Master. If he was displeased, he said nothing, yet he pinched my nipples, twisting them in his fingers.

I wasn't anticipating the shock of discomfort or the subsequent vibrations deep inside my pussy. A gasp left my mouth, a span of white light floating by my eyes.

"Good girl. I will take care of you."

His comforting words seemed odd, but I sensed he meant them. I'd never wanted anyone to take care of me before and the thought of starting now was difficult to stomach. He rubbed his palm down my stomach, his fingers flexed open. When he reached my pussy, he cupped my mound, curling a single finger to tease my clit.

The man was masterful in his actions, the temptation almost immediately pushing me to a sweet moment of bliss. As he continued to torment my nipple, he created a wave of pleasure by stroking my clit. Within seconds, my lungs screamed for air and I was gasping for it, my legs shaking. The combination was so intense that my body rocked against his.

"Oh…" My murmur seemed to echo and I closed my eyes as the wave of pleasure rushed over me.

Jameson pressed his rock-hard cock against my ass, a reminder that he had full control. I undulated my hips enough he lowered his head, growling in my ear. The teasing continued but he shifted his hand, plunging two of his fingers past my swollen folds. My entire body shivered, my legs threatening to give out.

I'd never experienced foreplay like this. No one had cared enough to push me into a spectacular frenzy, so wet and hot that I was certain I couldn't hold back an orgasm.

As I started panting, his strokes became more intensified. When he added rolling his thumb across my clit, I almost lost it, even though I knew I wasn't allowed to come without permission.

He nuzzled his head against my ear, his scorching hot breath searing my skin. "Very good girl. You're not allowed to come yet."

I wasn't certain his reminder would help, every nerve standing on end, a fire burning brightly inside my core. I grabbed a handful of his trousers, tugging to try to keep my mind from splintering into a thousand pieces. Every sound I made reminded of some wild animal in heat, my mind spinning out of control.

Just when I thought I couldn't take it any longer, he tossed me further over the railing, both his hands gripping my bottom as he kicked my legs apart. I grabbed the thick metal, half laughing from the force he'd used. I took deep breaths, the humid air and ocean breeze almost as stimulating as the man.

The hard crack across my bottom pushed a yelp from my throat but added to the series of tingles. I tipped my head over my shoulder, still amazed at the sight of his broad shoulders and sculpted chest that the loose-fitting shirt couldn't hide.

He dropped his trousers then wrapped his hand around my throat, immediately driving his thumb into my mouth. When he placed his cock against my swollen folds, my body tensed. He was so large that the anticipation kept the light floating in front of my eyes.

There was no pretense, no romantic words said before he pressed the tip inside. My muscles immediately clamped around his thickness, drawing him in even deeper. We both groaned collectively, my grip on the railing tightening. I sucked his thumb, tasting my juice and a hint of cognac. The combination was delicious.

"So tight," he muttered as he pulled out, thrusting into me again. The angle forced me onto my toes and for a few seconds, I felt as if I was flying. When he pulled out again, the thrust was more brutal and I loved every second of it. "The things I'm going to teach you."

Several of the kinks rushed into my mind, the thought of sharing them surprisingly tempting.

Moans slipped past my lips, my mind a beautiful blur of images and thoughts. I took shallow breaths, my heart continuing to race. He cracked his hand against my buttocks twice more, and I was shocked how much it added to the pleasure. A rush of adrenaline shot through my system, my blood almost boiling.

He slowed the pace as he squeezed his hand around my throat, not enough to choke me but just to the point I was even more aroused. How was that possible?

When I felt his face pressed against mine, the slight scruff of his beard delicately abrading my skin, I opened my eyes.

"In trusting someone and giving up control, you'll learn that falling free will take you to ecstasy."

Trust. I hadn't thought about it but he was right. And I did trust him. I thought I'd never be able to trust again.

His fingers tightened around my throat even more, this time stars in vibrant colors floating past my periphery of vision. The shock remained as he pushed me to new heights but the second I started to feel uncomfortable, he backed off instinctively, fisting my hair instead.

The hard crack of four additional smacks against my bottom only heightened the wetness, the scent of our combined desires swirling with the fragrance of the ocean.

I couldn't stop panting, the sweet blur of being driven into rapture the most amazing thing I'd ever felt. He rolled onto the balls of his feet, his plunges more brutal than before, driving me into the railing. I threw my arms out, allowing the cascading electricity to pass through both of us. There was such a ferocity about him, a need that neither one of us could understand.

He was on fire, every sound he made adding to my utter arousal.

When he started to slow down, I pushed up from the railing, meeting every thrust.

"Remember what I told you. You are not in charge. Grip the railing and do not let go."

I did as he commanded, uncertain what he was going to do.

"Now open your mouth."

Again, I did so without question. He drove three fingers inside.

"Suck them, Alexandra. I want them nice and wet. Use your tongue as well."

If it was possible, his voice was even deeper, as hypnotizing as it had been when he'd saved my life. I obeyed him without question, not flinching when he drove them in even deeper. The moment he removed them, I had a sense of what he was going to do, but as he vocalized it, I was throwing into a strange vacuum.

"Now, I finger fuck your tight little ass."

Whether or not he sensed I'd never done this before I couldn't determine, but he wasn't rough in his actions as he pressed the tip of one against my dark hole. The slight breach was stimulating, delicious in its pure sin. He slowly eased it inside, pumping several times. When he added his other fingers, I stiffened.

"Relax."

I wanted to scream at him to relax but I did what I could to control my breathing, my mind still a huge blur. Surprise rushed through me as he pumped several times. While there was discomfort, the pain was minimal. Once all three were inside, he flexed them open, pumping several times. I concentrated on the sound of his ragged breathing, which I knew was from building desire.

He took his time until I began to relax, finally removing his fingers and pressing the tip of his cock against my tight hole. I felt warm and fuzzy inside, my mind a beautiful blur as vibrations prickled my senses.

When he pushed an inch inside, I tensed. Then he cracked his hand across my bottom again and I almost instantly relaxed. He pushed inside more, driving past the tight ring of muscle. A true wave of pain blasted through me for a few seconds.

Moaning, I couldn't stop my body from shaking. He stopped moving, now caressing my aching bottom with tenderness until I stopped trembling.

"You're doing so well, Alexandra."

I wasn't certain whether he was being serious or not, but I took several deep breaths, jolted when he drove the remaining inches inside. I'd never felt so full, the tingling sensations entirely different. He shifted back and forth, allowing my muscles to stretch. Then he pulled out, slowly pushing into me again.

"Oh. Uh. Uh. Uh."

"Good girl," he whispered, and I felt like a good girl, remaining on my toes as he repeated the action, allowing me to get used to his size.

I was floating on a cloud, every muscle tingling. When he repeated the move, I pushed back against him.

"Insatiable," he muttered.

"Uh-huh. I mean yes, sir."

He brought his hand down again, pushing me against the railing. I'd heard that pleasure and pain were intricately weaved together but had never understood it until now. I was ignited with a fire I hadn't known existed, my entire body tingling as blood rushed through my veins.

Breathless, I concentrated on blinking and controlling my heartrate as he fucked me, pulling almost all the way out every time, slamming into me again.

"So tight."

I was shocked how incredible it felt, my mind spinning out of control as the pleasure continued rolling through me. I was pitched into an almost immediate moment of bliss as he continued his savage thrusts.

I would never have imagined how delicious it felt to be taken this way. I closed my eyes, falling into the rhythm he'd selected, pushing me harder with every brutal plunge of his cock. But I loved every second of it.

The light breeze shifted, becoming a howl that sounded mournful. As tiny grains of salt tickled my skin, I heard a slight rumble. A storm was rolling in.

His body tensed, enough so I pushed back from the railing, trying to bite back a moan. There was no way. When he pulled me against his chest, wrapping his hand around my forehead, I'd never felt freer in my life. In the next few seconds, I sensed him tensing.

There was no other warning before he erupted deep inside my dark hole, every muscle in the man's gorgeous frame shaking.

I was completely breathless, shocked that I'd enjoyed the round of sin as much as I had. He cradled me against him for a full minute, both of us watching the crackling of lightning pulsing in the sky.

Seconds later he pulled out, turning me around to face him. Where he'd been forceful before, there was a difference in him, the look in his eyes something I could no longer read. He lowered his head and I closed my eyes, anticipating he'd capture my lips. I sensed he was hovering over me, his hot breath skipping across my already heated skin. Then he pressed his lips against my forehead before gathering me in his arms.

There was no concept of saying no to him.

As he took long strides through the house, carrying me like a prized possession, the entire experience felt normal. Who was I to know what normal was any longer? I'd thought that's what I had, a guy I could fall in love with, eventually get married and buy the perfect little house. Maybe pop out a kid or two. When whoosh. It had all been destroyed by...

By a tragedy I couldn't allow myself to remember any longer.

I had no idea how he wasn't knocking into things as he carried me up the stairs since his eyes never left mine. They also never blinked, the color intense like steel after being heated to a thousand degrees, deep silver with pearlescent flecks. I had no doubt he was going to devour me, keeping the control he'd begun on that bright day that now seemed a lifetime ago instead of a couple of days.

Being brought to his house had been completely unexpected. Perhaps I was in shock that I'd garnered his attention more than just being the sad girl down on her luck. He kicked open a partially closed door, instantly flicking a switch.

The warm glow of light in the room did little to hide the shadows. But it did provide a spotlight on his impressive bed.

One complete with shackles.

Or was that my imagination getting the better of me?

He eased me onto the center of the bed, a slight smirk on his face. "Do not move."

"Or what will happen? "

"Or you'll learn to respect the feel of the leather strap." He wrapped his fingers around my arm, lifting it over my head.

I was right about the shackles. As he wrapped the thick leather around my wrist, I immediately fisted my hand. "I've never done this before."

"Relax," he said as he buckled the first one into place. "I have." The sly grin remained on his face and I was at the point of hyperventilating already. When the first strap was in position, he rubbed his knuckles across my cheek, slowly trailing them down between my breasts. Then he walked to the other side.

By the time he moved into position, I already had my arm over my head, but I couldn't seem to stop shaking. He was tender, brushing his fingers along the underside of my arm before grasping my wrist. As he secured the second one, I pulled on the first, the creaking sound of the leather giving me shivers.

"In giving up control, you place all your trust in your partner."

"Okay. I mean, yes, sir."

He lowered his gaze then placed the strap around my wrist, his eyes piercing mine as he buckled it. I could clearly tell he'd done this before, the well-worn leather an indication. "Do you trust me?"

"You did save my life."

When he laughed, I was thrown into a moment of panic, struggling with both arms. "Close your eyes and breathe."

I wanted to scream that he should take a breath and let me go, but I managed to hold myself together. "I'm trying."

"You're doing very well." Suddenly his heated breath was cascading across my face and I shuddered. "The act of letting go isn't about pain, although it does provide intense pleasure. You had a small taste of that."

From the way he'd described the various kinks, I wasn't certain I could handle but so much more. He continued touching me, calming my nerves, his footsteps reverberating into my ears. When he reached my leg, he bent it at the knee, which forced me to open my eyes just as he was reaching for another piece of bondage gear I hadn't noticed before.

As he secured my leg in place, I held my breath, conscious of the fact I was completely helpless. I couldn't imagine doing this with a stranger.

Every step he took was methodical, repeating the same tethering with my other leg. Now I was spread wide open and completely vulnerable to him. He returned to the end of the bed, staring down at me with complete lust in his eyes.

"You are so beautiful tied and waiting for me to devour you." The huskiness of his voice sent another shiver trickling down my spine. I was so wet, aching to have him touch me, yet I was embarrassed, which was a surprise. We'd already had sex, not once but twice. He'd seen all of me, every last curve and flaw. However, this was completely different. He could do anything he wanted to me and there would be nothing I could do.

He moved toward the dresser, unfastening his watch. I lifted my head, watching his every move, curious as to what he had planned. I thought for certain he was going to undress, but he merely rolled up his sleeves, staring at me in the mirror as he performed the menial task.

His forearms were so muscular and I concentrated on studying the ink covering one arm as he finished the task.

At least the concentration calmed my nerves to some degree. Next, he removed his tie, the act taking longer than it should. I had a feeling he was trying to keep me in suspense, testing my resolve.

As he started to unbutton his shirt, I realized my mouth was watering all over again. The word 'magnificent' entered my mind, not once but twice. He was truly a gorgeous specimen of a man.

"Have you ever had a girlfriend?" I asked, immediately following that with a nervous laugh. "Of course you have. You're what, in your thirties? That means you've had lots of girlfriends. Dozens. Were they all submissives? I would guess they'd have to be. Right? You couldn't handle a normal relationship being the way you are. I mean not that it's a bad thing, just that your needs are different than other men." At this point, somewhere in the back of my mind I knew my mouth was getting the better of me, but when I was nervous, and I definitely was freaking out, I couldn't stop.

I wasn't even looking at him by that point, just spewing off one question after another that I doubted he'd answer.

"Oops. I made that sound horrible. I didn't mean it that way. I just meant—"

"Ssshh…" he interrupted, placing his index finger across my lips. I hadn't noticed his approach. I'd been far too busy fighting with my bindings, the leather creaking like crazy. "Be quiet, Alexandra. I'll answer all your questions but not right now." He lifted my head and within seconds, a mask was placed over my eyes.

Now I thought for certain I would have a full panic attack and might have already if his hand hadn't remained on my arm.

"What is happening?" I demanded, the tone much stronger than I'd intended.

"Now, I'm going to share uncontrollable pleasure with you."

"That sounds good." My brain was spinning out of control. He must think I was an idiot, unable to put a coherent sentence together. I took several loud, gasping breaths, trying to hold my position. When I didn't hear anything for what were probably minutes but felt like hours, I jerked on all the bindings.

Then I felt the weight on the bed change, his intoxicating scent overwhelming. I tossed my head from side to side, trying to figure out what he had planned but the mask blacked out everything. As my breathing became more ragged, I was certain I'd soon be hyperventilating.

"What are you doing?" I asked after a few seconds had passed.

"Good things come to very patient girls."

"I have none. You should know that." What seemed like a half hour passed, although I knew my mind was exaggerating the time. Suddenly, I felt something between my legs.

"Everything you experience in the next few minutes should be heightened, your other senses taking over."

Now I was panting, my heart beating more rapidly than before. I heard a sound, one I couldn't identify. Then I felt what had to be his fingertips lightly rolling down the inside of my leg, coming dangerously close to my pussy. My entire body began to shiver and I jerked up as much as the shackles would allow.

Then his heated breath cascaded across my pussy, but the effect was entirely different than when he'd done so across the nape of my neck. I couldn't have stopped a moan if I'd wanted to. My mind was an entire blur of strange images.

Whips and chains and spanking benches, oh, my. The ridiculous thought almost bubbled to the surface in the form of another nervous laugh, but I managed to curtail it.

The hot breath was followed by wetness. It took me a few seconds to realize what he was doing. Oh, my God. He was licking my clit. I was immediately thrown into a beautiful trance, uncertain of where I was any longer. Nor did I care, the pleasure so intense.

When the sound seemed closer, I turned my head in the direction. Something was whirling. I tensed again, fisting my hands but within seconds, the vibrating whir was place against my clit, replacing his mouth. I jerked out so hard I was certain I'd popped the bindings. My mind was blown as a wave of pleasure jetted through me with enough power I couldn't hold back a scream.

"Oh, God. Oh… I can't… I…"

Jameson rubbed the instrument of rapture down the length of my pussy as he suckled on my clit, swirling his tongue around the already sensitive nub until I was bucking at the shackles. Nothing had prepared me for the intensity of sensations, leaving me aching, desire roaring through me with a tidal wave level of strength.

I was certain he was growling, the hum of his breath keeping me warm and wet. When he returned the vibrator to my clit, rolling it back and forth, there was no way I could hold back. "I need to come. Please. Oh, please allow me to come. Sir. Master. I'll call you anything you want."

"Not yet."

Was he freaking kidding me? I continued to struggle with my body, trying to be that perfect girl when I was certain I'd go completely off the rails. He alternated between the grueling pleasure of his mouth and tongue with the wretched yet wonderful vibrator, leaving me aching all over. I couldn't control my body more than I could my whimpers, the noise I made drowning out the whirring instrument.

As another wave of pleasure tore through me, I bucked hard, the lack of vision no longer a pressing thought in my mind.

"Oh, please. Oh… I can't. I can't. I can't."

"Yes. You. Can." His authoritative words were barely audible over my thumping heart but I did my best, biting my lower lip until I tasted blood, praying that would stop me from disobeying him.

I was aware he'd shifted positions, driving his tongue into my pussy while he tormented my clit with the vibrator. Every pant erupting from my mouth sounded like some animal in heat. I didn't care. As I drifted into some other plane of existence, my head lolled to the side. I was suddenly exhausted, unable to keep fighting the raw bliss.

"That's my good girl. Now, come for me."

He didn't need to tell me twice. As soon as he buried his face into my wetness, I exploded, the strongest orgasm I'd ever had driving all sense of being and rational thought from my mind.

"Yes. Yes. Oh…"

One wasn't enough for the man who called me his submissive, the single climax sweeping into a beautiful lust-filled haze. When I screamed, there was no sound other than a strangled breath.

As I finally came down from the beautiful high, I heard his husky voice.

"That's my good girl."

CHAPTER 13

 ameson

"What are we doing here?" Alexandra asked, her tone accusatory.

"Your car couldn't be saved." I cut the engine and immediately unfastened my seatbelt.

"I can't afford a new car."

"I can."

She slowly turned her head, eyeing me with uncertainty and her usual defiance. "I'm not that kind of girl. You're not buying me."

"Is that what you think is happening?"

"I don't know but I'm perfectly capable of making money and eventually purchasing something." I could tell her mind was processing the night before while morphing it into a simple gesture.

I opened the driver's door before answering her. "You need reliable transportation and I can afford helping you."

"I don't accept charity."

"If you're that concerned, we'll work something out." I had no intentions of asking her to repay me for the gift. I climbed out, heading for the other side, laughing when she locked the door. "Don't do this, Alexandra." I knew she could hear me.

She shook her head, mumbling to herself.

I gave her a stern look and she closed her eyes. Seconds later, she finally opened the door, climbing out with the same attitude riding her face. Then she folded her arms, crowding my space. "I'm not a whore."

"No, you're not. You're a young woman who needs a break and I happen to be a man with money I don't spend. Allow me to do this for you."

There were a half dozen emotions crossing her face. "Fine. But I will eventually pay you back. I will never owe anything to anyone."

"I'll accept that and for the most part, that's admirable. Come on. I hope that you like what I picked out."

As soon as we headed for the main building, a guy I'd done business with on several occasions popped out of his office.

"Mr. Stark. It's so good to see you again."

"Tony. How've you been?"

"Good," he answered, smiling broadly when he noticed Alexandra. "This must be the special lady."

"Alexandra Kingston and this is happening under duress," she answered, shaking his hand.

He belted out a laugh. "You told me she was tough."

"That I did," I answered.

"Let's see how she likes your selection. I had it washed and there's a full tank of gas."

I pressed my hand against the small of her back, forcefully pushing her to follow him. She gave me another hard glare and after we'd taken only a few steps, she grabbed my arm, pulling me to the side. "What about insurance? I can't afford the insurance at this point."

"I've taken care of that as well."

"What? How? You were spying on me? Do you have some burly hackers like you do bouncers?"

Her sarcasm was a reminder of how special she was. "You answered the question on your new hire form. Remember?"

"Oh. I did?"

"Yes, you did. I took the liberty of paying for a year just so you'd have time to get on your feet."

"Of course you did. Do you always go around doing anything you want?"

I shoved my hands into my pockets. "I'm used to getting what I want, Alexandra. Before you ask, I'll take it if necessary."

Her mouth twisted as she tried to think of a barrage of ugly words to counter it. Then she exhaled. "Being around you is exhausting."

"I'll take that as a compliment."

She walked ahead of me. I watched her for a few minutes and two thoughts entered my mind: fucking her in the backseat of her new car and turning her over my knee. Both would happen eventually. When I finally headed toward them, I sensed another outburst coming.

"You bought me a new truck." She tipped her head, the sunlight unable to hide the shock on her face.

"It's reliable and I like the visibility it offers."

"You're... crazy."

"I'll take that as another compliment. If you don't the color, I'm certain Tony has several others."

She stared at the red Dodge Ram, her mouth twisting more than before. "It's beautiful."

"I'm glad you like it."

I was surprised she didn't walk closer, still rooted to the ground as if it wasn't real. "No one has done anything so nice for me. I won't forget it."

"I had the liberty of getting your belongings from the other car. It's on the floor of the passenger seat." I could tell she wanted to find some snappy retort but remained floored.

She smiled, but I noticed pain in her eyes, the girl from behind the mask.

Only when she walked toward the truck did I finally take a deep breath. I'd sequestered myself for so long, I'd forgotten how much I'd enjoyed aspects of life I'd given up on while trying to block out the pain. The sound of my phone was an interruption that had become far too normal. As I yanked my cellphone into my hand, I noticed her smile and it added brightness to the gorgeous day.

I glanced at the screen and groaned. Lachlan was on the phone. The Scot was a ballbuster and always had been, the true playboy of our group of three. Thank God, he'd softened over the last few months, a spunky senator's daughter the reason.

"If you're calling this early in the morning, there must be an issue," I told him, half laughing.

"It's after ten. Are you still getting your beauty sleep?" Lachlan teased.

"No. I'm doing something good for a change. What's up?"

"We might have an issue in Paris that needs your attention."

"Do I want to know and why didn't Philip give me a call?"

My buddy snorted. "Maybe because his attorney called me instead. It would seem Mr. Dumas has gotten himself into some legal trouble. Apparently, his family also has ties to a ruthless crime syndicate overseas. From what I was told, if we don't want the workers to walk off the job, they need someone controlling them."

"Why would they walk off?"

"Because his funds have been put on hold."

"The reason?"

"Well, he's been accused of blackmail, extortion, and I'm sure a few other crimes as well."

I took a deep breath. "In order to get the land then the building designs approved."

Lachlan snorted. "You were always good at weeding through the bullshit."

One of my fortes. I rolled my eyes. Dumas. We'd all had our reservations about the secretive man, but he'd checked all the boxes enabling us to go forward, including the money he'd already put down on the project. "Why do I have a feeling we're the target?"

"That's what I was thinking as well."

"Let me guess. You nominated me to handle the mess."

"I wouldn't know the difference between a two by four and a header beam and you know it. We could send Grant, but somehow, I think Mr. Number Cruncher wouldn't do much good either. Besides, he has his hands full with issues of his own in LA. You have a strong connection with Dumas and with the folks in their government office. You up for it, buddy?"

I glanced toward the truck, exhaling as I watched Alexandra climbing into the cab. "How soon?" My thoughts drifted to the meeting I'd left. Obtaining the urban planning authorization hadn't been difficult, but I'd had the feeling Dumas had paved the way before my arrival eight months before. I only hoped he hadn't lined the official's pockets as well.

"A day. Maybe two. That's all the time the attorney thinks we have before things get ugly."

Fucking fantastic. "Fine. I'll figure something out. Email me the details and I'll get the jet ready. I'll call you after I'd read everything over."

"We'll do a conference call with Grant. I want to make certain we're all on the same page."

While the three of us were equal partners, as CEO, Lachlan had always been the front man, his always camera-ready presence adding to our credibility.

"Hmmm… Why does it sound like there's something preventing you from leaving swanky Miami?"

"Go mind your own business. How is that sexy almost wife of yours?"

"You know women," he chortled. "Everything must be perfect."

Perfect. It was a word not included in my vocabulary. "Better than you know."

Alexandra

. . .

Rarely did anyone surprise me. If they did, it was usually the kind of revelation that eventually became caustic. As I pulled down the street to the condo, I took another deep breath. I hadn't wanted to admit it to Jameson, but I was like a giddy kid inside, butterflies still swarming my stomach. The nagging voice was still in the back of my mind, but I'd sensed the powerful man was being generous, and that the gift didn't come with strings attached.

I thought I'd made myself perfectly clear that I wasn't selling anything, including my body for sex or something else. Laughing, I rolled into the garage, sliding my hand back and forth across the leather steering wheel.

He'd spared no expense. Even though the sticker with the price had been taken off the window, I'd found it in the center console. He'd paid almost sixty thousand for the special edition. In cash. That much I'd managed to get out of the nice but far too lecherous dealer. There was no way I could handle payments and I wasn't entirely certain I could pay Jameson back in ten years.

I'd checked with my insurance company and he'd been fibbing to me a little. He'd paid for two years of insurance up front. All the bells and whistles too. I remained floored yet cautious. No one ever did anything like this without wanting something in return. Maybe I was just jaded. I did have every reason to be.

After pulling into the designated parking space, I took a few minutes to sit and enjoy the new car smell. I'd had hand-me-downs since I'd learned to drive. The radio was still on, the heavy metal station I'd found on satellite radio jamming with my favorite tunes. I couldn't help but dance a little in my seat as the bass boomed from the eight speakers inside the cab. Eight. And satellite radio! I'd been lucky to find a station every fifth town on my drive to Miami.

I noticed Charlotte's car was parked in her regular spot. I had no idea what to say to her. *Hey, I was lucky enough to be given a brand-new truck. Why? Because I'm his little subbie.*

Oh, God. Was that what I'd become?

A few more minutes of enjoyment before I figured out what to say that wouldn't hurt anyone.

Exhaling, I closed my eyes, slumping down in the leather seat, running my fingers across the smooth grain. Why would he do something so incredible for a girl he barely knew?

Okay, so the sex was out of this world, the night before what fantasies were made of, but really? I'd never easily trusted anyone, especially when they tried to ply me with gifts. While I didn't think the man had a hidden agenda, I still couldn't wrap my mind around his generosity.

There was no reason a sudden moment of sadness swept through me. None at all. Maybe it was all about missing my brother. "You would have loved this truck, Matt. And red was your color." I could still envision his grin, the expression I'd called evil more than once. "I know. You'd have installed huge tires and rims right away. Then I could see you driving down the road with the stereo blaring. Full blast. Yeah. With a beer in your hand."

The sadness became almost overwhelming. I'd tried to put the ugliness behind me, but his closeness was missed so much, a hole would forever be in my heart. How many times had I asked why? If only we'd both made other choices that night. Yeah, if only. I took a deep breath and allowed the images to fade, squeezing the leather-covered steering wheel hard enough my knuckles turned white. Damn it.

The seat was so comfortable, I could have easily fallen asleep. And I would have if a loud screech of tires hadn't jerked me back to reality.

I glanced into the oversized side mirror, noticing a black SUV had pulled up about four lengths ahead and nearer to the elevator. While I didn't recognize the vehicle, that didn't mean anything given the comings and goings of residents and guests, most of whom I didn't know and from what I could tell didn't want to be seen.

When two doors opened, I unfastened my seatbelt, turning toward the activity. Three huge men dressed in dark suits popped out, each one of them obviously influenced by bad gangster movies. Their slicked-back hair had seen far too much hairstyling gel, their burnished cinnamon complexions adding a dangerous aura. And I could swear one of them held a weapon in his hand.

What. The. Fuck?

I'd seen my share of bad guys, including in Montana, although the rough dudes usually carried rifles, not handguns. The three stood outside the SUV, two of them keeping watch in either direction. Then the third opened the back passenger door. From the angle I didn't have a clear line of sight, but two sets of legs eased onto the concrete.

The brawny guy who'd opened the door almost completely blocked my view. When he threw a look in the direction of my truck, I turned off the radio and slunk down further. My instinct told me whoever they were didn't want to be seen.

I cut the engine, praying they hadn't noticed the exhaust. While my curiosity was nagging at me to crawl closer to the passenger door for another peek, the intelligent and rational side of me won out.

Seconds turned into full minutes. Then I heard the slamming of car doors and the revving of an engine. I refused to move from my spot until the driver sped off. If they were exiting the garage, they'd need to find a spot and turn around.

When it finally whizzed by thirty seconds later, I took a deep breath, counting to ten before lifting my head. Thank God they were gone.

For about a million reasons my legs were shaking as I stepped out, grabbing my bag. No one remained in the garage. Exhaling, I headed for the elevator, constantly looking over my shoulder. Maybe Jameson was right and living in the building wasn't such a good idea.

As soon as the elevator doors opened, I rushed inside, slamming my hand on the button for our floor, praying the doors would close. When they did, I let out a moan. I tapped my foot on the floor, staring at the panel over the doors as the steel box took its sweet time getting to its destination.

When it was finally close, I inched forward, ready to jump out. Then I noticed a spot on the floor. After eyeing it carefully, I bent down and swiped my finger though it. I didn't need to bring it to my nose to realize it was a large drop of blood. A slight chill coursed through me as I thought about Charlotte.

The girl needed to level with me about what was going on. I wiped it on my jeans, quickly heading to the door of the condo. It took me almost ten seconds to find the keys. At least my hand was steady as I shoved a key into the lock, yet I took a few seconds to open the door, listening for any sounds of activity.

Silence greeted me, but it eerie. Charlotte was a music lover, her stereo blasting when she was home. I walked inside, scanning the perimeter before closing and locking the door. I wanted to call out to her, but my gut told me it wasn't a good idea. I placed my bag on the foyer table, slowly moving through the living room toward the bedroom hallway.

Her door was closed, no sounds coming from the other side. It was entirely possible she was sleeping. Thankfully, no sound was made when I opened it, peering inside. She was on her bed fully dressed, her face pressed into her pillow.

"Charlotte?" My whisper seemed hoarse, my nerves the reason.

She didn't say a single word or move and I was about to leave when the covers were rustled.

"Go away. Okay? Just go away."

Her voice seemed distant, devoid of any emotions, but I sensed she was in pain.

"What happened?"

"Nothing. Just go."

I walked closer. "That's going to happen. You need to tell me what's going on. Right now. I won't leave until you do."

She didn't react right away nor was there any sound. Then I heard a sob, the sound so full of agony that I eased onto the edge of her bed. When I pressed my hand on her shoulder, she flinched.

"Don't," she moaned.

"What did they do to you?"

She sniffed, shaking her head slightly, refusing to allow me to see her face.

"Charlotte. Not only am I family but I'm your friend. You need to tell me what's going on. Please?"

The hesitation killed me. We'd trusted each other through boys and troubles in school, always able to count on each other.

Charlotte moved, then slowly turned her head. I couldn't see any damage or bruises, but I could only see half her face.

"I found blood in the elevator. Is it yours?"

"I don't know. Other stuff happened."

Stuff. Even the short answer wasn't like her. Fed up, I threw back the covers, gently rolling her over. Her lip was swollen, caked blood on her cheek. "Fucking Jesus Christ. Who did this to you?"

"It's complicated, but Diego took care of it. Or he will because he cares about me."

"Diego. As in Santiago the cartel leader?"

She nodded and my anger rushed to the surface.

"What in the hell are you doing around that man? He's a monster, a murderer. I've read articles on him. You're smarter than that."

"He's good to me. Mostly."

Mostly, my ass. I knew what I was talking about. "Is he your boyfriend?" I couldn't fathom how she'd gotten herself mixed up with a crime lord.

"I wouldn't call him my boyfriend exactly."

"Then what would you call him? Your pimp? Is he paying for this condo?"

"How dare you!" she snapped. "You don't seem to mind living in the lap of luxury."

"Let me guess. I'll be required to do favors like you're doing for this... pig?" The anger in her eyes quickly turned to sadness.

"No. Of course not. I would never do that to you. You're family."

But she had no issue sliding under the thumb of a man who could toss her aside at a moment's notice. The rage remained furrowing deep inside of me.

"Men like him don't care about anyone but themselves. I should know."

Charlotte chewed on her lower lip, which she did when she was nervous or afraid. She was both.

"What do you do for him?" When I asked the question, her entire expression changed, the mask she usually wore appearing. Even with her determination to hide her life from me, there was no disguising the amount of trouble she was in.

"Sometimes I work in his casino. Sometimes I work private parties. It all depends."

"Uh-huh. Are you running drugs?"

"No! Of course not."

"Then tell me what else. Now!" She jumped then recoiled, immediately placing her hands over her face. Why had she put up with this shit?

I did what I could to tamp down the increasing anger. "Honey. Look. I care about you. You need to tell me what you're mixed up in. Maybe we can go to the police."

"No police!" She snapped her head up, her eyes wilder than before. "I care about you, which is why it's better you don't know anything. But no, I'm not running drugs."

"Why is it easy for me not to believe you?" I knew the edge in my voice would keep her clammed up, but I was far too furious to tiptoe around what she'd gotten herself into.

When she raked her hand through her hair, I noticed it was shaking.

"You will stay away from him. Do you hear me? If you don't, I'm going to have a discussion with him. He can't beat up women."

"You can't." She jerked up and I was able to see her torn clothes. When she noticed my horrified reaction, she grabbed a handful of the sheet, pulling it around her. "Promise me you won't say anything to him. Ever. He didn't do this. One of his men did. Diego is going to take care of it. He's good to me."

"So you've said, which is why you have other bruises."

"I told you I was a bad girl."

"Jesus Christ. I can't believe you've sunk this low."

"What about you?" she threw out. "You're fucking a rich guy who's more powerful than Diego."

Why I wasn't shocked she'd thrown that in my face I wasn't certain. I gave her a nastier look than maybe she deserved. "As long as you promise to get away from whatever situation you're in then I won't approach the asshole."

"You can't."

"I will. You know it too."

Charlotte looked forlorn, her bruised mouth twisting. Then she nodded. I gathered her into my arms, holding her tightly.

"It's going to be alright." Somehow, it had to be.

"Just promise me, cuz, that you'll stay away from them," she said. "Diego will kill you if you interfere. Then he'll kill me."

CHAPTER 14

 *ameson*

"Motherfucker," Grant hissed as he stared into the camera, the Zoom call lasting longer than I'd wanted. "I knew Dumas was hiding something."

"Bullshit," Lachlan piped in. "You were behind him one hundred percent. Don't give me that crap." The brusque Scot was more agitated than normal.

I'd spent time going through every document Dumas had signed as well as the background documentation we'd required. He hadn't purposely hidden anything from us that I'd noted. "Let's not jump to conclusions just yet. I need to have a conversation with him."

"Once a liar, always a liar." Grant's attitude made me smirk. He'd used a few unscrupulous methods of skirting around a few county officials in LA. I doubted he wanted a reminder.

Whatever was going on, it was clear that Philip Dumas was a piece of work.

I was being kind.

He'd recently been arrested for possible extortion, including bribing several members of the government of the French Republic. From what Lachlan had sent via email, officials were doing everything in their power to shut down the project. Whether or not the accusations were true mattered only on the surface at this point. Carnal Sins had millions of dollars tied up in investments, loans to Dumas for construction. While his family had money, their wealth noted in the billions, he was considered the black sheep of the family.

That meant he'd obtained funds for the larger percentage of the project on his own. If I had to guess, I'd say using unscrupulous methods that he'd hidden well. Well enough neither Grant nor I had determined that it was in our best interest to refuse signing our names on the contract.

Lachlan had been more concerned but had deferred to the two of us and our judgments. I'd met with the Frenchman on several occasions, grilling him as I studied his financials. While I wasn't stupid enough to believe they couldn't have been doctored, my gut told me the guy was in the middle of a French war whose foes had used unfounded information to try to strong-arm him.

Something definitely smelled foul.

Not that I gave a shit about his well-being at this point, but I refused to lose the funds we'd provided. It looked like I would be heading to Paris for an undisclosed period of time.

I sat back in my seat behind my desk, closing my eyes and rubbing the scruff on my face. I'd ignored shaving, especially after Alexandra's comment about how much she enjoyed being stimulated by my beard. That had come after I'd taken her a second time, that time in the shower with her wrists secured to the showerhead. The thought of water trickling down the length of her body was enough to shove me into full arousal.

"Are you with us, lover boy?" Lachlan threw in.

I lifted my middle finger without hesitation, both men laughing.

"Is there something I should know?" While Grant's question was rhetorical, I wasn't in the mood to compare dick size or anything else at this point.

"Not a fucking thing." The statement was a bit terse, but the last thing I wanted to do was to leave Alexandra alone. Part of it was for selfish reasons, but I'd delved a little deeper into Santiago's business tactics, including his foray into human trafficking. However, the man was extremely good at keeping his name out of the press as well as greasing the palms of a number of officials.

Including Judge Garber. I'd discovered by accident a glossy photo of the two men shaking hands at a fundraiser of all things.

"I'll find out what's going on," I told them. "But as of now, the project is too far along to abandon. You both know it.

Up until this incident, everything was on track to open in three months. We owe it to him to provide our assistance." My dominating behavior was on full display this morning, likely given my determination to protect Alexandra.

Maybe I'd insist she come with me to Paris. Hmmm... The idea had merit.

"Listen to the construction god," Grant snarked.

"What's up your ass?" I retorted.

"You're one to talk. Did you get a bad batch of Wheaties this morning?" Grant had turned into quite the joker after all these years. When I glared at him, he acted offended, adjusting his suit jacket. "Fine. No sense of humor. Bad clients who think they can use the club as their personal conference room."

I knew what that entailed. The note on my desk indicated Judge Garber had requested a meeting. Like hell that was going to happen.

"Let's not get off track. Just see what you can do to eradicate the situation, Jameson," Lachlan suggested. "We don't need any bad press while trying to get the Milan project off the ground. The authorities are dicey enough, the Cosa Nostra sniffing around."

"How the hell would they know about the project unless the man interested in entering into business with us ignored his confidentiality agreement?" I barked.

Grant was pressing my last nerve, driving up his arms as if surrendering to my piss-poor mood.

Lachlan sighed. "That's a good question that will be answered, but the situation with Dumas needs to be rectified."

"Agreed. I'll give you a status update when I'm in Paris."

"I admit I'm curious. Are you going alone?" he threw in.

There was no reason for me to bristle as the three of us had tormented each other through the years regarding the choices in women we'd made. "Not you too."

"Call it a hunch. Maybe that's a way to defuse the situation. Take her with you."

The way Lachlan was leaning into the camera, his eyes pointed on mine meant he wasn't telling me everything about the problems I could face. "Maybe. I'll need to see. Now, if there's nothing else. I have a business to run." I was already out of my seat, ready to stop the meeting before either one realized I'd moved.

Grant hitched both eyebrows, his previous look of amusement shifting into annoyance. "Sure, buddy." He ended the call abruptly and Lachlan turned his full attention in my direction.

"Is there something else going on?"

I wanted to walk away without mentioning Pamela's death, but a part of me needed to mention it to someone. "Pamela was killed in a boating accident."

"What?" He looked at me quizzically. "You two were talking?"

"Oh, hell, no. I got a call from her brother."

"Well, how nice of him since he was the one who threatened your life years ago."

I'd all but forgotten about the ugly incident. It had been the single time I'd almost used my brawn to end a man's life. It had put a final wedge between me and Pamela. "He just wanted me to know."

Exhaling, he rubbed his jaw then offered the fatherly look that he'd grown accustomed to giving. "I won't ask about this girl because I have a feeling at this point you'll tell me it's none of my business. But I'm going to give you my opinion whether you freaking want to hear it or not. Move on. I know you cared about Pamela, but your relationship was toxic."

Anger immediately rose to the surface, but he was right. "I got it. It was just a shock from the past I didn't need."

"Go to Paris. Take this girl with you. Maybe what you found with her will turn out to be nothing. Maybe it's something. But maybe the damn universe is telling you it's time to let the past slide into hell."

"You have such a way with words, buddy."

"Aye," he chided, his Scottish accent suddenly stronger than usual. "Just remember. Paris is the city of love."

"Very funny. I'll call you when I know something." I ended the call, able to laugh. Then I rubbed my beard again. Maybe he was right.

Besides, I would enjoy taking her to a club in Paris.

My lovely submissive had no idea what she'd started.

*　*　*

Alexandra

No one could ever call me Florence Nightingale, but I knew my way around first aid. I'd taken CPR and a few other EMT classes prior to switching my major to elementary education, much to the chagrin of my father. He'd wanted me to be a doctor or lawyer, but his reasons had little to do with skill or what I wanted. He'd merely called my brother a fuckup then placed the burden on my shoulders to ensure the family's reputation would be upheld.

I'd often wondered as what exactly, card carrying hypocrites?

At least I'd been able to use the special training to determine Charlotte didn't have any broken bones. However, since she'd allowed me to help her remove her dress, mostly at my insistence, I'd finally seen the number of partially healed bruises she'd managed to hide.

She'd been used as a punching bag by some asshole. My bet was on Santiago, but she'd continued to insist he hadn't been the one to cause her pain. I bought it like I did little green men were about to invade the Earth. She'd clammed up after that and I'd spent time fuming, pacing the floor.

Her warning had rattled me, but not enough to reconsider finding out everything I could about what was going on.

After convincing Charlotte to take a bath, I'd put her to bed. When she woke up, she and I were going to have a long talk.

If not, I'd shake her until she confessed.

I'd returned to the living room, trying to think about what to do. That had been almost an hour before with no decent results.

Granted, I could say something to Jameson, but if I did, I had a feeling he'd be the big he-man all over again, getting himself killed while trying to protect me. What if I found us a different place to live?

Laughable at this point unless Charlotte had squirreled away money.

There was no way for me to solve anything this afternoon given I had to head to work in a few hours. When I heard a knock on the door, I immediately froze. Charlotte had plenty of friends. That much I knew. I moved closer to the door, eyeing the thick piece of steel as if it would provide answers as to who stood on the other side.

With no peephole and no chain like the doors on my parents' house, I'd get no advance warning. However, if it was a friend, maybe I could glean information. I took cautious steps closer, almost yelping with whoever it was pounded on the door.

"Who is it?" I barked, deepening my voice.

"Cut the crap, Char. It's me."

That meant she hadn't mentioned she had someone living with her. "I'm not feeling well."

"Yeah, I bet," the guy snorted. "Just open the fucking door. I will knock it down if I need to. Don't fuckin' piss me off."

Don't piss him off? I'd shifted into the livid side. "Hold on. Let me grab a robe." I coughed so the asshole wouldn't figure out he wasn't talking to Char. Then I grabbed my phone so I could call the police. After flying by the kitchen, I stopped. Then I moved toward the butcher block, grabbing a knife. A girl couldn't be too safe. I shoved the phone in my pocket then hid the knife behind my back before opening the door.

I was greeted with a dozen roses shoved in my face.

"Take these. I was told to bring them to you. The boss wants to make certain you're okay."

I backed away, allowing them to drop to the floor.

"What the fuck?" Whoever he was snarled, his angry glare not registering I wasn't Charlotte for at least five full seconds. Then he stomped on the flowers as he came inside, slamming the door behind him. "You're not Char."

"Oh, look. The Neanderthal has a brain larger than a pea." My rage was doing the talking but I was not going to allow her to stay mixed up with these animals.

He seemed confused I would dare talk to him that way. As we did our version of a stare off, I realized something just as sickening as the fact the killer was only a few feet away from me. He was also the driver who'd almost run me down.

"Who the fuck are you?" he demanded.

"I should ask the same question."

"My friends call me the Killer."

"And my friends call me the Slicer." What was I doing challenging him?

As he took another step closer, I refused to back away. "You're a funny girl."

"So I've been told. I'm going to ask you nicely to leave."

"Nicely, huh? I can't do that."

When his eyes flitted toward the hallway, I yanked the knife in front of me, pointing the blade at his jugular. "Yes, you can."

He threw up his hands, his golden tooth highlighting his love of fights. Maybe they were all the rage in the cartel. A fashion statement.

That's the moment he decided to slowly lower his gaze, the leer sickening. "I don't want any trouble, little girl."

Little girl? "Then don't ask for it. Just leave and never come back."

His sneer was followed by the ugly beast narrowing his eyes. "As I said, I'm afraid I can't do that. I'm here to make certain Char is okay. My boss told me to check on her. He heard there was a little… incident at her job."

"Right. If by incident you mean some ass-wipe beat her, then he heard correctly." I knew I was pressing my luck, but my gut told me that if he got to her, there was a chance I'd never see her again. I jammed the knife in his direction. "Tell your boss that no one is going to touch her again."

His laugh was riddled with amusement until he figured out I was serious. When he looked at me again, his expression was all about scrutinizing me as if I'd been recognized. Shit. "Don't I know you from somewhere?"

"Not a chance. I don't deal with termites and cockroaches." I could tell I'd finally insulted him. I lifted the blade, shifting it back and forth. "Leave. Now."

He sniffed, his expression darkening. "Fine, but you won't be seeing the last of me."

"Let me put it to you this way. If you dare try and come back, the police will lock you up."

There was something about his laugh that sent an icy chill down my spine. "You're a funny girl. Stupid. But funny." He backed away, stepping on the roses again as he opened the door. He studied me intently, memorizing every aspect of my body and face then issued a knowing grin.

I managed to wait for a full sixty seconds before racing toward the door, slamming and locking it. Then I slowly slid down the door to the floor, dropping the knife.

"Who was that?"

Startled, I lifted my head. Char had her arms crossed, glaring at me intently. "I guess a buddy of yours. Big guy with a gold tooth?"

When she broke into a smile, I was shocked. "Benny was here? I love Benny." She suddenly noticed the crushed flowers I was sitting on. "Get up. They're ruined."

Her tone sounded accusatory. "They're from a killer." I clambered to my feet, and she immediately gathered the flowers into her arms, cradling them against her.

"They're from Diego. I told you he cared about me."

"No, they were technically from Benny." I stood and watched her, a little sick to my stomach. Had this been the way I'd acted? God, I hoped not. "Incidentally, Benny was the driver of the car who hit me."

"That's crap."

"No, the license plate was registered to Diego Santiago."

She frowned and I could sense she was trying to make up some excuse. "Maybe he didn't know he hit you."

"My car is totaled, Charlotte."

At least she seemed shocked. "What are you going to do?"

It was my turn to feel embarrassed. "Jameson is allowing me to use one of his trucks until I can figure something out." I certainly couldn't tell her the truth at this point. I could only imagine what she'd say in chastisement. And she'd be right for a change. I'd accepted the truck without putting up enough fight against it. I'd told myself at least ten times that I had no other choice, but who accepted a sixty-thousand-dollar truck from someone they didn't know?

She studied me, a strange smile curling on her lips.

Charlotte had been a tough girl growing up. She'd been forced to be since her father remained in prison, her mother addicted to painkillers. That's why we'd tried to keep our friendship private. My father hated that side of the family with a passion. When her mouth twisted, I waited for a barrage of angry words, which had always been her defense mechanism.

Just never against me.

"Oh, so you don't mind getting a favor from a dangerous, rich guy but when I do it, then you condemn me."

"It's not the same thing and you know it."

"You don't have a clue how things work, Alexandra. You act all high and mighty, waltzing into my life acting like the way I live isn't good enough. Not that I need to explain myself to you, but I worked hard to get here. I struggled for two years. If you remember correctly, my mother didn't want me any longer. I lived in cardboard boxes for almost six months, fighting off drug addicts and rapists. Then Diego picked me up off the street after some asshole nearly beat me to death. He nursed me back to health then gave me a home. He's been good to me." She struggled to her feet, still wincing in pain. "I make five hundred thousand dollars a year now. This is my condo. I have a beautiful car and all the clothes I want. I eat in five-star restaurants drinking ten-thousand-dollar bottles of champagne. Don't you dare try and tell me what to do."

Charlotte had never acted this way, nor had she treated me as if I meant nothing to her. It was obvious she'd forgotten about the promises we'd made about making certain our lives were different.

She brushed past me into the kitchen, probably searching for a vase. I remained where I was for a few seconds before heading to my room to grab my purse. When I returned to the kitchen, she was arranging the flowers, a smile on her face. But it was plastic, just like the world we both had survived in.

There were at least a dozen things I wanted to say but at this point, what good would they do? She believed what she was going through was somehow justified.

When Charlotte shot me an unapologetic look, I was forced to face the fact there was nothing I could do except find a place of my own. I could tell by the glisten in her eyes that she truly believed she was in love.

As I'd thought before. Who was I to judge? I'd allowed myself to fall into the deep end of a cesspool. I understood better than most how tough it was to fight off the insecurities and other demons that plagued someone's mind.

I only hoped she'd come to her senses before she lost the battle.

And her life.

Traffic was a bitch and I remained nervous, constantly glancing in the rearview mirror. The truck was amazing, including the fact it sat high above a significant number of other vehicles. It allowed me to catch a glimpse at traffic several car lengths behind.

The dark SUV drew my attention immediately. There were hundreds of them in Miami, likely carrying various bad men from all walks of life in their attempt to remain as anonymous as possible. While I wasn't prone to worrying about boogeymen crawling out from under my bed, this time I was very much on edge. There were too many 'what if' scenarios floating in the back of my mind.

Benny had all but threatened me, although he'd done a damn good job of masking it as a nice little warning. I studied the area, remembering a turn I could use that would also get me to the club. I waited until the last minute, not signaling before making the turn. After a wave of blasting horns, I sped forward, my actions more daring than normal as I weaved my way around several other cars.

When I looked again, there was no sign of the SUV. Exhaling, I was about to chastise myself for being ridiculous when it appeared again. "Shit." A lump formed in my throat and the only hope I had was losing the asshole on the interstate.

With two miles still to go, I continuously glanced in the side mirror, my stomach in knots. When the onramp appeared, I did the same thing I had before, gunning the engine. As expected, the SUV followed me, keeping a distance but close enough to watch my every turn.

I wasted no time, trying to stay just five miles above the speed limit, but with the heavy traffic, it was almost impossible. The best I could hope for was losing them in the sea of vehicles.

Five minutes later, it was apparent I was losing the game they were playing. I wasn't in the mood to play cat and mouse, my anger increasing. I glanced at the sign indicating several exits, the one leading to Blackout three ahead. After taking another glance, I shifted to the right-hand lane. What I was thinking about doing would take luck. If I could get off at the exit prior to the one I needed then roar back onto the interstate immediately, I might lose them long enough to be able to get to the next exit.

Even if the assholes knew where I worked, all I needed to do was get to the door and one of the bouncers would help me.

Laughing nervously, I sped down the exit ramp, scanning the road furiously until I located the sign enabling me to get back on. Fortunately, luck was with me for a change, no vehicles or streetlights to hinder me. When I pressed my foot on the accelerator, heading back to the interstate, I held my breath until I made it to the next exit. Only then did I look up.

The SUV wasn't in sight.

Thank fucking God for small favors.

I didn't waste any time, also thankful the three lights I had to go through were all green. My throat was tight when I pulled into the employee parking lot, forced to take a space in the back. I barely managed to bring the truck to a stop, cutting the engine before I had the door open, and my hand wrapped around my purse.

The employees' entrance was twenty yards away. The only problem was that there was no bouncer on the other side, only a single camera over the door for security. I glanced over my shoulder then jogged toward it, shifting in between other vehicles.

I was almost there when I heard a sound and froze.

Suddenly, a hand was snapped across my mouth and I was shoved against the building.

A man leered at me, laughing under his breath. "Hello, Alexandra. It's good to see you again."

CHAPTER 15

 *ameson*

Jagger was whistling when he came into my office. As soon as he saw me, he sported a shit-eating grin. "So, I didn't get a chance to ask you how it felt to toss out some unruly customers. You haven't done that in years."

I heard a slight growl coming from my throat and grumbled under my breath. "Make certain those kids aren't allowed in here any longer."

"Well, I hate to remind you of this, but Matthew Garber has a full membership. As I seem to recall, that was again my recommendations."

"You're going to throw that in my face for a long time. Aren't you?"

"If necessary." He folded his arms as he walked closer. "I heard you're planning a sudden trip to Paris. Again."

"Word travels fast." I'd told Ginger for a single reason only: to ensure she didn't count on Alexandra working a shift for the next few days.

"Ginger wanted me to know." He kept his eyes on me as if my hair was on fire. "Besides, you know the employees often come to me because they're terrified of you."

"Terrified? That's crap."

Jagger shrugged. "You started losing your sense of humor about five years ago. Since then, you shifted into being a cranky old guy."

"Hey!" I pointed my finger at him. The dude was laughing. "I'm not old."

"No, but you are cranky."

I pushed the cup of coffee away, the bitter taste unusual. "Is that right?"

"I don't tell lies. I will say over the last couple of days, it's almost like you're a changed man. With the exception of almost killing that kid last night."

He wasn't wrong, although I wasn't going to admit it. I'd slowly fallen into a level of depression that had become close to impossible to ignore or fix. He said nothing, still remaining staring at me.

"What?"

He lifted a single eyebrow, the amusement on his face more irritating than normal. "You're taking the girl with you. Aren't you?"

Goddamn it. Nothing was private any longer. "I need an assistant."

"Take Sheila."

Sheila was a sweet girl who handled the books, working with Anastasia Wilde, who ran practically everything on the financial end out of the DC office. Coincidentally, Anastasia was also Grant's spunky younger sister. "I need her here. Business in Miami doesn't stop because I need to babysit a Parisian asshole."

He chuckled. "No, you're right. But are you hiring an assistant or a submissive?"

I gave him a hard look. "She'll be back to waiting tables after we return."

"Funny how you avoided the question altogether."

"Don't start with me."

"Who's starting anything? You were the one worried about whether she was of legal age or not."

I rolled back in my chair, swinging it from side to side. "She's very legal, thank you very much."

When we both heard a knock on the door, he swiveled around, but I could still see the smirk on his face when he noticed it was Sheila.

"I'm sorry to interrupt, Mr. Stark, but I found a personal piece of mail for you in the payments. I'm sorry. I'm usually better catching anything with the wrong address."

She acted as if I was going to be angry with her.

"You can come in. He won't bite, Sheila," Jagger said. "He's having a good day."

Her face flushed and I almost pitched the mug against the wall. Had I become that much of an ogre? Evidently so.

"You didn't need to bring it by now," I told her, hating the sheepish look on her face.

"No. I knew it was important. It says urgent. I'm so sorry. I'll be more careful."

"Sheila. If it was so important, then the sender should have known my correct address. Not the one for the club. Okay?"

She gently placed it on my desk and backed away, almost tripping. "True. Still. I'm sorry." When she turned and started to flee from the office, it wasn't before giving Jagger a very sensual onceover, her face turning a bright red. I also couldn't help notice that he'd returned the same salacious look.

I wasn't the Neanderthal he thought I was, waiting until she was safely tucked away in the elevator before laughing softly. "Is there something I should know?"

Jagger huffed. "Like any woman could handle this." He used all his fingers to point to himself. "*Moi?*"

"You're right. You're not fit for any woman."

"Speak for yourself."

We both laughed and I snagged the overstuffed envelope, eyeing the return address. Fuck. As I sat back, I rolled my finger across the address absently.

"By the way, I'm heading out early tonight. My sister flew in for a few days and I need to pick her up at the airport."

The man lived in the club. "Take a couple days off."

"We'll see. She drives me nuts when she's here," he gritted out then nodded toward the envelope. "What is it?"

"It appears to be a letter from an attorney."

"Maybe we're being sued."

As I eyed the address a second time, a moment of anger washed through my system. "No, we're not being sued. Just an inconvenience." I shoved it in a drawer with no intentions of handling it tonight.

Maybe ever.

Lachlan was right. It was time to start living again.

Jagger's Apple Watch made a noise and he instantly jerked his arm up, pressing his finger on the screen.

"Fuck. We've got a problem. One of the servers is being accosted in the parking lot."

My gut told me who it was.

He didn't wait for my instructions, yanking out his phone and contacting another one of the bouncers.

I bolted ahead of him, making it to the bottom of the stairs within seconds. I raced down the hallway then through the crowd of Blackout patrons, almost knocking over several. When I made it to the employees' entrance, I slammed both hands on the door, lunging outside.

The sight of Alexandra being pulled toward an awaiting SUV would remain emblazed in my mind. I lunged forward, pulling her from his arms, her scream as his hand released from her mouth bloodcurdling.

And it fueled the raw rage burning inside of me. I issued two hard punches, slamming the assailant into the passenger door.

"Jesus," Jagger said from behind me, immediately moving toward the driver's side.

The guy's head was lolled to the side, gasping for air. Blood seeped from his broken nose, as if I gave a shit. I wrapped my hand around his throat, ready to deliver several more in rapid succession.

That's when I recognized the son of a bitch who'd attacked Alexandra.

Matthew Garber.

"Hey. You broke his nose," the kid's companion said as he was dragged around the back of the SUV.

"Yeah?" I snarled. "I'm planning on doing a hell of lot more," I hissed then tightened my hold around Matthew's neck until he was choking.

"Hey, boss man. I don't think you want to do that," Jagger said from behind me.

I shot him a look then turned my head toward Alexandra. She appeared shaken but not hurt. At least I could still see the fire in her eyes.

"Yeah? What I want to do is to break his neck. That's exactly what he deserves." I kept the choke hold as I lowered my head, leaving him no room to look away. "But here's how we're going to play this. I'm going to let the police handle it from here."

"No. No!" he barked out as he slammed his fists against me. "Please."

"Please? You attempted to kidnap a woman and you say please don't have your ass arrested? Would you prefer I handled your penance, ass-wipe?" By now, a crowd had formed, including Danner and another employee. Both men flanked the sides of the SUV to prevent anyone from attempting escape.

"We didn't mean nothing by it," his worthless companion said.

I laughed. "And what exactly did you mean?"

"Let him go, Jameson. The putz isn't worth it." While Jagger's words of wisdom registered, I'd had enough of rich kids who were constantly let off the hook.

While a part of me wanted to snap the kid's neck, Jagger was right. I let him go, backing away and immediately heading for Alexandra. "Danner. Call the police. Let them deal with this scum. And take the keys."

Jagger grinned, shaking his head. I knew I'd be forced to deal with a shitstorm on my hands by having the judge's son arrested, but what did I care?

"Come on. Let's get you inside." I wrapped my arm around her waist, easing her into the door.

"What is it about men who won't take no for an answer?" she asked before I led her through the foyer of the club headed for my office. I waited until we were in the quiet of the private hallway before answering her.

"Because they grew up with silver spoons in their mouths. Did they hurt you?"

"No. The jerks just refused to take no for an answer. I can't believe they followed me from my apartment."

"They did what?" What the guys had done was wrong on every level, but I didn't see them as the type to follow her all the way to the club then accost her. "You're certain it was them?"

"A black SUV trailed behind me. I thought I lost them."

I led her into my office, still seething. "Either they antici-pated what you were doing, or you had two stalkers this afternoon. Either way, you're not returning to your condominium."

"That's not possible," she half whispered but from the change in her expression, my gut told me she already believed there'd been two possible assailants. "I need to be with Charlotte, especially after what happened." Her eyes opened wide for a few seconds, realizing she'd put her foot in her mouth. "Shit."

"What happened?"

"Nothing really."

I gently pulled her by her arm, tugging her in front of me. "Talk to me."

"You'll be angry with me."

"I'll be angrier with you if you don't explain."

Alexandra grimaced. "Charlotte was dumped off at the apartment by guys in a dark SUV. She was banged up pretty badly. She refused to tell me what was going on. However, one of Diego's men stopped by, acting as if he was sent by the cartel bastard to check on her. The fucker even brought roses. I threw him out."

"You did what?"

"I…" She sighed as she looked at me, faking doe eyes. "I don't take men barging into where I live kindly."

"Uh-huh." I glanced away, realizing she had no understanding of the people she was messing with. "I originally thought you had a death wish. Now, I know you do."

"That's not it. I just refuse to allow anyone to be abusive under any circumstances. I had enough of that in my life." By the look on her face, I sensed either her father or a love interest had been more than just vicious.

I gave her a stern look, waiting for her to come to terms with what could have occurred. "I put myself on their radar. Didn't I?"

"Absolutely. Neither Diego nor his followers take kindly to anyone attempting to tell them what to do. Especially a woman. In their world, women are used for fucking and creating heirs and nothing else."

"I'm sorry, sir, but she was crying and bleeding. I didn't know what else to do. If you need to punish me, then do it."

While it was tempting and something she needed, that wasn't going to happen just after she'd been accosted. "I will but only when you tell me you're ready."

She looked at me quizzically. "I'm supposed to tell you?"

"Yes."

Her nervous laugh pulled at the protective man inside of me all over again. Whatever claim this girl had over me, it was getting stronger. "Fine. Now, can I go to work? I don't want to disappoint Ginger."

"Yes, but the police will want to talk to you."

"What am I supposed to say to them?"

"Tell them the truth."

There was a wry smile on her face. "Isn't that some judge's son? Won't his father attempt to keep the police from pressing charges?"

"They will. Then they'll need to go through me."

"I'd like to be there for that."

The girl was far too resourceful for her own good. "We'll talk later."

She nodded, backing away. Then she moved forward quickly, kissing me on my cheek. "Thank you for saving me. You're very special too."

Special.

After she left, I pressed my hand against my cheek and sighed. There was a chance I could fall in love with her.

That wasn't in either of our best interests.

When she was gone, I immediately pulled out my cellphone before heading toward my desk. I'd insisted on obtaining every private phone number of my members, placing them in a separate secure database. That alone was worth a significant amount of money. I sat back, putting my feet on my desk as I typed the number. I would giftwrap Judge Garber's son to him with a single warning.

There wouldn't be a second.

* * *

Alexandra

Men.

I wasn't certain I could ever understand them. I'd watched Jameson throw several hard punches without hesitation and I'd sensed his fury from where I'd been standing. If he'd been given the chance or had carried a weapon in his jacket, the arrogant ass with the gleaming white teeth would now have several bullets in him.

While the police officers had been cordial, the fact they'd continuously glanced at each other while I retold the story for the third time meant they either didn't believe me or were planning on losing the case number. Besides, they hadn't written down more than a few notes. That didn't bode well for my level of confidence.

The club was packed, every table full of people enjoying the evening. I had a bad taste in my mouth that refused to go away, still angry with both Charlotte for her ridiculous behavior, but also furious with myself for falling victim to fear and insecurity. Plus, I was worried about her.

And finally, I was second guessing whether Matthew and his friend had been the ones following me or if Benny had wanted to provide me with another warning.

Ginger had given me a small section to wait on, which I was grateful for. The first couple of hours had gone without a hitch, the tables turning twice, the tips fantastic. I'd calculated my percentage and I'd already earned over two hundred dollars. No wonder the job was highly sought after. At this rate, I would be able to afford a place of my own in a couple of weeks. Okay, maybe four given the market rental prices. At least it gave me hope.

I hadn't asked myself if I wanted to stay. I'd fled Montana to the first place that had provided a smidgeon of hope.

Stop feeling sorry for yourself.

I headed back to the bar, placing the empty used glasses in the dirty bin then turning in another order.

"You're getting the hang of it," Troy said, beaming as he'd done before.

"I think I am."

"I told you so. Are you all recovered from the scuffle?"

I rolled my eyes. "The jerk actually thought I'd agree to go party with him. Can you believe that?"

"Yeah, I can. What I find absolutely fascinating is that Mr. Stark almost pulverized him, which would have been spectacular. Is there something you're not telling me, girl? Are you two dancing under the sheets? We are best friends after all. Right?"

His teasing tone always made me laugh. "There are some things a girl will never admit to." I wagged my finger at him on purpose.

"Such a bad girl. And don't look now but there comes Ginger." He nodded and I glanced in the direction.

The look on her face was one of concern.

"Hi," I said, fearful something was wrong.

She moved closer, glancing at Troy. "I meant to come out sooner. Are you okay?"

"Never better. The creep got what was coming to him."

She laughed with me. "Hopefully, that's the end of his illustrious membership. There's been a request for you to be the server for a private party."

Ginger's tone had suddenly changed. "I'd be happy to. Where are they?" I asked.

"There's a section that allows members of the Carnal Sins side of our establishment enjoy being behind closed doors. The rooms are intimate where conversations can be held in private."

I wasn't certain what to say. "I'm not ready for... I mean I'm not submissive."

Ginger laughed. "No. This has nothing to do with the activities. They're just private rooms and nothing more. Some have stocked bars and others require servers. You must have impressed one of our members. You should take that as a compliment."

"I don't know how. Are they special as well?"

"I dare say I have yet to meet a single member who doesn't think they need to be catered to." I'd yet to see this kind of discomfort on her face. "I'll also add that some members on the private side have dubious backgrounds."

"I knew that was possible. Mr. Stark was open about members who used the gray area in business."

She seemed relieved. "I personally think some do more than that. However, they are required to follow the rules like everyone else. That means no touching. You are their server and nothing more. What I can share with you is that the tips are much higher. Partially because they are required to be. And usually, the men are very generous."

"Then I have no problem handling any of the private parties."

"They already ordered drinks, which Troy is preparing right now. Just check on them every once in a while."

"Sounds easy enough."

"You just need to go through the main private entrance that you were shown. Your hand scan will work. There's a hallway on the floor and they're in the Red Room. So you're aware, the members are considered important clientele. If for any reason you can't handle the room and your tables, let me know and I'll get one of the other servers to take over in Blackout for you."

"Got it. Let's see what I can do."

"I do love your spirit. Good luck. You got this."

"Wow. You are requested on your second night. What exactly did you do last night?" Troy teased as he continued making drinks.

"You mean other than almost start a fight? Then almost get myself kidnapped for a wild party?"

"Honey, you did both and in record time I might add." He laughed and I growled as I grabbed a fresh tray. "Just take a piece of advice. Be careful with the private rooms. The men are holier than thou jerks. I've even had to punch a few in the... nuts myself."

I couldn't help but laugh around the man. "Now, that would have been a sight."

"He hasn't come back for more. I warned him that he didn't want my kind of strange, but he refused to listen. That's how they are. They take what they want."

Why did my thoughts drift to Jameson?

"Maybe I need a sugar daddy."

"Girl, you and me both."

Winking, I leaned over the bar. "I'll see what I can find for you and trust me, I can take care of myself."

"Somehow, I think you can."

After adding all the drinks to the tray, I headed for the special room. I took a deep breath and walked inside. Within seconds, I realized I'd walked into a lion's den.

"I was hoping that we'd have a chance to meet."

I remained in the doorway, studying the four men inside, my eyes falling to the one who'd been inside Charlotte's place only a few hours before. Benny. The fucker had tracked me down. I did what I could to keep a straight face, although it was difficult not to notice Diego Santiago as he continued to stare at me.

"My lovely Charlotte mentioned that you were her new roommate. I thought I'd slum it tonight so I could meet you," Diego said.

"I assure you that wasn't necessary." I guessed on the drinks, smacking the Budweiser down in front of Benny first.

"I believe it was especially since I heard of your unfortunate accident." Diego tossed Benny a harsh look. Then he reached into his pocket, pulling out an envelope and sliding it in my direction.

"What's that?" I lifted my gaze, trying to keep from clawing his eyes out. While the man was good looking, the scar on the side of his face marred what others might call his beauty. To me, he was a disgusting pig.

"Payment for the trouble Benny caused."

"Trouble?" I pressed, the bad girl inside of me curious what he wanted in return.

"It would seem my... friend was exceeding the speed limit. I would hope this will be enough to repair any damages or provide any medical attention necessary after such an inconvenience."

"In exchange for exactly what?" I was seething, still glaring at Benny who didn't seem bothered in the least. Obviously, Charlotte had told him what I'd said.

Diego shifted in his seat. After placing both elbows on the arms of the leather chair, he steepled his fingers. "Merely in exchange for your understanding."

The laugh that bubbled to the surface annoyed him. Oh, darn.

I said nothing, my stomach churning. Then I noticed Benny's hand was bandaged. I didn't need to look closely to see he was missing his little finger. I placed another drink on the table, no one reaching for it. I would guess the great cartel leader was supposed to give his approval for his men to enjoy their libations. From the thickness of the envelope, it was easy to tell there was a wad of cash inside.

The four men were staring at me, waiting to see how I'd react. While I wanted nothing more than to toss a drink in Diego's face, I found enough restraint to place the tray on the table away from me. Then I slammed one hand on the surface while I tossed the envelope in his face. "Let me make this very clear. I don't want payment from scum like you.

And I will tell you this. If you ever lay another finger on my cousin, I will hunt you down and ensure you never touch another woman again. You got that?"

Diego looked smug, leaning back in his seat. The smile curling on his lips was unnerving, but I refused to be intimidated. When he said nothing, I plastered on a plastic smile, holding his seething gaze before backing away. "Enjoy your drinks, gentlemen. It's the last you're going to get in this club. We don't allow trash."

"Oh," one of the men muttered, chuckling as if I'd just made a snappy joke.

I continued to back toward the door, daring Diego to do something. He sat calmly, the same look on his face, but his eyes moved as I did, watching me intently. I was able to hold my own as I opened the door, stepping into the hallway. Then my legs began to shake.

"Sweet Alexandra. I'll forgive your behavior this once but keep something in mind. I am a dangerous man, someone you don't want to cross."

It was my turn to say nothing.

After taking several deep breaths, I headed toward the door, half expecting to be followed and yanked into one of the rooms. When I made it to the crowded main room, I made a beeline for the bar.

Troy watched my approach, stopping what he was doing and taking long strides toward me. "What the hell?"

"They came here to find me. Me! I told them I wouldn't serve them, and I won't. They can't threaten me or my cousin. I won't allow that to happen."

"Whoa. Slow down. You're not making any sense. Who were those guys?"

I threw a look over his shoulder, my nerves remaining on edge. I was a stupid girl for doing what I did, but someone needed to take care of Charlotte. "Diego Santiago and his men. Are they even supposed to be in here?"

He took a deep breath then hissed. "I can't believe Ginger allowed you to wait on them."

"Do not tell me they are members." I thought about the room they'd selected and hissed. The Red Room. How appropriate. It was another subtle warning. Who did these assholes think they were?

"Not unless Mr. Stark changed the rules. He doesn't allow known criminals inside the place. Although," he said as he half laughed, "I assure you there are plenty of members who work the morally gray zone on a regular basis. You'll need to talk to Mr. Stark about how Santiago was allowed to step foot in the place. He's obviously a guest of a regular member. I am surprised the group was allowed in. I don't like it at all."

"Why?" I could tell his concern went far beyond what I'd just experienced.

"Santiago is bad news for everyone. He has a firm hold on far too many members of law enforcement if you ask me." He threw up his hands. "The city is corrupt as fuck."

"Great. And I just moved here."

"How did they threaten you?"

I took a deep breath, fighting another round of anger. "It's a long story but he tried to give me money for something that happened the other day."

"Please don't tell me you're involved with those guys. They'd eat their own young if it they thought it was prosperous."

"Are you crazy?" I snorted. The man continued to have a flair for the dramatic. "Not a chance. I tossed the money in his face and told him to shove it. The attempted payoff was for a hit and run involving my car. It's obvious they don't want me going to the police. Too late."

"Whew. Somehow, you managed to get mixed up with the wrong people. Thank God you didn't take the money."

"I will never owe anyone, especially a criminal."

He exhaled, glancing into the crowded bar. "Come on. I'm taking you to the breakroom. You just sit and wait."

"What are you doing?"

"Handling this."

As he led me to the small area designated for the staff, I couldn't stop shaking all over. Both Jameson and Ginger would likely be disappointed, but I didn't care. If it cost me my job, so be it.

I was finished with being used as a doormat.

CHAPTER 16

 achlan

"Mr. Stark. I'm sorry to bother you but it would seem we have another issue."

I glanced at Troy as he stood just inside the doorway. When he couldn't handle a problem, I knew the issue was something I'd need to deal with. If I had to guess, I'd say Alexandra was involved in another situation. The girl did bring trouble with her. I was immediately on my feet, buttoning my jacket as I headed toward him. "What's wrong?"

"Diego Santiago managed to crawl his way inside the club and he brought some of his buddies in tonight?"

His question was one that required answering. What the fuck? My thoughts drifted to Senator Collins and his insistence Santiago be allowed past my doors. Then I thought about the fact Alexandra had been followed. Diego was sparring for a fight. But why? Was he that nervous Alexandra had seen or overheard something? Or was he merely pissed she'd tossed one of his soldiers from Charlotte's place? "Friends? Who are they?"

"No clue, but they requested Alexandra, the new girl, to wait on them. Apparently, she was threatened and handed cash, which she didn't take, for some incident with her car?"

Anger immediately swelled in my veins, my blood boiling. "Where are they?"

"Not sure but I thought you'd want to handle this. She's pretty angry." Troy laughed. "Actually, I think she gave them the riot act. She's one tough girl."

My little pet was determined to get herself killed. While I was infuriated that she'd ignored my command, trying to handle a situation herself, what I really wanted to do was break Diego's neck. Perhaps I hadn't been forceful enough with the man the last time. If Collins was behind his guest appearance, he'd soon learn he'd fucked with the wrong man. The fact the fucker threatened anyone, especially Alexandra, meant he would face my wrath.

"You were right to track me down, Troy. I will handle it from here."

"Good deal. Just out of curiosity. Why was he allowed to enter the premises in the first place? Isn't that something Jagger should have stopped?"

"Jagger isn't in the club right now, but it's a very good question and one I'll also find the answer to." One guest only. It had been a rule since the beginning. If Santiago had one of his men with him, another member was also involved.

Nodding, he backed away. "Don't be angry with her, Mr. Stark. She's good people if you know what I mean."

"I know exactly what you mean, Troy. I appreciate you protecting her. Where is she?"

"She's in the breakroom in Blackout."

"Keep her there. Don't let anyone approach her."

"You got it, boss."

I walked with him toward the stairs. While he raced down them, I took my time heading to private entrance, where Diego had likely entered. I always had at least one employee on the door in case members had questions or for situations just like this one.

Danner had been left on duty, the son of a man I'd known for almost as long as the club had been in existence. He was a good guy, accommodating the correct word. As soon as I walked closer, he stood immediately.

"Good evening, sir."

"Danner." I tried to curtail the continuing fury. "Diego Santiago and one of his men were brought in as guests. Who are the two members?"

He quickly checked the computer system. "Senator Collins and the police chief, who made certain I knew who he was. What an asshole."

Fuck me. It would seem my buddy, Manuel Gonzalez, the illustrious chief of police had taken the report straight to Santiago. What the fuck was my friend trying to do, issue a warning to stay away from the cartel? I couldn't rule anything out. For him to be seen inside the club by anyone was risky as fuck. Why would he do that?

I found it interesting he'd shouted to anyone who would listen that he planned on eradicating crime in the city. Including the vicious cartels. What in the hell was going on? While I could go on the assumption either he or his family had been threatened by the brutal cartel leader, I also couldn't ignore the fact the man I'd respected could have taken a bribe. Did he really think Alexandra was a threat of some kind?

"Where are they?" I snarled.

"Senator Collins asked for the Red Room in particular."

I almost laughed. A warning had been issued. "That's all I needed to know."

Whether this was all about Alexandra or a threat to my organization didn't matter. Perhaps this was my week to ban members. That didn't bother me in the least.

There was no hesitation before entering the room. I barged in, immediately turning my full attention toward the senator. "Gentlemen." I'd used the term loosely, shifting my heated gaze toward the chief of police.

He kept his eyes on mine, refusing to look away. Sadly, that told me he wasn't under any immediate duress.

"Why, what a treat seeing the club owner in person," Diego said as he swirled the liquid in his glass. "What can we do for you?"

The fact the man was obviously baiting me, while irritating, also made a statement that either the group wanted my support, or they were afraid of what I could do. While I was curious as to the issue they were facing, at this point I refused to allow it to matter in the least.

"As at least two of you know inside this room, I'm a man of few words. I also don't like wasting time as my schedule is very busy, my time highly sought after. Therefore, I'm going to make this easy on you, Mr. Santiago. It is not only inappropriate but repulsive that you come into my club as a guest, which is a significant privilege I might add, and attempt to provide payoff to one of my employees. That kind of behavior will not be tolerated."

Just as I'd finished the words, something Lachlan had said to me years before filtered into my mind.

"You're like a bull in a china shop, dude. In this world, you need to learn panache and sophistication instead of using all that muscle."

After I'd laughed in his face, I'd asked him the reason why. For a man who'd been brought up with a silver spoon in his mouth, believing the world to be his personal playground, his answer had made sense. It remained so today.

"Because doing so will alienate your enemies, leaving them in a beautiful fog and they won't see the strike coming."

Words to live by.

It was a shame he didn't take his own advice. I made certain I made eye contact with every man in the room, leaving the chief of police until the last. As least he'd had the good graces to finally look away as if embarrassed. I was a keen observer, and it was easy to tell he was under at least minimal duress. Senator Collins, on the other hand, appeared as smug as he usually was.

He'd likely arranged the meeting if for no other reason than to send me a message that he had more power than his predecessor, my threats meaning nothing.

He didn't seem to understand I wasn't the kind of man who could be shoved into a corner.

Diego's jaw clenched, his dark eyes attempting to hold me hostage. I almost laughed. He obviously had no idea how many situations of this nature I'd been faced with.

"I don't believe I was doing anything illegal by offering her restitution for her pain and suffering. Was I, Manuel?" He turned his head toward the police chief, purposely using the man's first name.

"He was making a genuine offer, Jameson," Manuel stated. While there was no emotion on his face, I noticed a single bead of perspiration trickling down from his forehead.

"That's good to know, but in my club, my rules apply. Now, please feel free to finish your drinks and your business. You're welcome to order from the bar in the Blackout Club or within the privacy of Carnal Sins. But make note that after this evening, your guest privileges have been revoked permanently, Mr. Santiago. That goes for your associate as well."

I'd finally riled him, enough so he started to rise from the table. The senator threw his hand in front of the Puerto Rican.

"There's no need to be contentious, Jameson. Manuel and I asked for a meeting with Mr. Santiago to try and mend fences with our various organizations," Senator Collins said casually, as if this was a traditional meeting between corporate moguls. "Your establishment has always been a welcoming respite as to keep concern from outside individuals to a minimum. You do want to keep violence out of our beloved city and from inside your club. Don't you?"

I took a deep breath, holding it for several seconds. The backhanded threat didn't bode well but given I would be out of town for a few days, I had no intention of throwing gasoline on the fire.

Yet.

"I'm certain our chief of police has a very pointed game plan for handling gang warfare. However, no one has control over any aspect of this club," I answered.

The smug look on Collins' face remained, which meant it was possible he'd taken up the previous senator's cause of attempting to shut me down.

"What a pity you can't seem to control the violence inside or outside your own club," the senator added. "I heard about the incident tonight. What a pity your young protégé attacked Judge Garber's son. He has a broken nose to prove it."

I almost scowled but could tell he was also attempting to goad me. I laughed instead.

Out of the corner of my eye, I noticed Manuel's discomfort had changed, as if he was issuing a warning of his own not to indulge in further conversation.

"We all do what we can to keep the peace. Now, as I have other business to contend with, I'll leave you to enjoy the rest of your evening." I made another round of eye contact before leaving the room. I hadn't signed onto this adventure to play political games yet that's what I'd been faced with over the last five years in particular.

Maybe it was time to diversify.

Hopefully, both Diego and the good senator realized I couldn't be bought, nor did threats bother me in the least. I hadn't anticipated being followed but when I heard footsteps seconds after rounding the corner, I abruptly stopped.

"Jameson," Manuel said as he flanked my side. "We need to talk."

I tilted my head, waiting for him to launch into the conversation. "I don't think we have anything at talk about."

He laughed halfheartedly, scratching his head. "Jesus, Jameson. You don't want to push this."

"Push what exactly?"

"Whatever point you're trying to make. You're making enemies everywhere you go, including Judge Garber. Why the hell did you have his kid arrested?"

"For attacking one of my employees."

His eyes opened wide. "That fucking kid has been an issue for two years."

"That's your problem. It's not going to be mine. I think you should reconsider the company you're keeping."

"You don't understand."

I laughed, shaking my head. While I still considered him a friend, I had no intentions of allowing him to goad me into following along like some lapdog. I closed the distance, my height allowing me to peer down at him. This time, he was intimidated. "I find it curious that you don't seem to care about the fact Santiago is attempting to get in bed with a state senator. Or is this just business as usual, Manuel? One corrupt politician after another."

"You're a smart man, Jameson. The bad blood between the Bratva and the cartel is getting worse. People are taking sides. You can't turn a blind eye to what's happening."

A blind eye. I found it interesting he'd purposely changed the subject.

"How exactly did they get to you, Manuel? We've always been straight with each other. You were a man who refused to kowtow to any criminals in this city. What happened? How much did it take to sell your soul?"

He was instantly incensed. "Get off your moral high ground, Jameson. We've all done things we wouldn't rush home and tell our families about. I'm merely trying to keep the peace in a city where war is imminent. Collins might have his issues, but he cares about the city."

I wanted to laugh but I knew his concern was justified. "Right. I can see that. I own a club, Manuel. I'm not interested in politics or playing games. However, I won't have rival gangs starting a war in my club."

"Don't insult me. I know how much information you have on every member within Carnal Sins. I'm no fool. I've watched you use it to your benefit. You're a very dangerous man, Stark. Did you ever stop to think you might have a target on your head?"

"Are you threatening me, Manuel?" I'd been called many things over the years. Was I dangerous? I had all the qualifications of being a ruthless bastard, but I'd chosen the high road the majority of time.

He chuckled. "I'm a man of the law whether you believe me any longer or not."

"Then what are you driving at?"

"I'm not driving at anything. But people know you're sitting on a powerful empire."

It was impossible not to laugh at this point. "Let me guess. If I were to divulge information for certain purposes, I would be well rewarded. Choose one side over the other? Would I be a rich man?"

"I'm not suggesting you sell out, Jameson. That's not the kind of man you are. Just be careful. There are new players who wouldn't mind taking you down in the process of rising to the top. It would seem you managed to piss off several influential people, your partner Lachlan as well when he eliminated the former senator."

"Lachlan had nothing to do with Marshall Winston's demise and you know it."

"That's not the way people remember it."

I laughed again, allowing my thoughts to drift to the issues in Paris. "I'll keep that in mind. Incidentally, a young woman is possibly being held against her will in Santiago's domain. Charlotte Darlington? Name ring a bell?"

He glanced over his shoulder. "She's a drug runner, at least that's what I've heard on the streets. Who's she to you?"

I thought about Alexandra and sighed. "A friend of a friend."

"She's being used, which means when her resourcefulness runs out, she'll be eliminated."

"That's what I thought."

Manuel shook his head. "Stop meddling in things that don't concern you. But remember what I told you about the information you have stored in some magical vault. It could be worth more than you think."

"I'm not for sale and I thought up until this point neither were you. Whatever they promised or threatened, you need to think about how you're going to look your kids in the eyes when you go home at night." With that, I turned around to leave.

Alliances were typical, including with those in power who had no issue delving in the murky gray waters of morality. While I couldn't consider myself entirely moral, there was no amount of money or the promise of power that would allow me to get into bed with a bastard like Santiago.

The trouble was he knew it.

That meant he'd do everything in his power to find a weakness.

There hadn't been one to find.

Until now.

I headed to the main floor, barely acknowledging anyone along the way. I found Alexandra pacing the floor, a lioness in a cage. When she noticed me, I sensed more than just irritation. She was afraid of Santiago but not for herself. I'd been right about her cousin.

"Come with me," I told her, waving off Troy when he attempted to flag me down. I waited as she moved in front of me, keeping my hand pressed on the small of her back as I guided her to my private elevator.

Once inside, she remained rigid, her mouth twisted as fury continued to consume her.

"You're angry with me for a second time tonight," she said, her usual defiant voice devoid of any emotion.

"I'm not angry with you at all. Disappointed that you didn't leave the room immediately, but you were blindsided."

"Why would they offer me money?"

"I'm not certain, Alexandra. Perhaps to keep you quiet regarding your cousin." As soon as she looked away, I realized she knew more than she was willing to tell me. "Perhaps as a warning that they can take you anytime they want after your incident with one of his men earlier."

"Fucking bastard."

The simple acknowledgement was the first step in helping her. I led her into my office, closing the door. "Talk to me. How deep is your cousin in Santiago's world?"

She sighed, her body starting to tremble as the adrenaline rush began to fade. "I think she's in love with him."

I moved to my desk, sitting on the edge. When I reached for her hand, she didn't try to pull away. I tugged her closer until she was between my legs. "Listen to me. I know you care about her but at this point you can't force her to leave the situation."

Her jaw was clenched and she tried to pull away but I wouldn't allow her to. "She's smarter than this but I didn't know how bad life had gotten for her. She didn't tell me. When she left Montana, she was following the second or third guy she thought she was in love with. That was after a huge fight with her drug-addicted mother. The guy was supposed to be her knight in shining armor. She'd call me occasionally telling me about all the exciting locations she'd been. Then I didn't hear from her for almost a year. When she called me out of the blue, she seemed so happy not to have a boyfriend. It was all a lie."

"A small part of you feels responsible."

"To a point. I had my own issues to deal with, ignoring several of her calls. Maybe if I'd been there. She had a terrible life, my aunt and uncle basically abandoning her. You don't need to know the sordid details. She was a broken kid."

I squeezed her hand, rubbing my thumb across her knuckles. "You can only do but so much for someone you care about. Ultimately, how they live their life is entirely up to them."

"I know that somewhere in the back of my mind."

"Yet you felt you needed to remain her protector."

She laughed. "I know that sounds ridiculous. My mother used to call it the lost puppy syndrome."

"It's an admirable trait. But in this case, the puppy has wolves for friends."

"I'm painfully aware of that now, although I'm not going to simply let her fall into the hands of a monster."

"You're not going to risk your life. I'm going to help ensure Charlotte is safe, but that's not something I can do right away."

"What can you do? Not to seem disrespectful, but from what little I've seen and heard already, Diego has extreme power in this lousy city."

I continued to find her defiance refreshing, although the protector in me was fully aware she'd continue to place herself in jeopardy. I refused to allow that to happen. "You underestimate me, Ms. Kingston. I'm going to make a few phone calls to some powerful friends."

Alexandra exhaled, nodding after a few seconds. "I'll be curious what you can do."

"You might be surprised."

"Who were those men with Mr. Santiago?"

"The chief of police for Miami and a newly elected senator from Florida."

"What an interesting combination. Is there a power play going on between them?"

Perhaps I'd underestimated her as well. "You're too smart for your own good, but yes, there is a possibility of war between the Russians and Santiago's cartel. It's in everyone's best interest to attempt to keep the peace."

"The club is considered neutral ground."

I nodded. "As intended. However, certain lines are being crossed I won't accept."

"They're worried you're even more powerful." Her mischievous smile was enough to drive my hunger to a predatory point.

"I am. So you're aware, I've taken the liberty of having you removed from the schedule at Blackout."

"Wait a minute. I have to work. I need to make a living. I've already decided I'm going to find a place of my own, but I can't do that without money. I'm sorry I refused to serve them, but no job is worth being treated like an object. Maybe I should look for another job. It's about time I email another round of resumes for teaching positions."

I walked closer, allowing the extreme connection between us to speak for me for a few seconds. "You've caused quite a stir in the last few days. You're on a couple radars that could make your life difficult."

"Where am I going to stay?"

"I have an opportunity I think you'll enjoy, and I need assistance for a few days. As far as tonight, you're coming home with me."

She narrowed her eyes, tilting her head and all I could concentrate on was her plump, delicious lips, hungering to spend time kissing them for an extended period of time. "Are you always this possessive?"

"I don't take no for an answer."

"You're trying to protect me."

"I will protect you, Alexandra, but that's not the only reason."

"What did you have in mind, Mr. Stark?"

"You're coming with me to Paris. A situation with a new club being opened in a couple months requires my attention. As business doesn't stop when I'm out of the country, I require someone to keep track of emails and other correspondence while taking notes at meetings."

"I've never been anyone's secretary before. I'm not qualified."

"You're intuitive, organized, and have a keen sense of what's going on around you."

"I still don't know how I can help you."

"You'll be my eyes and ears. Part of being a business owner is keen observation. You have that in spades."

"I don't know. I'd love to go to Paris with you, but I can't leave Charlotte. Besides, I don't have any appropriate clothes to become your... special assistant or whatever you'd call me."

Her continued pushback was another admiral trait, but she didn't seem to comprehend or accept that she now belonged to me. I cupped her chin, lifting her head until she was required to look me in the eyes. "Logistics is my forte and as I promised, I'll make some calls to ensure Charlotte is protected while we're gone. I'll also have Jagger go by the condo a couple of times. Now, I don't think you understand, my little pet. I'm not asking you to go with me. I'm telling you."

CHAPTER 17

lexandra

Paris.

The city of love.

Or as I've read in dozens of romance books, the city of multiple orgasms. The thought was ridiculous but brought a shudder tingling my system. I wanted to pinch myself that I was being whisked away in a gorgeous Italian sports car driven by perhaps the most handsome man in the world through a city I thought I'd never visit in my lifetime.

As I stared out the window, I could see the Eiffel Tower in the distance, the city streets creations of beauty. While crowded, I'd already gotten a sense of excitement in the air. Or maybe it was just me. I allowed my thoughts to drift to Charlotte, hoping and praying she would be okay while I was gone. I'd stayed with Jameson the night before. He hadn't disciplined me and I hadn't asked. However, the passion had been even more incredible, a taste of the forbidden fruit.

After he'd fallen asleep, all I'd done was think about incidents that I'd somehow gotten myself in the middle of. When he'd gone with me to the condo, there'd been no sign of Charlotte. From what I could tell, she'd left and never returned. The fact Santiago had been at the club part of the night unnerved me even more.

Since then, I'd left her two voice messages and no return call. Maybe he was right in that there was little I could do. Hopefully, Jagger would keep an eye on her.

Jameson had been unusually quiet, making several business calls during the flight. I'd been able to tick off another item on my bucket list. Flying in a private jet, champagne served with smoked salmon and brie. It had been an unexpected slice of heaven.

"We're almost there," he said quietly, his deep voice sending a shower of tingles into my core.

"If I haven't told you yet, thank you for bringing me with you."

He chuckled. "Don't worry, my little pet. You'll be hard at work for the majority of the trip."

"And the rest?"

As he tipped his head toward me, the carnal look in his eyes sent another penetrating jolt of electricity into every cell and muscle. "I think you'll enjoy what Paris has to offer."

I bit my lower lip, my fingers tingling from anticipation. When he pulled into an alcove in front of valet parking, I sucked in my breath. Hotel Plaza Athénée. The building was gorgeous, dozens of years old, the exterior full of charm with balconies protected in iron railings against every window. Bright crimson awnings adorned the windows and several sets of French doors, the classic yet gothic architecture hinting of romance and affluence.

"This is beautiful," I told him.

"The hotel just celebrated one hundred and ten years of operation, the recent renovation one of the finest I've seen."

"You've stayed here before?"

He chuckled as he shifted the gear into park, opening his door. "Every time I come to Paris."

I took a deep breath as gorgeous young man opened my door, extending his hand and helping me from the car. It was difficult not to gawk given the incredible surroundings.

Jameson handed the man his keys, speaking in fluent French. Another surprise and I had a feeling there were dozens of them when it came to Jameson.

The man who'd claimed he owned me.

The thought was both riveting and terrifying. I was out of my element but determined to enjoy the perks of being in his company.

A bellman quickly advanced with a gold-plated cart, grabbing our luggage. We were whisked inside, Jameson's hand placed firmly on the small of my back as he always did. The gesture was controlling yet comforting. At least I'd had the forethought of wearing one of the few skirts I owned, a nice blouse and heels instead of my usual comfortable attire.

Every man and woman inside the hotel was dressed as if prepared to head off to a fabulous event. Money oozed from the luxurious surroundings, the interior likely photographed for various upscale magazines.

After another short conversation in French with the girl behind the marble counter, Jameson headed toward the bank of elevators.

Once we stepped inside, the bellman pressed his hand on the button. The top floor. I should have guessed.

"How are you, Charlie?" Jameson asked.

"Very well, sir. It's good to see you again. And you brought a lovely guest with you." Charlie nodded in appreciation, his smile genuine. The man spoke perfect English.

"This is my assistant, Alexandra, a very important person in my life."

"Then I will make certain and take good care of her," Charlie answered.

"You're very sweet," I told him.

"Thank you, miss. If I may say, you are the first person Mr. Stark has brought with him. We are honored."

The power Jameson exuded was equaled by his genuine care of others. I'd always thought men of extreme wealth were ruthless, horrible versions of the rest of the world. It would seem I had a lot to learn.

When we were taken to the room, I wasn't certain what I'd expected, but the moment I walked inside, I couldn't keep from squealing. The Eiffel Tower seemed steps away, the view absolutely perfect. We were in a suite and I was standing in an art deco living room, a small dining area off to the side. I also noticed a set of curved stairs. The furniture was stunning, as artistic as the works of art adorning the walls. I couldn't imagine what it cost per night, but more than I made in a month.

I moved toward the window, the late afternoon sun providing a perfect backdrop to the entire city.

Charlie appeared behind me, leaning over and opening a window. "This is a very special time of year."

"It's gorgeous. Thank you."

"I hope you enjoy your stay."

I remained where I was, amazed that I was standing in a gorgeous suite in such a beautiful city. The sights. The smells. The music coming from an unknown location. Everything was perfect.

"Thank you again, Charlie. Say hello to your lovely wife. Perhaps we can catch dinner together while I'm here."

"Oh, Sasha would love that, sir."

"Charlie, you can call me Jameson."

"No can do, sir," Charlie answered, which made me smile. "At least not while on duty."

"Understood."

I turned just in time to witness Jameson handing him a wad of cash. The man who wanted me to call him Master was also a generous tipper.

Note to self. You fell into the hands of a good man.

My inner voice was right, but I reminded myself this was a taste of a fairytale, but at some point, I'd be forced to come back to the real world. Girls like me didn't have all their dreams come true.

When the door was closed, he slowly removed his jacket, his expression one of amusement, his eyes sparkling in the slender stream of sunlight.

"Come with me," he said in his usual commanding tone.

I trailed behind him as he headed for the staircase. When he opened the doors, another surprise awaited me.

The terrace was breathtaking, incredible outdoor furniture surrounded by views of the city. Vines crawled the exterior wall attached to metal trellises, plants and flowers hanging in boxes secured to the railing. There was even a small fountain on one end, the trickle of water adding to the alluring atmosphere.

While I was normally terrified of heights, the draw to the outlying city was enough to squelch my fears. I weaved my way through the loveseat and chairs to the corner; the pristine illumination of the Eiffel Tower was what dreams were made of. While my grip on the iron railing was tight, I had no fear of falling, especially since Jameson crowded my space, placing his massive hands over mine.

The light breeze added to the ambience, every scent fresh and inviting. But it was the man whose body was pressed against mine who kept me in awe as well as suspense.

"I don't know what to say," I whispered a few seconds later.

"There's no need to say anything."

"Why do you care about me?"

"The answer is easy. Because you're special."

"I'm just a girl with no lease on life as of yet."

He lowered his head, nuzzling his face against my neck. His aftershave sent another wave of desire scouring my system, my mind still processing the events of the last few days. "You're a woman who awakened the man inside."

The statement brought another wave of desire, my fully aroused nipples uncomfortable in the lace bra I'd selected for the trip. My panties were already damp, my muscles clenching and releasing several times.

I wanted to ask him why he'd felt so dead, but opening old wounds wasn't what this trip was about. While business was required, I sensed he was letting go of a part of his past that had haunted him. It would seem we were two damaged people striving to find a different way of healing.

When he turned me around to face him, the way he brushed the back of his hand across my cheek was entirely different. The touch was tender, yet his eyes told an entirely different story. One of darkness in his hunger, a longing to devour every inch of me.

He fisted my hair suddenly, keeping my head tipped toward the sky as he hovered over me. I pressed my hands against his chest, marveling in the ability to feel his carved muscles through the crisp white shirt he'd worn.

With his lips only a few centimeters from mine, I yearned to drag my tongue around his mouth. His heated breath ignited the embers deep inside and as he yanked on my hair, I issued a whispered moan.

"The things I'm going to do to you, Alexandra." He crushed his mouth over mine, immediately thrusting his tongue inside. The taste of him was sweet yet spicy, his hold so possessive that it took my breath away. I was thrown by the insanity of so many emotions rushing through my mind. He'd also provoked an intense darkness that terrified me.

I wanted to submit, allowing him to take full control. I didn't care what that meant or what people thought. He'd managed to calm my fears while enticing the woman who'd been locked inside a cage. As he explored my mouth, taking his time dominating my tongue, I melted into him. Our connection wasn't just about physical needs but emotional ones as well.

And somehow, I sensed he needed me too.

I clung to his shirt with one hand as I wrapped my other arm around his neck, sliding my fingers in his thick hair. This felt right, being in his arms special. And for the first time in as long as I could remember, I felt free of the chains that had weighted me down for so long.

How could one man do this in only a few days?

I also felt the weight of being reckless.

The kiss became a wild roar of need shared between us. Being here with him was a dream come true, but I knew in the back of my mind reality would come crashing down.

When he broke the kiss, he pressed his lips against my forehead as he'd done before. The action was tender, as if the protector was reminding me that he was here.

Suddenly, I couldn't stand the guilt that I'd carried for disappointing him.

As well as myself.

"You asked me to let you know when I was ready for discipline."

"I did."

"Okay."

He grinned and slid a stray strand of hair from my eyes. "Okay. What?"

"You can."

When he moved his hands to my arms, I felt more like the bad little girl than ever before. "I want you to embrace the reason you need regular discipline in your life. It's not about pleasing me as much as it is about accepting the fact of what is best for you. As I said before, when the time is right, you'll know what to say to me."

As he eased past me, I was dumbfounded. He was putting all the weight on my shoulders for asking for a spanking?

Didn't dominating men take control? I watched him walk toward the door and groaned inwardly.

"Wait." My voice seemed so small that I almost didn't recognize it. "You're right. May I please have a spanking?"

"Why do you feel you need one?"

I wasn't entirely certain what he was looking for. "Because I've been out of control."

He turned around to face me and there was no condemnation on his face, just appreciation that I'd managed to ask him for what I needed. The thought would have been ridiculous only a week before. But now? Everything I'd experienced up to this point made me feel cared for as well as comfortable. It was as if he knew what I needed before I did.

"Is this what you really want, Alexandra?"

I shuddered as I always did when he said my name. "Yes, it is."

"Then go into the bedroom and remove your skirt and panties. Place a pillow in the center of the bed and lie across it."

He gave me a simple command, lifting his eyebrows when I remained where I was.

"Yes, sir." If I dared tell anyone I not only accepted punishment from a man but a part of me looked forward to it, they'd call me crazy. Charlotte would laugh at me, especially given what I'd been through less than a year before.

However, as soon as I walked past him into the suite, I felt a sense of relief.

Maybe I wanted an excuse to cry my eyes out, releasing all the tension that had built up over the last two weeks since I'd arrived. I certainly felt lighter than before, my mind no longer a foggy mess of worry and fear. Would this single act change anything? No, of course not, but it would provide an entirely different kind of relief and that was very important to me.

I headed into the bedroom, taking a few seconds to admire the room itself. The furnishings were definitely meant for lovers, the king-sized bed covered in a stunning violet comforter, at least a half dozen fluffy pillows waiting for respite or something a little kinky.

As I kicked off my heels, unbuttoning my skirt, my mind drifted to images of the club and the way he'd presented several of the kinky acts. In doing so, I allowed a series of tingles to drift down the back of my legs. I wanted to experience everything with Jameson.

If only he would allow it.

I folded my skirt neatly, catching a glimpse of myself in the mirror while placing it on the dresser. I'd made myself a promise while still in Montana that no man would ever control me again. In doing so, I'd shut down my feelings, pretending that no one could ever hurt me again. That had only led to my assertive side taking over. While good in concept, I hadn't been thinking things through lately. If at all.

What was I doing living in Miami? I doubted it would ever be my home.

As I slipped my fingers under the elastic of my thong, shimmying it down my legs, I realized I wanted more than anything to let go of the past.

With my panties on top of my skirt, I turned toward the bed, grabbing one of the pillows. There was something cathartic about lying across the bed, waiting for my own private hero to discipline me. I folded my arms under my chin, thinking about the events of the last few days. I'd managed to attract the attention of the worst kind of people. Who knew I was a shit magnet?

A nervous laugh bubbled to the surface. I hadn't been lying across the pillow for ten seconds and I was already antsy. And nervous.

And excited.

The scent of my desire was strong, which also confused me. Perhaps it was true that with pain comes the ultimate pleasure.

After what seemed like several minutes had passed, I closed my eyes, trying to relax. It was nearly impossible to stop thinking about how sexy Jameson was or that with every touch, fire erupted all through my body.

I didn't hear his footsteps, but I sensed his presence directly behind me. Then I heard rustling and tipped my head over my shoulder. He was gazing at me intently as he unfastened his belt. My mouth suddenly went dry as I realized he was going to use the thick leather on my backside.

A trickle of apprehension mixed with the rush of desire, the combination keeping my stomach in knots. His eyes never left me, dark and hooded as the afternoon sun dipped below the horizon. He seemed even more powerful than when I'd first met him, and not just because he'd challenged people intent on harming me. He exuded domination in the way he walked, the words he spoke and from the way he dealt with people.

It was easy to see he was comfortable in his skin, yet the sadness in him remained. He was beautifully dangerous in every aspect.

At times, I felt like a lost lamb when I was next to him. Other times, he allowed me to feel as if I could take on the world. And I'd only known him for a few days. No one else had such a profound effect on me.

Not my father.

Not any teachers.

And certainly not the pig I'd allowed to take my virginity.

He rolled a portion of the strap around his arm then pressed his hand on my back, caressing my skin. "I'm glad you asked for this. Some of your tension will be released."

I wasn't certain if he was right but at this point, I wanted nothing else as much. When he repositioned my legs, I pressed my face into the pillow.

The whooshing sound caught my attention, grabbing it with force. When he brought the belt against my backside, I jerked up from surprise, not from pain.

At least a full five seconds passed before he issued another strike, the strap slapping against my sit spot. Almost instantly I bent my knees, the reaction involuntary. That's the moment explosive pain jetted through me like rocket fuel.

"Oh. My. God." I clenched the bedding with enough force I yanked several inches.

"Breathe. You're doing beautifully."

My bratty personality almost took over, nasty words forming in my mind. I bit my inner cheek instead, trying to keep my composure.

Jameson delivered four more, one coming so quickly after the one before I didn't have time to breathe. I hadn't been prepared for the surge of wetness between my legs, my muscles clenching as if his glorious cock had already been shoved inside.

I took several gasping breaths, wiggling against the pillow until I was able to create friction on my clit. The next four strikes I concentrated on the sound more than anything, even while the rush of pain turned into a moment of anguish.

I was wet and hot, the scent of my desire stronger than before. He pressed his hand against my back again and I could easily tell his breathing was heavier than before. The crazy sensations only continued to build until I was lightheaded.

Then he started another round, bringing the thick strap down at least six times. I was no longer thinking clearly, allowing the savagery of his actions to help me drift into a peaceful place. There were no ugly memories, no fears that his actions would turn abusive. He was a different man and this was a new life.

When he placed the belt on the bed beside me, I took several shallow breaths. I wasn't surprised when he gathered me into his arms, holding me tightly against him. Nor was I shocked by his whispered words as he lifted my chin, first kissing my lips before sliding them to my ear.

"You're my perfect baby girl and you are all mine."

CHAPTER 18

 ameson

The effect of human touch was incredible. I'd felt that my entire life, but having Alexandra in my arms, I understood the breathtaking moment where two people who'd collided together were close to being one. There was a significant chance I was blowing what we shared out of proportion, but I didn't subscribe to anything others would consider normal. Maybe it was because of my chosen way of life or the fact I hadn't been involved with anyone for so long.

My long hours prevented me from indulging in normal activities such as boating or reading. I wasn't the guy who wanted to spend time with other dudes talking sports and drinking beer, even if my background had been all about sports. What I wanted precluded most terms of dating no matter how I tried to disguise it.

Alexandra had become a beautiful yet disastrous reminder of everything I hadn't allowed myself to experience.

A home with a family.

Dinners out with friends.

Date nights that didn't involve handcuffs.

As she pushed away from me, I wanted nothing more than to curl up in bed with her, but even the lights and atmosphere of Paris couldn't hide the reason for my trip. I'd spoken with Dumas twice, insisting on a meeting. He hadn't been charged with anything and he'd insisted that the authorities were on a fishing expedition, although he hadn't wanted to talk over the phone.

Between the mess in my own club as well as this, I remained on edge. I'd had years of unrest followed by others with no instances in the club and no reason to toss anyone to the curb. What I'd learned over the years was that everything has a progression, including the merciless criminals who huffed and puffed until they got their way. They'd be destroyed by another powerful predator only to make a resurgence at a later time.

It was an inevitable, vicious cycle that every large, diverse city had gone through. LA and DC weren't any different. And in truth, I'd grown weary of the games people played.

If the Bratva and the cartel wanted to duel in the streets, I couldn't care less, at least until it was brought inside my club. It would seem I didn't have the ability to shut them out this time.

My mind continued to process the information, but I had a feeling the issues with the Paris club was all about revenge. Every city had what was called an Old Boys' Network, men who originally controlled everything that went on. Over time, it morphed into allowing women into the fold, but few and far between. If anyone truly believed mafia organizations were in control, they'd be wrong. There were others even more powerful that used the crime syndicates to do their dirty work.

Carnal Sins had come into focus with the elimination of one of the key players—Marshall Winston. It didn't matter he'd been dirty, committing white collar crimes for years. He'd been beloved because he could manipulate power whatever way he wanted.

"What now, sir?" she asked, her voice still breathless.

"Now, we dress for our meeting and the night afterward."

"And where are we going?"

"A club in the heart of Paris."

"A BDSM club?" she asked. The way her eyelashes skimmed across her cheeks was entirely too sexy. My cock was already completely aroused, enough so I doubted we'd make it to dinner before I took her again.

I rolled my fingers down her arm, crawling my hand under her blouse to squeeze her nipple. "Yes, my beautiful submissive." Her slight moan was a sinful reward. "You will stay very close tonight." I lifted my index finger when she gave me a pouty look. "If you're good, we might find time to play."

"I'm always good."

"If only that were true. I am serious about staying with me. The clubs in Paris are entirely different."

"You have my blood pumping," she cooed. "I'm curious. How do you know Charlie?"

"He was the first person I met in Paris. I've had dinner with him and his wife at their quaint cottage. The woman is an amazing cook."

"I would think you'd prefer dinners in expensive restaurants."

"There's a lot you need to learn about me."

"I can't wait to uncover all your secrets." When I lifted her blouse, she threw her head back, her moan more ragged than before.

Growling, I yanked her bra away, leaning over and suckling on her rosy nipple, swirling my tongue as I pulled the tender tissue between my teeth. When I bit down, she shuddered in my hold. I could enjoy spending hours learning every nuance of her luscious body.

When I heard a text on my phone, I sighed and pulled away. I'd yet to tell her what Manuel had told me about her cousin, although I guessed that it was something that had already come to her mind.

"Always working," she said quietly.

"Unfortunately, yes." I glanced at the text from Jagger. "Your cousin is safely locked behind closed doors. It would appear nothing happened." I'd also contacted a police officer I knew for certain had no connection with Santiago. His instructions were to call me if anything happened.

A look of relief crossed her face. "Thank you for checking on her."

"I told you I'd take care of things." I backed away further, yanking on my tie. "I took the liberty of having a few items purchased and placed in the closet."

"More surprises."

It was good to smile, the moment of contentment more pleasurable than I could explain to anyone. I headed toward the closet, throwing open the door. I slowly yanked off my tie as I stood in front of the full-length mirror secured on the back of the door. When I noticed her moving behind me, every muscle tensed. She'd removed the remainder of her clothes, peering at me over her shoulder with a mischievous look on her face.

"I'm curious. Do you ever go anywhere without wearing a jacket and tie?" She rolled her fingers along my shoulder, slowly brushing them down the length of my back then tugging on my shirt.

I finished removing it, sliding the silky material in between my fingers. "The reason I wear a tie is because you never know when you might require shackling a beautiful submissive at a moment's notice."

"Is that so? Sir?" Her purr was far too enticing.

"Absolutely. Allow me to demonstrate." I moved away from the mirror then guided her back against the reflective surface. As I lifted first one arm over her head then the other, the shimmer in her eyes turned to a wildfire that kept my balls tight. I wrapped the thick silk around her wrists, enjoying the heat she exuded as well as the way goosebumps appeared across her arms.

When I jerked the material tight, she struggled and laughed. "Now what, sexy sir?"

I glanced at the hook meant for at least two robes, breathing in her scintillating perfume as I maneuvered the tie until I was able to secure her to the door. Then I took a step back, admiring my work. "That's perfect. Maybe I'll just keep you that way for the duration of the trip."

Alexandra looked up, twisting her hands as her body writhed. The sight was glorious, pushing me toward a wave of desire that couldn't be contained. My hunger required being sated.

"This isn't fair."

"I'm your master. Did I ever tell you that the relationship is completely fair?"

"No, but…"

I pressed my index finger against her luscious lips, shaking my head. "Shush. You aren't in control and never will be." As I allowed my gaze to fall to her painted toes, filthy things crossed my mind. I'd been remiss in not packing a few of my implements to use on her. That could be rectified easily but for now, I'd enjoy taking a few minutes indulging in my needs.

She continued fighting with her bindings as I raked my fingertips down her chest, pinching one nipple between my thumb and forefinger. When I flicked my finger against the other, her tremors intensified.

"I think piercing your nipples will be next on the agenda. Would you like that?"

The way she dragged her tongue across her lips was far too inviting. "Yes." I barely heard the slight whisper and her eyes were glassy.

"That's not an answer, my little pet." I lowered my head, sucking on one nipple as I twisted the other. "I will have your nipples and clit pierced, a beautiful chain between the three."

She laughed nervously, wiggling in the bindings. "God, yes. I would love that."

"Good girl. Then I'll make that happen." The thought was riveting, enticing the darkness furrowed deep inside. I could imagine the feel of flicking my tongue back and forth across a gold stud or diamond.

I lifted my gaze, studying her reaction before moving to the other. When she whimpered from the hint of pain, my cock pressed so tightly against my trousers that I was instantly in distress. I continued my exploration, rolling my fingers down to her stomach, slowly encircling her bellybutton.

"The things you do to me," she whispered.

"As I said. The things I will do. Only if you're a very good girl." I slipped my hand between her legs, cupping her wet mound. The second I swirled my finger around her clit, she jerked away from the door.

"Oh… my." Her eyes were already glassy, her need as intense as my own.

After teasing her for a full minute, I took long strides backwards, my skin tingling from the sweet fragrance of her need. I took my time unbuttoning my shirt, rolling the material over my shoulders. After kicking off my shoes, I retreated altogether.

"Where are you going?"

"Patience, my beautiful pet. That you will learn."

She moaned when I walked out of the room and the grin on my face became wider. I wanted her so hot and wet that she was ready to scream out my name.

I headed for the fully stocked bar, taking my time selecting a scotch before yanking a glass from the shelf. After preparing the drink, I added two ice cubes, taking a few moments to gaze out at the incredible view. Paris was a dazzling city by day and night.

The taste of the scotch was exquisite, but the lingering kiss was the reason every cell in my body was on fire. My desire was at the point my cock was throbbing. I shifted my hand to my crotch, stroking to offer some relief. A few seconds later, I realized my actions were useless. I needed to drive my shaft deep inside of her sweet pussy.

When I returned to the room she moaned, still fighting the tight hold. I loved to see the way her body thrashed, her skin glistening in the last vestiges of sunlight. I took another swig then placed the glass on the closest table, standing in front of her as I finished undressing.

"You're a terrible man to keep me waiting." Her voice was breathless and so alluring my cock twitched even more.

"For keeping you waiting?"

"For making me want you so much."

When I was fully undressed, I retrieved the drink, gulping a good third before grabbing one of the melting ice cubes. As I approached, she shivered visibly, her eyes drifting to what I held in my hand. I rolled it across her lips, smirking when she darted her tongue across the surface. Every sound she made brought an additional level of excitement, the longing to introduce her to various acts of BDSM weighing heavily on my mind.

She never blinked as I dragged the cube between her breasts, cocking my head and enjoying the sight of her pebbled nipples. As I swirled the ice around the already hardened bud, she gasped, bucking hard against the bindings.

The explosive heat of her body almost instantly melted a portion of the ice, water trickling down my fingers. I brushed what was left across to her other nipple, taking my time encircling her areola. Then I dropped my head, sucking on the tip. She moaned loudly, still thrashing in the firm hold. My mind was full of darkness as I slipped the remaining cube between her legs, driving the thick shard past her swollen folds.

"Oh, God. Oh…" She laughed nervously, her eyes now half closed.

I dropped to my knees, spreading her legs wide open. When I darted my tongue around her clit, she gasped, still fighting. Still bucking. I spread her pussy lips wide open, my patience running out. As I lapped her cream, burying my face into her wetness, she couldn't stop shaking. Her ragged murmurs continued, fueling the fire building to an out-of-control blaze.

There was no possibility of focusing as the dangerously hungry man inside feasted. I drove my tongue inside, flicking it several times.

"Yes. Yes. Yes," she whimpered, her leg muscles tensing.

I adored the way her body reacted, the way she molded to my desires, driving my hunger to a frenzied point. I wanted to consume every drop of her liquid gold. I needed her scent covering every inch of my skin. And I longed to cover her with my cum. I plunged several fingers inside, rolling my thumb around her clit.

"Uh. Uh. Uh. Uh. Jameson."

The way she uttered my name spurred me on, my actions becoming more savage. Within seconds, I sensed she was close to coming. This time, I wouldn't control her orgasm. I wanted her eager to submit to anything I demanded. Maybe I was an evil man after all.

I closed my eyes, concentrating on giving her divine pleasure and the second her body started to convulse, I yanked her legs over my shoulders. I drove four fingers inside, matching their action to the brutality of my lashing tongue. Her climax brought breathless screams, the taste of her so sweet I couldn't stop ravaging her delicious pussy.

"Oh. My. God. Yes. Yes!"

As a single orgasm shifted into a beautiful wave, I licked every drop until my tongue and throat were covered in her sweet cream. I refused to let her go until she stopped writhing. As I rose to my feet, she lolled her head, dragging her tongue across her lips.

I cupped her chin, digging my fingers in as I captured her mouth. She hungrily sucked on my tongue, writhing in my hold. She was without a doubt the most beautiful creature I'd ever set my eyes on. And fucking her made me insatiable.

The kiss was explosive as usual, the taste of her like fine red wine mixed with strawberries. When I pulled away, she nipped my lower lip, her tooth piercing my skin. She laughed as I broke away, rubbing my index finger through the single drop of blood.

"You like it rough, baby?" I asked, no longer recognizing my gruff voice.

"Yes, I do, sir. The rougher the better."

After taking a deep breath, I rolled my fingers against the skin of her waist, taking a few seconds to study her with relentless eyes. I tapped my cock against her stomach, slowly allowing my gaze to return to her eyes. "Be careful what you ask for, my pet." I'd never wanted to fuck anyone as badly as I did at that moment. I'd never been much of a romantic guy, my dominating side too influential for pretend foreplay or feathered kisses for hours.

While being with her had broken all the rules I'd set in place for myself, I no longer cared. I wrapped her legs around my hips, placing the tip of my cock against her slickened folds and refusing to hesitate for a second. As I drove my cock inside, we both shuddered uncontrollably. The feel of having her muscles constricting around my cock was powerful, so much so I had difficulty breathing.

I planted my hands on either side of her, pulling almost all the way out then driving into her again. There was no way I could or would be gentle. I needed satisfaction and she was the only woman who could give it to me.

Alexandra gasped for air, her chest rising and falling as I rose onto the balls of my feet, fucking her hard and fast. The angle was utter perfection, allowing me to drive so deeply inside I was certain I'd entered her womb.

"Oh. Oh." Her eyelids were half closed as she tossed her head back and forth.

Goddamn, I adored her reaction, her breathless sounds making me even more of a crazed animal. When she squeezed her knees against me, I wrapped one hand around her throat, squeezing until she dragged her tongue across her lips. Her eyes were lit with a fire I'd never seen, the roughness satiating the sadist inside. She had no idea the beast she'd lured from the cage, my actions no longer those of a sane, decent man.

Perhaps I'd never been one.

In my mind, the same words replayed constantly. She belonged to me.

As I sensed she was close to another mind-blowing orgasm, I slowed my actions, rubbing my thumb across her jaw. "No man will ever touch you again."

"No," she managed.

"Say it for me. Tell me you belong to me."

Her eyes were dilated, her luscious lips twisting. "I'm yours. No one else... will ever... touch me again."

I squeezed my hand around her long throat, thrusting in deep, even strokes as the new wave of pleasure jetted through her. I was so alive that the electricity crackling between us paled in comparison. As the wave tore through her, I plunged long and deep, waiting until she closed her eyes.

After I pulled all the way out, I wiped my arm across my face then spun her around, immediately grabbing both sides of her rounded buttocks. When I pressed them open, she gasped as she'd done before, doing everything she could to arch her back. Now standing on her tiptoes, she couldn't have been more ravishing.

"Yes. Fuck me. Please, fuck me."

I cracked my palm against her bottom twice before wrapping my hand around my cock, pressing the tip to her dark entrance. She sucked in her breath, her eyes remaining closed. As I pushed the tip inside, I struggled to keep from driving it all the way in. I was suddenly more predator than anything else, already losing some of the rigid control I usually had.

Every sound I made was more of a growl, my pulse skyrocketing. This is what the woman did to me. As I pushed past the tight wall of muscle, I threw my head back. Nothing had ever felt so damn good.

When I finally plunged the remaining inches inside, I wrapped my hands around hers, allowing her to get used to the thick invasion.

She was shaking, her body melding against mine. I was lightheaded, my cock swelling, the tightness of her muscles almost too much to take. I needed release, my balls already swelling. As I nuzzled against her neck, biting on her earlobe, she squirmed in my hold.

"Yes," she whispered, every sound like a soft purr.

I pulled away, smacking her bottom until she squealed. Then I couldn't hold back any longer, fucking her so savagely the door slammed against the wall. And still, I refused to stop.

Lights flashed in front of my eyes, and I gritted my teeth, the sensations roaring through my body boiling my blood. After four additional brutal thrusts, I lost all control, erupting deep inside.

She lolled her head, half laughing, entwining her fingers with mine. "Do it again."

I laughed as I pressed my lips against the side of her neck. "Soon. Very soon."

CHAPTER 19

 *ameson*

If you'd asked me twenty years before if I would ever consider myself a businessman, having discussion about financials and quarterly returns, I would have laughed. I'd grown up in an environment where working with my hands was valued more than solving problems with my brain. Fortunately, my mother had encouraged the use of my mind as well as my body, which had also allowed me to obtain the scholarship to the university. Even my coach had been impressed I'd maintained an A average the four years I was there.

I might not have the affinity for number crunching that Grant did or the finesse in handling members and clients that came naturally to Lachlan, but I knew how to spot a lying sack of shit in one minute flat.

I'd learned a long time ago that looks could be deceiving and that people were most comfortable hiding behind a computer screen where they could be anyone they wanted. Often that's why I required a face-to-face meeting rather than by phone or God forbid email. I preferred to cut through the bullshit immediately. Once I did, either I walked out without reservation or joined in the conversation.

Dealing with Dumas was no different.

I'd found him to be cordial, intelligent, and cunning, but I'd always known that he kept a part of his life in secrecy, which was fine by me. He'd checked all the boxes during the discovery phase when discussing the possibility of working together. That's all that had mattered.

At least on paper.

What I hadn't expressed to my partners was my continued concern about his family background. The reports of their ties with the mafia shouldn't matter since given his status within the family, but it continued to nag at me. Lachlan would find it laughable given his father's connection to the Scottish crime syndicate, something he almost never talked about.

"What exactly is this meeting about? You just mentioned some issue with the club itself," Alexandra asked as I pulled into the parking lot of the location Dumas had selected for a meeting. He'd suggested what would be the true opposing BDSM club when Carnal Sins opened later in the year. Perhaps I should say *if* it opened.

"My partners and I sold a franchise almost a year ago to a powerful Parisian businessman. As with any land development in most countries, there are county or city requirements, the approvals obtained before the contracts were signed. Now, we're within a couple months of opening and there's been some accusations made regarding his handling of the applications."

"Accusations? Like blackmail?"

"And extortion."

"Fantastic," she said. "Which will sully the reputation of the entire corporation."

"Absolutely."

She looked at me as I pulled into a space, the overhead lighting adding a shimmer to the cab of the Maserati. "What do you think you can do?"

"First, I'm going to find out if it's true or not. I'll know that by talking with him."

"If it is?"

I yanked the keys from the ignition. "There is a clause in the contract that will immediately be acted upon if he's found guilty of any crimes. It will be terminated, the money he's put into the project forfeited."

"But you'll lose millions as well because you'll have an unfinished building and a tarnished rep."

Laughing, I scrubbed my hand across my jaw. "You have a complete understanding of what I'm facing."

"I took the opportunity of looking up Mr. Dumas on the plane."

"Oh, you did? And what did you find?"

"His family is highly respected in the wine industry, but it would appear his grandfather was involved with some very bad people."

"That is correct," I told her. There was no reason to keep it from her. "It was made clear that his family business in no way could be connected to the club."

"Why do I have a feeling you think there's an outside influence that has little to do with Mr. Dumas and more to do with your corporation itself?"

I opened my door, easing onto the pavement. I'd been at the club once before at Dumas' suggestion. While it was a gorgeous location, they didn't have the strict rules set in place as we'd established early on.

She climbed out, smoothing down the dress I'd selected for her myself. I took long strides around the back of the vehicle until I was in front of her. "Tonight you observe. I will be eager to see your reaction. And the answer is that you're right. There are too many interesting coincidences going on and I don't believe in them."

"Santiago? Could he have connections this far?"

"That's what I'm going to find out."

"Then what are you going to do?"

I thought about her question. "I might need to pull out my little black book."

"You are full of surprises."

"You have no idea." Dumas had already secured our entrance. However, after finding out where we were going once inside, I was surprised at his choice. The club's design allowed for a loft overlooking several of the specialty rooms, available only to very special members. It was also in the center of the club, the acrylic walls surrounding the three sides allowing anyone to view who was meeting whom.

There was very little difference in Paris versus what were considered the power cities in the US. The rich and influential made up the membership. Dumas was sending a message, attempting to draw out who was responsible for putting his life and his career on the line.

I guided her through the crowd, allowing her to stop long enough to watch a scene being played out. Nothing shocked me any longer, but the use of a bullwhip would never occur in my club or any attached to the Carnal Sins name.

"That's crazy," she said, her body stiffening.

"And not allowed inside my walls."

She turned away and even in the shimmer of neon lights, I sensed her nervousness was shifting into raw fear. "Are you alright?"

"I can't do that."

I lifted her chin, studying her eyes. "I would never subject you to something remotely that harsh. I need to ask you. Did something happen in your past?"

Her mouth twisted before she laughed. "Why would you ask that? No man has ever used a whip on me."

By the way she made the statement, her words stilted, my anger rushed to the surface. She had been hurt terribly. Now wasn't the time to find out what she'd endured but I would make it my mission to learn.

Then I would destroy whoever had hurt her.

As soon as we walked out onto the platform, Dumas rose to his feet. The man had balls, which I appreciated. The table he'd selected was nestled against the railing. Maybe I liked the man after all.

He moved closer to Alexandra, taking and kissing her hand. *"Une belle créature honore ma présence,"* he said as he glanced into my eyes.

"Thank you for the compliment, Mr. Dumas. I must admit I've never been called a beautiful creature before and I am happy to be in your presence. However, you should know that in additional to being Mr. Stark's administrative assistant, I am also his submissive."

Philip pulled away, giving a respectful nod. "Mr. Stark is an extremely lucky man. Where did you find her, Jameson?"

"At a traffic accident."

His eyes opened wide and he laughed as we all sat down. "I'll need to consider that in the future. I took the liberty of ordering wine. I hope you don't mind."

"Perfectly fine." I waited until he'd poured two additional glasses before leaning forward. "I need to hear what happened detail by detail."

"There's little to tell. I was at the site one afternoon and had a visit from the French police. While they didn't arrest me, they encouraged me to talk with them. Only after I was inside the station did I realize what accusations were being leveled at me."

"And those are?"

He sat back, taking a sip of his wine. "My father has been good friends with two French officials. Their relationship goes back two decades. Suddenly, that relationship was brought into light as being the reason I won the bid for the land as well as was able to reduce the approval time for the plans from the usual four months to thirty days."

"Is there any truth to this? Did your father make a phone call for you?" I could tell he was disturbed by everything that had occurred.

"I confronted my father on two occasions and he assured me that he didn't interfere. I believe him since he isn't a fan of what I'm doing."

"Do you have any enemies?" Alexandra asked.

He tipped his head in her direction. "My family certainly does."

"Do any of them extend to America?" she continued.

"That's a very good question. Quite possibly."

I reached into my suit jacket, pulling out an envelope. "I took the liberty of preparing a list of names you should have checked, perhaps with your father." I slipped it across the table. "I believe what you're telling me, Philip. I think that you're caught in an attempt to shut down our corporation in its entirety."

"Why?"

Laughter almost bubbled to the surface. "Because of some power-hungry people who are terrified of the information that could be leaked to the press."

"Ah. Let me take some time with the list. If there is anyone in question, I'll let you know."

"What about the workers on the project? Are they remaining on the job?"

"So far," he said. "I was able to offer bonuses."

"Were your funds restored?"

He chuckled under his breath. "I have various sources of income and bank accounts in several offshore locations. While the main fund for the project is still being held, I planned ahead. We have as many corrupt politicians as you do in your country."

"Wise thinking. Let me guess. You purposely chose this location to issue a warning of your own."

Dumas leaned forward. "You're not the only man with secure, substantiated data on those who might cause trouble. My father taught me that information is the key to survival, one of the few aspects of my childhood that I still use today."

"A wise man. What can I do to provide assistance?" I kept my hand on Alexandra's leg, stroking her skin. While she attempted to keep her concentration on the meeting, I sensed her increasing nervousness. The scenes were out in the open, some more brutal than others. While there was nothing more I wanted than to enjoy spending time introducing her to additional acts of kink, I sensed an entirely different level of reservations. Whatever she was keeping locked away in her past prevented her from letting go entirely. Maybe a change in plans was necessary.

"Take a look around you, Mr. Stark. We have people watching us as we speak. It is entirely possible that prior to you returning to the States, we'll know who is behind the obvious attempt at derailing everything I've worked for. I don't take being threatened kindly."

"When were you threatened?" This I didn't know.

"The day I won the auction for the land. And before you ask, it came in the form of an anonymous source."

"But you suspect who it is," Alexandra piped.

"Yes, *cherie*, I do, although I can't prove it."

I had the distinct feeling he wasn't going to share with us who he believed was behind the threats. "It may be necessary to talk with the French officials on your behalf."

"Trust me. You don't want to do that. They will only dig in deeper. However, if information is discovered, I know the right people to talk with in order to make this problem disappear."

I studied Dumas for a few seconds before leaning back in my chair, tapping my fingers on the table. "I think it's prudent to have a meeting with the officials. However, take the evening to see if you can make connections. Then we talk in the morning. I'll need to return to Miami as soon as possible so this incident must be solved."

He dragged his gaze toward Alexandra and for the first time, I noticed real emotion on his face. He'd been stoic, cold for almost every meeting.

"Very well, Jameson. I need this club to work. It's the only thing that is truly mine and I won't let it go down in flames. Now, may I suggest you enjoy some of what Club Noir has to offer. I should make a few phone calls. Whatever you would like will be taken care of. It's the least I can do for dragging you to Paris."

"It's always enjoyable to come to this vibrant city." I lifted my glass in recognition, noticing we'd drawn more attention. There were several men at another table watching us intently. I could only imagine what they were concluding.

He took another gulp of his wine then moved back from the table. "Alexandra, you are a true beauty in a sea of loneliness. I hope you find my beloved city to your liking."

"Very much so," she said. "Thank you."

Dumas smiled, giving me another nod before moving away from the table.

Alexandra settled into her seat, turning toward me. "Are we staying?" Her question was hopeful but laced with uncertainty.

"I was originally planning on indulging your fantasies, but I have a better idea."

* * *

Alexandra

The powerful man was full of surprises.

He'd made a phone call once outside the club, refusing to allow me to hear what was being said. I was excited and nervous, wondering what he had in mind. The look on his face gave me goosebumps, as if we were entering into another realm of our kinky relationship.

The word seemed strange, as if I was living another life. I'd been a sheltered girl, not allowed to go wild like my friends. I'd told myself I'd fall in love with a nice boy, live on a small ranch, and have three kids and a dog, along with the picket fence. I'd learned the hard way that typical fantasies weren't in my future.

Maybe that's why I'd gravitated toward Jameson, longing to be taken care of, treated like a princess.

He said nothing as he drove away from the club, keeping his hand firmly planted on my knee. My thoughts drifted to the scene with the bullwhip. While the look on the girl's face as every lash was cracked against her naked body indicated the highest form of pleasure, I remained sick to my stomach. In truth, I was glad that we'd left the club.

"How much further?"

He squeezed my leg. "Patience, my dear girl."

"You know I don't have any."

"You will learn."

"And you're my teacher?"

"In all things."

The man was so dominating yet kind, but I sensed the protective side of him was just under the surface. He didn't like anyone even looking in my direction. I'd loathed everything about possessive men after what I'd endured. I'd run away on purpose, promising myself that I would never enter into any kind of dominating relationship. Now this. Now... him.

As he continued to drive through the brightly lit streets, a realization hit me hard.

I was falling hard for the man. It wasn't just about lust, although the passion we shared was undeniably incredible. The way I felt about him gripped my heart and soul, my need to be around him increasing. He had a way of making me feel beautiful even when I felt such ugliness. And he made certain I was comfortable in every situation, watching my reaction closely.

I'd noticed the way Philip Dumas had looked at me, as if he could be allowed even a single taste. Jameson would never allow anyone else to touch me. A single shiver trickled through my body, the moment shared special. I couldn't predict the future but I knew one thing with certainty.

I could see a life with this man.

Oh, God. Was that even possible? What did I have to offer someone of his stature?

When I looked away, his breathing changed. I could swear he read my mind and my moods better than anyone ever had.

"You know I'll never force you to do anything you don't want to do. Correct?" His deep voice rumbled in the dense space, filling me with tingles.

"I know that, but as strange as I find it for myself, I want to please you."

"You do. I don't need you to be anything but what your heart tells you is right. Always follow your instincts. They will never steer you wrong."

Little did they know my instincts had betrayed me once. Never again.

"I'm curious. What's your favorite flower?"

His question caught me off guard.

"A beautiful sterling silver rose. The delicate purple is spectacular. Why?"

"I want to learn everything about you."

The deep vibe to his voice was entirely different, the tone keeping a fire burning deep within. He had a way of making me feel special.

Moments later, he pulled into a parking lot, the sign secured on the brick surface brightly lit neon. "What does that say?"

"Picturesque Ink."

"A tattoo place?"

"Yes," he said, half laughing. "As well as piercings."

My stomach did a series of flipflops. "You were serious about piercing my nipples."

He pulled into a space and tipped his head, his grin easy to see in the glow of the sign. "I was. However, I've wanted another tattoo. I thought now was the perfect time."

I pressed my fingers against my mouth, trying to decide if I was excited or terrified. Both. I would never have considered something so… sinful a few months before. Good girls didn't get their nipples pierced. Or did they?

"I'll ask you one more time. Is this something you want?"

There was no pressure, no insistence that I do something I couldn't stand. The answer was far too easy. "Yes."

I could tell by the smile on his face that I'd pleased him. When he helped me out of the car, wrapping his arm around my waist, I'd never felt so cared for or protected in my life. Maybe moving to Miami wasn't such an irresponsible decision after all.

"Mr. Stark," the girl behind the counter said. "We've been expecting you."

She spoke English, her accent lovely. The shop was beautifully decorated with colorful photographs of tattoos from clients, and other art to inspire designs and creations. It was bright and clean, leather sofas in the corner of the room with what had to be design books placed on a glorious coffee table.

"My beautiful Alexandra is very special," he said in response.

The girl turned her attention to me, her smile remaining. "We'll take very good care of her. Would you like to be in the room while the piercing is done? We can have your ink done at the same time."

"Absolutely. I wouldn't miss it for the world."

As we were led into another room, I realized I was holding my breath.

"I'll need you to remove your dress. Don't worry. You can have a sheet to cover you. If at anytime you feel uncomfortable, just let the technician know. We want this to be a pleasurable experience for you." The girl guided me to a small room to change and I almost panicked. This was the craziest thing I'd ever done in my life.

"I don't know anything about this," I admitted.

She patted my arm. "My name is Julie. I didn't either. My dom was insistent and I almost ran out of the store. But now I wouldn't consider going anywhere without my piercings. Would you like to see them?"

Heat rushed to my face, but I nodded. She wasn't shy about lifting her top, exposing her diamond-studded nipples.

"You'll have a wide variety of choices once you heal. Your master was very specific in his selection. You won't have any issues. Just come out when you're ready."

"I'm not having my clit pierced today?"

Julie laughed. "That wasn't listed on the instructions. I have that as well. It's very sexual. I hope your master will allow that one day for you. You won't be disappointed."

I nodded, a lump forming in my throat. Ready. Would I ever be ready to let go of the past entirely? After taking several deep breaths, I removed my dress. Already braless and wearing only a thong, I stood in front of the small mirror, studying my breasts. They were considered voluptuous yet fit perfectly in his hands. I squeezed them, pinching my nipples until pain forced me to wince.

My nipples were already hard, aching from our rough round of passion. I tried to imagine what the sensations would feel like once they were pierced. The strangest thing of all was that I no longer recognized the girl in the mirror. She'd grown by leaps and bounds, her eyes sparkling and her skin flushed from excitement.

There was never a dull moment being around Jameson.

I took another minute before grabbing one of the sheets folded on a shelf, tying it around my waist. A rush of embarrassment forced me to fold my arms over my chest as I left the dressing area.

As soon as I exited, Jameson lifted his head, the desire in his eyes sending a wave of adrenaline into my system. A single look from the man caused my pussy to clench and release.

An older man entered the room, conversing with Jameson in French. I only knew a few words from my high school French class, but I could easily tell the technician was being instructed to take good care of me.

Or else.

"My name is Pierre. Please move to the table. This won't take very long."

I did as requested, unable to take my eyes off Jameson as he removed his shirt, moving to another chair as someone else entered the room. I'd never felt so exposed yet free in my life. As I leaned back against the incline, Pierre adjusted it then studied my breasts.

"At any time if you're uncomfortable, just give me the word and I'll stop. You'll feel a pinch from pain but that will go away quickly. Are you ready to begin?"

Was I? "Yes."

He nodded, adjusting the swinging light overhead. As he pulled what looked like an antiseptic bottle into his hand, I sucked in my breath. Pierre was gentle, taking his time cleaning both nipples. When he pulled a marker into his hand, I almost laughed from nervousness.

His grin was kind, as if knowing I was struggling with embarrassment. Then he marked a spot.

"Now, I will clamp your nipple to make it easier. You'll feel some pressure."

I nodded, uncertain I could find my voice.

Jameson never took his eyes off me, piercing mine even from the distance.

As the tattoo artist began whatever design Jameson had selected, I barely felt the pinch as the needle went through my nipple. I only glanced down after the gold piece was secured, the delicate barbell shimmering in the light. The technician moved to the other side and I arched my back, struggling with the various emotions skittering through me. Pierre repeated the same actions, only lifting his gaze from his task once.

This time, I felt the slight hint of pain, exhaling to try to ease the tension. When the other bar was clipped into place, I felt the difference in weight, almost laughing from the instant sensations.

When Pierre was finished, allowing me to rise from the table, I sensed a change in Jameson, his aura darker than before.

I knew then that the promises he'd made, the intentions he'd shown could not be denied.

He intended on owning me. Not just for an extended timeframe or until he grew bored with the ecstasy we shared.

The man with the gorgeous face, eyes that continued to roam over my half naked body had made a decision that I couldn't ignore even if I wanted to.

I belonged to him.

My body, my soul.

And my heart.

CHAPTER 20

lexandra

The cool breeze tickled my skin, the view of Paris even more incredible at night, the streets quieter given the late hour. I stood with my hands gripping the railing, terrified yet exhilarated. The soft strains of guitar music floated from the open set of French doors, keeping me electrified as I gazed from the Eiffel Tower to the stars twinkling in the sky. The moment was magical. It felt like all the fairytales I'd had as a little girl had come true.

I sensed Jameson's approach as I always did, taking a deep breath of his lingering aftershave. As usual, the exotic spices infused with sandalwood and just the perfect hint of orange created another significant wave of desire. I don't know why I felt like this was a turning point, but when he'd finally

286

revealed the tattoo he'd selected, I'd felt honored, and strangely giddy.

The creation was beautiful, the sterling silver rose woven with a single letter—a capital A. I'd been shocked and still was, uncertain what adorning his skin with my initial meant to him. I'd watched the creation coming to life, enjoying the process as much as the finished product.

I tipped my head, noticing he'd brought two glasses of champagne. How could I keep from smiling?

"You're spoiling me," I told him.

"And the issue is?" He laughed softly as he laid the glasses on the coffee table, quickly moving behind me, placing his hands over mine. "I enjoy indulging you."

"Why?"

"Why? Because you should be made to feel special."

"I'm just a girl who lost her way."

"Haven't we all done that at least once in our lives?" His question wasn't rhetorical but very personal. As he moved beside me, leaning over the railing, I sensed he'd lost himself in whatever moment in the past was continuing to haunt him.

"Who was she?"

He didn't respond or seem as if he'd heard me for a few seconds. When he lowered his head, glancing over his shoulder, the look in his eyes was both primal as well as cautionary. "She?"

"The woman who broke your heart."

His reaction was slow but intended. Then he glanced toward the Eiffel Tower. "Her name was Pamela. She was my assistant several years ago, originally from a temp service."

"What happened?"

"She was very good at what she did, keeping me on track as no one else had managed to do before. We were working late one night. I took her to dinner. Sparks flew. We found out we had more things in common than we'd originally thought. Her father worked in construction like mine did. She came from a small town. We enjoyed spending time together."

"Then what happened?"

"I became too dominating for her. She finally admitted she didn't like the club, the kink and wanted no part of the life I shared. By then, her brother had arrived in town to take her home. We had a confrontation and things were testy after that. She was very tight with her family."

I had a feeling there was much more to the story. "So she broke it off."

"Not before I found her sharing special time with a bartender." He laughed, the sound bitter.

"That's terrible."

"I was incensed, of course, becoming the jealous man. I beat the guy before throwing him out. That was the end."

"But it wasn't. Was it?"

Jameson laughed. "What I learned much later was that she'd set up the encounter so I'd find her. She wanted to make certain I broke it off."

"Did she tell you that?"

"No. Another employee did but that was months later. I tried to call Pamela, but she refused to talk to me."

"I'm very sorry."

"It was my fault. I'd tried to push her into a lifestyle she wanted no part of, which is why I will never do that with you. The club is my job. It doesn't need to be my life."

"But it is your life, something that's very important to you. I wouldn't try and take any of that away."

"You're wise beyond your years." He shifted toward me, pressing the tips of his fingers against my cheek. A shiver bolted through my muscles and I pressed my hand against his chest.

"Not really. You don't know me that well."

His grin was full of dark hunger. "I think I do. In fact, I know I do."

"Have you talked with her since?"

"No. She made it perfectly clear she didn't want to continue a friendship. She left the job. Left the state. Unfortunately, I heard from her brother recently that she died."

"Oh, God." Another death. Another tragedy. I couldn't believe how we'd managed to find each other.

PIPER STONE

I pulled away, fisting my hand. He'd exposed a part of him that I doubted few people knew about. I wasn't prepared to do the same. It was far too painful.

"Don't run away from me as you did from Montana, Alexandra. I'll never hurt you."

"I never said you would, but what I went through I wouldn't wish on anyone." I heard the edge and the sadness in my voice and cringed. "I'm sorry. I'm not angry with you, just with my life."

He wrapped his arm around me, tugging me close. I didn't want to pull away any longer. He'd been the only comfort I'd felt in so long that I melted against him.

"Talk to me, Alexandra."

I took a deep breath, holding it for a few seconds. The feel of his hard body pressed against mine was scintillating, so much so I wrapped my arm around his. "Does your arm hurt from the tat?"

"Just tender. Your gorgeous nipples?"

"They ache." I wanted so much to share with him everything that had occurred. My fear wasn't about dredging up the past but about what he'd think of me.

"It will take time." He said nothing else, merely holding me as we gazed out at the city together.

Suddenly, I couldn't stand holding back the truth from him any longer. If he thought less of me, then I'd understand. I continued to blame myself and likely would for some time.

"I've had a single boyfriend, a guy I met in high school. He was the all-American athlete, determined to perform in rodeos. Tall, muscular, and popular. I was the shy kid with overprotective parents. I was asked to help tutor him in English and we became friends. Then he asked me to my senior prom, which shocked me."

"It shouldn't. You're a beautiful woman."

"Not in high school." I allowed myself to laugh. "He didn't seem to care. We had a wonderful time that continued through the summer after my senior year. I went to a college close to home while he started the rodeo circuit and was very successful. We dated. I was certain we'd marry and have a huge family."

"What happened?"

"The more famous he got, the angrier he became. The circuit was brutal, not only on his body but his mind as well. He started being more aggressive, demanding. We argued more."

His hold became firmer. "He became abusive."

"Yes. It was little things at first. Breaking a glass, punching a wall, but things escalated. I tried to push him away, but that made him angrier. After the first time he hit me, I said no more. I blocked his number and refused to see him."

"But he didn't take no for an answer."

"No. I went back to him once, but by the end of the night, I had a black eye. By that point my older brother knew what was happening. Matt had been my protector growing up, so he took it upon himself to act like he needed to deal with it.

I tried to stop him, but there was no talking to him. He was a rebel, almost landing himself in prison for beating a guy in a bar for touching his girlfriend." I heard the ugly glitch in my voice and did everything I could to keep the tears away. I'd promised myself that I'd never cry again.

"Baby, you don't need to say anymore. I understand."

I broke the hold he had on me, turning around to face him. This time, I pressed my hand against his face, enjoying the feel of his beard. "It's okay. I need to tell you. The only other person besides my parents who know is Charlotte."

He placed his hand on my hip, digging his fingers into my skin through the robe I'd changed into. His face was pensive, his eyes never blinking. No one had ever looked at me so intensely or taken me so seriously.

"My brother was a hothead. When he saw my face, he went ballistic. He'd been drinking and I tried to keep him from going but there was no stopping Matt when he set his mind to something. He took my keys so I couldn't go after him. In my heart, a part of me wanted him to beat the shit out of Daryl, even though I knew it was wrong." I looked away, struggling with finding the right words. "My parents were out of town, so I waited alone. Matt didn't come back. I tried calling both Matt and Daryl but neither one answered. Somehow, I fell asleep only to be awakened by the sheriff stopping by."

Jameson slipped his hand behind my head, wrapping his fingers around my neck. "Oh, baby."

"I learned that Matt had attacked Daryl. They'd fought. Daryl was left with a broken nose and jaw. Then Matt left.

He had a..." A sob tore from my throat, a single tear falling. "He ran into a tree and was killed instantly."

He refused to allow me to stop him from pulling me against his warm body, cradling me as he rubbed his hand up and down my back. "Jesus. Christ."

"My parents were devastated and blamed me. That's okay because I blamed myself. I still do. They bickered constantly and it broke apart their marriage. That's why I came to Miami. I couldn't bear to live in the same city any longer."

Growling, he jerked back, lifting my chin. "Do not do that to yourself. You weren't to blame for your boyfriend being an asshole or the bad decision your brother made even if he was trying to protect you."

"I know, but..." My entire body was shaking, the heartache as if it had just happened yesterday. "Why didn't he listen to me? Why?"

"Because he loved you. He wanted to protect you."

"That's why this can't happen. I don't want you to get hurt. I care too much about you." I was trembling, my emotions all over the place. I'd never wanted to be with anyone as much as I did the man holding me, keeping me calm and protected. I hungered so much for him that I ached inside, but the fear had returned with a vengeance.

"Baby. No one is going to hurt either you or me, definitely not ghosts from the past. You need to hear something. You managed to do something that I never thought would happen again. You stirred my heart. Then when I least expected it, you grabbed ahold and refused to let go. Now, I know you're thinking that we haven't known other long enough, but I am the kind of man who knows what I want and from the moment you crashed into my life, you're all I've been able to think about. If you dare try and run away from me, I will find you."

I grasped his shirt, clinging to him as another tear rolled down my cheek. "I didn't expect you in my life. I'm falling in love with you and that scares me to death."

He lowered his head, allowing his hot breath to cascade across my face. "Don't let it. I'll catch you when you fall." As he slipped the tip of his finger through the tear, his eyes narrowing, I could see such love in his eyes that I was taken aback. He slid his finger into his mouth, issuing a low and husky growl. "Always."

As he captured my mouth, I closed my eyes and shoved all the memories away. He held me gently, aware of the piercings when I honestly didn't care about the physical pain. It was nothing in comparison to the emotional anguish we'd both been through. I slid my arms under his, pressing myself tightly against his chest as he thrust his tongue inside. Just being in his arms felt safe, as if nothing and no one could ever hurt us.

The moment of passion shifted into something even deeper. This wasn't about sex as much as it was about a connection that needed nurturing, like a beautiful flower requiring water and sunlight in order to survive.

He swept his tongue back and forth across mine, every action demanding yet not forceful. I was lightheaded, no longer capable to thinking about anything else but the time we were spending together on such a glorious night. My legs trembled, my panties soaked from the longing spiraling through me.

When he slipped his arm under my bottom, lifting me into his arms, he refused to break the kiss. Every move deliberate, he took long strides into the suite, easily finding the bedroom. He finally pulled away long enough to ease me to the floor, yanking the sash on my robe.

His expression now carnal as he rolled the silky material over my shoulders, allowing the material to drop to the floor, he shook his head. "Magnificent." He cupped my breasts, being careful to avoid my nipples, but I could tell his mouth was watering.

"You make me feel that way."

After nipping my lower lip, he backed away, taking his time to remove his clothes. I never tired of seeing his sculpted body, muscles that cried out to be caressed. His cock was fully engorged, his balls hanging low, creations of utter beauty.

When he approached, I was unable to resist tracing the beautiful image on his upper arm, watching his reaction. "This is perhaps the most special thing anyone has done for me in my life. When do I get one?"

"Oh, no. Piercings only."

"So, I'm still under your rules," I teased.

"Always. I am your master, after all." Everything about the man was breathtaking, leaving me wondering how many delicious experiences we'd have in the future. Shifting, he yanked down the covers, lowering me onto the bed. As he crawled onto the sheet, he raked his eyes down the length of me.

"Arms over your head."

I did as he commanded, shivering as he rolled his fingers down my chest. He took his time, creating a path of goosebumps along the way. I bit my lower lip, my body continuing to tremble. He issued a series of low growls as he slipped his fingers under the thin elastic of my panties, ever so slowly lowering them past my hips.

When he pulled them free, tossing them aside, I arched my back, the offer blatant. He was in full control, studying me so intently I was breathless with anticipation, so lightheaded my vision was foggy. He purposefully planted each hand on either side of me, hovering above as he used his knee to kick my legs apart.

The concentration on his face was incredible, his dark eyelashes floating across his cheeks keeping my mouth watering. When I lowered one arm without thinking, he shook his head, placing his index finger across my lips.

"You will obey me at all times. That's something you need to keep in mind. Keep your arms over your head or I'll tie them to the bed. Then I won't release you until morning."

I shuddered audibly, longing for his touch. "Yes, sir." A part of me wanted to disobey him to see what he'd do, but my hunger was too strong. I intertwined my fingers to help remain obedient, but the way the moonlight from the wide-open windows highlighted his gorgeous physique made it difficult.

He lowered his head, nuzzling against my neck, nipping my earlobe. Then he rolled his lips from one side of my jaw to the other, slowly lowering until he breathed across my nipple. It was extra sensitive, yet I longed for him to suck it, swirling his tongue across the slender bar of gold. Instead, he dragged his tongue between my breasts, moving ever so slowly to my stomach.

I couldn't stop shaking, the electricity coursing from his body through mine keeping my pulse racing. When he dipped his head lower, I pulled back my knees, opening my legs as wide as possible.

"My little pet is hungry."

"Yes, sir."

"What do you want?" How could his voice be any deeper, the seductive tone sending a roar of desire straight to my core.

"Everything."

He chuckled darkly before swirling his finger around my clit, lifting a single eyebrow. "That's not an answer."

"Lick me. Suck me. Fuck me."

His grin widened and he immediately gathered my legs into his arms, lifting my bottom off the sheets then burying his head into my pussy.

The instant he did, I was certain I'd go mad. I was crazed with longing, twisting my head back and forth as he drove his tongue inside. Even the animalistic sounds he made were powerful, pushing me into a completely blissful state within seconds.

"Oh, God. Oh, you are so good."

Stars floated in front of my eyes, my mind completely devoid of any thoughts other than the yearning to wrap my lips around his cock.

He lifted me even higher until my toes were barely touching the sheets. I writhed in his hold, gasping for air and it took everything I had not to reach for him. Sweet Jesus, I wasn't certain I could contain the climax that was just about ready to erupt.

"Hold it, sweet girl."

"I can't."

"You will."

"You don't understand," I moaned. When he smacked his fingers against my pussy, I let out a strangled wail. Not from pain. Not from shock. From the way my pussy reacted, clenching and releasing several times. Now I was certain madness was right around the corner.

I had no idea how he managed to spread me even wider, but he did. Then he cracked his fingers against my pussy three more times before returning his mouth, feasting as if he was famished.

A crazy buzz started in my ears and I lolled my head to the side, doing everything I could to continue obeying. Within seconds, I was panting and laughing nervously. The intensity of what he was doing had created a live wire inside my body.

"Please," I finally begged. "May I come?" I could no longer recognize my voice. I bucked up from the bed when he didn't answer immediately, panting so hard I was about ready to scream.

"Come for me, baby. Coat my tongue before I fuck you, driving my cock deep inside."

The man could talk dirty to me all night long. I bit down on my lower lip to keep from screaming, the orgasm rushing into me like a tidal wave, the pleasure so intense. I was certain I would pass out as a single climax roared into a second, my skin on fire. He kept me from thrashing, his fingers digging into my skin.

"Oh. Oh. Yes. Yes. Yes."

When he lifted my feet off the sheets, switching the angle, I shifted directly into ecstasy. He continued licking until I stopped shaking, slowly easing me to the bed. My mind was as blurry as my eyes, but I wanted to see all of him. He rose to his knees, dragging his tongue across his lips. There was something devilish about his smile, his eyelids half closed. He slowly lowered his body down once again, remaining aloft on his elbows.

"Do you want my cock buried inside of you?"

Was he insane asking me these questions? "Yes. Yes, God, yes. Please."

He cocked his head, his nostrils flaring, and placed the tip of his cock against my swollen pussy. The ache was extreme and I was so wet, my thighs were coated with my juice. He kept a sly smile on his face, using his powerful arm muscles to keep himself hovering a few inches away from me.

Struggling, I managed to lift my body enough, catching and biting down on his lower lip. He laughed, shaking his head three times. "You don't always get what you want," he told me.

"And why not?"

"Because only I know what's good for you."

I hadn't seen his playful side, but I knew the dominating alpha inside would always take full control. He jutted his hips, driving his cock in by an inch, maybe two, toying with me. He shifted his hips back and forth, his features turning darker.

"All mine."

There was something so provocative about the way he claimed me, the piercings just the beginning of how he'd mark me as his. He remained where he was for far too long, driving me to the point of disobeying him.

But I was able to stay a good girl, taunting him by licking my lips, purring several times. As if he couldn't take it any longer, he thrust the remainder of his cock inside, both of us instantly issuing ragged moans. I still couldn't believe how large he was, swelling almost immediately as my muscles stretched.

I wrapped my legs around him, tangling my feet together and pulling him tightly against me.

As he lowered his head, purposely glancing at what I'd done, I couldn't help but laugh.

"You're determined to get yourself into trouble. Aren't you, my little pet?"

"Why, yes, sir."

He dropped his forehead against mine, taking several deep breaths. "As soon as your nipples are healed, a chain will be attached."

The thought made me shudder and I darted my tongue across the seam of his mouth, lifting my head until our lips were able to touch.

His breathing was as labored as mine and as he pulled out, holding just the tip inside, I took several tiny gasps. His actions were gentle, driving his cock inside then holding it for a few seconds, but I could tell he wouldn't be able to hold back and I didn't want him to.

His lips curled slightly as he continued to stare into my eyes, remaining aloft so he wouldn't crush me with his weight. Being able to look into his eyes as he made love to me was amazing and I felt as if I was looking directly into his soul.

Seconds later, his thrusts became more powerful, every muscle in his body tensing. With his jaw clenched, the shimmer in his eyes drifted to darkness. I did what I could to meet every brutal thrust, the breathless moment leaving me dizzy.

Seconds turned into minutes and still he refused to release. As beads of sweat trickled down from his forehead to mine,

I couldn't stop moaning. He finally crushed his mouth over mine, capturing the sounds as he thrust hard and fast.

When I knew he was close to losing control, I squeezed my muscles, his body spasming almost instantly as he erupted deep inside.

After both of us took gasping breaths, he rolled me over, gently molding me against his side. I was covered in his scent, longing for even more, but all I could think about was how two damaged hearts had managed to find one another.

CHAPTER 21

 *ameson*

The call from Dumas wasn't necessarily what I'd expected but it was a relief to know which player had been determined to destroy Carnal Sins in its entirety as well as me personally. From what little Philip had told me, he'd been required to contact his father for a second time. How the senior Mr. Dumas had known hadn't been disclosed but to find out just how close the French politician was with the responsible party was just as amusing as it was irritating.

Lachlan had no idea what he'd started when he'd picked a fight with a branch of the Florida government. I snickered at the thought that the glass house several of the politicians lived in was cracking day by day. Corruption was everywhere. Maybe Manuel was correct in that I was sitting on a box of dynamite. If I was a better man, I wouldn't consider using what I'd learned over the years.

I was no longer that man, the fresh-faced kid who believed in the betterment of mankind. It was a dog-eat-dog world.

What Philip's father had provided was photographic art that would be used to clear the case against his son.

Maybe the good judge believed that he was above the law. Garber would find out otherwise after my return to the States. For now, it was time to shut down the Parisian accomplice. I was still curious if he'd sent his son in as a distraction as well as to keep an eye on the club. I wouldn't put it past the son of a bitch.

I'd learned a great deal about French politics over the years, each municipality handling their jurisdiction slightly differently. Louis Visage was a minister within the parliament, considered a man who ruled with an iron fist. He held control over Paris and the surrounding areas. What he said mattered. He'd done his buddy, Judge Garber a favor by making two phone calls.

One to have the municipality begin the paperwork to shut down the project and a second to the local police planning on filing extortion charges. It didn't matter if Visage provided evidence or not.

The Frenchman lived in a sinfully large estate, one that took up an entire city block. As soon as Dumas pulled up in front of the sprawling location, I eased from the vehicle, eager to get back to my lovely submissive. Her story had lingered in my mind well into the night, preventing me from getting more than a couple of hours of sleep. I couldn't imagine what she'd gone through, but it explained her initial reckless behavior and the reason she'd moved so far away.

It wasn't just about running but trying to find herself while eliminating guilt. Sighing, I shoved my hands into my pockets and headed toward Dumas. He'd somehow managed to secure a meeting with Visage. I didn't ask how. I didn't care. Whatever influence he'd used was in our favor. I was only here to ensure the Frenchman knew I'd use my weight within the States to bring down his glorified empire if necessary.

Philip had a sly grin on his face as he headed in my direction. "I see you had no trouble finding the location."

"None at all. How could you miss a pink house sitting on the top of a knoll?" I squinted from the sun, glaring at the massive stone gargoyles adorning the front windows. Garish was the word for the style.

"Well, be warned. He's a holier than thou asshole."

"I know the type. Let's get this over with."

As he started to head toward the house, I stopped him, pulling him back. "I am curious what your father has on him."

Philip laughed. "Let's just say Louis enjoys going to Spain for his recreation." He tugged an envelope from his pocket, allowing me to look inside.

My reaction was the same, laughing from the ridiculousness of the costume he wore while being punished by a huge man with a whip in his hand. "Colorful."

"And not something he'd want to get out in the public."

"Why didn't your father supply this before?"

Philip sighed. "You don't understand my dad. He wrote me off years ago."

"Then how did you convince him?"

He grinned. "I returned my share of the winery."

"Interesting."

I trailed behind him as he walked to the door, knocking twice. When the housekeeper opened it, they spoke for a few seconds before she allowed us in.

Mr. Visage was waiting for us outside in the sunroom. He didn't bother looking up from the book he was reading as we walked in.

I leaned against the doorway, keeping my hands in my pockets while Philip moved to the chair across from him, sitting down without being invited. I was beginning to appreciate his way of doing business more than I originally thought. After sliding the envelope in front of the man on the table, he sat back, crossing his legs and sliding one arm over the back of the chair.

Two minutes passed. Then two more.

Neither one of us acted antsy and I was surprised I continued to be amused.

Finally, Louis looked up, barely acknowledging Philip's presence before glancing at the envelope.

He spoke in French, his greeting gruff.

Philip didn't respond for a few seconds then nodded in my direction. "English in honor of my business associate. I'm sure you know Jameson Stark."

Louis tilted his head, studying me with hard, cold eyes. "I've heard of him, yes."

It apparently didn't matter that I was in the room. I finally walked closer, taking the small sofa located off to the side. "We've come to conclude business with you, Mr. Visage. I hope you'll understand that we anticipate the troubles my associate has been forced to endure will end as of today."

Louis laughed, the booming sound of his voice echoing in the room. "Your associate has a long list of grievances against him, Mr. Stark. I'm afraid that I can't be but so helpful in his endeavor to clear his name."

To Philip's credit, he didn't respond as I normally would with anger, choosing to remain where he was, acting as if he had all the time in the day.

"As you might imagine," I continued, "I'm well aware of your friendship with Judge Daniel Garber. I believe not only do you go way back prior to you accepting your position, but you've been friendly enough to go on lengthy vacations together."

My carefully selected words grabbed his attention. He finally allowed his gaze to linger to the photographs neatly tucked away. He leaned forward, placing the book on the table with tender loving care before grabbing the envelope. With great finesse, he opened the flap, pulling out the colorful images. I was glad to see he wasn't immune to embarrassment, his face turning bright red.

When he jerked to his feet, neither Philip nor I were certain what to expect. He simply closed the sunroom door, taking a few seconds before facing us.

"Where did you get these?"

Philip brushed nonexistent lint from his jacket before answering. "I have my sources as you have yours. And so does Mr. Stark. I'm certain we can come to a suitable arrangement that will keep your name out of the papers and your marriage intact."

When Louis stared at him, gawking for a few seconds, Philip continued.

"Although perhaps you'd prefer to have the people you work with and the entirety of France learn about your enjoyment of dressing up as a dog for your male master."

The look of horror was brief but enough to denote he knew we were serious.

"This is blackmail," he sputtered.

"Yes, it is," I answered. "Certainly not meant with malintent." I grinned after issuing the lie. I couldn't care less about the man or what leaking the information would do to his illustrious career or his marriage. I only had one intention in mind.

Clearing Philip's name and our reputation.

His anger had already increased. Now he was shaking as he shoved the photographs into his pocket. Then he pointed his finger in my direction. "You will pay for this."

"I look forward to the honor of you trying, Mr. Visage. However, you should know that I'm privy to incredible volumes of information that I've amassed over the years. I also know enough people on both sides of the pond that you could find yourself in seclusion for the rest of your life."

Philip's smile matched mine. We were both conniving men when we found it necessary.

"Are you prepared to have your men drop the case against me?" Philip asked casually.

Louis sputtered a second time, raking his hand through his thinning white hair. "How do I know that you won't release this once I've complied with your request?"

Philip used that as a cue to rise to his feet, heading in my direction. I was the one who supplied the answer.

"You don't."

As we left, a bitter sound drew our attention the moment I closed the door. Philip grinned a second time, shaking his head.

"You are much different than I believed you'd be the first time I met you," he said.

"How so?"

As we walked toward the vehicles, he seemed to be lost in thought regarding how to answer. "You hide your power behind a kind smile but inside you're a ruthless beast of a man. I would hate to be on the receiving end of your anger."

"I'll take that as a compliment."

"Please do. I don't give them often."

I laughed as I took long strides toward the Maserati.

He opened the door to his SUV, hesitating and leaning over the top of the door. "Is there any chance I would be allowed to spend time with Alexandra?"

I grabbed my sunglasses, shoving them on my face before answering. "None."

"That's what I thought. You Americans are all alike, possessive and not into sharing. You should learn to be more giving like the French."

He had a way with words. "Thanks for the hospitality and the recommendation, but I'll take a hard pass. I take what I want and I keep it. Alexandra belongs to me."

* * *

Alexandra

Back in the United States.

The day of leisure spent in Paris hadn't been enough to satisfy my yearning to learn everything about the beautiful city. What the time spent with Jameson had done was confirm the reason I longed to be with him and had since the moment I'd laid eyes on him.

He'd briefly told me about the solution used to keep Mr. Dumas from seeing the inside of a prison cell. The methods of business used in Miami were cutthroat, but I suspected that was true everywhere. Even my father had crossed the line more than once when dealing with the purchase of cattle.

Did that make it right? Who was I to say one way or the other. I stood in the kitchen of Jameson's house, marveling at the view from the oversized window. Seeing the ocean first thing in the morning was better than any cup of coffee, although the mug of dark brew I had in my hand was my second cup.

I felt at peace since exposing the ugly secret that I hadn't wanted anyone to learn. Jameson's reaction had been so unexpected that even now, I had butterflies in my stomach. How many times had he called me his good little girl? Enough to know I was addicted to the praise. Maybe this was a continuation of a sizzling fantasy, nothing more than a vivid dream, but if so, I never wanted to wake up. I glanced at my phone on the kitchen table, angry with Charlotte.

I was antsy and out of sorts after calling Charlotte several times and always getting her voicemail. If she really was home, why wasn't she picking up the phone? There were still so many questions about her involvement with Diego that had yet to be answered.

And I continued to fear for her safety.

At some point, I needed to return to the condo. However, I'd been forbidden, another rule that had been imposed by the man I had no issue calling my master.

I heard Jameson's deep voice and my heart fluttered. He was on a phone call, one of many since we'd left Paris. He was in control of every aspect of his business from logistics to financials. His power and prowess seemed never ending.

And that made me hunger for him even more.

His footsteps sounded right behind me, his call ending. I remained where I was, able to see a hint of his reflection in the morning light.

There was such an air of authority anytime he walked into the room. As always, my skin tingled, the tiny bars piercing my nipples keeping them pronounced. The way they shifted against the thin shirt I'd worn, the fact I couldn't wear a bra because of the sensitivity was a reminder that he'd claimed me as his. His possession. His submissive.

I turned to face him, exhaling the hot air that had built the moment he'd walked into the room. His expression was one of longing, his eyes dangerously sensual as he perused my entire body. I placed the mug on the table, moving to the other side then dropping to my knees.

He lifted a single eyebrow, remaining where he was as I slowly crawled in his direction. The fact he was already dressed for the business of the day stirred something carnal deep within, filthy thoughts taking over. I lowered my head, remaining on all fours, crawling closer and closer.

When I was finally only a few inches away, I sat back on my legs, my arms out in front of me. He took a deep breath, holding it for a few seconds.

"Utterly perfect," Jameson muttered then rubbed his hand across the top of my head several times. "And such a good girl." He rolled his fingers down the side of my face, sliding a single finger under my chin, lifting my head so I was able to look into his eyes.

I didn't need to be told what to do. As I rubbed my hands on the insides of his trousers, he returned to stroking my head, his action loving and nurturing. I crawled my fingers to his thighs, my mouth watering at the sight of the thick bulge between his legs. The moment I pressed my hand against his cock, he issued a husky growl of appreciation.

"You make me crave doing very bad things to you, my little pet. I can tell you want that."

"Yes, sir."

"Perhaps I'll ink you with my name so no other man will be able to touch you."

There was no doubt my face expressed excitement as I envisioned all the filthy things he'd do to me.

Feasting on my pussy.

Shackling me to his bed.

Punishing me with his belt.

Fucking me in the ass.

The excitement continued to build until I was in a frenzied state, my hunger knowing no bounds.

He fisted my hair, tugging my head until I was forced to look in his eyes as I unbuckled his belt, running my fingers along the smooth grain of thick leather. It was the same belt he'd used to discipline me. Now I was no longer afraid of the pain it caused, the need to obey him growing stronger every day.

As I unfastened his trousers, tugging on the zipper, his eyes became hooded, desire roaring through him. When I freed his cock, running a single fingernail along the thick vein on the side, he muttered something under his breath.

I slipped one hand between his legs, cupping and squeezing his balls. The scent of him was musky, infused with the fragrance of his timber-laced aftershave. I could easily become drunk off the smell alone. He had full control over me, guiding my head to the tip of his cock. I darted my tongue across the sensitive slit, the taste exploding in my mouth.

There was nothing sweeter than the taste of his cum. I wanted my body covered in it, keeping his scent covering my face and every inch of skin the entire day. I slid my tongue down the underside as I wrapped one hand around the base, stroking and twisting my fingers until I created immediate friction.

"Jesus, woman. You make it difficult to leave."

His deep voice penetrated every cell and muscle, leaving me tingling all over. As I pulled one testicle into my mouth, swirling my tongue, he let off a series of animalistic sounds, forcing his pants over his hips so I had full access.

I hungrily sucked, shifting to his other swollen ball, using my jaw muscles to entice him even more. Then I dragged my tongue ever so slowly to the tip, taking his cockhead into my wet mouth.

"Fuck!" His exclamation was followed with a tighter hold on my hair, his fingers digging into my scalp.

I kept my eyes locked on his face, enjoying the way his brow furrowed, his mouth twisting as I provided pleasure. He allowed me to control the moment for a few seconds longer, gently pushing another inch inside my mouth.

"Fucking hot and wet. A new rule. You do this every morning." He grinned salaciously, teasing me but somehow, I knew it would be a new requirement and one I would eagerly enjoy.

I shifted my tongue back and forth, continuing to suck as he jutted his hips forward. There was nothing more delicious than hearing his ragged breathing or the way his muscles tensed.

Only seconds later, he shoved the remainder of his cock inside, the tip hitting the back of my throat. He held me there, the powerful man gasping for air as I gagged slightly. Then my muscles relaxed, accepting the thick girth.

After exhaling, he allowed me to take a deep breath, usurping full control, rocking on the balls of his feet as he fucked my mouth. I continued to swirl my tongue, rewarded with several drops of pre-cum. His actions became rougher, more demanding. He gripped my face with both hands, driving his cock hard and fast, lowering his head so I could see his glassy eyes.

Every sound he made was a dark and husky growl, his entire body shaking as he thrust deep and long. I planted my hands on his thick thighs, squeezing his muscles, my skin on fire and my heart racing. The man could fuck me every hour of the day and it wouldn't be enough.

"Fuck. Yes." He threw his head back, his actions more relentless but I sensed he was ready to explode. I would take every drop, licking him clean. Then I'd beg for more.

Jameson took several scattered breaths, finally lowering his head, dragging his tongue across his lips.

Then his body spasmed, his cum filling my mouth, trickling down the back of my throat. I clung to his legs, sucking, my tongue rolling back and forth.

He let out a deep exhale, finally releasing his hold, stroking the top of my head as he'd done before. "Clean my cock, baby."

I did so eagerly, allowed to grip the base, holding his shaft proud as I dragged the tip of my tongue up and down every inch.

When I was finished, I eased back, peering up at him once again. His eyes remained half closed and when he rolled his fingers down my cheek, my core was ignited. He rubbed the tip across my mouth, shoving his finger inside, forcing me to suck the last drop.

His laugh was subtle, one of satisfaction if not continued need. He stumbled back a couple of feet, taking a few seconds before sliding his trousers over his hips. I could easily tell he hungered for more. He pulled me to my feet, raking a single finger under my chin. "You've already made my morning."

"Then I've done my job."

Laughing, he didn't utter another word but by the look in his eyes, I knew what he was thinking. He rolled his hands over my skirt, sliding the material up my legs, shaking his head slowly as his nostrils flared. He lifted me onto the counter, raking his hands across the stack of mail he'd brought in the night before. As the envelopes and catalogs drifted to the floor, he pushed me back, yanking the skirt up even higher.

I couldn't stop shivering as he shifted his fingers to my thong, gently sliding the lace over my hips, tugging them away from my feet. Then he grasped my legs, bending and pressing my knees against the counter. My head was just over the edge of the other side, preventing me from watching anything he did.

"Now, it's time for breakfast," he half whispered, immediately lowering his head. As he pressed his face into my slickened pussy, I lifted my arms, both doing a creative dance. I kept my toes pointed, staring up at the ceiling as his fingers dug into my skin. There was something so sinful about being wide open for him, losing all control to the man prepared to eat his fill.

He lifted one leg higher, pressing his face into my wet mound. I smacked my hands against the top of the counter, struggling to arch my back. His actions became rough and unyielding, his tongue lashing my clit, his mouth sucking the tender tissue until I was left breathless and unable to think clearly.

As he shoved two fingers inside my pussy, flexing them open, I laughed nervously. The sensations were raw, exposing the desire that never seemed to abate around him.

Within seconds, he brought me close to an orgasm, my mind doing everything I could to shut down the need until I was allowed to come.

Jameson planted my heels on the edge of the counter, sliding his hand under my shirt. The force he used pitched my head further over the other side. I'd never felt such a loss of control, the electricity explosive. Every sound sliding past my lips was guttural, the pleasure so intense a fog developed over my field of vision.

He was fevered in his actions, pulling me to the purest moment of ecstasy.

"Come for me, baby."

A laugh bubbled to the surface as soon as he issued the command. As my muscles clamped around his fingers, pulling him in even deeper, I lost all control. The rush of endorphins was unimaginable, pushing me into pure rapture.

"Yes. Yes…"

He pressed his palms against my inner thighs, keeping me wide open as he licked and sucked, finally shifting his lips from one leg to the other.

I had no idea how long I was in the blissful fog but when he eased my legs from the counter, pulling until my head rested gently on the solid surface, I finally opened my eyes.

He stood over me, his hands on either side. "I have a meeting. We'll get your truck later."

"What about Charlotte?"

"I'll end up talking to Jagger. After this meeting, it will be made clear that she's not going to be made a pawn in whatever game Diego is playing with the judge." He pulled me into a sitting position, remaining between my legs.

"She won't answer my calls."

"That doesn't mean there's an issue. Let me handle it. You need to trust me."

When I hesitated, he gripped my chin.

"You do trust me. Don't you?"

"Of course I do. It's Charlotte I don't trust."

Nodding, he backed away, fastening his belt. "Everything will work out. Relax until I return."

I watched as he left the room and closed my eyes before jumping off the counter, jerking my panties from the floor. There was our fantasy. Then there was an uglier reality. I refused to allow Charlotte to be used.

As I grabbed the phone, hoping to see a text pop up and knowing I'd be sorely disappointed, I thought about the rules Jameson had issued the night before.

You will not leave the house unless I provide permission.

While you can return to work at the club, it will be in the position as my assistant.

You will obey my commands without question, or you will be punished.

There'd been others, all of which didn't seem obtrusive on the surface until today. I couldn't sit around waiting for him to return, hoping he'd had information on Charlotte. I dialed her number again, this time prepared to leave a terse message.

Her cheeky message was quickly followed by a beep. "Charlotte. You will call me. I'm sick to death of the silent treatment. I was trying to protect you whether you like it or not. If you don't call me in ten minutes, I'm coming to find you." I tossed the phone on the counter, struggling into my panties as I waited.

Ten minutes went by in a blip. No return call. No text. Nothing.

That's the moment I knew I would disappoint Jameson again.

I planned on finding her myself, one way or another.

CHAPTER 22

 ameson

Someone I no longer cared to remember had once called me a consummate actor. I'd taken it as a compliment but I doubted the pompous son of a bitch director who'd 'graced' my club with his appearance had offered it up as one. He'd laughed in my face afterwards, calling me a fake in the world of BDSM.

Granted, that had been six months after opening my doors, my mind still trying to wrap around the fact I owned a kink club. I'd never been a prude by any means, even with my typical middle-class upbringing; however, trying to explain to my mother what I did for a living in layman's terms had proven to be a nightmare.

Lachlan had known what amenities should be offered, his experience surpassing both myself and Grant's limited exposure. At first, I'd spent hours on the internet trying to learn the language and aspects of our offerings. Only after a few months had I ventured out to a rival club, taking a few classes and indulging in fantasies I'd tried my best to drive away.

Now I was considered a master dom, a colloquialism in the industry. Did I actually believe I'd mastered any technique? It wasn't possible given I'd enjoyed little since Pamela's departure. As I exited from my vehicle, adjusting my sunglasses given the cloudless day, my thoughts drifted to Alexandra. At this point, what we'd shared couldn't be considered a traditional dom-sub relationship by any means. She was far too fiery to tame her in a week. The fact she remained purposefully disobedient would need to be dealt with, but not until after the ridiculous threats had been removed.

I still wasn't certain what Garber had wanted to accomplish other than ruining me. Both he and Collins were up to something else. I felt it in my bones. As my father had told me more than once, the most effective way of bringing rats to the surface for elimination was to provide them with something they craved.

Or feared.

Perhaps today was a little of both.

I hadn't brought a weapon, although I owned several. I wasn't planning on threatening the judge with bodily harm to himself or his family. I wasn't a member of the cartel or some low-life mafia organization who was allowed to get away with killing indiscriminately. Had I crossed the line a few times of right versus wrong? Yes. Of that there was no doubt, and I would do so again, but there came a point when pushing an agenda for political or financial gain had to be stopped.

That was my intention today.

And if the good judge ignored my... recommendation? Then he would suffer the consequences.

I'd taken it upon myself to become a member of the Keystone Club, a popular watering hole only for the upper echelon of the male population in Miami and Fort Lauderdale. This was the safe zone where they could bring their wives or mistresses on rare occasions without receiving flak from anyone. I'd been here twice up to this point, unimpressed either time. The term stodgy came to mind.

I took long strides in through the club doors, already learning from the judge's secretary that he had lunch plans with a colleague.

The man was easy to find, his booming voice boasting about whatever poor soul who'd landed in his courtroom. Neither man saw my approach, barely acknowledging me until I'd pulled out the third chair, sitting down without being asked.

The judge stopped talking immediately, his face reddening and I hadn't even opened my mouth.

Yet.

I offered a lazy grin as I sat back in the chair, not bothering to acknowledge the other judge, who currently wasn't a member of Carnal Sins.

Judge Garber sucked in his breath and likely his rage, realizing making a scene wasn't in his best interest. "I hope, Mr. Stark, that you have come here to have a discussion about my son."

Maybe I was an evil man, taking my time before answering. "Not at all. That's a police matter now."

"Then why the fuck are you here?"

The other judge was almost instantly uncomfortable. "I thought I'd drop by and mention I had the liberty of seeing a good friend of yours while in Paris handling business. Louis Visage?"

For a man who was forced to mask his feelings on a daily basis, he was doing a piss-poor job of hiding them now. "What. Do. You. Want?"

"It's not what I want any longer, Judge Garber. It's what I am willing to do for you." I placed the envelope full of similar pictures given to Visage in front of him, keeping a grin on my face.

He glanced down twice then scowled as he lifted it into his fingers, keeping the brown envelope close to him. At first, he had no reaction, the photographs of his meeting with Santiago positioned on top. However, the pictures certainly became more risqué the further down he went. By the time he'd reached the fifth very vivid image of his time spent with a young man in Spain, I could tell his blood pressure had gone through the roof.

"This is…" The judge reached for his whiskey, almost knocking the glass over.

"Is something wrong, Dan?" the other judge asked.

"Nothing I can't handle. What do you want?"

I shifted my gaze to the other judge and Daniel huffed.

"Take a hike, Joe. Let me handle this… gentleman on my own." Daniel tossed his napkin onto the table, guzzling down his drink and immediately searching for the waiter.

"You sure?"

"Just go. This fucker I can deal with."

While Dan sounded reassuring, the way his other hand was clutching the envelope meant he knew I was deadly serious.

Joe gave me a nasty look before storming off. Then Dan leaned in. "I don't know what the fuck you think you're doing but you won't get away with it."

"I'm going to make this very easy for you. I'm finished with playing games. I had a nice discussion with Mr. Visage. All accusations leveled against Philip Dumas have been shoved under a fat rock. I am totally aware that both you and Senator Collins are responsible for making several phone calls to the French Parliament and members of law enforcement. Your plans to shut me down have been derailed. Here's what's going to happen. You're going to cease all communications with Santiago. You're going to make certain that Welsh Pharmaceuticals isn't pushed out of business and you're going to help our police chief with criminal investigations against the cartel and the Bratva. Given your influence, that shouldn't be a stretch for you."

"I can't do that. You're out of your mind if you think I can." He huffed and looked away. "They'll kill me."

"That's not my problem. You got into bed with criminal elements. That's entirely on you. Besides, you're more powerful than you give yourself credit for. I'll be happy to give you twenty-four hours to think over my proposal." I rose to my feet without providing the consequences should he not follow through with my request. He snapped his hand around my arm, hissing under his breath.

"What about my son? You can't ruin his entire life."

I gazed down at him, almost feeling pity. Almost. "Maybe it's time you deal with your son's punishment. If you do so, charges will be dropped."

"You'll pay for threatening me."

"I have no problem with watching you try, Judge."

"What if I can't?"

"Then as I said, it's simple. I'll hand over the photographs to a friend of mine at channel nine. Since he has a national syndicate, I'm certain he'll know what to do with the information provided." I yanked my arm away, grinning at him. Then I walked away.

There was no need for violence when valuable information was at my disposal. Perhaps Manuel was indeed correct that given the bank of knowledge I had, I could venture out in ways I hadn't allowed myself to imagine.

As I walked out into the sunshine, my grin widened. Today was going to be a very good day.

I was halfway to my car when my phone rang. "What's up, Jagger?"

"Did you drop Alexandra off to get her truck?"

Exhaling, I stopped before reaching my vehicle. "What did you just say?"

"One of my other men called saying Alexandra rushed into the club. He was coming in to open up and noticed her in the parking lot. Before he had a chance to say anything to her, she sped away in a hurry. Did something happen?"

Fuck me. "Where are you?"

"About to get some groceries. Why?"

"Meet me at her condo. Round up a couple of the other guys." I jumped inside the driver's seat, immediately starting the engine.

"What the fuck do you think happened?"

I twisted my hand around the steering wheel. "I think my sweet Alexandra has gotten herself into a mess."

"What the hell are we going to do?"

"We'll go hunting if necessary."

"About damn time."

After I ended the call, I immediately dialed her number. When it rang several times, I knew there was an issue. As I headed out of the parking lot, I reached into the glovebox. I'd also learned a long time to ago it was best to keep a weapon inside every vehicle.

Just in case.

* * *

Thirty minutes earlier

Alexandra

I almost pounded the elevator doors, they were going so slowly. What the hell was taking so long? I paced back and forth, cursing under my breath. Charlotte was possibly just ignoring me, but if that was the case then I'd smack her across the face. I couldn't believe she wouldn't return my calls.

God. What if something happened to her? I'd never forgive myself for going to Paris. No. It was my life and Jameson had been right. I couldn't force her to do anything she wasn't ready to do. I'd tried that once before. When the elevator beeped, I almost jerked it open with my fingers. I raced out, immediately struggling to find my key, almost tripping since I wasn't paying any attention to where I was going.

Even my hands were shaking when I finally managed to snag it from the bottom of my purse. I rounded the corner, half expecting to see the door busted open. Nothing seemed amiss but I remained rattled as I pushed the key into the lock. When I opened the door, I didn't notice a single sound.

Oh, my God. The place was trashed. My nerves rushed to an edge I'd never been to before, my mind fuzzy about what to do.

"Charlotte?" I closed the door behind me. Her car was parked in the usual spot in the garage, but it was obvious by her bad parking job that Jagger had been right that she'd returned at least once. After tugging the phone from inside, I tossed my purse onto the couch, glancing toward the kitchen. Then I heard something. What was it? Shaking, I took another step toward the bedrooms. This was bad, so very bad. "Charlotte?"

When the yelp turned into a scream, I started to run toward it.

"Run!" Charlotte yelled.

I backed away, bolting for the door when a hand grabbed my wrist, swinging me around. Before I had a chance to scream, a hand was placed over my mouth, the phone knocked from my fingers.

"You're not going anywhere, little dove." The guy was huge, his black eyes piercing mine. As other men walked into the room, Charlotte dragged behind them, I noticed the expression on her face.

One of utter terror.

I struggled in the asshole's hold, managing to kick him in the shins.

"You're a feisty little kitten. Aren't you?"

The son of a bitch had no idea. I twisted, almost able to get out of his hold.

"It looks like we have two of them to play with, boss," the guy holding me quipped, laughing in a deep, husky tone.

As another man walked closer, I recognized him almost instantly. Unfortunately, he also recognized me.

"Well. Well. We have two very valuable packages," he growled. "This must be our lucky day. Get them out of here."

Jameson

Jagger had managed to pull Danner and Gary, all three men well trained in both martial arts and weaponry. All four of us were armed, uncertain what we'd face. As soon as the elevator doors in the condo where the women lived opened, I took a deep breath, pulling the weapon into my hand. The hallway was quiet, devoid of any activity.

The others followed behind me, remaining quiet as I headed for the condo. When I rounded the corner of the corridor, it was obvious there was an issue. The door remained ajar. I took long strides, clutching the weapon with both hands then kicking open the steel surface.

"Jesus. Fucking. Christ," Jagger said from behind me.

The place had been torn apart, but I sensed the person responsible had no intentions of stealing anything. It was all about making a point.

We fanned out and immediately I noticed Alexandra's phone on the floor, her purse on the couch. I searched the living room then checked the kitchen.

Danner returned from the bedrooms less than a minute later. "No sign of them but there's blood on a dresser."

Rage kicked to the surface, the anger getting ready to tip me over the edge. I'd been a good guy for long enough. That would end today. If any harm had come to either woman, the son of a bitch responsible would face the kind of wrath where he'd beg for his life.

"What now? We call the police?" Jagger asked as he flanked my side.

"No. They'll be dead before the police get their ass in gear. Now comes the hunting part."

"You think you know who did this?"

"Not yet." I moved through the condo to the bedrooms, glancing in one then the other. I doubted Diego would have his men destroy his own property. That wasn't like the man at all.

As I returned, I studied the room then exhaled. "We're going to find Diego Santiago."

There was no time to waste. I bolted from the condo, determined to track Santiago down. I knew where he lived.

Where he partied. Where he fucked. And every business he owned.

I would find him one way or another.

However, I had a feeling my initial thought that Diego was responsible was wrong. There was a game being played and I hadn't been invited. However, if I was right then the responsible party knew how important Alexandra had become to me.

My beautiful submissive had fallen into a trap of her own making.

And because of her relationship with me. "We leave now."

We took two vehicles, heading toward Santiago's estate.

When I pulled up at the gate, iron railings surrounding the entire property, I rolled down my window and grinned for the camera as I pressed the button announcing our arrival.

It took almost a full minute before a voice came on the speaker. "Yes?"

"I'm here to see Diego."

"You are?"

"Jameson Stark. I'm not leaving without speaking with him. I have something of interest for him."

There was no indication that my demand had been accepted or even taken to Diego, who was obviously there.

"What if he doesn't bite?" Jagger asked from beside me. He glanced at the soldiers walking the roof of Diego's estate.

"He'll want to see me."

"You're awful confident."

I slowly turned my head. "That's what it takes to play with the likes of Diego. He'll be curious of my intentions."

"What do you have?"

"The ability to keep his ass out of prison."

"Now, you have me curious."

"Don't forget. Curiosity killed the cat."

He snorted. "We're out playing cops and robbers and you use that line?"

Two minutes passed. Then three. While I wanted to slam my car into the gates, I knew within a few seconds, twenty or so men would surround both vehicles, all pointing weapons in our faces. I couldn't risk lives.

When the gate started to move, he chortled. "You have more power in this town than people give you credit for."

"Perhaps that's the problem."

"Maybe it's time for you to be Mr. Badass."

"Maybe I already am."

He laughed as I headed down the long driveway, parking in front of the house. As expected, two armed guards were waiting.

When we exited the vehicles, one of the gruff-looking men came closer. "Leave your weapons here."

I turned toward Danner and Gary, both men as on edge as I was. This was a dangerous game, but Santiago wouldn't assassinate any of us at this point. He knew better than to chum the waters with blood. I put my weapon on the dashboard, giving the soldier a hard glare.

He frisked me, moving to Jagger as another man headed toward Danner and Gary.

"Fuck this shit," Jagger said under his breath.

"Let it go," I told him.

As we were led inside, I marveled at the beauty of Diego's home, although everything inside had been purchased with illegal drug and arms deal money.

The room where we were taken was obviously Diego's office. When I entered, he immediately stood, noticing the three men behind me.

"If I didn't know better, Jameson, I'd say you've turned to the dark side."

"If I didn't know better, Diego, I'd say you had a soul, but that's simply not the case."

His look of amusement faded. "You come to my home demanding to see me then insult me. I don't mind telling you that I've killed men for less."

"You're not going to do that because you want to know what I have."

He walked from around his desk, studying me intently. "Yes, I am curious."

"Answer me one question. Did you abduct Charlotte and Alexandra?"

His laugh wasn't one of admission or guilt, merely surprise. "Contrary to what you've heard, Charlotte is special to me. Why would you accuse me of something so egregious?"

"Because the condominium that you paid for is trashed and two women are missing, one obviously hurt."

I'd made it my business over the years to know by expressions and flinches if someone was guilty or lying. In this case, the anger on Diego's face was similar to mine.

And very real.

He threw his head back and roared, his second in command racing into the room.

"What the fuck, boss?"

"Time for a killing spree, Benny. Have our soldiers on standby."

Benny shifted his attention in our direction. "I'll handle those bastards myself." His statement indicated the four of us.

"Not Mr. Stark and his friends. Grigori Aleksei," Santiago advised. "Today they aren't our enemies."

"The fucking Russian?"

"He has Charlotte and her cousin. We *will* get them back." Diego walked closer, staring me in the eyes. "I promise you I will get your woman back. You will need to trust me, Stark. Is that possible for you to do?"

"More than the cops."

He seemed pleased with my answer, giving me a respectful nod. "Benny. Have two dozen soldiers poised at the marina. Grigori has a shipment expected to arrive in one hour. If there are any issues, I want them ready to strike."

Benny snickered. "Yes, sir."

Santiago wasn't a stupid man. I had to respect that, but I had just as much at stake as he did. "I'm going with you."

"Like fucking hell you are," Jagger snarled. "You're not some trained fucking soldier. I am. I'll go."

"No," I snapped. "The three of you leave. This is my fight, not yours."

"That's not gonna happen, boss," Gary said as he moved closer, glaring at Diego.

Danner did the same, flanking my other side. "I'm not leaving you to fight this alone."

Diego clapped his hands. "You have loyal men who work for you, Stark. Perhaps we can work together in the future, but you have no clue what to expect."

I crowded his space. "I don't know if you really give a shit about Charlotte, but she seems to think she's in love with you. I do love Alexandra and there isn't a goddamn thing on this earth that will keep me from saving her. So fuck you if you think otherwise. We are running out of time. The fucking scum will take out his anger on those two women and you know it."

Diego took a deep breath then glanced around me at my men. "You are right. We could use the muscle. But we do things my way."

I hesitated before answering. "Agreed."

I would do anything at this point to protect the woman I'd fallen in love with.

Even if that meant having blood on my hands.

CHAPTER 23

 *ameson*

The Bratva worked differently than the cartel. That much I already knew. Diego handled most of his business inside his home where he felt the most protected.

Grigori and his merry men worked out of a warehouse, using the front offices for their work. The Pakhan's home was considered sacred, only his closest people allowed behind his hallowed doors.

Diego had brought over thirty of his soldiers with him, prepared for a war if necessary. The women were being used as a bargaining chip for a war that I wanted no part of. Now I had no choice in the matter if I wanted to save Alexandra and Charlotte.

We were met by two of Grigori's men at the warehouse door, their cold expressions not giving away anything other than disdain.

"We're here to see Grigori," I told them. When they acted like they didn't understand, I half laughed. *"My uvidim tvoyego bossa ili moi druz'ya vsadyat tebe pulyu v cherep. Tebe reshat'."*

We will see your boss or my friends will put a bullet in your skulls. It's up to you.

The element of surprise was always helpful. One of the men glanced all the way down to my shoes, snorting then turning to his friend. I'd taken it upon myself to learn both Spanish and Russian, figuring both would come in handy one day.

"The infamous Mr. Stark. We shall see if the Pakhan will honor your request." He disappeared behind the door, the other man staying.

Diego turned his head toward me, lifting a single eyebrow. "It would seem I've underestimated you."

"That happens a lot." My weapon remained in my pocket, the itch in my fingers something I hadn't experienced before.

"Be careful with the Pakhan. He will test you," Santiago advised.

I glanced in his direction, chuckling under my breath. "Then he will undoubtedly underestimate me as well."

"I might be able to tolerate your presence, Stark."

As the Russian returned, he studied the army of men behind us before ushering us inside. There was no talk of removing our weapons, no discussion on protocol. There was an understanding that this was sacred ground.

For now.

The Pakhan sat in a chair that likely dated back to the nineteen seventies. However, he seemed comfortable behind the desk, making the drab room his palace. He drummed his fingers on the metal desk, his gaze falling from one of Santiago's four men allowed inside to the three I'd brought with me. Then to Santiago and finally leveling his angry gaze at me.

"What do I owe this unexpected pleasure to?" Grigori asked.

"I think we can cut to the chase," Santiago told him. "You have something that belongs to me."

Grigori scrubbed his jaw, acting as if he had no clue what the cartel leader was talking about. Then light penetrated his dark eyes. "Ah, yes. The lovely woman you've taken to over the past few months. What is her name? Char, I believe. She's delightful."

When Santiago bristled, I placed my hand on his forearm.

Santiago took a deep breath, cracking his neck. "We're not here to play games. I have no issue hijacking your shipment if necessary."

Grigori didn't flinch, only his eyes registering the information.

"No, we aren't. In addition, you also have something that belongs to me. We can do a fair trade," I stated without any inflection in my voice.

I sensed Santiago was curious what the hell I was getting at.

"What could you possibly have to offer me?" Grigori snorted. "A club membership? I get my kinks easily and without paying for them, club owner."

"You get your kinks from selling young women on the open market, Russian," I retorted back. I sensed the tension was increasing.

Grigori laughed. "You do keep up with what's happening in our beloved community."

"Yes, and I have valuable information locked away corroborating my statement. That goes for Santiago's illegal arms trades and pretty much every corrupt decision made by some of our sanctimonious state leaders."

The flash of anger in Grigori's eyes was paralleled by Santiago's heavy breathing.

"You've come to make threats?" the Pakhan threw out.

"As I said, I've come to make a deal. The women for your freedom."

Grigori glanced at Santiago, narrowing his eyes. Perhaps I'd stymied both men.

"I don't accept deals from someone who can't provide me with opportunities."

Without hesitation, I pulled out my weapon, pointing it at Grigori's head. Everyone in the room whipped out their guns, ready to start a bloodbath. I was well aware of the risk I was taking but at the end of the day, the two rulers in the room were still businessmen with families. Today wasn't a good day to die.

The quiet in the room was intense, pulses increasing. But I felt nothing inside, allowing my rage to fuel my actions in an entirely different way. I cocked my head, smiling at Grigori as he stood.

Then he slowly walked around the desk toward me, one of his men close behind. When the Pakhan was standing at the barrel end of my gun, he studied me for a full minute, searching my eyes while watching my body language. I'd played this game many times before, only without the weapon involved.

After another full minute, Grigori laughed then waved his soldiers down, requiring them to lower their weapons. "I will admit, Mr. Stark. I didn't expect a man of your... stature and good nature to remain completely calm in the face of a crisis. You have balls, which is rare, and something I can respect. Bring the women into the office."

His burly soldier looked at him strangely, huffing when he headed to another room following his Pakhan's orders.

"What do you offer my colleague and me?" he continued.

"I'm curious about that myself, Jameson," Santiago added.

I lowered my weapon, barely taking a breath then turning so both men could see me. "I took the liberty of putting together the information I have on both of you. As of this minute, it is poised to not only be handed over to someone in law enforcement I trust, but also to the press. I assure you I have colorful art to go along with substantial and proven allegations."

"What do you want in return?" Grigori asked. "The women only?"

"Yes, but also your cooperation that both of you will steer clear of the pharmaceutical business. I'm certain you're aware that because of mafia-related involvement, normal people are becoming addicted to painkillers, destroying their families. Children are dying. I doubt you want that on your conscience."

Santiago burst into laughter. "I should have you along for every negotiation."

Grigori shared in his amusement. "He is rather formidable. Isn't he?" He walked even closer and I refused to move a muscle. "I admire your tactic, Mr. Stark, so much so that I will consider your offer. However," he pressed as he lifted his hand, showing me his index finger, "you do not want to make an enemy out of either myself or my associate here."

The thought of the two of them working together under any circumstances was amusing if nothing else. They'd be at each other's throats again soon enough.

"I have no issue staying in my lane if you will in yours."

Grigori seemed to like my answer. "Very well. Will you agree to these terms, Santiago?"

Santiago locked eyes with mine. "It would seem neither one of us have a choice. But if you betray either one of us, there won't be a location on this earth where you can hide."

"I'm an honorable man, Santiago. That's something you should have learned by now." I wasn't certain how my reflection would affect me after today, but I would never regret my decision to risk my life in order to save the woman I loved.

The sound of the door drew his attention.

"They have not been harmed other than when one tried to escape. I apologize for marking her, Santiago. The woman you are infatuated with is fierce. So is yours, Mr. Stark. You should both consider yourselves lucky men."

When Santiago got a look at Char's bruised face, I was certain no one would leave the room alive. He cursed in Spanish, shoving Grigori across the room.

"Stop!" I shouted, waving my weapon from one side of the room to the other. Then I saw Alexandra's terrified face and almost lost it myself. "We have come to an agreement. Period."

"He's right," Grigori spit out. "Stand down, Santiago. I will promise you she will never be touched by one of my men again. You have my word."

The tension was even higher, the testosterone level as well. When it seemed the agreement would stand, I lowered my weapon then headed toward the two women, who were still being held by guards. "Let them go."

The soldiers didn't react.

"Delay, kak on govorit!" Grigori snapped.

Do as he says.

Char was released, immediately running toward Santiago. I was surprised at the change in the man's expression. He did care for her.

When the other soldier hesitated, I lifted my weapon again. The look in Alexandra's eyes shifted from terror to anger. Then her personality took hold, blowing her rational mind out of the water. She stomped on the soldier's foot.

The trained killer reacted as would anyone indoctrinated into the criminal world. He grabbed her around the throat, jerking her off her feet and placing the barrel of the weapon at her temple.

I'd critique my reaction later, but I lunged toward the man, the surprise of my reaction able to knock him to the floor, Alexandra pitched to the side. We rolled twice, fighting to keep our respective weapons from being able to get off a killing shot.

After cracking my weapon against the side of his head, I managed to scramble away, pushing Alexandra behind me, my gun still pointed at his head.

He roared as he jumped to his feet and it was obvious he was prepared to take a shot.

Pop!

The sound reverberated in the small space, both women screaming. As the soldier dropped to his knees, the single gunshot catching him between the eyes, I turned my head toward Grigori, who'd fired the killing shot.

Our eyes connected and he gave me another nod of respect. "No man inside my organization ignores my rules and lives. Take the women. The deal is made. I will trust you are an honorable man, Mr. Stark."

I grabbed Alexandra, pressing her head against my chest. "I assure you I will honor the deal made." I glanced at Jagger, who stared at me in amazement, my eyes directing him to lower his weapon.

"Charlotte is coming with us," Alexandra said defiantly.

I shifted my gaze toward Santiago, who was cradling Charlotte in his arms.

"Go, Char. I'll come for you later," Santiago told her, lifting her chin with a single finger. The two of them were obviously close and there was no mistaking the love in Santiago's eyes.

As I led Alexandra out of the office and the building, I realized how close I was to losing her. The thought left me angry and bitter inside. I'd lost sight of what was important to me.

That would never happen again.

Once outside and close to our vehicles, I cupped both sides of her face. "I almost lost you."

"I knew you'd come for me," she whispered, rising onto her tiptoes and pressing her lips against mine.

When I wrapped my arms around her, Jagger muttered under his breath.

"Get a room."

The kiss was tender, my tongue sweeping her mouth and my pulse racing. She was the most important thing in my life.

No one would be allowed to fuck with us again.

* * *

Alexandra

"You love him, don't you?" Charlotte asked as she moved beside me on the deck.

"Yes." We'd been home for over twelve hours, yet it felt like just minutes before I'd been held captive.

"He's good to you."

Exhaling, I studied the way the ocean water lapped against the shore, the anguish of being captured slowly fading. "He's amazing, so protective."

"That's what I have with Diego."

Her voice was hushed but there was such certainty in her words, full of emotion.

"I want you happy, Charlotte, but I can't say I approve of your choices."

"I know," she half whispered. "I didn't expect to fall in love with him."

"Were you running drugs?"

Her hesitation was an answer and one I hated. "For two months. Then he asked me to work his casinos. No, I didn't have to fuck anyone. I was just there, making certain there were no cheaters. I really was treated well and the money was fantastic. Then things got a little rough and Diego didn't like it. We started talking and one thing led to another and I was in his bed. He hadn't touched me until then even though I'd lived in his house after he'd saved me from the streets. I understand that he's a bad man, but he's good to me. That's all that matters."

I shifted toward her, brushing hair from her face. "I'm not condemning you, cuz. I've made horrible choices in my life, especially with someone I thought was a decent man. I will worry, but you know what you're doing."

"And I love you for that."

We hugged and the emotion running through both of us could be defeating, but we were strong women, both going through so much. "I love you too."

When I eased back, she wrinkled her nose. "So you... submit to Jameson?"

"I do."

"And you like it?"

I had to laugh. "When I came here, I had no intentions of becoming involved with anyone, but the way he touches me,

348

kisses me and his praise are things that I can't get enough of."

"Maybe I'll need to introduce Diego to the dom/sub lifestyle."

We both laughed. Whether she knew it or not, she was already living a different version of the same.

Suddenly, Jameson appeared in the doorway, a strange look on his face. "You have a visitor, Char."

"It's Charlotte. That's my given name," she told him.

He smiled. "Charlotte it is. Do you want to see Diego?"

Her eyes lit up and the moment was both sweet as well as gut wrenching. She gave me another look, asking for my approval. How could I not? The heart was unpredictable, refusing to obey rules. "Be careful, cuz. And you tell him that if he ever hurts you, I will hunt him down."

"I think he already knows that," she said, rushing by Jameson.

There were so many warnings I wanted to issue, advice that she would never accept, but I couldn't control her life. Only mine. I shifted my attention to the man standing with a twinkle in his eye. "I didn't know you were a superhero."

Jameson laughed and came closer. When he brushed the backs of his fingers across my cheek, I shuddered all the way to my core. "I did what was necessary to protect the woman I care about so much."

"You did, huh?" I grabbed his shirt with both hands, clutching onto him as if he'd disappear. I'd gone through so many emotions that I was drained as well as relieved. It was as if the last twenty-four hours were nothing more than a nightmare, one that I'd awakened from. He'd held me overnight, molding my body against his. I'd gathered strength from his hold, able to allow the horrible images to drift away, if only for a little while.

He lowered his head until our lips were touching. "I love you, even if you're reckless and determined to get your own way. I'll break that soon enough."

"You just think you will." I dragged my tongue across his lips, the taste of him sweet as ever.

"Oh, I will. Trust me."

"I trust you more than anyone in my life." I craned my neck, pressing my body against his. Everything about him was powerful and demanding, yet I felt safe and protected.

As he captured my lips, the swell of emotion coursing through me threatened to bring tears, but I refused to allow that to happen. He'd saved me. He'd saved my cousin. And I loved him with all my heart. The taste of him was incredible, scintillating every cell in my body, my heart thudding against my chest. How could one man cause so many sensations all at one time?

When he pulled away, he lifted a single eyebrow. "You disobeyed me. You constantly place yourself in danger."

"I couldn't allow Charlotte to be hurt."

"And what happened?"

"I know," I half whispered. "I deserve punishment."

He rolled his hands down my arms. "Yes, you do. Soon." As he allowed his gaze fall to my breasts, a wave of vibrations tore through me, the ache in my nipples slowly starting to subside. His smile was a promise of things to come.

"You're so mean."

His laugh was far too enticing. "Yes, I am. But fair."

"That remains to be seen." I nuzzled closer, my thoughts drifting from Charlotte to a few past memories. It was time to put them aside. Somehow, I knew my brother was smiling. He'd been the first real protector in my life, someone I could count on.

Now I had the man who I hoped would be my entire future.

My friend.

My boss.

My lover.

My master.

CHAPTER 24

ameson

Jagger didn't just enter my office, he swaggered in, the usual grin on his face. When he didn't say anything right away, I glared at him. "What?"

"What do you mean, what? You know what."

"No, I don't think I do."

He rolled his eyes. "I didn't know you had it in you."

"What exactly are we talking about?"

His snort almost made me laugh. "Taking on two crime syndicates singlehandedly. I didn't know you were capable of such violence, but I was damn glad you were there."

I allowed myself to laugh. "Part of the job."

"Right. Well, I'll tell you this. If you ever want to switch positions, I think I can get you a mercenary job with a couple buddies of mine from the Marines."

"Uh. No, thank you. I have other interests."

"The feisty woman who captured your heart?"

"Maybe."

"It's good to see you smile, buddy. Just don't let all this lovey-dovey stuff keep you from business. We have two bachelorette parties coming in later this week."

"Don't remind me. That's your baby, my friend."

"Oh, now you throw the ladies in my direction."

"Somehow, I don't think you mind."

He took a deep breath, rubbing his jaw. "Nope. You're right. Does that mean you're taking time off?"

"Soon. Very soon." I thought about the letter from Pamela's attorney still buried inside my desk. Avoiding it wasn't going to make dealing with her thoughts or wishes any easier. I suspected it was an apology for the manner she'd chosen to break my heart.

Jagger nodded. "What do you want me to do with the information you gave me to send to the press?"

I'd already contacted the judge, backing down on my threats. For now. As long as he walked the straight and narrow, his secret was safe with me. "Place it in the safe." Only my partners and Jagger had the code to the safe or knew what I kept inside. I had second copies of information and evidence I'd gleaned over the years at my house as well.

He looked at me for a few seconds then nodded. "Keep your friends close but your enemies closer?"

"Exactly." While the alliance I'd made with both the Bratva and the cartel left a bad taste in my mouth, I had a feeling their assistance might prove helpful in the future.

As with all things, time would tell.

"What about the kid?" he asked.

All I could do was smile. "It would seem the judge has taken his son's punishment on with a vengeance. He's no longer a member of the club, his trust fund on hold, and he'll be doing grunt work for a construction company for a few months. Talk about community service."

"It'll be good for the brat."

"Amen, brother."

Before he had a chance to leave, both Grant and Lachlan stepped through my door. "A full house today, I see," I said as I grinned at my friends.

Jagger winked at me before leaving.

"An unexpected surprise," I told my college buddies.

"We thought we'd take the opportunity to meet the woman that turned you into a badass," Lachlan said as he headed to the bar.

Grant shook his head. "This girl must be pretty damn special. I didn't know you had it in you, buddy."

I'd relayed the events briefly to them over the phone, amused at their surprise the country boy football star had it in him. "Maybe there's a lot you don't know about me."

"Maybe so," Grant said before turning his attention toward Lachlan. "Do you remember the first time we met this guy?"

I eased onto the edge of my desk, amused at both, curious as to what they did remember. Both arrived in fifty-thousand-dollar sports cars. I'd been lucky my beat-up old Chevy had made it to Pennsylvania at all.

"It was outside Gregor Hall. Jameson pulled up in some old Ford with a busted muffler," Lachlan mused then handed us both a hefty tumbler of scotch before retrieving his.

"That's right," Grant said as he nodded. "He had no clue where he was going and I had to give him directions. We became his heroes that day."

I lifted my eyebrows, trying to keep quiet. Heroes, my ass.

Lachlan took a sip of his drink then swirled the liquid in his glass. "He begged us to become his friends shortly there-after. Then he threatened us that if we didn't help him pledge the fraternity, he'd hunt us down with his big rifle."

"I guess we were smart in taking him seriously, huh?" Grant teased.

All I could do was shake my head. "The two of you acted like I was some freaking redneck from a Podunk town. First of all, it was my beloved Chevy. You didn't talk to me for thirty days, which was fine since you still had the silver spoons in your mouths. Only when you were failing your classes did you come to me for help."

The truth was somewhere in the middle, although even after all these years, as I looked back it was hard to believe the three of us had become friends.

"Then you needed relationship advice since I had all the hot women," I couldn't help adding.

"Oh!" both chimed in.

We laughed for a few seconds then Lachlan looked away. "You took a risk, buddy."

The very words I'd said to Alexandra. "Sometimes the risks are worth the rewards."

Grant caught the meaning first. "She's the one?"

"The beautiful but bratty Alexandra is absolutely the one."

Lachlan lifted his glass first. "'May you both be blessed with the strength of heaven, the light of the sun and the radiance of the moon, the splendor of fire, the speed of lightning, the swiftness of wind, the depth of the sea, the stability of earth, and the firmness of rock.'"

I turned my eyes, studying his expression. "That's beautiful."

"An old Scottish toast," he offered, taking a sip. "Usually for weddings." His eyes twinkled, his usual bad boy attitude returning.

"Hold on. Are you getting married?" Grant chortled.

The question was one I'd thought about more than once. "Maybe. We'll see. I just met the girl."

"Trust me, lad. That's all it takes." Lachlan lifted his glass again. "To the woman who managed to capture Jameson's heart."

"It's funny how your accent is heavier when you're taunting someone," I threw out.

I'd spent far too much time living in the darkness, remaining in an ugly limbo that I couldn't dig my way out of. Alexandra had brought the light that had guided the way back.

There was nothing I'd enjoy more than spending the rest of my life with her.

But that couldn't happen until I'd finally shut the door to the past.

* * *

Alexandra

I'd always heard that life could change on a dime. I'd learned in my short duration on Earth just how true that was. Tragedy could destroy everything in seconds, the insufferable damage lingering for years to come. I hadn't realized how deep the quicksand I'd allowed myself to succumb to had been until I'd met Jameson.

He was my rock, someone I could count on to keep me on the straight and narrow while reminding me to enjoy every moment possible. He didn't just do so in words, but also in actions and his expressions. With a single look, I could melt into a puddle or know that I'd done something wrong. Yet at the same moment, he'd shower me with compliments, making me feel like the most beautiful woman in the world.

Even the way he was looking at me now was a mixture of domination and raunchy hunger, the combination irresistible.

I knew exactly what he was waiting for: my acknowledgement as well as my request for discipline. Admitting I needed guidance and correction for my bad behavior would never be easy for me. However, I was at the point I just wanted to get it over with.

As I walked closer, he lifted his eyebrows. "How is my gorgeous pet doing?"

"Fantastic. I have a lead on a position at a local elementary school." The ocean breeze drifting in through the open doors was invigorating. I loved being in his house. In the five days since the attack at the condo, he'd helped me move my things into his house. There'd been no question as to whether I would, the understanding from the day he'd saved my life.

Now I couldn't imagine being anywhere else.

"You were keeping things from me," he said in his gravelly voice, the one that encouraged the fire to grow, the wetness to increase between my legs.

"I just wanted it to be a surprise."

Jameson grinned. "And it is. I'm very proud of you. However, I'm curious. You don't enjoy working at the club?"

"Don't you have a strict rule about no fraternization among employees?" The fact he was proud of me meant a great deal. I'd wanted nothing more than to have the opportunity to work with children, nurturing them into becoming good humans. Plus, I loved their laughter and their bright eyes. Maybe one day I'd be lucky enough to have a family of my own.

"I do but I'm the boss."

"Oh, no. You must set the standard."

He laughed and moved closer, his presence as overwhelming and intoxicating as it always was. "Perhaps you are trainable."

"Only under your… tutelage," I teased and rolled the tips of my fingers down his cock.

"I can tell my precious submissive is hungry. Aren't you forgetting something?"

"No, I don't think so."

He gave me a stern look and I wrinkled my nose.

"Okay, fine. I've been a very bad girl. May I please have a spanking?"

"Are you certain that's what you need?" he asked, his voice sending another wave of heat through every cell.

I started to be sarcastic then thought about the question. The strange truth was that his firm hand was exactly what I needed. It brought peace and relieved tension. "Yes, I am."

"Then remove your clothes and bend over my desk."

Every time he spoke about discipline, his tone dipped into the delicious darkness that I adored. "Yes, sir."

I backed into his office, brushing my hand along the edge of his giant desk. The ornate wood and carved legs reminded me of him. Sophisticated yet tough. I removed my dress, folding it neatly, not nearly as self-conscious about removing my panties as I'd been before. When I leaned across the desk, I still had a magnificent view of the ocean to help calm my nerves.

I doubted I'd get over being antsy and nervous any time soon. Maybe that was the entire point. In order to become his good little girl, I would need the heightened anticipation.

As I expected, he kept me waiting, allowing me to wrestle with demons inside, questioning why I'd gone off half-cocked in heading to the condo. I'd been lucky.

When Jameson finally entered the room, he remained quiet, walking behind me. I sensed he was selecting an implement. I'd learned that he kept several in one of his drawers. I could only imagine what today's choice would be.

My nerves continued to increase, and an insane urge to laugh bubbled to the surface. I'd actually started requesting to be spanked like a bad girl. Never in my wildest dreams would I have anticipated doing something so... crazy.

When I heard a drawer close and his footsteps, every muscle tensed. Now I felt exactly like that bad girl longing for forgiveness.

He was completely silent, which made tiny goosebumps pop all over my skin. Yet as he caressed my back, taking his time sliding the pads of his fingers down my spine, nervousness turned into swooning.

"Do you realize what could have happened when you disobeyed me the other day?"

"Yes, sir."

He tapped my bottom, hearing the slight hint of rebelliousness. It was ingrained in my system. "I can see we have a long way to go before you understand the word 'consequences' but I'll make certain to remind you from time to time. Hands over your head, gripping the edge of the desk."

I obeyed him without hesitation, closing my eyes and taking a deep breath. When the first strike came, the dull echo surprised me, the pain immediately more than I'd experienced before. Yelping, I pushed up from the desk, immediately realizing I'd broken the rules.

Jameson said nothing, merely pushing his hand against the small of my back, rubbing his thumb up and down until I settled against the cool wood. Then he started again.

But by the third or fourth brutal smack, I realized he had a thick piece of wood in his hand. Wait a minute. I was being spanked by a paddle? The thought was both scintillating and slightly offensive. Didn't they used to use paddles in school in ancient times?

"That's it. As I said, you can be a good girl when you want to be."

I cringed inside while my pussy reacted to every strike of the thick wood, clenching far too many times. If I wasn't careful, I'd orgasm right here and now. The thought was as embarrassing as it was the first time but was becoming the norm. Maybe it was all about the man providing the discipline.

When he issued four in rapid succession, my mind drifted into a fabulous place of peace. Although the anguish was insufferable, I knew it would be over soon enough. He continued the round of discipline for at least another ten or twelve smacks, enough I'd lost count, my bottom on fire.

Strangely enough, I wasn't even aware he'd finished until he'd gathered me into his arms, cupping my breasts tenderly. As he nuzzled into my neck, the endorphins kicked in and I was swaying on my feet, so wet I was terrified I'd stained the surface of his desk.

"Perhaps later we can talk," he murmured.

"Mmmm… always."

"You did very well. I'm proud of you."

His praise almost made me giggle. My emotions were still all over the place. "Thank you, sir."

"Why don't you get dressed and we can talk a walk on the beach." He turned me around and brushed hair from my shoulders.

"Is something wrong?"

"Nothing is wrong, baby. When I'm around you, nothing could be. I'll grab us a couple glasses of wine. Meet me on the beach when you're ready."

When he moved away, giving me privacy, I was certain he was going to break off the relationship. A dull ache already formed in my heart, so much so it was difficult to catch my breath. I hadn't considered that what we'd shared, the trouble he'd been forced to go to because of my reckless behavior would finally be too much to handle.

As I slipped into my dress, the material scratching my bruised bottom almost immediately, I was shocked that he'd end our... fling now. No, I couldn't call it a fling. Or should I? I hated second guessing myself, but at this point, I couldn't handle a breakup. If that's what he'd call it.

After easing my panties over my hips, I fluffed my hair with my fingers, determined to keep from becoming emotional. There was no reason to. I was a big girl and could handle anything. Well, almost.

I moved to the deck, shielding my eyes from the late afternoon sun with my hand as I searched for him. He was standing inches away from the water, which was the first time I'd seen him bother to step foot on the sand. Something was definitely wrong. I moved down the stairs, tossing my sandals on the steps before heading toward him.

When I moved beside him, he didn't acknowledge my presence at first. "Jameson?"

It took a full five seconds before he realized I was there, trying to shake off his odd behavior with a smile. "I'm sorry. Here's your wine. Let's walk."

"Why don't you just tell me what's going on. I mean if you're going to break up with me, go ahead and rip that bandage off. I can take it. Well, I'm not certain I can take it. I'll probably shatter into a dozen pieces, but that won't be in front of you. Nosiree." I was doing it again, so nervous I was prattling on.

He cocked his head. Whereas I expected amusement or even a stern look, his expression was so serious that I was even more terrified. "Baby. Did anyone ever tell you that patience isn't your virtue?"

The wind continuously whipped hair in my face and I was ready to yank it out at the scalp. "More than once. Just tell me what's wrong. Please?"

"Do you like it here?"

"Here? You mean the beach? Your house?"

"That and in Miami. Or would you prefer to return home?"

I hadn't anticipated the question. He deserved a decent, well thought out answer. "If you'd asked me this just after meeting you, I would have said I was a fool for moving here. But now, I can't imagine being anywhere else. I want to make this my home." I placed my hand on his chest, taking a few shallow breaths. If I was going to make a fool of myself, I might as well go full force. "You're my home. I know we haven't known each other for very long. I'm infuriating to you at times, but I think you understand that I haven't been grounded in a long time."

Jameson seemed pleased with my answer, rubbing his fingers across my shoulder. "I do realize that and I'm glad you consider me a part of the home you desire to be in."

"Where is this going?"

He finally chuckled, although the sound was full of an emotion that I couldn't read. "We'll continue to work on patience. I didn't tell you that Pamela's attorney sent me a letter a couple weeks ago."

"What did it say?"

"I didn't open it until this morning. I was hoping to put an end to a chapter of my life before continuing another and one that quickly became so important to me."

My stomach was instantly in knots.

"I'm glad you did. It's none of business what it said. If you need time alone, I'll understand. I'll get another place to live."

He wrapped his hand around the back of my neck, holding me exactly where I was. "I don't want you going anywhere, but it's your choice to make."

I wasn't certain where he was going with this at all. After kissing my forehead, he backed away, reaching into his pocket. When he handed me an envelope, my entire body began to shake.

"You have your entire life ahead of you. I want you happy and comfortable with every decision you make. I refuse to hold you back, Alexandra. Not now. Not ever."

I took a few seconds doing nothing but gazing into his eyes. Whatever was inside the letter could hold a valid reason I'd want to leave him. The thought terrified me. I struggled to pull the envelope into my hand, taking a sip of wine before opening it. I was aware he was watching me intently. Then he turned back toward the water, one hand in his pocket, the grip of the other around the crystal firm.

As I read the first few lines, I wasn't certain why he was concerned. Then I flipped to the second page and my heart stopped.

When I'd lost my brother, that's when I'd realized how precious life truly was. It was a gift and one that shouldn't be taken lightly. People came into your life often by happenstance, creating a life-altering event. That's the way I looked at this moment and the man standing a few feet away.

If my car hadn't totaled and a big he-man hadn't opted to save the day, this moment wouldn't have occurred. I was lightheaded, uncertain about our future with a single exception. I'd meant what I said now more than ever. He was my home, my family.

And our future would be as bright as we made it.

Together.

As I rushed toward him, he seemed surprised when I rose onto my tiptoes, wrapping my arm around his neck and whispering in his ear, "I love you."

* * *

Two weeks later

Jameson

I love you.

Alexandra had whispered those words several times over the last two weeks, but the moment on the beach was one I'd always remember. It had meant a change, an acceptance and hope for a future I never believed possible.

I kept my hand on her leg as I drove. We both remained quiet. She'd gotten the job at an elementary school closest to the house, which would work out beautifully. At least she wouldn't be starting for another three weeks, which would allow for some additional time.

She'd been a godsend, helping me accept the required changes, making the house more of a home for all of us. I had no idea what I was doing, but I suspected with her help, we'd muddle through just fine.

As I slowed down, she shifted closer, fighting the seatbelt to do so. I pulled down the driveway of the small but pristine house, trying not to become emotional. I'd been angry, furious with Pamela for days, my rage almost getting out of control, but the beautiful woman by my side had insisted on being right there. And somehow, she'd calmed the beast.

I stopped the car, cutting the engine, staring out the windshield.

"Are you okay with this?" I asked.

"You've asked that ten times. Maybe twenty." She laughed softly when I gave her a harsh glare.

"Spanking later."

"Somehow, I think you'll have your hands full."

"Somehow, I think you're right." I ran a powerful business, more so than I'd realized until recently. I had more money than I could spend in a lifetime, investments that would continue to build my wealth. I had big boy toys and could go out to dinner every night if I wanted to.

And I had the perfect woman.

Everything was going to change. Everything.

In truth, I couldn't have been more excited.

I eased out of the car, taking a deep breath of the humid air. She waited a few seconds then joined me, her smile refreshing. She was completely calm while I was crawling out of my skin.

"It's time," she encouraged, gently pushing me.

"Aren't you coming?"

"I'm right here. This is something you need to do first."

"You're right."

"I'm always right."

Cocking my head, I gave her another authoritative look and she blushed. Then I started walking toward the door.

"Wait. You forgot something."

I heard activity and remained where I was until she rushed to my side.

"Take this," she told me. "Trust me."

"Baby, I do with my life." I waited until she backed away then walked up the stairs, ringing the doorbell.

As soon as the door was opened, the woman smiled. "Mr. Stark? I'm Beverly Jones. We spoke on the phone."

"Yes. I hope I'm not too early."

"Right on time. Just give me a second. Why don't you wait right here?" She backed away and I heard muttered voices later.

Finally, she returned with a suitcase in one hand and the fingers of her other wrapped around a little boy's.

He was staring at me intently with his eyes open wide. I hunkered down, shifting the new stuffed bear from one hand to the other.

The woman also dropped to his level, giving me an encouraging nod. "Jacob. This is the man I was telling you about. This is your daddy. He's going to take you on a wonderful adventure and you'll live in a brand new home."

When he didn't react, my heart was crushed, but I couldn't blame the little boy. He was a little over four years old and had recently had his entire world ripped apart. Then he'd been told a big, gruff man was his father. I couldn't imagine what the little man was thinking. Why Pamela hadn't told me was somewhat of a mystery, although the letter she'd obviously prepared at least a year before in the event of her death had attempted to explain. Only she hadn't known her words would ever be read.

She'd hated my lifestyle, but more important, her parents had forbidden her to see me again, threatening to have her child taken if she ever told me.

"Do you remember, honey?" Beverly pushed.

Finally, Jacob nodded yet remained where he was.

"This is for you, little man. You have an entire room full of toys." This wasn't going so well. He continued to stare at me. "Do you like the ocean? I live on the water."

He nodded, allowing his gaze to fall to the bear. Then he tentatively reached out, taking it from my hand and cradling it against his chest.

"It's okay, Jacob," Beverly said softly. "He's really your daddy."

He turned his little head toward her then looked at me again. And in a flash, he flew into my arms, wrapping one of his around my neck, still clutching the bear. As I rose to a standing position, I was rewarded with a giggle.

"You're big."

I laughed, smiling at Beverly. "Why, yes, I am. I have a feeling you're going to be huge."

"Really?"

"Yes, sir. How about we go home? Would you like that?"

"Do I get my own room?"

"You certainly do. Now, I want you to meet someone very special."

"O-tay!"

As I walked out into the sunshine, not a cloud in the blue sky, I realized that I was a very lucky man. The love of my life beamed, walking toward us slowly, tears in her eyes. There would be difficulties and tragedies, concerns and fights, but we'd handle everything that came our way.

As a family.

The End

AFTERWORD

Stormy Night Publications would like to thank you for your interest in our books.

If you liked this book (or even if you didn't), we would really appreciate you leaving a review on the site where you purchased it. Reviews provide useful feedback for us and our authors, and this feedback (both positive comments and constructive criticism) allows us to work even harder to make sure we provide the content our customers want to read.

If you would like to check out more books from Stormy Night Publications, if you want to learn more about our company, or if you would like to join our mailing list, please visit our website at:

http://www.stormynightpublications.com

BOOKS OF THE RUTHLESS EMPIRE SERIES

The Don

Maxwell Powers swept into my life after my father was gunned down, but the moment those piercing blue eyes caught mine I knew he would be doing more than just avenging his old friend.

I haven't seen him since I was a little girl, but that won't keep him from bending me over and belting my bare backside… or from making me scream his name as he claims my virgin body.

He's twice my age, and he's my godfather.

But I know I'll be soaking wet and ready for him tonight…

The Consigliere

As consigliere of New York's most ruthless crime syndicate, Daniel Briggs rules with an iron fist. But here in Los Angeles, he's just my big brother's best friend, forbidden in every way.

This stunningly handsome billionaire may be the most eligible bachelor on the West Coast, but to him I'm still just a little girl in need of protection from men who would ravage her brutally.

Men like him.

But he'll soon realize I'm all grown up, and then it won't be long before my teenage crush finally shows me the side of him he's kept hidden from me—the savage side that will blister my bare ass for talking back and then take what has always been his with my hair gripped in his fist.

I don't know what comes after that. I just know everything he does to me will be utterly sinful…

BOOKS OF THE TAINTED REGIME SERIES

Cruelest Vow

D'Artagnan Conti was born into poverty, raised to be a soldier in my father's savage regime. I grew up in luxury, longing to escape my family's cruel machinations, and the young man with sapphire eyes and the voice of an angel became not just my forbidden crush but my everything.

Then he was taken from me, killed in a brutal attack by our enemies. Or so I was led to believe…

For twenty years I did my best to forget him, until a devilishly handsome stranger awakened my desire in a way that I hadn't thought possible, baring my body and soul and setting them both ablaze with passion so intense it burns hotter than the lash of leather across my naked backside.

Every taste of his lips, every whisper in my ear, and every quivering climax pulled me deeper into this dark, twisted rapture, and only when I was already under his spell did I learn the truth.

The man I thought I'd lost is the one who has made me his.

BOOKS OF THE CARNAL SINS SERIES

Required Surrender

My first mistake was agreeing to participate in a charity auction. My second was believing I could walk away from the commanding billionaire with a brogue accent and dazzling green eyes.

It was supposed to be one date, but a man like Lachlan McKenzie plays by his own set of rules.

As the owner of Carnal Sins, DC's exclusive kink club, his reputation is as dark and demanding as his desires, and before I knew it I ended up his to enjoy not for just one night but a full week.

I fought his control, but I knew I wouldn't win… and in my heart I don't think I even wanted to. Not after he called me his good girl, stripped me bare and spanked me with his belt, and then made me blush and beg and come so hard I forgot all about being his only for a few more days.

That didn't matter anyway. We both know he's keeping me forever.

planned to end this arranged marriage before it even began.

But it wasn't Diego waiting for me at the altar.

By all appearances the man who laid claim to me was the mafia heir to whom I'd been promised, but I sensed an entirely different personality, one so electrifying I was swept up by his passion.

A part of me still wanted to escape, but then he took me in his arms and over his knee, laying my deepest, darkest needs bare and then fulfilling them in the most shameful ways imaginable.

Now I'm not just his bride. I'm his completely.

King of Depravity

When Brogan Callahan swept me off my feet, I didn't know he was heir to a powerful Irish mafia family. I didn't find that out until after he'd taken me in his arms... and over his knee.

By the time I learned the truth, I was already his.

I went on the run to escape my father's plans to marry me off, but it turns out the ruthless mob boss he had in mind is the same sinfully sexy bastard who just stripped me bare and claimed me savagely.

He demands my absolute obedience, and yet with each brutal kiss and stinging lash of his belt I feel myself falling ever deeper into the dark abyss of shameful need he's created within me.

At first I wondered if there were bounds to his depravity. Now I hope there aren't...

King of Savagery

I knew Maxim Nikitin was a man to be reckoned with when I went undercover to help the FBI bring him down, but nothing could have prepared me for his raw power... or his icy blue eyes.

He caught me, and now he's determined not just to punish me, but to tame me completely.

Every kiss is brutal, every touch possessive, every fiery lash of his belt more intense than the last, yet with every cry of pain and every scream of climax the truth becomes more obvious.

He doesn't need to break me. I belong to him already.

King of Malice

When I met Phoenix Diamonds, I didn't know anything about him except that he had a body carved from stone and a voice that left me hoping he'd order me to strip just so I could obey.

By the time I learned he's the head of a Greek crime syndicate intent on making me pay for the sins of my father, he'd already mastered me with his touch alone, belted my bare ass for daring to come without permission, and ravaged me thoroughly both that night and the next morning.

All I can do is try to pretend he isn't everything I've always fantasized about...

But I think he knows already.

In my late-night hunt for the perfect pastry, I never expected to be the victim of a brutal attack... or for a brooding, blue-eyed stranger to become my savior, tending to my wounds while easing my fears. The electricity exploded between us, turning into a night of incredible passion.

Only later did I learn that Valentin Vincheti is the heir to the New York Italian mafia empire.

Then he came to take me, and this time he wasn't gentle. I shouldn't have surrendered, but with each savage kiss and stinging stroke of his belt his beautiful seduction became more difficult to resist. But when one of his enemies sets his sights on me, will my secrets put our lives at risk?

Beautiful Obsession

After I was left at the altar, I turned what was meant to be the reception into an epic party. But when a handsome stranger asked me to dance, I wasn't prepared for the passion he ignited.

He told me he was a very bad man, but that only made my heart race faster as I lay bare and bound, my dress discarded and my bottom sore from a spanking, waiting for him to ravage me.

It was supposed to be just one night. No strings. Nothing to entangle me in his dangerous world.

But that was before I became his beautiful obsession...

Beautiful Devil

Kostya Baranov is an infamous assassin, a man capable of incredible savagery, but when I witnessed a mafia hit he didn't silence me with a bullet. He decided to make me his instead.

Taken prisoner and forced to obey or feel the sting of his belt, shameful lust for my captor soon wars with fury at what he has done to me... and what he keeps doing to me with every touch.

But though he may be a beautiful devil, it is my own family's secret which may damn us both.

BOOKS OF THE BENEDETTI EMPIRE SERIES

Cruel Prince

Catherine's father conspired to have my father killed, and that debt to the Benedetti family must be settled. Just as he took something from me, I will take something from him.

His daughter.

She will be mine to punish and ravage, but when she suffers it will not be for his sins.

It will be for my pleasure.

She will beg, but it will be for me to claim her in the most shameful ways imaginable.

She will scream, but it will be because she doesn't think she can bear another climax.

But when she surrenders at last, it will not be to her captor.

It will be to her husband.

Ruthless Prince

Alexandra is a senator's daughter, used to mingling in the company of the rich and powerful, but tonight she will learn that there are men who play by different rules.

Men like me.

I could romance her. I could seduce her and then carry her gently to my bed.

But that can wait. Tonight I'm going to wring one ruthless climax after another from her quivering body with her bottom burning from my belt and her throat sore from screaming.

She will know she is mine before she even knows she is my bride.

Savage Prince

Gillian's father may be a powerful Irish mob boss, but he owes a blood debt to my family, and when I came to collect I didn't ask permission before taking his daughter as payment.

It was not up to him... or to her.

I will make her my bride, but I am not the kind of man who will wait until our wedding night to bare her and claim what belongs to me. She will walk down the aisle wet, well-used, and sore.

Her dress will hide the marks from my belt that taught her the consequences of disobeying her husband, but nothing will hide her blushes as her arousal drips down her thighs with each step.

By the time she says her vows she will already be mine.

BOOKS OF THE MERCILESS KINGS
SERIES

King's Captive

Emily Porter saw me kill a man who betrayed my family and she
helped put me behind bars. But someone with my connections
doesn't stay in prison long, and she is about to learn the hard way
that there is a price to pay for crossing the boss of the King
dynasty. A very, very painful price...

She's going to cry for me as I blister that beautiful bottom, then
she's going to scream for me as I ravage her over and over again,
taking her in the most shameful ways she can imagine. But leaving
her well-punished and well-used is just the beginning of what I
have in store for Emily.

I'm going to make her my bride, and then I'm going to make her
mine completely.

King's Hostage

When my life was threatened, Michael King didn't just take
matters into his own hands.

He took me.

When he carried me off it was partly to protect me, but mostly it
was because he wanted me.

I didn't choose to go with him, but it wasn't up to me. That's why
I'm naked, wet, and sore in an opulent Swiss chalet with my
bottom still burning from the belt of the infuriatingly sexy mafia
boss who brought me here, punished me when I fought him, and
then savagely made me his.

We'll return when things are safe in New Orleans, but I won't be
going back to my old home.

I belong to him now, and he plans to keep me.

King's Possession

Her father had to be taught what happens when you cross a King, but that isn't why Genevieve Rossi is sore, well-used, and waiting for me to claim her in the only way I haven't already.

She's sore because she thought she could embarrass me in public without being punished.

She's well-used because after I spanked her I wanted more, and I take what I want.

She's waiting for me in my bed because she's my bride, and tonight is our wedding night.

I'm not going to be gentle with her, but when she wakes up tomorrow morning wet and blushing her cheeks won't be crimson because of the shameful things I did to her naked, quivering body.

It will be because she begged for all of them.

King's Toy

Vincenzo King thought I knew something about a man who betrayed him, but that isn't why I'm on my way to New Orleans well-used and sore with my backside still burning from his belt.

When he bared and punished me maybe it was just business, but what came after was not.

It was savage, it was shameful, and it was very, very personal.

I'm his toy now, and not the kind you keep in its box on the shelf.

He's going to play rough with me.

He's going to get me all wet and dirty.

Then he's going to do it all again tomorrow.

King's Demands

Julieta Morales hoped to escape an unwanted marriage, but the moment she got into my car her fate was sealed. She will have a husband, but it won't be the cartel boss her father chose for her.

It will be me.

But I'm not the kind of man who takes his bride gently amid rose petals on her wedding night. She'll learn to satisfy her King's demands with her bottom burning and her hair held in my fist.

She'll promise obedience when she speaks her vows, but she'll be mastered long before then.

King's Temptation

I didn't think I needed Dimitri Kristoff's protection, but it wasn't up to me. With a kingpin from a rival family coming after me, he took charge, took off his belt, and then took what he wanted.

He knows I'm not used to doing as I'm told. He just doesn't care.

The stripes seared across my bare bottom left me sore and sorry, but it was what came after that truly left me shaken. The princess of the King family shouldn't be on her knees for anyone, let alone this Bratva brute who has decided to claim for himself what he was meant to safeguard.

Nobody gave me to him, but I'm his anyway.

Now he's going to make sure I know it.

BOOKS OF THE MAFIA MASTERS SERIES

His as Payment

Caroline Hargrove thinks she is mine because her father owed me a debt, but that isn't why she is sitting in my car beside me with her bottom sore inside and out. She's wet, well-used, and coming with me whether she likes it or not because I decided I want her, and I take what I want.

As a senator's daughter, she probably thought no man would dare lay a hand on her, let alone spank her thoroughly and then claim her beautiful body in the most shameful ways possible.

She was wrong. Very, very wrong. She's going to be mastered, and I won't be gentle about it.

Taken as Collateral

Francesca Alessandro was just meant to be collateral, held captive as a warning to her father, but then she tried to fight me. She ended up sore and soaked as I taught her a lesson with my belt and then screaming with every savage climax as I taught her to obey in a much more shameful way.

She's mine now. Mine to keep. Mine to protect. Mine to use as hard and as often as I please.

Forced to Cooperate

Willow Church is not the first person who tried to put a bullet in me. She's just the first I let live. Now she will pay the price in the most shameful way imaginable. The stripes from my belt will teach her to obey, but what happens to her sore, red bottom after that will teach the real lesson.

She will be used mercilessly, over and over, and every brutal climax will remind her of the humiliating truth: she never even had a chance against me. Her body always knew its master.

Claimed as Revenge

Valencia Rivera became mine the moment her father broke the agreement he made with me. She thought she had a say in the matter, but my belt across her beautiful bottom taught her otherwise and a night spent screaming her surrender into the sheets left her in no doubt she belongs to me.

Using her hard and often will not be all it takes to tame her properly, but it will be a good start…

Made to Beg

Sierra Fox showed up at my door to ask for my protection, and I gave it to her… for a price. She belongs to me now, and I'm going to use her beautiful body as thoroughly as I please. The only thing for her to decide is how sore her cute little bottom will be when I'm through claiming her.

She came to me begging for help, but as her moans and screams grow louder with every brutal climax, we both know it won't be long before she begs me for something far more shameful.

I was warned about Frederick Duvall. I was told he was dangerous. But I never suspected that meeting the billionaire advertising mogul to discuss a business proposition would end with me bent over a table with my dress up and my panties down for a shameful lesson in obedience.

That should have been it. I should have told him what he could do with his offer and his money.

But I didn't.

I could say it was because two million dollars is a lot of cash, but as I stand before him naked, bound, and awaiting the sting of his cane for daring to displease him, I know that's not the truth.

I'm not here because he pays me. I'm here because he owns me.

BOOKS OF THE CLUB DARKNESS SERIES

Bent to His Will

Even the most powerful men in the world know better than to cross me, but Autumn Sutherland thought she could spy on me in my own club and get away with it. Now she must be punished.

She tried to expose me, so she will be exposed. Bare, bound, and helplessly on display, she'll beg for mercy as my strap lashes her quivering bottom and my crop leaves its burning welts on her most intimate spots. Then she'll scream my name as she takes every inch of me, long and hard.

When I am done with her, she won't just be sore and shamefully broken. She will be mine.

Broken by His Hand

Sophia Russo tried to keep away from me, but just thinking about what I would do to her left her panties drenched. She tried to hide it, but I didn't let her. I tore those soaked panties off, spanked her bare little bottom until she had no doubt who owns her, and then took her long and hard.

She begged and screamed as she came for me over and over, but she didn't learn her lesson…

She didn't just come back for more. She thought she could disobey me and get away with it.

This time I'm not just going to punish her. I'm going to break her.

Bound by His Command

Willow danced for the rich and powerful at the world's most exclusive club… until tonight.

Tonight I told her she belongs to me now, and no other man will touch her again.

Tonight I ripped her soaked panties from her beautiful body and taught her to obey with my belt.

Tonight I took her as mine, and I won't be giving her up.

MORE MAFIA AND BILLIONAIRE ROMANCES BY PIPER STONE

Caught

If you're forced to come to an arrangement with someone as dangerous as Jagger Calduchi, it means he's about to take what he wants, and you'll give it to him... even if it's your body.

I got caught snooping where I didn't belong, and Jagger made me an offer I couldn't refuse. A week with him where his rules are the only rules, or his bought and paid for cops take me to jail.

He's going to punish me, train me, and master me completely. When he's used me so shamefully I blush just to think about it, maybe he'll let me go home... or maybe he'll decide to keep me.

Ruthless

Treating a mobster shot by a rival's goons isn't really my forte, but when a man is powerful enough to have a whole wing of a hospital cleared out for his protection, you do as you're told.

To make matters worse, this isn't first time I've met Giovanni Calduchi. It turns out my newest patient is the stern, sexy brute who all but dragged me back to his hotel room a couple of nights ago so he could use my body as he pleased, then showed up at my house the next day, stripped me bare, and spanked me until I was begging him to take me even more roughly and shamefully.

Now, with his enemies likely to be coming after me in order to get to him, all I can do is hope he's as good at keeping me safe as he is at keeping me blushing, sore, and thoroughly satisfied.

Dangerous

I knew Erik Chenault was dangerous the moment I saw him. Everything about him should have warned me away, from the scar on his face to the fact that mobsters call him Blade. But I was drawn like a moth to a flame, and I ended up burnt... and blushing, sore, and thoroughly used.

Now he's taken it upon himself to protect me from men like the ones we both tried to leave in our past. He's going to make me his whether I like it or not... but I think I'm going to like it.

Prey

Within moments of setting eyes on Sophia Waters, I was certain of two things. She was going to learn what happens to bad girls who cheat at cards, and I was going to be the one to teach her.

But there was one thing I didn't know as I reddened that cute little bottom and then took her long and hard and oh so shamefully: I wasn't the only one who didn't come here for a game of cards.

I came to kill a man. It turns out she came to protect him.

Nobody keeps me from my target, but I'm in no rush. Not when I'm enjoying this game of cat and mouse so much. I'll even let her catch me one day, and as she screams my name with each brutal climax she'll finally realize the truth. She was never the hunter. She was always the prey.

Given

Stephanie Michaelson was given to me, and she is mine. The sooner she learns that, the less often her cute little bottom will end up well-punished and sore as she is reminded of her place.

But even as she promises obedience with tears running down her cheeks, I know it isn't the sting of my belt that will truly tame her. It is what comes next that will leave her in no doubt she belongs to me. That part will be long, hard, and shameful... and I will make her beg for all of it.

Dangerous Stranger

I came to Spain hoping to start a new life away from dangerous men, but then I met Rafael Santiago. Now I'm not just caught up in the affairs of a mafia boss, I'm being forced into his car.

When I saw something I shouldn't have, Rafael took me captive, stripped me bare, and punished me until he felt certain I'd told him everything I knew about his organization... which was nothing at all. Then he offered me his protection in return for the right to use me as he pleases.

Now that I belong to him, his plans for me are more shameful than I could have ever imagined.

Indebted

After her father stole from me, I could have left Alessandra Toro in jail for a crime she didn't commit. But I have plans for her. A deal with the judge—the kind only a man like me can arrange—made her my captive, and she will pay her father's debt with her beautiful body.

She will try to run, of course, but it won't be the law that comes after her. It will be me.

The sting of my belt across her quivering bare bottom will teach Alessandra the price of defiance, but it is the far more shameful penance that follows which will truly tame her.

Taken

When Winter O'Brien was given to me, she thought she had a say in the matter. She was wrong.

She is my bride. Mine to claim, mine to punish, and mine to use as shamefully as I please. The sting of my belt on her bare bottom will teach her to obey, but obedience is just the beginning.

I will demand so much more.

Bratva's Captive

I told Chloe Kingstrom that getting close to me would be dangerous, and she should keep her distance. The moment she disobeyed and followed me into that bar, she became mine.

Now my enemies are after her, but it's not what they would do to her she should worry about.

It's what I'm going to do to her.

My belt across her bare backside will teach her obedience, but what comes after will be different.

She's going to blush, beg, and scream with every climax as she's ravaged more thoroughly than she can imagine. Then I'm going to flip her over and claim her in an even more shameful way.

If she's a good girl, I might even let her enjoy it.

Hunted

Hope Gracen was just another target to be tracked down… until I caught her.

When I discovered I'd been lied to, I carried her off.

She'll tell me the truth with her bottom still burning from my belt, but that isn't why she's here.

I took her to protect her. I'm keeping her because she's mine.

Theirs as Payment

Until mere moments ago, I was a doctor heading home after my shift at the hospital. But that was before I was forced into the back seat of an SUV, then bared and spanked for trying to escape.

Now I'm just leverage for the Cabello brothers to use against my father, but it isn't the thought of being held hostage by these brutes that has my heart racing and my whole body quivering.

It is the way they're looking at me…

Like they're about to tear my clothes off and take turns mounting me like wild beasts.

Like they're going to share me, using me in ways more shameful than I can even imagine.

Like they own me.

Ruthless Acquisition

I knew the shameful stakes when I bet against these bastards. I just didn't expect to lose.

Now they've come to collect their winnings.

But they aren't just planning to take a belt to my bare bottom for trying to run and then claim everything they're owed from my naked, helpless body as I blush, beg, and scream for them.

They've acquired me, and they plan to keep me.

Bound by Contract

I knew I was in trouble the moment Gregory Steele called me into his office, but I wasn't expecting to end up stripped bare and bent over his desk for a painful lesson from his belt.

Taking a little bit of money here and there might have gone unnoticed in another organization, but stealing from one of the most powerful mafia bosses on the West Coast has consequences.

It doesn't matter why I did it. The only thing that matters now is what he's going to do to me.

I have no doubt he will use me shamefully, but he didn't make me sign that contract just to show me off with my cheeks blushing and my bottom sore under the scandalous outfit he chose for me.

Now that I'm his, he plans to keep me.

Dangerous Addiction

I went looking for a man working with my enemies. When I found only her instead, I should have just left her alone… or maybe taken what I wanted from her and then left… but I didn't.

I couldn't.

So I carried her off to keep for myself.

She didn't make it easy for me, and that earned her a lesson in obedience. A shameful one.

But as her bare bottom reddens under my punishing hand I can see her arousal dripping down her quivering thighs, and no matter how much she squirms and sobs and begs we both know exactly what she needs, and we both know as soon as this spanking is over I'm going to give it to her.

Hard.

Auction House

When I went undercover to investigate a series of murders with links to Steele Franklin's auction house operation, I expected to be sold for the humiliating use of one of his fellow billionaires.

But he wanted me for himself.

No contract. No agreed upon terms. No say in the matter at all except whether to surrender to his shameful demands without a fight or make him strip me bare and spank me into submission first.

I chose the second option, but as one devastating climax after another is forced from my naked, quivering body, what scares me isn't the thought of him keeping me locked up in a cage forever.

It's knowing he won't need to.

Interrogated

As Liam McGinty's belt lashes my bare backside, it isn't the burning sting or the humiliating awareness that my body's surrender is on full display for this ruthless mobster that shocks me.

It's the fact that this isn't a scene from one of my books.

I almost can't process the fact that I'm really riding in the back of a luxury SUV belonging to the most powerful Irish mafia boss in New York—the man I've written so much about—with my cheeks blushing, my bottom sore inside and out, and my arousal soaking the seat beneath me.

But whether I can process it or not, I'm his captive now.

Maybe he'll let me go when he's gotten the answers he needs and he's used me as he pleases.

Or maybe he'll keep me…

Vow of Seduction

Alexander Durante, Brogan Lancaster, and Daniel Norwood are powerful, dangerous men, but that won't keep them safe from me. Not after they let my brother take the fall for their crimes.

I spent years preparing for my chance at revenge. But things didn't go as planned…

Now I'm naked, bound, and helpless, waiting to be used and punished as these brutes see fit, and yet what's on my mind isn't how to escape all of the shameful things they're going to do to me.

It's whether I even want to…

Brutal Heir

When I went to an author convention, I didn't expect to find myself enjoying a rooftop meal with the sexiest cover model in the business, let alone screaming his name in bed later that night.

I didn't plan to be targeted by assassins, rushed to a helicopter under cover of armed men, and then spirited away to his home country with my bottom still burning from a spanking either, but it turns out there are some really important things I didn't know about Diavolo Montoya…

Like the fact that he's the heir to a notorious crime syndicate.

I should hate him, but even as his prisoner our connection is too intense to ignore, and I'm beginning to realize that what began as a moment of passion is going to end with me as his.

Forever.

Bed of Thorns

Hardened by years spent in prison for a crime he didn't commit, Edmond Montego is no longer the gentle man I remember. When he came for me, he didn't just take me for the very first time.

He claimed my virgin body with a savagery that left me screaming... and he made me beg for it.

I should have run when I had the chance, but with every lash of his belt, every passionate kiss, and every brutal climax, I fell more and more under his spell.

But he has a dark secret, and if we're not careful, we'll lose everything... including our lives.

Morally Gray

Saxon Thornburg is known to the world as a reputable businessman, but I knew his true nature even before he kidnapped me, bared, bound, and punished me, and then shamefully ravaged me.

He is not just the billionaire boss of a powerful crime family. He is the Patriarch.

Women drop to their knees on command for him, but he chose me because I didn't surrender.

Until he took off his belt...

BOOKS OF THE MISSOULA BAD BOYS SERIES

Phoenix

As a single dad, a battle-scarred Marine, and a smokejumper, my life was complicated enough. Then Wren Tillman showed up in town, full of sass and all but begging for my belt, and what began as a passionate night after I rescued her from a snowstorm quickly became much more.

Her father plans to marry her off for his own gain, but I've claimed her, and I plan to keep her.

She can fight it if she wants, but in her heart she knows she's already mine.

Snake

I left Missoula to serve my country and came back a bitter, broken man. But when Chastity Garrington made my recovery her personal crusade, I decided I had a mission of my own.

Mastering her.

Her task won't be easy, and the fire in her eyes tells me mine won't either. Yet the spark between us is instant, and we both know she'll be wet, sore, and screaming my name soon enough.

But I want more than that.

By the time my body has healed, I plan to have claimed her heart.

Maverick

When I found her trapped in a ravine, I thought Lily Sanborn was just another lost tourist. Then she tried to steal my truck, and I realized she was on the run... and in need of a dose of my belt.

Holed up in my cabin with her bottom burning and a snowstorm raging outside, there's no denying the spark between us, and we both know she'll soon be screaming my name as I take her in the most shameful of ways.

But when her past catches up to her, the men who come after her will learn a hard lesson.

She's mine now, and I protect what's mine.

backside, then she'll scream my name as she takes every single inch of me.

This naughty girl needs to be put in her place, and I'm going to enjoy every moment of it.

Mustang

I tried to tell him how to run his ranch. Then he took off his belt.

When I heard a rumor about his ranch, I confronted Mustang about it. I thought I could go toe to toe with the big, tough former Marine, but I ended up blushing, sore, and very thoroughly used.

I told her it was going to hurt. I meant it.

Danni Brexton is a hot little number with a sharp tongue and a chip on her shoulder. She's the kind of trouble that needs to be ridden hard and put away wet, but only after a taste of my belt.

It will take more than just a firm hand and a burning bottom to tame this sassy spitfire, but I plan to keep her safe, sound, and screaming my name in bed whether she likes it or not. By the time I'm through with her, there won't be a shadow of a doubt in her mind that she belongs to me.

Nash

When he caught me on his property, he didn't call the police. He just took off his belt.

Nash caught me breaking into his shed while on the run from the mob, and when he demanded answers and obedience I gave him neither. Then he took off his belt and taught me in the most shameful way possible what happens to naughty girls who play games with a big, rough Marine.

She's mine to protect. That doesn't mean I'm going to be gentle with her.

Michelle doesn't just need a place to hide out. She needs a man who will bare her bottom and spank her until she is sore and sobbing whenever she puts herself at risk with reckless defiance, then shove her face into the sheets and make her scream his name with every savage climax.

She'll get all of that from me, and much, much more.

Austin

I offered this brute a ride. I ended up the one being ridden.

The first time I saw Austin, he was hitchhiking. I stopped to give him a lift, but I didn't end up taking this big, rough former Marine wherever he was heading. He was far too busy taking me.

She thought she was in charge. Then I took off my belt.

When Francesca Montgomery pulled up beside me, I didn't know who she was, but I knew what she needed and I gave it to her. Long, hard, and thoroughly, until she was screaming my name as she climaxed over and over with her quivering bare bottom still sporting the marks from my belt.

But someone wants to hurt her, and when someone tries to hurt what's mine, I take it personally.

BOOKS OF THE EAGLE FORCE SERIES

Debt of Honor

Isabella Adams is a brilliant scientist, but her latest discovery has made her a target of Russian assassins. I've been assigned to protect her, and when her reckless behavior puts her in danger she'll learn in the most shameful of ways what it means to be under the command of a Marine.

She can beg and plead as my belt lashes her bare backside, but the only mercy she'll receive is the chance to scream as she climaxes over and over with her well-spanked bottom still burning.

As my past returns to haunt me, it'll take every skill I've mastered to keep her alive.

She may be a national treasure, but she belongs to me now.

Debt of Loyalty

After she was kidnapped in broad daylight, I was hired to bring Willow Cavanaugh home, but as the daughter of a wealthy family she's used to getting what she wants rather than taking orders.

Too bad.

She'll do as she's told or she'll earn herself a stern, shameful reminder of who is in charge, but it will take more than just a well-spanked bare bottom to truly tame this feisty little rich girl.

She'll learn her place over my knee, but it's in my bed that I'll make her mine.

Debt of Sacrifice

When she witnessed a murder, it put Greer McDuff on a brutal cartel's radar... and on mine.

As a former Navy SEAL now serving with the elite Eagle Force, my assignment is to protect her by any means necessary. If that requires a stern reminder of who is in charge with her bottom bare over my knee and then an even more shameful lesson in my bed, then that's what she'll get.

There's just one problem.

The only place I know I can keep her safe is the ranch I left behind and vowed never to return.

BOOKS OF THE ALPHA DYNASTY SERIES

Unchained Beast

As the firstborn of the Dupree family, I have spent my life building the wealth and power of our mafia empire while keeping our dark secret hidden and my savage hunger at bay. But the beast within me cannot be chained forever, and I must claim a mate before I lose control completely...

That is why Coraline LeBlanc is mine.

When I mount and ravage her, it won't be because I want her. It will be because I need her.

But that doesn't mean I won't enjoy stripping her bare and spanking her until she surrenders, then making her beg and scream with every desperate climax as I take what belongs to me.

The beast will claim her, but I will keep her.

Savage Brute

It wasn't his mafia birthright that made Dax Dupree a monster. Years behind bars and a brutal war with a rival organization made him hard as steel, but the beast he can barely control was always there, and without a mate to mark and claim it would soon take hold of him completely.

I didn't know that when he showed up at my bar after closing and spanked me until I was wet and shamefully ready for him to mount and ravage me, or even when I woke the next morning with my throat sore from screaming and his seed still drying on my thighs. But I know it now.

Because I'm his mate.

Ruthless Monster

When Esme Rawlings looks at me, she sees many things. A ruthless mob boss. A key witness to the latest murder in an ongoing turf war. A guardian angel who saved her from a hitman's bullet.

But when I look at her, I see just one thing.

My mate.

She can investigate me as thoroughly as she feels necessary, prying into every aspect of my family's vast mafia empire, but the only truth she really needs to know about me she will learn tonight with her bare bottom burning and her protests drowned out by her screams of climax.

I take what belongs to me.

Ravenous Predator

Suzette Barker thought she could steal from the most powerful mafia boss in Philadelphia. My belt across her naked backside taught her otherwise, but as tears run down her cheeks and her arousal glistens on her bare thighs, there is something more important she will understand soon.

Kneeling at my feet and demonstrating her remorseful surrender in the most shameful way possible won't bring an end to this, nor will her screams of climax as I take her long and hard. She'll be coming with me and I'll be mounting and savagely rutting her as often as I please.

Not just because she owes me.

Because she's my mate.

Merciless Savage

Christoff Dupree doesn't strike me as the kind of man who woos a woman gently, so when I saw the flowers on my kitchen table I knew it wasn't just a gesture of appreciation for saving his life.

This ruthless mafia boss wasn't seducing me. Those roses mean that I belong to him now.

That I'm his to spank into shameful submission before he mounts me and claims me savagely.

That I'm his mate.

BOOKS OF THE ALPHA BEASTS SERIES

King's Mate

Her scent drew me to her, but something deeper and more powerful told me she was mine. Something that would not be denied. Something that demanded I claim her then and there.

I took her the way a beast takes his mate. Roughly. Savagely. Without mercy or remorse.

She will run, and when she does she will be punished, but it is not me that she fears. Every quivering, desperate climax reminds her that her body knows its master, and that terrifies her.

She knows I am not a gentle king, and she will scream for me as she learns her place.

Beast's Claim

Raven is not one of my kind, but the moment I caught her scent I knew she belonged to me.

She is my mate, and when I claim her it will not be gentle. She can fight me, but her pleas for mercy as she is punished will soon give way to screams of climax as she is mounted and rutted.

By the time I am finished with her, the evidence of her body's surrender will be mingled with my seed as it drips down her bare thighs. But she will be more than just sore and utterly spent.

She will be mine.

Alpha's Mate

I didn't ask Nicolina to be my mate. It was not up to her. An alpha takes what belongs to him.

She will plead for mercy as she is bared and punished for daring to run from me, but her screams as she is claimed and rutted will be those of helpless climax as her body surrenders to its master.

She is mine, and I'm going to make sure she knows it.

MORE STORMY NIGHT BOOKS BY
PIPER STONE

Claimed by the Beasts

Though she has done her best to run from it, Scarlet Dumane cannot escape what is in store for her. She has known for years that she is destined to belong not just to one savage beast, but to three, and now the time has come for her to be claimed. Soon her mates will own every inch of her beautiful body, and she will be shared and used as roughly and as often as they please.

Scarlet hid from the disturbing truth about herself, her family, and her town for as long as she could, but now her grandmother's death has finally brought her back home to the bayous of Louisiana and at last she must face her fate, no matter how shameful and terrifying.

She will be a queen, but her mates will be her masters, and defiance will be thoroughly punished. Yet even when she is stripped bare and spanked until she is sobbing, her need for them only grows, and every blush, moan, and quivering climax binds her to them more tightly. But with enemies lurking in the shadows, can she trust her mates to protect her from both man and beast?

Millionaire Daddy

Dominick Asbury is not just a handsome millionaire whose deep voice makes Jenna's tummy flutter whenever they are together, nor is he merely the first man bold enough to strip her bare and spank her hard and thoroughly whenever she has been naughty. He is much more than that.

He is her daddy.

He is the one who punishes her when she's been a bad girl, and he is the one who takes her in his arms afterwards and brings her to one climax after another until she is utterly spent and satisfied.

But something shady is going on behind the scenes at Dominick's company, and when Jenna draws the wrong conclusion from a poorly written article about him and creates an embarrassing public scene, will she end up not only costing them both their jobs but losing her daddy as well?

Conquering Their Mate

For years the Cenzans have cast a menacing eye on Earth, but it still came as a shock to be captured, stripped bare, and claimed as a mate by their leader and his most trusted warriors.

It infuriates me to be punished for the slightest defiance and forced to submit to these alien brutes, but as I'm led naked through the corridors of their ship, my well-punished bare bottom and my helpless arousal both fully on display, I cannot help wondering how long it will be until I'm kneeling at the feet of my mates and begging them take me as shamefully as they please.

Captured and Kept

Since her career was knocked off track in retaliation for her efforts to expose a sinister plot by high-ranking government officials, reporter Danielle Carver has been stuck writing puff pieces in a small town in Oregon. Desperate for a serious story, she sets out to investigate the rumors she's been hearing about mysterious men living in the mountains nearby. But when she secretly follows them back to their remote cabin, the ruggedly handsome beasts don't take kindly to her snooping around, and Dani soon finds herself stripped bare for a painful, humiliating spanking.

Their rough dominance arouses her deeply, and before long she is blushing crimson as they take turns using her beautiful body as thoroughly and shamefully as they please. But when Dani uncovers the true reason for their presence in the area, will more than just her career be at risk?

Taming His Brat

It's been years since Cooper Dawson left her small Texas hometown, but after her stubborn defiance gets her fired from two jobs in a row, she knows something definitely needs to change. What she doesn't expect, however, is for her sharp tongue and arrogant attitude to land her over the knee of a stern, ruggedly sexy cowboy for a painful, embarrassing, and very public spanking.

Rex Sullivan cannot deny being smitten by Cooper, and the fact that she is in desperate need of his belt across her bare backside only makes the war-hardened ex-Marine more determined to tame the beautiful, fiery redhead. It isn't long before she's screaming his name as he shows her just how hard and roughly a cowboy can ride a headstrong filly. But Rex and Cooper both have secrets, and when the demons of their past rear their ugly heads, will their romance be torn apart?

Capturing Their Mate

I thought the Cenzan invaders could never find me here, but I was wrong. Three of the alien brutes came to take me, and before I ever set foot aboard their ship I had already been stripped bare, spanked thoroughly, and claimed more shamefully then I would have ever thought possible.

They have decided that a public example must be made of me, and I will be punished and used in the most humiliating ways imaginable as a warning to anyone who might dare to defy them. But I am no ordinary breeder, and the secrets hidden in my past could change their world... or end it.

Rogue

Tracking down cyborgs is my job, but this time I'm the one being hunted. This rogue machine has spent most of his life locked up, and now that he's on the loose he has plans for me...

He isn't just going to strip me, punish me, and use me. He will take me longer and harder than any human ever could, claiming me so thoroughly that I will be left in no doubt who owns me.

No matter how shamefully I beg and plead, my body will be ravaged again and again with pleasure so intense it terrifies me to even imagine, because that is what he was built to do.

Roughneck

When I took a job on an oil rig to escape my scheming stepfather's efforts to set me up with one of his business cronies, I knew I'd be working with rugged men. What I didn't expect is to find myself bent over a desk, my cheeks soaked with tears and my bare thighs wet for a very different reason, as my well-punished bottom is thoroughly used by a stern, infuriatingly sexy roughneck.

Even though I should have known better than to get sassy with a firm-handed cowboy, let alone a tough-as-nails former Marine, there's no denying that learning the hard way was every bit as hot as it was shameful. But a sore, welted backside is just the start of his plans for me, and no matter how much I blush to admit it, I know I'm going to take everything he gives me and beg for more.

Hunting Their Mate

As far as I'm concerned, the Cenzans will always be the enemy, and there can be no peace while they remain on our planet. I planned to make them pay for invading our world, but I was hunted down and captured by two of their warriors with the help of a battle-hardened former Marine. Now I'm the one who is going to pay, as the three of them punish me, shame me, and share me.

Though the thought of a fellow human taking the side of these alien brutes enrages me, that is far from the worst of it. With every searing stroke of the strap that lands across my bare bottom, with every savage thrust as I am claimed over and over, and with every screaming climax, it is made more clear that it is my own quivering, thoroughly used body which has truly betrayed me.

Primitive

I was sent to this world to help build a new Earth, but I was shocked by what I found here. The men of this planet are not just primitive savages. They are predators, and I am now their prey…

The government lied to all of us. Not all of the creatures who hunted and captured me are aliens. Some of them were human once, specimens transformed in labs into little more than feral beasts.

I fought, but I was thrown over a shoulder and carried off. I ran, but I was caught and punished. Now they are going to claim me, share me, and use me so roughly that when the last screaming climax has been wrung from my naked, helpless body, I wonder if I'll still know my own name.

Harvest

The Centurions conquered Earth long before I was born, but they did not come for our land or our resources. They came for mates, women deemed suitable for breeding. Women like me.

Three of the alien brutes decided to claim me, and when I defied them, they made a public example of me, punishing me so thoroughly and shamefully I might never stop blushing.

But now, as my virgin body is used in every way possible, I'm not sure I want them to stop…

Torched

I work alongside firefighters, so I know how to handle musclebound roughnecks, but Blaise Tompkins is in a league of his own. The night we met, I threw a glass of wine in his face, then ended up shoved against the wall with my panties on the floor and my arousal dripping down my thighs, screaming out climax after shameful climax with my well-punished bottom still burning.

I've got a series of arsons to get to the bottom of, and finding out that the infuriatingly sexy brute who spanked me like a naughty little girl will be helping me with the investigation seemed like the last thing I needed, until somebody hurled a rock through my window in an effort to scare me away from the case. Now having a big, strong man around doesn't seem like such a bad idea…

Fertile

The men who hunt me were always brutes, but now lust makes them barely more than beasts.

When they catch me, I know what comes next.

I will fight, but my need to be bred is just as strong as theirs is to breed. When they strip me, punish me, and use me the way I'm meant to be used, my screams will be the screams of climax.

Hostage

I knew going after one of the most powerful mafia bosses in the world would be dangerous, but I didn't anticipate being dragged from my apartment already sore, sorry, and shamefully used.

My captors don't just plan to teach me a lesson and then let me go. They plan to share me, punish me, and claim me so ruthlessly I'll be screaming my submission into the sheets long before they're through with me. They took me as a hostage, but they'll keep me as theirs.

Defiled

I was born to rule, but for her sake I am banished, forced to wander the Earth among mortals. Her virgin body will pay the price for my protection, and it will be a shameful price indeed.

Stripped, punished, and ravaged over and over, she will scream with every savage climax.

She will be defiled, but before I am done with her she will beg to be mine.

Kept

On the run from corrupt men determined to silence me, I sought refuge in his cabin. I ate his food, drank his whiskey, and slept in his bed. But then the big bad bear came home and I learned the hard way that sometimes Goldilocks ends up with her cute little bottom well-used and sore.

He stripped me, spanked me, and ravaged me in the most shameful way possible, but then this rugged brute did something no one else ever has before. He made it clear he plans to keep me…

Auctioned

Twenty years ago the Malzeons saved us when we were at the brink of self-annihilation, but there was a price for their intervention. They demanded humans as servants… and as pets.

Only criminals were supposed to be offered to the aliens for their use, but when I defied Earth's government, asking questions that no one else would dare to ask, I was sold to them at auction.

I was bought by two of their most powerful commanders, rivals who nonetheless plan to share me. I am their property now, and they intend to tame me, train me, and enjoy me thoroughly.

But I have information they need, a secret guarded so zealously that discovering it cost me my freedom, and if they do not act quickly enough both of our worlds will soon be in grave danger.

Hard Ride

When I snuck into Montana Cobalt's house, I was looking for help learning to ride like him, but what I got was his belt across my bare backside. Then with tears still running down my cheeks and arousal dripping onto my thighs, the big brute taught me a much more shameful lesson.

Montana has agreed to train me, but not just for the rodeo. He's going to break me in and put me through my paces, and then he's going to show me what it means to be ridden rough and dirty.

Carnal

For centuries my kind have hidden our feral nature, our brute strength, and our carnal instincts. But this human female is my mate, and nothing will keep me from claiming and ravaging her.

She is mine to tame and protect, and if my belt doesn't teach her to obey then she'll learn in a much more shameful fashion. Either way, her surrender will be as complete as it is inevitable.

Bounty

After I went undercover to take down a mob boss and ended up betrayed, framed, and on the run, Harper Rollins tried to bring me in. But instead of collecting a bounty, she earned herself a hard spanking and then an even rougher lesson that left her cute bottom sore in a very different way.

She's not one to give up without a fight, but that's fine by me. It just means I'll have plenty more chances to welt her beautiful backside and then make her scream her surrender into the sheets.

Beast

Primitive, irresistible need compelled him to claim me, but it was more than mere instinct that drove this alien beast to punish me for my defiance and then ravage me thoroughly and savagely. Every screaming climax was a brand marking me as his, ensuring I never forget who I belong to.

He's strong enough to take what he wants from me, but that's not why I surrendered so easily as he stripped me bare, pushed me up against the wall, and made me his so roughly and shamefully.

It wasn't fear that forced me to submit. It was need.

Gladiator

Xander didn't just win me in the arena. The alien brute claimed me there too, with my punished bottom still burning and my screams of climax almost drowned out by the roar of the crowd.

Almost…

Victory earned him freedom and the right to take me as his mate, but making me truly his will mean more than just spanking me into shameful surrender and then rutting me like a wild beast. Before he carries me off as his prize, the dark truth that brought me here must be exposed at last.

Big Rig

Alexis Harding is used to telling men exactly what she thinks, but she's never had a roughneck like me as a boss before. On my rig, I make the rules and sassy little girls get stripped bare, bent over my desk, and taught their place, first with my belt and then in a much more shameful way.

She'll be sore and sorry long before I'm done with her, but the arousal glistening on her thighs reveals the truth she would rather keep hidden. She needs it rough, and that's how she'll get it.

Warriors

I knew this was a primitive planet when I landed, but nothing could have prepared me for the rough beasts who inhabit it. The sting of their prince's firm hand on my bare bottom taught me my place in his world, but it was what came after that truly demonstrated his mastery over me.

This alien brute has granted me his protection and his help with my mission, but the price was my total submission to both his shameful demands and those of his second in command as well.

But it isn't the savage way they make use of my quivering body that terrifies me the most. What leaves me trembling is the thought that I may never leave this place… because I won't want to.

Owned

With a ruthless, corrupt billionaire after me, Crockett, Dylan, and Wade are just the men I need. Rough men who know how to keep a woman safe… and how to make her scream their names.

But the Hell's Fury MC doesn't do charity work, and their help will come at a price.

A shameful price…

They aren't just going to bare me, punish me, and then do whatever they want with me.

They're going to make me beg for it.

Seized

Delaney Archer got herself mixed up with someone who crossed us, and now she's going to find out just how roughly and shamefully three bad men like us can make use of her beautiful body.

She can plead for mercy, but it won't stop us from stripping her bare and spanking her until she's sore, sobbing, and soaking wet. Our feisty little captive is going to take everything we give her, and she'll be screaming our names with every savage climax long before we're done with her.

Cruel Masters

I thought I understood the risks of going undercover to report on billionaires flaunting their power, but these men didn't send lawyers after me. They're going to deal with me themselves.

Now I'm naked aboard their private plane, my backside already burning from one of their belts, and these three infuriatingly sexy bastards have only just gotten started teaching me my place.

I'm not just going to be punished, shamed, and shared. I'm going to be mastered.

Hard Men

My father's will left his company to me, but the three roughnecks who ran it for him have other ideas. They're owed a debt and they mean to collect on it, but it's not money these brutes want.

It's me.

In return for protection from my father's enemies, I will be theirs to share. But these are hard men, and they don't just intend to punish my defiance and use me as shamefully as they please.

They plan to master me completely.

Rough Ride

As I hear the leather slide through the loops of his pants, I know what comes next. Jake Travers is going to blister my backside. Then he's going to ride me the way only a rodeo champion can.

Plenty of men who thought they could put me in my place have learned the hard way that I was more than they could handle, and when Jake showed up I was sure he would be no different.

I was wrong.

When I pushed him, he bared and spanked me in front of a bar full of people.

I should have let it go at that, but I couldn't.

That's why he's taking off his belt…

Primal Instinct

Ruger Jameson can buy anything he wants, but that's not the reason I'm his to use as he pleases.

He's a former Army Ranger accustomed to having his orders followed, but that's not why I obey him.

He saved my life after our plane crashed, but I'm not on my knees just to thank him properly.

I'm his because my body knows its master.

I do as I'm told because he blisters my bare backside every time I dare to do otherwise.

I'm at his feet because I belong to him and I plan to show it in the most shameful way possible.

Captor

I was supposed to be safe from the lottery. Set apart for a man who would treat me with dignity.

But as I'm probed and examined in the most intimate, shameful ways imaginable while the hulking alien king who just spanked me looks on approvingly, I know one thing for certain.

This brute didn't end up with me by chance. He wanted me, so he found a way to take me.

He'll savor every blush as I stand bare and on display for him, every plea for mercy as he punishes my defiance, and every quivering climax as he slowly masters my virgin body.

I'll be his before he even claims me.

Rough and Dirty

Wrecking my cheating ex's truck with a bat might have made me feel better... if the one I went after had actually belonged to him, instead of to the burly roughneck currently taking off his belt.

Now I'm bent over in a parking lot with my bottom burning as this ruggedly sexy bastard and his two equally brutish friends take turns reddening my ass, and I can tell they're just getting started.

That thought shouldn't excite me, and I certainly shouldn't be imagining all the shameful things these men might do to me. But what I should or shouldn't be thinking doesn't matter anyway.

They can see the arousal glistening on my thighs, and they know I need it rough and dirty…

His to Take

When Zadok Vakan caught me trying to escape his planet with priceless stolen technology, he didn't have me sent to the mines. He made sure I was stripped bare and sold at auction instead.

Then he bought me for himself.

Even as he punishes me for the slightest hint of defiance and then claims me like a beast, indulging every filthy desire his savage nature can conceive, I swear I'll never surrender.

But it doesn't matter.

I'm already his, and we both know it.

Tyrant

When I accepted a lucrative marketing position at his vineyard, Montgomery Wolfe made the terms of my employment clear right from the start. Follow his rules or face the consequences.

That's why I'm bent over his desk, doing my best to hate him as his belt lashes my bare bottom.

I shouldn't give in to this tyrant. I shouldn't yield to his shameful demands.

Yet I can't resist the passion he sets ablaze with every word, every touch, and every brutally possessive kiss, and I know before long my body will surrender to even his darkest needs…

Filthy Rogue

Losing my job to a woman who slept her way to the top was bad enough, and that was before my car broke down as I drove cross country to start over. Having to be rescued by an infuriatingly sexy biker who promptly bared and spanked me for sassing him was just icing on the cake.

After sharing a passionate night, I might have made a teensy mistake in taking cash from his wallet in order to pay the auto mechanic, but I hadn't thought I'd ever see him again…

Then on the first day at my new job, guess who swaggered in with payback on his mind?

He's living proof that the universe really is out to get me… and he's my new boss.

ABOUT PIPER STONE

Amazon Top 150 Internationally Best-Selling Author, Kindle Unlimited All Star Piper Stone writes in several genres. From her worlds of dark mafia, cowboys, and marines to contemporary reverse harem, shifter romance, and science fiction, she attempts to delight readers with a foray into darkness, sensuality, suspense, and always a romantic HEA. When she's not writing, you can find her sipping merlot while she enjoys spending time with her three Golden Retrievers (Indiana Jones, Magnum PI, and Remington Steele) and a husband who relishes creating fabulous food.

Dangerous is Delicious.

* * *

You can find her at:

Website: https://piperstonebooks.com/

Newsletter: https://piperstonebooks.com/newsletter/

Facebook: https://www.facebook.com/authorpiperstone/

Twitter: http://twitter.com/piperstone01

Instagram: http://www.instagram.com/authorpiperstone/

Amazon: http://amazon.com/author/piperstone

BookBub: http://bookbub.com/authors/piper-stone

TikTok: https://www.tiktok.com/@piperstoneauthor

Email: piperstonecreations@gmail.com

Printed in Great Britain
by Amazon